# KILLING KAREN

"They aren't dreams, Chris." Jessie sighed. "It's the house. There's something living in that house. And I don't mean people."

"Then what do you mean?"

"Unless you help me, I won't be able to stop them."

"Stop them from what?"

She turned away, then looked back at Chris. "Have you ever heard of Lettie Hatch?"

*Lettie Hatchet took a butcher knife, and with it took her father's life . . .*

"Yeah," Chris said. "Everyone has. She killed her parents."

"I live in her *house*, Chris. Lettie Hatch's mother killed herself. And two years later her father got remarried to this young bitch and then Lettie killed her father and her stepmother." She walked over to the window where the rain was still pounding the earth. "And my dad just got married again . . . to Karen, a girl way younger than he is. Are you starting to follow my line of reasoning?"

"Uh, yeah . . ."

"It's going to all happen again, Chris, I know it is. I dream about it. I dream about the knife and the blood. And last night—"

Gooseflesh crawled up Chris's arms. "What happened last night?"

"Last night I dreamed about killing Karen." Jessie laughed. Almost a funny ha-ha kind of laugh, but Chris knew she wasn't joking. "I dreamed I went into the kitchen and got the knife and went into her bedroom and started stabbing . . . *and it felt so good!*"

Books by Robert Ross

WHERE DARKNESS LIVES

DON'T CLOSE YOUR EYES

CAUSE OF FEAR

NEVER LOOK BACK

Published by Pinnacle Books

# ROBERT ROSS

# Never Look Back

**PINNACLE BOOKS**
**KENSINGTON PUBLSHING CORP.**
http://www. kensingtonbooks.com

PINNACLE BOOKS are published by

Kensington Publishing Corp.
850 Third Avenue
New York, NY 10022

All Kensington Titles, Imprints, and Distributed Lines are
available at special quantity discounts for bulk purchases for
sales promotions, premiums, fund-raising, educational or in-
stitutional use. Special book excerpts or customized printing
can also be created to fit specific needs. For details, write or
phone the office of the Kensington special sales manager: Kensington Publishing Corp., 850 Third Avenue, New York, NY
10022. Attn: Special Sales Department, Phone: 1-800-221-2647.

Pinnacle and the P logo Reg. U.S. Pat. & TM Off.

First Pinnacle Books Printing: May 2005

10 9 8 7 6 5 4 3 2 1

Printed in the United States of America

With thanks to Greg H., my New Orleans expert

# Book One

# THE CIRCLE OPENS

# Chapter 1

"I miss you."

Karen spoke the words into the telephone as she ripped open another box. *More books*, she groaned inwardly, almost dropping the phone. She glared down at the dog-eared paperbacks nestled snugly in the box. The bookcases in the bedroom were already full. She tilted her head to grip the phone tighter between her head and shoulder and folded the box flaps back down. *Another box for the attic*, she thought, cursing herself for not throwing more away. *You're never going to read these again. Why did you have them shipped here?*

"I'll be home before you know it." Her husband's deep voice was reeassuring. "And the house? You like the house, don't you?"

"Well, sure. What's not to like?"

She walked over to the window and stared out at the bay. Apparently there was a good breeze—the horizon was edged with sailboats moving across the surface. The house was certainly much different from what she was used to, her cramped, roach-infested studio apartment in New Orleans' French Quarter. Now she was living in an old white-clapboarded Victorian, weather-beaten but still grand, on the far east end of Commercial Street, the main drag through town. The house was two stories high—three if you counted the partial attic—with a small green yard in front and in the back, stone steps that led almost immediately down to the beach. Huge picture windows took up almost the entire second story, with an elegant, recently renovated bathroom complete with a Jacuzzi bathtub and a three-headed shower. From wherever she stood the view of the bay was breathtaking.

"I still wish you were here," she said into the phone.

She heard the whiny tone in her voice and winced. Philip didn't like weak women. She'd known that from the beginning. *The only reason he married me was that I've pretended to be one hell of a lot stronger than I really am. But surely it's not too much to expect that my husband would be here—in the house we're supposed to be making our home—when I arrived?*

He sighed, not responding to the suggestion of neediness in Karen's voice. "Is Jessie behaving?"

Yet again, it was Jessie—Philip's sixteen-year-old daughter from his first marriage—whom he was most concerned about.

"She hasn't said two words to me since I arrived last night." Karen looked out over the bay. The house was so still; if she didn't know Jessie was downstairs, she'd swear she was alone in the house. Jessie never had friends in to see her, she never spoke on the phone, she couldn't be bothered watching television.

Other than a mumbled "hello" when Karen first walked into the house, Jessie had pretty much given her the silent treatment. She hadn't known what to really expect after her three-day drive from New Orleans, but she hadn't expected such rudeness. *Of course, I was kind of cranky from the drive*, she amended, *and it can't be easy to have your new stepmother foisted on you like that.* She'd arrived in the early afternoon, after spending the night in Providence. After the brief greeting, Jessie had scampered up the stairs and shut her bedroom door with a resounding slam that shook the old house. It wasn't an auspicious beginning.

"In time," Philip promised, "she'll grow to love you."

*Yeah, right, when I sprout wings and fly,* Karen thought. She sat down on the window seat. The window was open. A breeze carrying the tangy scent of a salty low tide gently fluttered the sheer curtains.

"Listen, Karen, I have to get going. I'll call you tonight. I love you."

"I love you, too," she said to the dial tone.

She hugged herself as she stood and headed across the room to the opposite side of the house that looked out over Commercial Street. The sidewalk was packed with people heading toward town. It was August, the height of the tourist season. She stood there for a moment watching the pedestrians, laughing and joking with each other as they strolled up the narrow street.

If someone had told Karen Donovan a year ago she'd be settling into a beautiful old house in Provincetown with a new husband and a stepdaughter, she would have laughed in their face. Back then, she was living in New Orleans, barely eking out an existence waiting tables at night in a restaurant that catered to tourists and spending her days slaving away at her novel. Marriage was the furthest thing from her mind. Sure, she wanted to get married someday, but that someday was far off in her future. The guy she was sort of seeing, Dave Trask, was no more marriage minded than she was. Neither one of them saw much future in the relationship; they were more friends with a strong sexual attraction than anything else. Dave was too selfish, for one thing, and for another, he didn't have enough time for her. He was going to Tulane, majoring in prelaw—she suspected that sleeping with a local girl gave him some kind of "cool" credibility with his fraternity buddies. And she doubted she was the only one sharing his bed. They barely saw each other, which was fine with her. She liked devoting her free time to her laptop computer and the world she was writing about, the world where she was in complete control of everything that happened.

She'd always wanted to be an author from the time she was a little girl and first discovered the magic world of books. As soon as she got her first library card, she was at the library every Saturday, going through the shelves and finding things to read. She would come home every time with an armload of books, and spent the rest of the weekend in a secluded spot reading. She read about anything that struck her fancy, until her tenth birthday when her mother gave her a book called *The Secret of the Old Clock*. She became hopelessly addicted to Nancy Drew. She devoured the series, then found others: Trixie Belden, the Dana Girls, Judy Bolton, and even the Hardy Boys.

By the time she was thirteen she was certain she could write those books better herself, and started writing her first book as a freshman in high school: *The Secret of the Haunted Carousel*. Her heroine, Vicky Knight, was very similar to herself—a high school freshman, pretty but kind of bookish and quiet, with an older brother into sports and parents who didn't seem to quite know what to make of her. She wrote the book in longhand, in spiral notebooks she carried with her everywhere. Her father, a mechanic, would tease her whenever she would bolt from the dinner table to head to her desk, "There goes the writing fiend." Whenever she couldn't think of anything to write or how to get Vicky out of her latest predicament, she would lie on her bed and stare at the water-stained ceiling, thinking about her future when she was a rich and famous writer. She dreamed about having lunches with other writers, where they talked about books and writing. She dreamed of Paris, London, and Rome, of sitting in coffee shops and drinking espressos, plotting out her next novel.

There hadn't been money for college, and she wasn't a good enough student to get a scholarship—she spent too much time in classes that bored her, daydreaming about what she was writing. Math and science were nightmares for her. Algebra might have been a language from another planet for all the sense it made to her. Her parents thought her dreams were just that—daydreams that wouldn't come true. "Writing is for dreamers, Karen," her mother had told her once, "not for people like you. You have to get some kind of training and get married, have children. You'll never support yourself as a writer." She knew her mother wanted her to go to beauty school and join her at the hair salon, just like her older sister, Vonda.

Karen would rather die than end up like Vonda. The thought of being like her sister was her worst nightmare. She was going to be different. She wasn't going to lose her virginity in the bed of a pickup truck to some guy who was going to wind up working on an oil rig, getting knocked up and forever trapped in a life that meant more kids and doing other people's hair. Vonda, at twenty-three, looked as if she were going on forty. Her figure was gone, her hair a mess, and she just didn't care.

No, Karen planned to escape from Chalmette, the little town just outside New Orleans on the St. Bernard highway, if it killed her. No tired little old house with an unkempt lawn and a statue of the Virgin Mary stained with dog urine for her, thank you very much.

Much as her mother's lack of support had hurt, it made her more determined. She'd show her mother, her father—all of them. She didn't *need* a man. She didn't need a backup career. She was going to be rich and famous and write books that made the *New York Times* best-seller list and got made into movies with big stars that won Oscars. She was nineteen when she moved out of her parents' house and into the tiny apartment she could afford on her tips. She bought a used laptop computer and began working on her first adult mystery novel. She used Vicky as her main character still, only now Vicky was grown up and worked as a reporter for the *New Orleans Enquirer*. It took her a couple of years to finish it; and when it was ready she spent about a hundred dollars she could ill afford to make five copies and mail it off to agents in New York she'd found in *The Writer's Market*. As she dropped each copy through the package mail slot at the post office on Loyola Avenue, she said a little prayer to her patron saint, Teresa of Avila.

Over the next five months, every copy came back to her. The first rejection letter had seemed encouraging.

> *You're a very talented young writer, and I can see a bright future for you, but this isn't the book. I'm afraid that I can't see a way to sell this book in today's highly competitive marketplace. But your characters are good, your sense of place is excellent—New Orleans really comes to life in your hands—but there are some problems with the plot that I think will hurt it in the eyes of the editors.*
>
> *Keep writing, and the best of luck to you in your future endeavors.*

Despite the rejection, Karen chose to see the letter as a positive. She hadn't expected to be represented by the first agent she'd approached—that would have been too much for her to even fantasize about. All the little sections in *The Writer's Market* written by award-winning best-selling writers talked about how difficult it was to get started but to keep plugging away. And the agent thought she had talent—which was the first time anyone other than her high school English teachers had said so. This was from a publishing professional! She was certain she was on her way. She'd gone out that night after work to celebrate.

Then the next letter came, and said almost exactly the same thing as the first, only in different words.

When the third came, again the same thing in slightly different words, she was crushed. It was a standardized form letter all agents used, nothing more, nothing less; the same as the rejection letters from editors to whom she sent her short stories.

Maybe she didn't have talent.

Maybe she couldn't make it as a writer.

The fourth rejection letter made her cry.

Written in ink on the back of a torn-off piece of recycled office stationery, it said simply:

> *Ms. Donovan:*
> *I find your plot and your characters to be neither interesting or compelling. It is, to say the least, the work of an immature writer and no publishing house would be interested in publishing such a thing. I suggest you try another line of work.*
> *Best of luck to you.*

Even though she noticed the agent's incorrect usage of "neither" with "or," it still hurt. That night after she got off work she did something she rarely did: she went out and got drunk. That was the night she met Dave. He'd sat down next to her at the bar after her third tequila sunrise and said something stupid like "What's a pretty girl like you looking so sad for?" She'd laughed in his face. Just the act of laughing broke the depression she'd been feeling, and about an hour later she took him back to the sad little apartment with her. He was good looking, with blue eyes and ragged blondish hair and a crooked grin that made him look like he was up to something. He wasn't her first; she'd lost her virginity shortly after moving to the Quarter to a bartender at the restaurant she worked at. She hadn't really seen the big deal about sex—nor did she feel the need to run to confession the following Sunday. She hadn't been to Mass since she moved out of her parents' house. There had been a few others since the bartender—but they all turned out to be mostly disappointments. Dave was different. Dave played her body like a musical instrument, and she finally understood what the big deal really was.

They fell into their routine of seeing each other once or twice a week, when the mood struck or, as she suspected, he had nothing else—or more likely, nobody else—to do. She might not have loved him, but he could always make her laugh.

Karen shivered. *Why am I thinking about Dave, of all people, today?* She looked around at the piles of unopened boxes and sighed. She'd managed to get through most of them, and she hoped there weren't any other boxes of books. She got up and walked over to the box of books she'd just opened.

*Might as well move this to the attic*, she figured, *since it isn't going to move itself.*

She sighed and knelt down, using her knees to lift it. It was still heavy, and she staggered a little as she carried it through the door to the hallway. The attic staircase was at the other end of the hall. As she walked down the hallway she passed her stepdaughter's room.

She glanced in, thought about saying something, and decided not to. There didn't seem to be much point. Jessie was sitting at her desk, headphones on, writing away in her journal. Karen wondered what music she was listening to. If Jessie was anything like Karen's younger sister, she was listening to Justin Timberlake.

Somehow, Karen didn't think so.

*It doesn't help that Jessie is only eight years younger than I am*, she thought again as the stairs groaned and creaked beneath her weight. *If my dad had brought home a stepmother just eight years older than I was, I sure as heck wouldn't have wanted much to do with her either. I should have waited to come here until Philip was back.*

But Philip hadn't wanted her to wait. "It's your home now," he'd said after the brief ceremony at City Hall, "and I won't be able to get back home for about another month."

Against her better judgment, Karen finally gave in—especially after Philip bought her the new white Lexus SUV for the drive up. The platinum American Express card was also a nice touch.

She put the box down to turn on the attic light before heading up the stairs, cursing herself for not thinking to have the boxes of books moved to the attic while the two local teenaged boys she'd hired to unload the rental truck were still there.

*Philip was wrong*, she thought again. *I should have waited to come until he was back.*

Her parents had agreed with her.

"Philip, you just can't spring a new mother on the girl," Mrs. Donovan had said, shaking her head over their wedding dinner at the Napoleon House. Her parents hadn't exactly been thrilled about the wedding either. "Karen doesn't know anything about being a parent—especially to a teenager." Mrs. Donovan was by that time on her third glass of wine, and her words were getting a little slurred.

But Philip wouldn't budge. "You're wrong, Mrs. Donovan," he'd said. "Besides, Karen has a younger sister—so she knows how to deal with teenagers."

"But, Philip—I don't know. I mean, she's never even met me," Karen protested, waving off the hovering waiter who was trying to refill her mother's wineglass, giving him a frown.

Philip wasn't hearing any of their arguments. "She'll love you. Besides, Mrs. Winn will be there." Mrs. Winn was the private tutor who was schooling Jessie at home. "Jessie loves Mrs. Winn, and Mrs. Winn won't let her pull any nonsense." Mrs. Winn had come to work for Philip when his first wife had died, and Jessie's grades started falling. She pretty much had run the household. But now that was going to be Karen's job.

Karen remembered her mother's embrace standing beside the Lexus just before she left New Orleans. "I still think this is a mistake, Karen," she said, "but you know you can always come home."

"Mom, please."

"That man," her mother said darkly, "likes to get his own way."

Karen couldn't help but smile. She still couldn't believe she was Mrs. Philip Kaye.

Philip Kaye was her favorite writer, bar none. One day she'd gone to the Garden District Bookshop to pick up the latest Julie Smith and Sue Grafton mysteries. After the horrendous experience with the agents—she'd never heard anything from the fifth—she had tossed the Vicky Knight book aside once and for all and started from scratch. She still wanted to write mysteries—but she'd been casting about for a new topic, a new character, *anything*, to write about. She'd started a horror novel about a haunted beach resort in Florida, but it didn't seem to work. "Who's the best horror writer?" she'd asked Deb, the woman working at the cash register.

Deb had come out from behind the counter and picked up a paperback called *Out of the Darkness* by Philip Kaye. Karen bought it with the others, and when she got home from the store, she'd lain down on her bed with her new books. On the back cover of Philip's book was a photo of the author, and she found herself staring at it. He was drop-dead handsome—probably in his late thirties with a thick shock of black hair starting to gray a bit at the temples, piercing green eyes, a strong jaw, and a slightly crooked nose. She started reading the book, and only put it down to use the bathroom or to get a Diet Pepsi. It was around two in the afternoon when she started, and when she finally finished, it was three in the morning.

The next morning, she'd gone back to the store and bought all the rest of his books. All sixteen of them.

Three months later, she saw in the paper that Philip Kaye would be giving a reading at the Garden District Bookstore to promote his newest hardcover, *The Whisperer*. Not knowing what to expect, she'd put on her most flattering outfit, styled her red hair, and changed her makeup three times before heading to the store.

He'd been sitting at a table when she arrived; there were four people ahead of her in line. In her purse she'd crammed several of his paperbacks—she was going to get everything signed. When it was finally her turn, she approached the table hesitantly.

"Well, aren't you pretty?" he said in his deep voice, smiling at her, his eyes flashing.

"Th—thank you," she stammered, hating herself for sounding stupid, and knowing she was blushing like a

starstruck teenager. He was even handsomer in person
than in his jacket photos, and those green eyes— "I'm
a big fan," she managed to say.

He took a copy of the new book off a stack and
opened it to the title page. "What's your name?"

"Karen Donovan."

He wrote something with a flourish, signed and dated
his name, and handed the book over to her. "There you
go."

There was no one in line behind her, so she opened
her purse and started removing the tattered paperbacks.
"Would you, um, mind—"

He grinned. "You *are* a fan," he said as she started
stacking the books in front of him. As he started signing, he asked without looking up, "Which one is your
favorite?"

"*Out of the Darkness.* I loved the character of
Barbara."

His pen stopped moving and he looked up at her.
"Why is that?"

"Um, well—" She became aware of the passing seconds as she tried to come up with an intelligent answer.
It was Philip Kaye, for God's sake! Finally, she just
smiled at him. "I just couldn't believe that a man could
create such a convincing female character. I could identify with her, want her to succeed. You really captured—
oh, this is going to sound stupid, but you really captured
what it's like to be a woman who wants something she
can never have."

His eyes danced. "And is there something you want
that you can't have?"

She tilted her chin up. *What the hell?* she thought.
"Yes," she said. "I want to be a writer."

"And who says you can't have that?"

"At least five agents."

He patted the chair next to him. "Have a seat, and let's talk."

She stayed there with him through the whole signing, having an in-depth conversation about writing, books, and the publishing business—occasionally interrupted whenever another fan showed up. She told him about the painful rejection letter, and he snorted. "I know that man—he's a complete asshole who wouldn't have represented Mark Twain." He asked her about her current book, and she started explaining the plot to him, the characters, and then the store manager walked up to have him sign the rest of the stock. Two hours had gone by and she hadn't noticed. She didn't want it to end. She was talking about books with her idol. And he was taking an interest in her writing!

They left the store and he took her to dinner across the street at Commander's Palace—one of the best restaurants in the city, and definitely not in her budget. So he was a playboy, a flirt. So maybe he flattered lots of his pretty young female fans like this. Karen didn't care. If she did, she wouldn't have worn the low-cut blouse at which Philip kept surreptitiously glancing.

"If you like mysteries, you should write mysteries," he was saying to her. "That's where your heart is. You have to write about what interests you—not about what you think will sell. That's the road to becoming a hack writer—and you're much too pretty and intelligent to be a hack."

He thought her mystery novel showed promise. "I like the premise, and what you say about the main character—it sounds like there's no other character out there like her, and that's a key to help sell the book."

"Really? Do you really think so?"

He just grinned and winked at her.

When the after-dinner coffee arrived, he said, "Would

you mind letting me read your manuscript? I'd be glad
to look it over and give you some pointers. I don't usually do this—but I'll make an exception in your case."

"You'd do that for me?" She couldn't believe her
luck. She thought she was going to die on the spot.

He patted her on the leg. "It's my duty to the reading
public."

She'd taken him back to her little apartment and dug
out one of the copies. He sat down on her desk chair
and read the first page, whistling as he did so. "This is
really pretty good, actually," he said, looking up at her
and giving her the same smile that stared out of his author photos. He glanced at his watch. "Well, I've got an
early flight tomorrow. This tour is really out of control,
the schedule they've got me set up for—but give me
your phone number and e-mail address."

She wrote them down for him and then walked him
down to the street. She was surprised: she really thought
he was going to make a move on her, expect something
in return for all the attention he'd given her, the promises
he was making. She wasn't sure how she would've responded.

Oh, who was she kidding? If he'd made a move, she
would've made a move right back.

At the door, she gave him a kiss on the cheek. "Ah,
pretty Karen Donovan," he said, smiling down at her.
"Let's keep this professional—at least for now."

*And six months later, I'm his wife*, she thought, setting the box down in a corner and looking around the
attic. Somehow, it still didn't seem real to her.

The attic looked like no one had set foot in it for
months—years, maybe. Dust and cobwebs were everywhere, and old furniture was scattered and stacked
with no sense of rhyme or reason. There were several
old trunks shoved into one corner covered in a layer of

dust. The roof of the house came to a peak directly in the center of the big room, and the dormer windows let in a surprising amount of light. Dust motes were floating gently in the path of the sunbeams.

She put her hands on her hips. *Maybe I'll make a project out of this attic*, she thought, *clean it out, get rid of this junk—it might just make a nice work space.* She wasn't comfortable at the thought of sharing Philip's office with him. She liked solitude when she worked, usually putting on headphones and listening to a CD— Stevie Nicks, preferably—to shut out all outside noise. *I'd hate to be a distraction to him.*

The more she thought about it, the more she liked the idea. She walked over to one of the windows that faced the bay. There were plenty of electrical outlets, and no phone jack. *Perfect*, she thought, a grin spreading across her face. *I'll ask Philip about it tonight when we talk again.* She knelt down and felt the raw wood. *Sand it down and cover it in varnish and it'll be gorgeous.*

She heard the front door slam downstairs.

*Jessie*, she thought. She opened the nearest window and glanced out just in time to see Jessie disappearing down the street.

*Great, just great*, she moaned to herself. *Where is she off to? I guess we're going to have to set up some ground rules.*

She sat down on a trunk, sending up a cloud of dust. *Rules. Me setting up rules. She'll probably think I'm a wicked stepmother.* She laughed out loud, remembering how easily she'd evaded her parents' rules whenever she wanted. With a sigh, she got up and went back downstairs.

She caught a glimpse of herself in the hall mirror. Her face was smudged with dust and there were cobwebs in her brown hair. She ran her fingers through it, but just succeeded in making the tangles worse. She groaned and walked down to the kitchen.

"Where's Jessie off to?" she asked Mrs. Winn, seated at the kitchen table.

The older woman pushed her glasses up her nose. She was looking over a paper Jessie had written, a red pencil shoved behind her right ear. It might be August, but Jessie was behind in her studies. There were state guidelines for homeschooling, and on the latest test Jessie hadn't scored all that well. No summer vacation for her.

"Off to the library, I suspect," Mrs. Winn replied, getting up to stand opposite Karen. "That's pretty much the only place she goes. Well, that and the bookstores. Her research on this"—she gestured to the smudged computer printouts—"leaves a lot to be desired."

Mrs. Winn was a short woman, barely five feet tall in her stocking feet, and her hair was iron gray. Her brown eyes were perceptive and intelligent. Karen had liked her almost from the minute she'd arrived yesterday.

"Been up in the attic?" Mrs. Winn smiled, reaching over to pluck a cobweb out of Karen's hair.

Karen sank into a chair at the table and nodded. "I swear, I don't know where all this junk came from. If you'd seen my old apartment back home—"

"Ah, whenever I move, I think the same thing." Mrs. Winn moved over to the stove. "Would you like a nice cup of tea? I was just thinking I'd like one."

*What I really need is a shot of tequila*, Karen thought, but aloud said, "That'd be nice."

Mrs. Winn put the kettle on to boil, taking down two cups and some packets of tea. Sitting back down at the table across from Karen, she gave her a sympathetic look. "Are you settling in okay?" Her voice was so kind. She reminded Karen of her freshmen English teacher from high school.

Karen shrugged. "It's a lot to handle."

"Change is hard for everyone." The teakettle whistled and Mrs. Winn was up again, pouring the boiling water into the teacups. "And this house is hardly the best place." She shivered. "So much tragedy."

"Tragedy?" Karen stirred her tea.

"My dear, you don't know?" Mrs. Winn hesitated. "Oh, maybe it's not my place—"

*Mrs. Winn was a godsend after Jessie's mother died.* Karen heard Philip's voice in her head. *I don't know what we would have done without her.*

"Please, Mrs. Winn."

"Call me Alice." Mrs. Winn sipped her tea. "You know this is the old Hatch house, don't you?"

Karen shrugged. "Hatch house? What does that mean?"

"Oh dear. Mr. Kaye must have told you. It was why he bought the house! Because of the associations. Because of the legends. You know, with him being a horror writer and all . . ."

"Mrs. Winn, I don't know what you're talking about."

She seemed flabbergasted. "My dear Karen. Have you never heard of Lettie Hatch?"

An old child's rhyme floated suddenly through Karen's head:

*Lettie Hatch took a butcher knife, and with it took her father's life. To put an end to all her strife, she used it then on her father's wife.*

She shivered. "I—I always thought that was just a nursery rhyme."

"Well, Lizzie Borden was more famous, but Lettie Hatch was very real, our very own local version." Mrs. Winn sighed. "And this was the house—where it all happened. It stood empty for years until Mr. Kaye bought it." She shook her head. "Hardly the atmosphere to raise a child, you know?"

A cold chill went down Karen's spine.

"I'm surprised Mr. Kaye never told you."

"So am I. . . ."

"And Jessie's so sensitive." Mrs. Winn reached across the table and took Karen's hand. "It's important that you and I get along—for her sake. I'm worried."

Karen held the older woman's gaze. "Tell me about her. Philip hasn't said much about Jessie, except that she's homeschooled, and—" What were his exact words? She couldn't remember; she hadn't really paid much attention. But he had told her something else about Jessie. What was it? All she'd been thinking about was becoming Mrs. Philip Kaye. Karen shrugged. "I know he dotes on her. That much is obvious."

*More perhaps than he dotes on me,* Karen thought, immediately regretting it. Still, she couldn't help but feel that just two weeks after getting married she shouldn't be here all alone, her husband off on yet another book tour—with how many other pretty young female fans in low-cut blouses approaching him at his readings?

*But he married me. I am Mrs. Philip Kaye.*

She focused again on Mrs. Winn and talk of Jessie.

"She trusts me, I think," Mrs. Winn was saying. "But she doesn't *talk* to me—I don't know that she talks to anyone. We talk about her schoolwork, but that's about it." She sighed. "After the first Mrs. Kaye's, um, unfortunate accident, Mr. Kaye took Jessie to some therapists in Boston, but she wouldn't talk to them either, so he finally gave up on that."

"How did her mother die?" Philip had been vague about his first wife; whenever Karen had brought the subject up, he'd responded with an abrupt *It's too painful to talk about, I'm sorry, Karen.*

Mrs. Winn's jaw dropped. "You don't know?"

Karen shook her head.

"Well, I'm sorry to be the bearer of so many unpleasant secrets. . . ."

It began to dawn on Karen just how short a time she had known her husband before she married him. It's what made her parents so anxious about the marriage. There was so much she didn't know about him and his life—and had been too in awe of him to push for answers. *I'm his wife*, Karen told herself. *Not some starstruck fan. Not anymore. I have a right to know these things*.

"Tell me, Mrs. Winn. Please."

The older woman looked uncomfortable, then seemed to make a decision. "For Jessie's sake, you should know." She took a breath. "The first Mrs. Winn hanged herself. Jessie was alone in the house with her. Jessie was the one who found her."

# Chapter 2

*There she is again,* Chris Muir thought.

He was sitting on a bench on Commercial Street, bored out of his mind, drinking a protein smoothie. He'd already been to the gym that morning, lifting weights and riding the bike. His red T-shirt was stuck to his back with sweat, and his curly dark hair was damp from the exertion.

He watched as the girl in black hurried along the sidewalk, sidestepping dawdling pedestrians. Her long dark hair hung, uncombed, in tangles and knots past her shoulders. She had a heavy canvas bag thrown over her right shoulder, her eyes cast down on the redbrick sidewalk. Her skin was pale with dark circles under her large brown eyes, and her face was free of makeup. She was wearing a plain black T-shirt over black jeans and heavy black combat boots that weren't tied, the laces flapping as she walked.

*Don't be shy, dumb-ass, say something to her.*

He sat up straighter, pulling his stomach in a bit. He slid his headphones, blaring the latest Kenny Chesney CD, down from his ears. This time he was going to talk to her. *What's the worst thing she can say? It's not like she can kill me or anything.*

He steeled his courage. Biting his lip, he took a deep breath, stood up, and stepped right into her path.

She stopped, looked up at him, and stepped around him without a word, her eyes dropping immediately back down to the sidewalk again.

Mentally, he smacked his forehead as he turned and watched her continue on her way. *Smooth move, stud*, he berated himself, and started walking after her. *You're only going to be here for a few more weeks, and if you don't talk to her soon, you'll never get a chance.*

Almost six feet five, Chris had just turned sixteen a few months earlier. He'd always been tall and skinny, always the tallest boy in his class, and kids who didn't like him called him "Ichabod Crane" or "Beanpole." When he was ten years old, he was already six feet. He didn't understand where the height came from—both of his parents were under five eight, and none of his relatives were tall. *I'm just some kind of genetic freak*, he thought whenever he was at a family gathering. His relatives always teased him—more kindly than the kids at school, but it was still teasing. *Do you play basketball? How's the weather up there? Can you see the Pacific Ocean?* So funny. Har-de-har-har-har.

He tended to slouch, so as not to seem as tall, but his mother, Lois, always made him stand up straight. "Don't hunch like that, Chris," Lois lectured, "you'll end up with a hunched back. You're tall; be proud of it." *Easy for her to say*, he always thought resentfully.

His parents had bought a house in Truro the previous spring. But as beautiful as the Truro beaches were, there was no *there* there—no downtown, no shops, no anything—so most days Chris hitched a ride on the shuttle and headed into P-town for the day. Here the crowds were crazy to watch: wacky drag queens, leather-clad lesbians, freaky clowns that ogled the tourists and made grabs for the girls' tits. Chris had spent the whole summer watching the crowds. Especially the girl dressed all in black.

His parents both taught at Boston College—his father in philosophy, his mother in women's studies—and both were secure in their positions enough to not teach summer sessions. Their little house tucked away into the Truro woods was nothing like the big house in Boston they called home; it was snug and cozy and, in Chris's opinion, a little cramped. His mother was working on a book about the suffragette movement; he wasn't really sure what his father was doing, but he spent hours in front of his computer typing away at something.

Chris didn't pay any attention when his parents talked about things—his mind just drifted away. He'd learned early on that as far as they were concerned, he just had to listen—or at least give the impression he was hanging on every word. Mostly they talked to each other about any number of things, subjects either that he didn't care about or that went straight over his head. All he to do was just tune in for a little while, nod his head, then tune back out again. They didn't really want his opinion on anything—their discussions, their work, or his life. He'd heard his mother tell a colleague once how proud she was that she wasn't "one of those domineering mothers who made her child goose-step along with her decisions about his life. Chris fully participates in every decision about his future."

Chris couldn't help but laugh. He'd just rolled his eyes—behind her back, of course—and nodded assent as though it were gospel. But every decision affecting his life had been made for him—all that was required of him was to meekly bow his head and go along with it. He didn't want to go to Thomas More Prep—he was painfully shy and had trouble making friends, and he wanted to stay with the kids he'd been with since grade school. But going to Thomas More Prep would almost certainly get him "into Harvard," his mother said, "and then your future will be assured."

He didn't really want to go to Harvard, either, but that was another story.

He was also a virgin, a deep secret he kept from his classmates at Thomas More Prep, the all-male boarding school in Connecticut he'd begun attending as a freshman. He was relatively certain that most of the other boys were virgins too—all the talk around the dorm and the locker room was just talk. The boys bragged about their girlfriends back home, about the easiness of the local town girls, or scoring with the girls at their sister school, St. Isabelle's. Chris was shy around girls, could never think of the right thing to say, and always flushed with embarrassment. Instead, he channeled his sexual frustrations and energies into his workouts. The gym was a release for him, a way to go into his own little world where he didn't have to worry about having friends or getting laid or what his mother wanted him to do. There, he just was able to focus on what he was doing, on the effort and energy he needed to move the weights, to push the pedals on the stationary bike, and build his muscles up.

He didn't play any of the sports at Thomas More Prep, either—his mother didn't believe in team sports ("they don't teach individuality—just a pack mentality, and no son of mine is going to be in a pack"). That was fine with his father, who was short and overweight and completely blind without his glasses, and who had no interest in sports at all—other than to complain about all the money Boston College poured into its athletics department at the expense of academics. It was one of the few things Chris had in common with his dad, the total indifference he felt toward athletics. Most of the guys on the sports teams at More Prep were the biggest assholes at school. But Chris's height and his devotion to weight training made him seem desirable to the coaches.

There were times, late at night in his dorm room, wide awake and staring at the ceiling, when he thought it might be nice to belong somewhere.

His roommate, Josh Benton, had no such qualms. Josh played football, was on the wrestling team, and pitched for the baseball team in the spring. Josh spent as little time in their room as possible, which was fine with Chris. Josh was always out with his teammates, and spent as much of his time as possible in the nearby town of Suffolk, trying to get into local girls' pants—and if he was to be believed, he scored more off the football field than on it.

*Josh is okay*, Chris thought as he tried to keep his eye on the girl in black as she pushed through the throngs of people, *if a little sex-crazy*. Josh didn't tease him or call him beanpole the way some of the other boys did—although, Chris realized, a little smile stretching across his face, since he'd started lifting weights he wasn't tall and skinny anymore. He was filling out quite nicely, his muscles thickening and hardening.

Too bad the girl in black hadn't noticed.

He'd seen her the week he'd arrived—saw her walking up the street with her bag and her head down. He'd been exploring, and had just gotten an ice cream cone at the Ben & Jerry's when she walked by. Something about her stuck in his head; there was something about her eyes that seemed to pierce into his soul. He knew that sounded weird, but he couldn't help it. It was just a reaction he had; he couldn't deny it. It wasn't just that she was pretty—she was, even though she didn't seem to care about styling her hair. She had a heart-shaped face with a strong chin, a nice little nose, and her eyes were round and big and pretty. More than her looks, however, it was the air of loneliness about her that he recognized. So he'd followed her, just to see where she was going. He had nothing else to do, and it would help kill some time before he had to get back home. Maybe he'd be able to talk to her, ask her out, make a connection with her, and they could date all summer, and maybe she'd be able to help make this summer bearable. He was smiling as these thoughts filled his mind—and then in front of the post office, a group of kids across the street starting yelling at her as she passed.

"Hey, Spook, where you off to?"

"Spook, do you have anything that's not black?"

"Going a-haunting, Spook? There's a house on the east end that needs haunting!"

"It's not Halloween yet, Spook, why ya wearing a costume?"

And then they started laughing. It was a cruel laugh, like the kids who made fun of him. His stomach clenched into a knot.

The girl ignored them, didn't look at them, acted as if she hadn't heard a word they'd said. But she walked just a little bit faster.

The laughter made him angry. He wanted to punch the smiles right off their asshole faces. He knew what it was like to be made fun of—which was part of the reason he worked out so hard. When he'd arrived at Thomas More, he'd already been six feet tall and weighed a hundred and forty wiry pounds. His bones showed through his skin, and he could count his ribs in the mirror. Then one of the gym teachers, who heard a bunch of boys calling Chris the "Jolly Green Giant" in the locker room one afternoon, suggested he start lifting weights. It turned out that Chris liked it, and he started getting up early in the mornings to lift before class, when the weight room was deserted.

He liked having it to himself, liked the sound the weights made when he set them down in the otherwise silent gym. He'd grown another three inches since then, but had put on thirty pounds. But getting his mother to buy him a gym membership so he could keep working out during the summer had been a battle.

"Shouldn't you be spending the summer expanding your mind?" she'd insisted. "I gave you your reading list, didn't I? I can add more books if you need more things to do. And I thought you were going to be my research assistant." She'd offered to pay him five dollars an hour to look up information on the Internet for her.

But for once his father intervened. "I don't see what it can hurt. Come on, Lois, he can't spend the whole summer cooped in here with a book. He has to keep his body sharp, too—remember? Body, mind, spirit?"

His mother, startled by this rebellion, had stared, her mouth opening and closing. She wasn't used to being opposed by anyone, and finally she just threw her arms up in the air. "Fine! But if it interferes with your reading or your work, it's over."

Chris sat back on the bench and wished again he had worked up the nerve to say hello to the girl. It had been more than a month; the summer was almost over. Would he ever get to meet her?

*Why did they call her Spook? Just because she wore black all the time? That's just stupid. It's not like she's ugly or anything. She's pretty even if she doesn't do anything with her hair or wear makeup. Why are the kids so mean to her? What did she do to them? Can't they see how pretty she is?*

He wanted to say to her, "Don't listen to them— they're assholes. They're gonna grow up and be garbagemen or something like that, and have rotten little lives with wives who can't stand them and kids who won't listen to them." Chris closed his eyes, imagining himself reaching out and stroking her hair. "They don't know what they're talking about. They're idiots, ignore them."

He'd practice in the mirror at night before bed, before brushing his teeth and washing his face, trying to see which facial expression would be the most reassuring, the friendliest, the studliest—which one might make the girl respond to him. He'd stare at himself, wondering how she would see him. Would she think he looked like Ichabod Crane? Would the goddamned Adam's apple that stuck out so far from his long thin neck make her recoil? Would she think he was tall and dumb-looking? Would he be able to get the words out, or would he stammer and blush and make an ass out of himself like he did at the dances at school?

Every day, he'd venture out into the streets, keeping an eye out for the spook-girl, steeling his nerve to actually talk to her. And every day, he'd see her. He'd sometimes walk behind her for a while as she looked into store windows or stopped into a coffee shop. He'd get a cup of coffee himself and sit on the steps of Spiritus Pizza, keeping his eyes on her, drumming up his courage to say something. *Maybe she's gay*, he got to thinking. *After all, so many people in P-town are*. But she never said a word to anyone, male or female.

Not once had she ever acknowledged his presence. Day in, day out, as more and more tourists filled up the town, as the shops and restaurants and cafés filled, as the beach became wall-to-wall bodies glistening with oil.

Now he was leaving in less than three weeks, and he still hadn't said a word to her. He cursed himself as a dork, loser, jerk, at every missed opportunity. He worked his way through his reading list—Simone deBeauvoir, Germaine Greer, Jane Austen, Charles Dickens, and all the other books his mother felt were mind-expanding and "important" for him to read.

*It's now or never, you big loser,* he thought, getting up off the bench and following her yet again.

She turned in at the library, a narrow three-story building with peeling white paint shaded by an enormous oak tree, and he followed her inside. Up she climbed to the top floor, heading without pause to a section in the back, started scanning the titles in the stacks. Outside he could hear the whoops and whistles of the tourists on vacation, but inside the library all was quiet and still. Keeping his eye on the girl, he fumbled through the magazine rack, scanning the covers of *Time, Newsweek, U.S. News and World Report, Good Housekeeping,* and *Oprah.* He had to move quickly when the girl headed back downstairs with three books in her arms.

The older lady at the counter didn't even look at the girl as she processed the books. "Find everything you needed?"

"Yes, thank you," Spook said so softly that Chris barely heard her. She shoved them into her bag and started back toward the front door.

"Hey," Chris said as she walked past him, leaning up against the wall in what he hoped was a sexy pose. He forced a big smile on his face.

She stopped, looking at him. "Hey," she replied. She searched his face for a moment, then turned and walked out the front door.

Feeling stupid, Chris started after her. *Nice move, slick,* he told himself as he turned to follow her.

She stopped and sat down on a bench, withdrawing a crumpled pack of Parliaments from her bag. She lit one.

*Okay, big guy, this is your shot.*

Taking a deep breath, Chris sat down next to her. "Those are bad for you," he said.

She took a deep inhale, blew the smoke out through her nose, and looked at him without expression. "Are you stalking me?" she asked. Her voice was low, quiet, soft, and feminine.

He flushed, losing what little composure he had. "Um, no." He stuttered a bit. "My name's Chris."

She didn't answer, just kept staring, the cigarette burning between her fingers.

"What's your name?" he asked, knowing that his face was surely as red as his T-shirt. He wiped sweat off his brow. *Come on, come on, answer me, please!*

She kept staring, then turned her head and pitched her cigarette into the street. "I don't know why I smoke. They taste like shit." She shrugged. "Kind of a stupid thing to do."

"Well, then why do you do it?" *What the hell am I saying? Smooth move, idiot. You're lucky she doesn't laugh in your face.*

"Jessie," she said finally, still looking at him. "My name's Jessie Kaye."

"Nice to meet you." He held his hand out, but she ignored it until he finally let it drop back to his side.

"Yeah, whatever." A group of shirtless men in their midthirties passed, laughing and joking.

"This place sure is full of queers," he said.

She turned and looked at him. "*Queers* are people." She tilted her head to one side. "Everyone's got something about them that's not normal." She barked out a small laugh. "Trust me on that."

"Oh, I don't hate gay people or anything like that." He shrugged, flaying himself mentally for coming off like a homophobic jerk. His parents had long made a point of preaching tolerance. Half of their colleagues were gay or lesbian, and Chris knew them all, even called one lesbian couple Aunt Pat and Aunt Sally. He started to feel again that Jessie might be gay herself. "It's all good," he heard himself say. "I just don't understand it myself, but it's all good."

"Nobody's asking you to understand. Nobody's asking for anything—except to be left alone."

*Change the subject, quick, before she asks* you *to leave her* alone. "So," Chris said, "what'd you check out from the library?"

"You *are* stalking me." A ghost of a smile flitted across her face. She was really pretty when she smiled. "Don't you have anything better to do on a nice summer day? Like go to the beach? Rollerblade? Don't you have a girlfriend or anything?"

"No."

"I find that hard to believe," she said, arching an eyebrow.

"Why?"

She sighed. "You're cute. I'd think you'd be beating them off with a stick. Especially since most of the guys in town are gay, right? Hunky straight boys are in short supply."

"You think I'm cute?"

"You didn't answer my question. Why are you stalking me?"

His heart pounding, he wiped sweat off his forehead. "What else is there to do?"

She shook her head. "You can't find anything better to do than stalk the local freak show?" She rolled her eyes. "Don't you swim or sail or fish or all the other things guys are supposed to like to do?"

"No."

She smirked. "Maybe you're gay and you just don't know it yet."

"I highly doubt that."

"I was joking. Not very quick, are you?"

"Guess not." He turned his head and watched a sail-boat on the bay.

She laughed. Her laugh sounded rusty, like she didn't use it very often. "Well, Chris, I like that in a boy. Quick is way overrated."

He relaxed a little, finally. "I've always thought so, too."

"So what brings you to Provincetown for the summer? Since you're not gay, I mean."

He tensed, and then realized she was teasing him. "My parents bought a summer place here. Well, in Truro."

"What do they do?"

"They teach at Boston College."

"Oh." She was distinctly not impressed.

They sat in silence for a minute, watching the tourists. Chris was trying to think of something else to say when she said, "So what do you want to be when you get all grown up into a big bad adult?"

He eyed her. "Promise you won't laugh?"

She held up her right hand, and he noticed her fingers were stained with blue ink. "I swear."

"I want to be on *Road Rules*."

"Road rules?" She stared at him. "What the hell is that?"

"It's a show. On MTV." He felt his face starting to turn red again. Why was he telling her this? He hadn't told anyone; it was his deepest secret. He knew the kids at school would make fun of him if he said anything—and God forbid he tell his mother. She hated MTV—she hated television in general. He could only watch when she wasn't around.

"They put like six kids in an RV and send them all over the place," Chris said. "Like South America, or the Pacific Islands, or Australia or Europe. It's always some place really, really cool, and they have all these really cool but hard missions, like bungee jumping or walking tightropes, or learning how to kickbox, you know, cool stuff that's really hard to do. They have to face their fears, like heights or bugs and stuff, and if they complete all their missions they win prizes. It's really cool. They have to learn how to work as a team and get along with each other, and they're all complete strangers in the beginning, and they're always really different types, and—"

Her face was completely blank.

"Don't you watch MTV?" he asked.

She gave him a withering look. "I don't watch any television."

"Now you sound like my mom."

"Maybe she's on to something."

Once again they'd hit a stalemate. Her cigarette was almost gone; Chris worried that she'd be getting up to leave.

"So what do your parents do?"

She looked away from him. "My father writes books. He's away on a book tour now, leaving me with my brand-new stepmother." Her voice sounded bitter. "She's probably nice enough—but she's like only twenty-two or something. It's gross."

"Where's your mom?"

"Dead." Jessie let out a ring of blue smoke. "She's dead."

"Sorry." He swallowed. Much as his mother annoyed him, he didn't know what he'd do if she weren't around anymore. "I didn't mean to—"

She shrugged again. "It was a couple of years ago." She sighed. "She was pretty cool. I mean, she pissed me off now and then, but overall, she was cool. We used to do stuff together, you know? Just me and her. She was into all kinds of stuff—like birds and the sea and stuff. She wrote poetry. She liked to play the guitar and sing—and she had the best laugh." She stared at a man walking his dog for a moment, and then turned back to him. "Do your parents know? About this road show thing?"

"No. They'd think it was stupid. Especially my mom. She'd think it was a waste of my time."

"Why do you want to do it, then? To piss her off?"

"I just think it would be cool." He stretched his long legs out in front of him and crossed them at the ankles. "Pissing my mom off would just be an added bonus." He grinned at her. "What about you? What do you want to be when you grow up?"

Jessie didn't answer right away. She tossed her cigarette down to the sidewalk and ground it out with her black boot. "Alive," she said finally. "I want to be alive."

He searched her face to see if she was teasing him, but he couldn't read her. She was idly pulling on her lower lip.

She withdrew another cigarette and lit it, blowing out a stream of smoke through her nose. "Do you have dreams?" she asked, turning her brown eyes back to him. "I mean, everyone dreams, but do you remember yours?"

"Sometimes." Most of them were erotic, about beautiful naked women who kissed him and stroked his chest and let him—but he didn't want to tell her that.

"What do you dream about?"

"I don't know." He folded his arms. "Sometimes they're really weird, you know, like riding an elephant on the beach or something like that, but usually I don't remember them."

"Do you ever have nightmares?" she asked.

"Um, I guess, sometimes."

"Do you remember them? What are they about?"

*Okay, she's getting weird on me.* Maybe she was trying to shock him. Girls like her did that a lot. Tried to come off all weird and alternative and shit, just to be in control.

"Well," Chris said, not willing to let that happen, "the only one I ever really remember is one where I'm bouncing on a trampoline."

"That doesn't sound so bad."

"But I keep bouncing and I get higher and higher, until I get so high that the trampoline is only about the size of a postage stamp and I know that I'm too high up, and then I'm falling, and I know the trampoline isn't going to be able to hold me and bounce me back up, and it's just coming toward me faster and faster and just as I'm about to hit it I wake up."

He shivered. He couldn't believe he told her about that. He *hated* that dream. He always woke up sweating and trembling when he had it. He didn't understand the dream; he wasn't afraid of heights or anything, but it always scared him, made his heart race, and it took a long time for him to get back to sleep.

"Nightmares occur for a reason," Jessie said. "I've pretty much determined that."

"What, are you an expert?"

"You could say that." She shook her head. "I wish— I wish I could forget my nightmares, but they won't go away. I try everything—my psychiatrist gave me pills once, but they didn't help." She shuddered. "I mean, they were supposed to make me sleep without dreaming, but it only made things worse."

"You were seeing a psychiatrist?" He was starting to think he might be learning too much, too fast, about this strange girl in black.

"Isn't everyone?" Jessie's tone was bitter. "My dad thought I needed one when my mother died. Everybody thought I was crazy." She gave a bitter bark of a laugh. "They still do. That's why they call me 'Spook.' That's why I'm homeschooled. That's why I don't have any friends."

"Wow." He felt stupid. "I don't think you're crazy."

"Thanks." She stubbed out her cigarette. "I'll give you this. You might not be quick, but you're kind of sweet."

He grinned widely. "I try."

"And now I have this stepmother." She lit another cigarette, her third. "She's not even ten years older than me. How gross is that? But *I'm* the crazy one. Dad goes out and marries some total stranger young enough to be his daughter, for Christ's sake—and doesn't even tell me about her until they're married—but *I'm* crazy." Her fingers twitched. "Doesn't he know—" She broke off and looked away.

"Know what?"

"Nothing." She stood up. "Nice meeting you, Chris."

"Can I walk you home?"

"You don't mind being seen with the town whack-job?" She raised her eyebrows. "Think of your reputation, Chris. *Everyone* thinks I'm crazy—and everyone can't be wrong, can they?"

"I don't care what anyone thinks."

"Not even your mom?"

He stopped and stared at her. A weak smile twitched at the corner of her lips. He grinned back at her. "Especially not my mom."

They started walking in silence up Commercial Street. "You wanna go see a movie or something sometime?" he blurted out, his face reddening again. *Smooth move, stud man*, he cursed himself.

"I don't know if that's such a good idea. You're a nice guy, and there's a lot about me . . ." Jessie paused and didn't continue.

"A lot about you what?"

"Never mind." She started walking again.

"You never said what books you checked out." He changed the subject, figuring he'd ask her again later.

"Are you sure you want to know?"

"Why wouldn't I? They're just books."

"Books are very powerful, Chris. The pen is mightier than the sword, after all." She stopped and opened her bag, pulling the three books out and handing them over to him. He looked at the spines. *Demonic Possession. The Golden Bough. By Bell, Book and Candle: Exorcism Rituals.* He handed them back to her.

She stared into his face. "Aren't you glad you asked?"

He just stared at her, not sure what to say. Who was this girl?

A taunting half smile crept across her face. "Do you want to know why I checked these out? Do you really want to know?"

He stood firm. "Yes," he said.

"I'll make a deal with you, Chris. I'll tell you why, and then, after that, if you still want to take me to a movie, I'll go with you."

"Deal," he said.

She leaned close to him. "I think I'm possessed," she whispered.

She pulled back to look up at him. Her crooked little half smile came back. "So, do you still want to take me to a movie?"

He stared down at her. Who was this girl? he asked himself again.

His face betrayed his thoughts—his feelings of confusion, weirdness, revulsion. What kind of a girl would say such a thing? What kind of a girl would want to check such books out of the local library?

"That's what I thought," she said.

And she turned, running away from him.

"Hey, wait, I wasn't—"

*Wasn't what?* he asked himself. *Wasn't just getting a*

*little bit freaked out by you?* If that was her intention—
to shock him, to freak out—she'd finally succeeded.

He thought about running after her, to prove to her
that he wasn't so easily weirded out.

But somehow, he couldn't. He just stood there, watching her run down the street with her crazy-ass books.

*Possessed? What the hell is that supposed to mean?*

He turned, letting out a long sigh of disappointment
and heading for the shuttle stop to take him home.

# Chapter 3

*Vicky struggled against the ropes binding her hands behind her back to no avail. The sadistic bastard who'd chloroformed her and brought her to this strange place in the middle of nowhere had tied the knots too tightly. There was barely enough room for her to even wiggle her hands about.*

*She heard footsteps outside the door, which swung open, light spilling into the room. A form was outlined in the door. "Ah, Ms. Knight, have you reconsidered your foolish position?"*

*The tape over her mouth kept her from responding, but she shot daggers out of her eyes at him. Brick Baldwin! She might have known he was behind her kidnapping—who else would be so vile, so purely evil? Wasn't it bad enough he was trying to steal the election? Was there no low to which he wouldn't stoop in his insane bid for power? She had to get away, she had to finally expose his evil to the light of day—too much depended on it. The fate of everyone in Louisiana was depending on her. . . .*

He flicked the light switch on, briefly blinding her as the room flooded with light. She glanced around quickly, looking for something, anything, that could help her to escape. She had to get away—she couldn't remain his prisoner. The information she had was too crucial. The evidence had to reach the authorities in time. "Of course, how silly of me." He chuckled, raising the hackles on the back of her neck. His eyes glinted malevolently as they swept up and down her bound form, his eyes lingering on her heaving breasts. "You can't answer because your mouth is taped." In three steps he was in front of her, and she could smell the sour whiskey and stale sweat. He always stank. He narrowed his eyes, then reached up and ripped the tape off her mouth, taking skin with it. She let out a howl of pain. "You'll never get away with this, you scum."

"On the contrary, Ms. Knight, I've already gotten away with it." He smiled, showing his crooked teeth, yellowed from years of smoking. His breath was so foul she almost gagged. He reached down and cupped her left breast in his hand. The lust in his eyes was unmistakable.

Vicky spat defiantly in his face. "I'll never tell you who my source is, you bastard."

"Oh, you'll tell me, Baldwin said with an evil leer, pulling a bottle out of his jacket pocket. "You see this? It's sulfuric acid, Ms. Knight. Have you ever seen what sulfuric acid does to skin? It eats right through it, like a warm knife through soft butter." He stroked her cheek. "Pretty as you are, it would be a shame to spoil your looks forever, now, wouldn't it?" He uncorked the bottle and stepped back a few steps. "Now, tell me. Who in my organization is the traitor? All you have to do *is tell me and you can walk away from all of this. If you don't"—he smiled viciously at her—"you will become so ugly no one would look at you, except with pity in their eyes."*

*Vicky started to scream. . . .*

"This is crap!"

Karen ripped the headphones off her head and threw them down on her desk in disgust. She stared at the blinking cursor. Maybe that agent was right and she really *was* a no-talent hack. She rubbed her eyes.

No, Philip believed in her. *Philip has read my work and he says I'm good.*

*Philip Kaye.*

*The famous Philip Kaye.*

*My husband.*

With a sigh, Karen highlighted everything she'd just written and then hit the Delete key. It all vanished in the blink of an eye.

She was having trouble concentrating, that was the problem. She sighed and stood up, stretching, her back cracking in a couple of places. She walked over to the window. From the distance the neon lights of Commercial Street glowed.

She knew why she couldn't focus on the book.

Because she couldn't forget that the first Mrs. Kaye had died in this house.

Why hadn't Philip told her?

And why hadn't Philip told her about the Hatch family? All that death in this very house! It freaked her out.

*That's why he didn't tell you*, she thought. *He didn't want to frighten you. He'll be angry with Mrs. Winn for spilling the beans before he had a chance to let her in, gently, gradually . . .*

In the two days since Alice Winn had told her about

all the death in the house, Karen hadn't been able to focus on anything. She had hoped by now that the place would feel like home to her. But it didn't. Her boxes might be up in the attic, her clothes might be hanging in the closet, but the place was not home to her.

She couldn't stop thinking about the Hatches, their grisly bodies strewn across the floor downstairs, blood on the walls. *Lettie Hatch took a butcher knife, and with it took her father's life. To put an end to all her strife, she used it then on her father's wife.*

Somehow, even worse was thinking about Ivy Kaye. Alice Winn didn't know any details about Karen's predecessor's suicide—she'd been hired afterward. All she knew was gossip she'd heard around town, and she refused to spread gossip, she said. Karen had just smiled wryly, remembering how quickly she'd told her about Lettie Hatch.

Karen certainly couldn't talk to Jessie about it. In fact, she couldn't talk to Jessie about anything. Every time she tried to make even the slightest conversation with the girl, all Jessie would do was stare at her with her big brown eyes and shrug. Outside of her schoolwork, all Jessie seemed to do was write in that notebook of hers. Her fingers seemed to be permanently stained with blue ink.

"Do you want to be a writer?" Karen asked her that afternoon at lunch, hoping to finally draw something—anything—out of her stepdaughter.

But there was only a shrug.

"You know that I'm a writer, too," Karen said, still trying. "I'm writing a novel."

Nothing this time. No response of any kind. She might as well have been talking to her plate. Jessie finished eating her sandwich, picked up her notebook, and headed back up to her room. The door slammed behind her.

*It's not healthy to stay cooped up in the house all the time,* Karen thought. *Doesn't she have any friends? Isn't she interested in boys? Isn't she interested in anything at all?*

And if that wasn't enough, Philip hadn't called all day. She'd tried his cell phone a few times, always getting his voice mail. She tried to keep her voice light, as if there weren't anything wrong—*Philip doesn't like needy women,* she kept reminding herself, *he's said that many times.* She even left messages for him at the hotels he'd been staying at—and he still hadn't called.

*Who have I married? What have I gotten myself into here?*

But she stopped that line of thought dead in its tracks—that would be admitting her mother was right, that they should have waited to get married, that Karen was making a mistake rushing into this marriage.

Even if he was Philip Kaye.

Her hero.

Her husband.

She'd rather die than admit her mother was right.

After she'd finished drinking her tea, she'd gone straight to the computer and searched the Internet for information about the Hatch murders. What she'd found had chilled her. There was a site called lettiehatchet.net that some scholar from Boston had put together; she didn't know how true any of the information on the site was, but if even half of it was true—she shuddered and hugged herself tightly.

She picked up the stack of printouts.

*The Hatch murders were among the most noto-rious in Massachusetts history; at the time the*

Hatch murders were all anyone on Cape Cod—
and Boston—could talk about. The Hatches were
not only wealthy but politically connected. Horace
Hatch, the father of Lettie Hatch, had served several terms in the U.S. Senate, and was said to have
presidential aspirations. After his murder, a memo-
rial service was held in Washington attended by
President Coolidge and his wife. President Coolidge
himself spoke in glowing terms of all the "great
work" Senator Hatch had done, not only for his
Massachusetts constituency, but for the country
as a whole:

"Senator Hatch will surely be remembered by
history as one of the great Massachusetts patri-
ots, on a level with President Adams, John Hancock,
and Paul Revere," he'd said during his speech.

Modern historians don't quite agree with President Coolidge's assessment. Senator Hatch's
voting record was not only spotty but often contradictory. He opposed women's suffrage, for example, despite the fact that he married a suffragette.
He was also against American involvement in
World War I, opposed almost any legislation that
originated in the Wilson White House, and was
credited at the time as one of the legislators who
led the fight to defeat American ratification of the
Treaty of Versailles. He was a vocal opponent of
American involvement in the League of Nations—
and most historians agree that this doomed the
League of Nations to failure and ineptitude, which
resulted in the Second World War and the rise of
Hitler.

His much younger second wife, Sarah Jane
McConnell, had been a suffragette and quite a famous one, at that. She had written several articles on the subject of women's suffrage, had been

*arrested several times in protest marches, and had participated in the notorious hunger strikes. There is no record of how the suffragette met the senator, nor of any romance between the two. Their marriage, from all accounts, was sudden and unexpected—particularly from the point of view of Washington hostess Eliza Washburn, whom most Washington insiders thought to have the inside track on becoming the second Mrs. Hatch. A letter from the widowed Mrs. Washburn to her sister has survived; in it, Mrs. Washburn is quite frank about her anger at being so unceremoniously jilted for a much younger, far less socially connected woman. She went so far as to call the second Mrs. Hatch a "scheming viper." After the murders, Mrs. Washburn wrote her sister again to say that the senator "certainly received his just deserts."*

*Except for her suffrage work, nothing much is known of the second Mrs. Hatch. She seems to have appeared in Washington from nowhere, taken up residence at a women's boardinghouse, and started working on the suffrage movement. Her surviving writings show her to be a lucid thinker, capable of making and defending arguments, with no small skill at the use of language. Once she married Senator Hatch, however, her writings stopped. She certainly never published again.*

*Little is known, either, about the first Mrs. Hatch, born Ellen Chamberlain into a prominent Boston family who traced their history back to the Mayflower. This first Mrs. Hatch never resided in Washington, choosing to remain in Boston or in Provincetown, where the senator had a summer house. She didn't campaign for her husband, and most gossip from the time holds that the marriage had been over for quite some time. Publicly, the senator always claimed that his wife was an invalid—although Provincetown gossip claimed otherwise. Ellen Hatch died rather suddenly from unknown causes several years before his remarriage; there was only one child from his first marriage—the soon-to-be notorious Lettie. Even after her mother's death, Lettie remained in Provincetown with her governess rather than going to live with her father.*

*Witnesses from the time testified at Lettie's trial that she had hated her stepmother—which her governess, Anna Windham, claimed was just "malicious gossip." Miss Windham claimed that the Hatch family had gotten along beautifully—that Lettie and her stepmother, while not having a "mother-daughter" relationship (which, she claimed, would have been absurd given the closeness in their ages), were very close. Lettie herself never gave any testimony other than to protest her innocence; and it is very likely that without the alibi Miss Windham gave her she would have been convicted and hanged. Public sentiment was definitely against young Lettie—she was crucified in the newspapers, people crossed the street rather than come face-to-face with her; the Hatch house was frequently vandalized. At one point, an angry mob showed up on the doorstep, shouting epithets and throwing bottles and rocks, and the local constabulary was forced to disperse them.*

*Was Miss Windham telling the truth? Most newspapers and citizens of Provincetown at the time didn't believe so. Miss Windham's story held that at the time someone was inside butchering Horace and Sarah Jane Hatch, she and Lettie were walking along the sand dunes on the other side of the Cape. Miss Windham claimed that Lettie had never been out of her sight that entire day, and so someone else must have committed the murders.*

No witnesses ever came forward to corroborate their story, however, and indeed, contradictory testimony was presented at the trial—testimony claiming Lettie had not been with Miss Windham for at least an hour around the time the crimes were committed. Yet that testimony—from a gardener who was known to drink heavily and to have a grudge against both Miss Windham and Lettie—was shaken up by Lettie's attorney at the trial; ultimately the jury chose to believe Miss Windham rather than the gardener. The gardener, a young man of Portuguese descent named Pedro Fournier, claimed that he'd seen Lettie go into the house by herself shortly after Sarah Jane had returned from the grocer's. Lettie's attorney brought to light the fact that young Pedro had attempted to court Lettie and been spurned.

The butcher knife used to commit the crimes was never recovered, although a particularly large one was missing from the Hatch kitchen. Investigators believed the missing knife was the one used in the commission of the crime. The best the prosecution could do was show a knife "similar" to the one used in the commission of the murders.

It also hurt the prosecution's case that the clothes Lettie was wearing at the time the bodies were found showed no trace of blood, and there was no way—given the bloodbath the Hatch house was turned into—that she could have committed the murders without becoming completely drenched in blood. And several people testified that the clothes she was wearing at the time of the bodies' discovery were the same clothes she had on that morning. The prosecution insisted she *had changed clothes to commit the crime, then destroyed the blood-spattered clothes and bathed, dressing again in the clothes witnesses had seen her in that morning—but it was only a theory they couldn't prove, since they were unable to recover the clothes they theorized she'd changed into.*

*So, was Lettie Hatch indeed "Lettie Hatchet"— a notorious murderer—or merely a victim of circumstance? The secret died with Lettie in 1962, forty years after the crimes were committed. Many thought the fact she continued to live in the house where her parents were murdered was evidence of her guilt. "How," people asked, "could anyone live in that house?" was their line of reasoning. Others, however, saw it as proof of Lettie's innocence. Miss Windham, who died in 1947, lived with Lettie until her own death.*

*After the verdict of not guilty was returned, both women refused to ever discuss the case again. No killer was ever brought to justice for the crimes that were the talk of Cape Cod that winter of 1922. Whatever the two women knew, they took it to their graves with them.*

*As a side note, another, less well-known murder had occurred only a few weeks before the Hatch murders—that of a young artist named Orville Axelrod. His body was found hacked to death a few blocks from the Hatch house. Axelrod was known to be quite a ladies' man, and no one was ever arrested for that crime, either. Many theorists have conjectured that the two crimes were somehow related—but no link could ever be conclusively drawn between the crimes. It is doubtful if Axelrod, who was part of the artists' colony at the time and certainly not on the social plane of*

*the Hatches, even was acquainted with the sena-*
*tor or his family.*

Karen had read all of this, over and over. There was
more she had printed out, too, more speculation, theories, and even photographs of all the principals in the
case. The photograph of Lettie Hatch was from 1943.
No longer a teenager, she looked serious and severe.
She looked as though she never laughed, never smiled.
She stared grimly at the camera, her hair pulled back
into a tight bun behind her head, her blouse buttoned
up to her chin. Her eyes were cold and distant. It wasn't,
Karen thought, hard to imagine her taking a butcher
knife to her father and stepmother.

*Stepmother.*

That was the part that bothered Karen the most, even
though she knew she was being stupid and irrational. A
prominent father, a second wife almost the daughter's
age, a governess, and a teenaged girl—all living in this
house over eighty years ago. The similarities—

*Stop it, Karen*, she commanded herself. *Jessie is not
Lettie Hatch, and I'm not Sarah Jane.* In spite of herself,
she shivered. She picked up the page with the photos of
Horace and Sarah Jane. Horace was a frightening-look-
ing man with intense eyes and a grimace on his face. *It
couldn't have been easy to be married to him*, she thought,
and looked at the image of Sarah Jane. She wasn't smiling either, but it was easy to see she had been quite a
beauty—long curling blond hair, and a pert cupid's bow
mouth. She put the printouts down and shivered. *So
much death.*

It brought her mind back to the first Mrs. Kaye. Her
predecessor.

*Why had Ivy killed herself?*
*And why didn't Philip call?*
*Why the hell did I come up here?*

*Why did I marry him?*

She closed her eyes and took a deep breath. From the back of the house the waves kept up a steady crash on the beach. It was so quiet, so still. Not a mile away the town was a raucous party of life, but here, in this house, it was quiet . . .

Quiet as a grave.

Both Alice and Jessie were in bed. It was after ten. They'd had dinner together; Alice had made a nice chicken salad with vegetables on the side. They'd eaten in silence. Karen had again tried to draw Jessie out, get her to say something, anything, but she was either given a shrug in response or just ignored. The air of tension made her almost want to scream.

Finally, she stopped trying.

She tried to feel compassion for the girl. *If I'm to be her stepmother, I'm going to have to try to feel something for her.* Karen tried to imagine what it would be like to find her mother's body, hanging lifelessly from some beam, and couldn't. Her own mother was so vital and alive, always in motion, always talking or cleaning or cooking or doing *something*. She couldn't imagine coming into a room and seeing her hanging from the rafters—

*Stop it, Karen, you're scaring yourself.*

"I need to get out of this house," she said aloud.

She headed into the bathroom and turned on the shower. She loved the shower—the three heads with strong sprays of water always felt so good. Feeling a little foolish, she locked the door behind her. She stepped into the water and let it flow over her. *You need a break from this place, Karen*, she commanded herself. *It'll do you some good to get out of the house.*

She finished her shower, put on some clothes—a black T-shirt reading *It's not the heat, it's the stupidity*, and a pair of jean shorts—and crept down the stairs.

Jessie's bedroom door was shut, her lights out. Karen grabbed her purse and checked for her keys and wallet.

She slipped out the front door into the warm night and walked down the street. By August vacation time, it was still early; the tourists were out in force on the sidewalk. Karen breathed the warm night air and tasted salt from the sea. She hadn't really explored the town yet. It was high time she did so, if this was going to be her home.

She walked past several clubs, crowded full of people drinking, music blaring. She paused outside one of them, felt tempted to go inside, but finally just kept walking. The crowd was her age, early- to midtwenties, but she was different now. She wasn't a single woman out for a good time anymore. She was a married woman.

Despite the warmth of the night, she felt cold and hugged her arms around herself. *What was I thinking coming out tonight? I don't want to deal with getting hit on or anything. I just want to drink something—drink a few somethings and forget about everything, forget that—*

*—forget that maybe marrying Philip was a mistake.*

"Stop it, Karen Kaye." She shook her head. Loud music was coming out of a bar just ahead of her. She held her head up high and paid a five-dollar cover to a bald-headed man with muscles bulging under his tight black T-shirt who smiled at her. She smiled back and entered the darkness.

She paused for a moment to get her bearings. Buoys, fishing nets, and other maritime paraphernalia hung from the aged weathered wooden walls. The place smelled of beer and sweat. Two pierced, tattooed men were slinging drinks at a long bar to her immediate left, and another couple of bars were placed throughout the room. There was a small dance floor off to the side, but few were actually dancing.

*Here goes,* Karen thought, and walked determinedly up to the bar and ordered a beer. She took a swig from the bottle and leaned back against the bar.

That's when it hit her she was the only woman in the place.

*Perfect*, she thought, smiling to herself, *a gay bar.*

She had nothing against gay bars—back in New Orleans, she and Dave had often gone dancing at the gay bars in the Quarter. In fact, this was perfect. Absolutely perfect. Nobody would probably talk to her, but she'd be in a crowd of warm bodies nonetheless, and she sure didn't have to worry about being hit on. She took another swig.

The music stopped, and the lights dimmed. "Ladies and gentlemen, the A House is proud to present the vocal stylings of Miss Zsa Zsa Lahore!"

*Zsa Zsa Lahore?* Karen stifled a giggle.

"Hello, everyone!" A small figure climbed up onto the small stage, wearing a black leather miniskirt over fishnet stockings and spike heels. A huge blonde Dolly Parton–esque wig towered over the performer's head, and long curly thick blond ringlets dropped down to bare shoulders. Dangly rhinestone earrings swung wildly with every movement, and a teardrop necklace dropped itself right down into the cleavage inside a red satin shirt.

"Welcome to my fans and all of you wonderful tourists who keep our li'l town alive! Bless you and spend all your money! We *need* it!"

The crowd cheered, and Karen found herself smiling. She'd been to drag shows before in New Orleans, but without exception she almost always could tell the performers were men in dresses. Zsa Zsa, though, was a master illusionist. If Karen didn't know better, she would have sworn Zsa Zsa was a woman.

She recognized the opening bars of Shania Twain's "Man! I Feel Like a Woman!" as Zsa Zsa began her act. And what an act it was. Zsa Zsa had the song down perfectly. She didn't just stand there making minimal movements, she actually danced around, every once in a while letting loose with a high kick Karen wouldn't have thought possible in that tight miniskirt. People crowded up to the stage to offer dollar bills, which Zsa Zsa gratefully accepted and tucked into her cleavage. The song ended, and another started—Karen recognized "Bootylicious" by Destiny's Child—and she couldn't help but laugh as Zsa Zsa worked her "booty" for the crowd, turning her back to them and bending over and slapping it.

At the end, she finished and bowed to thunderous applause, thanking the crowd before introducing the next performer—Floretta Flynn, a three-hundred-pound drag queen in full Nashville regalia. She launched into "You Ain't Woman Enough to Take My Man" as Zsa Zsa disappeared into the crowd.

Karen turned back to the bar, finishing her beer and putting the empty down. The bartender was at the other end of the bar mixing what looked like kamikazes. She fished a five out of her wallet and tried to get his attention, to no avail.

"Hello, gorgeous," a deep voice said next to her.

She turned her head and found herself looking right into Zsa Zsa's heavily made up face. Zsa Zsa had the deepest green eyes she'd ever seen.

Karen smiled. "Hi," she managed to say. "You were wonderful—and you look *fabulous*."

"Aren't you sweet?" Zsa Zsa adjusted her breasts with a dramatic roll of her eyes. "God, I can't wait to get home and out of these fucking shoes!" She glared at the bartender, who was talking to a shirtless blond in his early twenties. "*Joey!*" she screamed in her cracked falsetto. "Who does a bitch have to blow in this bar to get a fucking drink?"

Joey walked down to them with a scowl on his face. "How many times do I have to tell you, Zsa Zsa, that you use your teeth too much for that offer to work?" He winked at Karen, who smiled.

"You hear what I have to put up with from the trash in this bar?" Zsa Zsa said to Karen, throwing her hands up to the sky. "Do you think Shania has to put up with this kind of crap?"

"Shania probably knows not to use her teeth," Joey quipped as he mixed Zsa Zsa a vodka tonic without asking. He gave Karen a dazzling smile. "Another beer?"

"Thanks," she said.

"Put it on my tab," Zsa Zsa commanded regally.

"About your tab—"

"You have customers," Zsa Zsa said pointedly. He laughed and moved back down the bar.

"Thank you," Karen said, toasting Zsa Zsa with her bottle.

"You're welcome." Zsa Zsa took a long swig of her own drink. "So, tell me, where you from?"

"New Orleans originally." Karen couldn't help but smile. One of Zsa Zsa's long false eyelashes was loose. "But I live here now—I just arrived yesterday."

"A new local?" Zsa Zsa's eyebrows went up. "I didn't hear about anyone new. Where do you live, honey?"

"In the east end. A gorgeous old Victorian on the water."

"Hmmmm." Zsa Zsa's eyes lit up. "Don't tell me you're the new Mrs. Philip Kaye? I heard you were young, but you're practically *jailbait*."

Karen bristled. "I'm twenty-three."

"Honey—it's your business. Personally, I adore older men. Younger ones don't really know what they're doing in the sack, and I'm *tired* of breaking them in." Zsa Zsa winked at her, and sighed. "You want to get out of here and get some pizza? I'm fucking starving. I was afraid to eat—this outfit is getting a little too tight, if you know what I mean. No offense, but this hardly seems like your kind of dive."

*What the hell, I wanted safe company, and it doesn't get much safer than a drag queen*, Karen thought, finishing her beer. "Lead on, Zsa Zsa."

Spiritus Pizza wasn't yet crowded—Karen had heard the stories of the place becoming a mob scene once the bars let out—so they were able to actually find a table inside. Zsa Zsa devoured her slice of pepperoni before Karen had finished putting red pepper on hers. "So, New Orleans girl, what do you think of our little town?"

"It's nice." Karen took a bite, and sighed. "I mean, I've only been here a few days, and I've been unpacking, but from what I've seen—"

"Different from New Orleans." Zsa Zsa sighed and waved at a couple of men who walked in holding hands. "I've only been down there twice—I performed at Mardi Gras a couple of times—and I loved it there. Such a fun place. I've always wanted to go back when I wasn't working, to really enjoy it, you know—but never managed to."

"Well, if you ever need a tour guide, Zsa Zsa . . ."

"Call me Bobbie. That's my real name—Bobbie Noble, when I'm not in this getup." She laughed. "Bobbie Noble, carpenter by day—Zsa Zsa Lahore, superstar by night."

"You're a *carpenter*?"

"What can I say? I like working with wood." Bobbie winked.

It took Karen a couple of seconds to get the joke. Then she laughed.

"Though I have to say," Bobbie said, "it's a bitch on the hands." He held up his callused palms. "Hardly the hands of a lady, right?" He laughed. "So what do you do, Mrs. Kaye?"

*"Karen."* She hesitated for a moment, then said, "Well, I want to be—" She stopped herself. She heard Philip's voice in her head. *Never say you want to be a writer—you* are *a writer.* "I'm a writer," she said obediently.

"Of course. Would Philip Kaye marry anything but?"

It hit her that she didn't know what the first Mrs. Kaye had done.

"So have you published anything?" Bobbie waved over at a guy who had just walked in. "By the way, stay away from that one. She's a crystal head." Bobbie made a face. "Tweaking all the time."

Karen smiled. The crystal head was gorgeous all the same. What gene did gay guys have that made them all so sexy?

"To answer your question," she said, moving her eyes back to Bobbie, "I haven't published anything yet, but I'm writing a murder mystery."

Bobbie made a face. "Weeeeelll, I'd say you certainly live in the right house for that."

"You mean the Hatches."

"I don't mean the Munsters."

"I've heard all about the grisly murders. In fact, I came out tonight trying to forget them."

"Consider the subject closed then."

"Actually," Karen said, "how long have you been in Provincetown?"

"Oh God, girl. Too long. Sometimes I think I was here before the Pilgrims got off their boat."

Karen played with the crust of her pizza. "Well, by any chance, do you know anything about the first Mrs. Kaye?"

Bobbie gave her a look. "Didn't your husband tell you?"

Karen blushed. "All I know is that she hanged herself. I just found out about it a couple of days ago."

Bobbie looked at her with compassion. "Ivy Kaye was a strange lady. She was a poet, but I never read anything she wrote, you know? But she looked like one—she always dressed in black and had this tortured look on her face. She liked to hang out in coffee shops, and always had a notebook with her."

*Just like Jessie.*

"That poor Jessie," Bobbie said, shaking his head. "The kids around her call her 'Spook,' you know. After her mother died, she started dressing like her and acting like her—like she's trying to *be* her mom or something."

"Well, I'm going to be a good stepmom. At least, I hope I will be."

"Oh, she needs it, honey. She needs something. Nothing against your husband, of course, because I'm a huge, huge, huge fan, but . . ." Bobbie paused. "It's just that he's gone so much, and I see poor little Jessie roaming all over town, all by herself." He took a sip of his Diet Coke. "I take it Mr. Kaye is out of town now, huh? Otherwise, you wouldn't be out prowling gay bars."

Karen smiled weakly. "A book tour."

Bobbie nodded. "Well, you'll be good for Jessie. I mean, imagine what it must have been like to come home and find your mom hanging in the living room. No note, no explanation, nothing."

Karen covered her face with her hands, then removed them, looking over at Bobbie's heavily madeup face. "I have to admit the house kind of creeps me out. All of its history. Ivy Kaye. Lettie Hatch . . ."

"Honey, the Hatch murders were more than eighty

years ago. It's just a house where some bad things happened. You're bringing new energy in that's gonna push all that bad shit right out." He leaned in closer to her. "You know, I've always wanted to see the inside of that house."

Karen smirked. "There's no blood on the floor, if that's what you're looking for."

"Karen." Bobbie placed a hand over his heart. "You wound me for thinking my motives so crass. It's just that it's a classic example of New England Victorian architecture, that's all."

Karen laughed. "Sorry." She thought of something. "You're a carpenter, right? Do you do renovations?"

"My bread and butter." He pulled off his wig. For the first time Karen saw his own short, thick black hair. "This is just for fun."

"Well . . ." Karen hesitated, but then remembered Philip saying, *It's your money now, too.* "I'd like to fix the attic up into an office. Would that be something you'd be able to do?"

Bobbie beamed. "Honey, I have the feeling this is the start of a *beautiful* friendship."

They knocked together the paper cups of Diet Coke.

# Chapter 4

The full moon glowed in a cloudless night, giving off almost enough light to make it seem like midday. He trudged through the dunes, looking from side to side. Her note had said she'd be here, but there was no sign of her anywhere.

"She's playing you for a fool," went through his mind, and he kicked at the yellow sand in frustration. Why would she meet him? What did he have to offer her other than his love? He was crazy to think she would actually come. It had been a trick, something for her to laugh about with her friends later—the dumb fisherman she'd duped into meeting her at the dunes, who probably waited all night in vain for her to appear. But he couldn't just take the chance and leave. What if he was wrong, and he missed a chance to see her? To talk to her? To look into her beautiful eyes and hold her in his arms, maybe even kiss her?

No, that was too much to hope for. A girl like her, who could have her choice of men, would never share a kiss with the likes of him. Which was exactly why she wasn't here. He was a fool to think—

"Hello," she said as she stepped around into sight. "I didn't think you would really come." Her face was smiling.

He gave out a sigh of relief, and gave her his warmest smile. "I was beginning to think you weren't going to come."

"It wasn't easy to get out of the house. They're watching me like a hawk." She made a face. "No one can know I'm meeting you." She stepped forward and took his hand. Hers was moist with sweat, and he brought it to his lips and kissed it. She smiled up at him, and put her arms around him, clinging to him. "I don't know how much longer I can stand it."

"We're together now, that's all that matters."

"If he finds out, he'll kill us both." She tilted her head back. "I'm frightened, Samuel. Really and truly frightened. There's something—" She broke off, her eyes wide. "Did you hear that?"

He had heard it, and the goose bumps rose on his arms. Someone was coming.

"We've got to hide!" she whispered, her head turning from side to side frantically. But they were out in the open, on the beach—anyone coming through the dunes would see them clearly.

She broke away from him and started to run back through the dunes without waiting for him. With a sigh, he started after her—

—and then he heard an earsplitting scream.


A clap of thunder woke Chris with a start.

He sat up in bed, sweating. Rain pelted against his bedroom window, which rattled in the wind. His heart was pounding. The clock on his nightstand showed just past eight—an hour before his alarm was set to go off. "Just a dream," he said out loud, "just a dream."

He took several deep breaths. His heart rate was slowing down. He got up, stretched, and walked into the bathroom. As he brushed his teeth, he tried to remember the dream he'd been having. The vestige of fear he'd felt was starting to drain away as his mind cleared. It hadn't been as bad as the trampoline dream, but he'd just as soon not have it again.

*It's her fault*, he thought as he washed his face. *All that nonsense about being possessed—she's a nutcase for sure.*

He hadn't seen her since. He knew he should just forget about her, but somehow he couldn't get her out of his mind. *You're being a dork, she said she didn't want to go out with you, and why would you want to go out with a nutcase anyway? Do you think a nutcase is the only kind of girl who'd go out with you?*

He'd spent the rest of the day doing mundane things— helping his father trim the rosebushes, taking out the garbage, cleaning the house—but try as he might, he couldn't forget the look on Jessie's face when she'd said those crazy things to him.

After dinner, he went to his room and watched MTV for the rest of the night—they were running a *Road Rules* marathon—but still he couldn't get her out of his head. The look in her eyes was so haunting. Finally he signed on to the Internet and did a search for "possession." As he clicked through the Web sites, he only became more and more convinced she *had* to be crazy. Demonic possession was just like werewolves, witches, vampires, and ghosts—remnants of a superstitious past when science wasn't evolved enough to explain the unusual. Finally, he'd given up and gone to bed.

He'd gone back to the library the next day and checked out one of her father's books—*Philip Kaye's Missing Pieces*. So famous they'd actually stuck his name in the title. He took it down to the beach and sat directly on the sand as he started reading it. The protagonist was a teenaged boy who lived at a boarding school and saw ghosts. Chris kept reading, paying no attention to the time. Philip Kaye was a good writer—the young hero reminded him a lot of some of the kids at More Prep. Five hours passed while Chris read, hooked into the story—and his mother had been furious when he got home with the book under his arm.

"Where have you been?" she demanded. "I was worried sick!" She liked to track his every movement. "You know you're supposed to call if you're going to be late." Her lips were compressed tightly, the lines in her forehead prominent.

"I lost sense of time," he replied. "I was reading, down at the beach. I don't see what the big deal is."

Her mouth opened and closed a few times; then she grabbed the book out from under his arm and examined the jacket. "You were reading *this*?" Her eyes narrowed. "This is trash, Chris!" She handed him back the book. "How many times have I told you not to read this kind of garbage?"

He stuck out his jaw. "I liked it. Besides, Philip Kaye lives here. I got it from the library."

She shook her head. "Go to your room and stay there. We'll talk about this tomorrow when I'm not so angry." That was one of her rules of good parenting. Arguments were counterproductive and did no one any good. If someone was angry in the Muir family, discussions were to be tabled until everyone had calmed down and could talk rationally.

The following morning, when Chris came down to breakfast, his mother had sat down with him at the table and told him, in a calm, reasonable voice, why he shouldn't read those kinds of books. He knew what was required—he shut his mind off and didn't listen to anything other than her vocal inflections, taking her cues to nod and agree when called for.

It was the same old lecture, anyway, the one he always got when he was late, whether it was five minutes or an hour. *Kids disappear all the time, Chris, so when you don't come home when we're expecting you, we fear the worst. Yes, I know you're a big boy and you think you can take care of yourself, but that's probably what all those kids on the milk cartons thought, too. Do you understand me? We gave you a cell phone so you could call us from anywhere, at any time, so we wouldn't worry. And when you have it turned off and we can't reach you, well, of course we expect the absolute worst. We don't want to have to go down to the police morgue and identify your body sometime. You know we worry— do you enjoy making us worry?*

And on and on it would go, until she finally wound down. Finally, Chris mumbled an apology and slipped out of the house to the gym. As he went through his workout, he wondered, for maybe the thousandth time that summer, why his parents couldn't be more *normal.*

That night, when he was getting ready for bed, his mother stuck her head in his bedroom door. "Your father and I are going into Boston tomorrow, and probably will just stay the night there. Do you want to come in with us?"

Her face was slathered with some green gunk that was supposed to keep her skin young and wrinkle-free; her long blond hair (he suspected she dyed it) was pulled back into a ponytail.

"No. I want to go to the gym in the morning."

"Chris . . ." She walked into the room and put her hands on his shoulders. "I'm a little concerned about this"—she fumbled for a moment—"*obsession* you're developing about exercise. Your father and I think maybe you shouldn't go every day—"

"I like going." He stuck his jaw out firmly. "And besides, it's not a bad thing to exercise. Isn't that better than just lying around and getting fat?"

He smiled to himself. He knew his mother was terrified of losing her figure, but would never admit it. That would be admitting she bought into the "patriarchal, impossible standard of female beauty foisted on women by Madison Avenue and Hollywood." She thought he didn't know, but she took aerobics classes regularly in Boston. *You're a hypocrite, Mom*, he thought. *It's not about me working out, it's about control—you just want to control my life, and it kills you that you can't. The older I get, the less control you have, and you just hate it, don't you?*

"It's not that we think it's a bad thing, Chris, but anything in excess isn't good for you. You need more social interaction. You've been here all summer and you haven't made any friends . . ." Her voice trailed off.

*If you're so worried about me not having any friends, why did you ship me off to boarding school?*

Chris bit his lip. No point in bringing up that he'd had a lot of friends in grade school, but after being shipped off to prep school he'd lost touch with them all. And the kids at More Prep—he didn't have much in common with them. They were all spoiled rich kids who spent their summers in Europe. If he'd known it wouldn't cause a nuclear blowout, he would've told his mother: *You sent me to More Prep so I would mix with a better class of people, but they're worse than any kids from the city. They're mean, for one thing, and selfish and spoiled and arrogant, and they drink and use drugs and treat girls like dirt—if you could just hear them talking in the locker room, you'd pull me out of there so fucking fast my head would spin. They make fun of me, and surely that can't be good for the self-esteem you always seem to be so goddamned concerned about.*

But he knew better than to say anything to her. His mother never changed her mind once she'd made it up. She knew what was best for everyone. Her whole life was predicated on being right.

The silence grew more pointed, until finally she threw up her hands and walked out of the room, muttering to herself. He knew she'd complain about him to his father, and Joe would just listen to her, the way he always did. Dad had obviously learned early in their marriage that there wasn't much point in disagreeing with her.

Chris washed his face and pulled on a pair of crimson sweatpants with BOSTON COLLEGE in gold lettering running up the left leg. His parents had already left. The house was silent, other than the sound of the rain. There was another loud crack of thunder. He switched on the kitchen light and started a pot of coffee. There was a note on the refrigerator from his mother, in her scrawling script: *Chris, honey, didn't want to wake you up, we probably won't be back until tomorrow morning, Love, Lois.*

He sighed. *Why can't I have normal parents who just want me to call them Mom and Dad, like everyone else?*

Joe and Lois considered themselves to be "enlightened parents"—which meant he'd always been able to call them by their first names since he turned ten. The rule about yelling was just another example. Nothing he ever did was "bad," either—*nothing* was bad. Things were merely "inappropriate." Once, when he was seven, he'd taken his crayons and started doodling on his bedroom wall. Rather than screaming at him—like other kids' parents would have—they merely sat him down and reasoned with him. *We don't want to interfere with your need to express yourself creatively*, Lois had said, *it's just inappropriate to color on the walls. Crayons are for use on paper, not walls—that's the appropriate way to express your artistry. That way you can show your art to other people so they can appreciate it.*

Of course, the "appropriate" punishment for him was to paint over it so the walls all matched again, but she'd given him a sketchbook. All the same, Chris never used his crayons again.

Lois also wanted him to be self-sufficient as an adult, so he always had chores. He knew how to do the laundry, how to cook, how to iron, how to dust and vacuum. "We're a team," Lois was fond of saying. "Joe and I make the money and provide a nice home for you, and you keep the house going for us so we don't have to worry about that."

Of course, when he was in the wilds of rural Connecticut at Thomas More Prep they had a maid come into the town house in Back Bay. Chris suspected Lois just didn't want to be bothered with doing her own housekeeping. That's what his grandmother thought: *Why do you make him do all the housework, Lois? He's just a child, let him have some fun!* Chris had never seen his mother turn quite that shade of purple before, but rather than yelling she'd merely taken a few breaths and started mouthing her mantra about teaching him "responsibility."

He walked into the living room while the coffee brewed and pulled the curtains on the big picture window to let in some more light. He started to turn away, when he saw something out of the corner of his eye that drew him back to the window.

"What the hell?"

He wiped some of the fog off the window to get a better look.

A figure was standing across the street in the pouring rain, staring at the house.

He opened the front door and stared through the rain.

"Jessie?"

It *was* her.

She crossed the street, came up the walk, and stood on the porch, shivering and dripping.

"Are you crazy?" Chris shook his head. "Get inside! How long you been standing out there?"

He shut the door behind her. She was dripping water on the carpet. "Come on, get into the kitchen." There were dry towels in the dryer, he remembered, and hurried to get her one.

She accepted the big green towel from him. "Thanks." Her teeth were chattering as she began rubbing her hair.

"You'd better get out of those clothes—I'll get you something." He went back up the stairs.

*She's crazy. She's like so totally and completely crazy! Why the fuck did I let her in the house? What kind of weirdo stands around in the pouring rain like that!*

He pulled a sweatshirt from his drawer and found another pair of sweatpants in his closet. He headed back down to the kitchen.

She was sitting at the table with a steaming coffee mug clutched in her hands. He noticed her nails were bitten down to the quick, and the skin around them looked chewed. "I helped myself," she said. Her teeth were still chattering.

He handed her the sweats. "Here. Go change. The bathroom's through that door."

She gave him a ghost of a smile and disappeared into the bathroom. He poured himself a cup of coffee and sat down at the table. When she came back out, he looked at her. Her face was a blank.

"Don't you have enough sense to get out of the rain?" he asked, fretting just a little that he was sounding like Lois.

She sat down and brushed a lock of wet hair out of her face. "I needed to talk to you."

"How did you know where I lived?"

"Truro's a small place. All I had to do was get off the shuttle at the post office and ask where the two profs from Boston College lived."

"Why?" Chris looked at her. "Why did you come all the way out here to find me?"

"Chris—" she said, biting her lip.

"What?"

"Like it or not, you're a part of this now."

The hair on the back of his neck stood up. "A part of what?"

"All of this." She looked at him. "Chris, I know you've been watching me all summer." She scratched her arm absently. "I didn't know why—I just figured you had really weird taste in girls or something. I didn't think you were a perv or anything like that." She gave him another ghostly smile. "I've been thinking about it since the other day, and I realized that you're here to help me, somehow."

"Help you?" He scratched his head. "With what? You aren't making any sense, Jessie."

"You think I'm crazy, don't you?" Her voice sounded defeated, and she seemed to literally shrink in front of him. "*Everyone* thinks I'm crazy. Even my shrink did." She looked out the window and sipped her coffee. "But I'm not, Chris, you have to believe me—I'm not crazy!

Strange things are happening, weird things, and I don't know what to do. You've got to help me!"

"You think you're possessed, I know." He looked at her. She was pretty, he thought. If she wore makeup and did something about that wild tangle of hair, she'd be beautiful. He reached across the table and took her hand. "But there's no such thing as possession, Jessie."

"I thought I was crazy, too." She got up, removing her hand from his and walking across the kitchen. She refilled her coffee. "Do you believe in ghosts?"

"There's no such thing as ghosts either." He crossed his arms.

"And how do you know that? For sure?"

"I—" He stopped. "I guess I don't know. Everyone says that." *She's crazy. I need to get her out of here. I should maybe call the police or something. . . .*

"Two years ago, my mother committed suicide." Jessie sat back down, sipping her coffee while keeping her dark eyes trained on Chris. "It was on a day like this. I was in my room, reading. I heard something—a noise that didn't make any sense, you know? I got up and went to see what it was—and she was hanging from the ceiling. Her eyes—" Jessie shivered. "Her eyes were open and her tongue was sticking out."

"Jessie, look—"

"I just started screaming and screaming—I guess one of the neighbors heard me and called the police." She shrugged. "Dad was gone—he's always gone, you know—and he had to fly right back home." She laughed bitterly. "He acted like it was this huge inconvenience to him, you know? He had to cancel some *appearances*. Like his wife dying might lose him some book sales."

"You don't really think that."

"He's an asshole," Jessie said vehemently. "He doesn't

care about me, he never cared about Mom . . . he won't admit it now, but I think he was going to divorce her. I think that's why she did it." She shuddered and wiped at her eyes. "It was so fucking weird, Chris, I mean, she made me lunch that day like nothing was wrong. Two hours later she was dead. Everything was fine . . . and then—" She closed her eyes again and took a deep breath. "And then of course dear Daddy decided I needed therapy."

Chris couldn't think of anything to say. He just kept staring at her.

"And that's, you know, when the dreams started."

"The dreams?"

"I thought they were dreams, anyway." The girl took a deep breath. "I kept seeing my mom. She was trying to tell me something, to warn me . . ." She finished her coffee. "And I made the mistake of telling my shrink about it. She thought I was crazy. And she told my dad . . . I was *this* close to being committed." She held her index finger and thumb about a centimeter apart. "And that's when I knew I couldn't tell them anything. So I started lying to them both. Dad pulled me out of school and hired Alice to homeschool me. Which is fine." She laughed. "School sucked, anyway. You know how well I get along with other kids."

He was softening toward her. Maybe she wasn't crazy. Just lonely. Weird, but harmless . . .

"Look, I don't get along with other kids my age any better. They call me Ichabod Crane." *And Beanpole*, he thought. *And Jolly Green Giant. And . . .*

"I don't care about them," Jessie said. "They're all idiots anyway."

"Jessie, why are you here?"

"You don't believe me, do you?" She stood up. "I don't know why I thought you would. You're just like everyone else."

There was so much despair in her voice, such sadness and defeat that he couldn't help himself. "Okay." He stood, looking up at her. "I believe you." He wasn't sure that he did, but it was the right thing to say.

She sat back down. "You have no clue how awful it is. . . ."

He stood, walking around her and placing his hand awkwardly on her shoulder. Her narrow shoulders shook. She stood once more, turning into him, placing her cold face against his bare chest. He slid his arms around her.

"It's okay," he heard himself saying.

*You are so lame, Chris Muir. Here's a pretty girl crying in your arms, and all you can do is hold her and say stupid things. No wonder you're still a virgin. Lame, lame, lame.*

She pulled out of his embrace, wiping her face. "Sorry." She gave him a weak smile. "You still want to help me?"

"Sure." *If it means I get to put my arms around you again.*

"Well, I should warn you. It's worse now."

"What do you mean?"

"I know they aren't dreams, Chris." Jessie sighed. "It's the house. There's something living in that house. And I don't mean people."

"Then what do you mean?"

"Do you promise to help me?"

"Jessie, I don't know what you're talking about!"

"Unless you help me, I won't be able to stop them."

"Stop them from what?"

She put her fists up to her ears in frustration, scrunching up her face. She turned away, then looked back at Chris. "Have you ever heard of Lettie Hatch?" she asked.

*Lettie Hatchet took a butcher knife, and with it took her father's life. . . .*

"Yeah," Chris said. "Everyone has. She killed her parents."

"I live in her *house*, Chris. Lettie Hatch's mother killed herself. And two years later her father got remarried to this young bitch and then Lettie killed her father and her stepmother." She walked over to the window where the rain was still pounding the earth. "And my dad just got married again . . . to a girl way younger than he is. Are you starting to follow my line of reasoning?"

"Uh, yeah . . ."

"It's going to all happen again, Chris, I know it is. I dream about it. I dream about the knife and the blood. And last night—"

Gooseflesh crawled up Chris's arms. "What happened last night?"

"Last night I dreamed about killing her." Jessie laughed. Almost a funny ha-ha kind of laugh, but Chris knew she wasn't joking. "I dreamed I went into the kitchen and got the knife and went into her bedroom and started stabbing . . . *and it felt so good!*"

She looked over at him with wild dark eyes.

"It's Lettie, Chris. She's still in the house, somehow. She's in my mind. Unless I stop her, unless I can do something, she's going to do it again. She's going to make me do it."

"Whoa." Chris's mind raced. "Let's just take a breather here, okay?"

*She's nuts, she has to be, she's telling you she's going to kill her parents, this is all so fucking crazy, get her out of here, she's not stable, Lois and Joe are going to come home and find me carved up . . .*

"You have to believe me, Chris."

Something about her eyes, wild as they were, made Chris keep looking into them.

"I don't *want* to do this. That's why you've got to help me."

*Humor her, Chris, tell her what she wants to hear, but get her out of here.*

"Okay. What do you want me to do?"

"I don't know." Jessie buried her face in her hands. "I don't know what to do."

"Maybe . . ." He hesitated. "Maybe you should go back to your therapist."

"That would be totally brainless, Chris. If I told her—anyone else—they'd just lock me up somewhere, medicate me—and *that won't change anything!*" She looked at him sadly. "It's not that simple!"

"Isn't it? Come on, Jessie—maybe you're wrong. Maybe—maybe the . . ." He cast about in his head for the right words. "Maybe your mom's death—"

"Unhinged me? Made me crazy?" She sighed. "Chris, crazy people don't think they're crazy. They don't even wonder about it. And I do. Every day." She sank back into her chair. "Every fucking day I wonder if I'm crazy. *But what if I'm not, Chris? What if I'm not?*"

He looked down at her, not knowing what to do, what to say. How had he gotten into this mess?

"You do think I'm crazy. I can see it in your face."

She ran into the bathroom and got her wet clothes. "Don't worry," she called, slinging them over her shoulder. "I'll mail these sweats back to you. I won't ever darken your doorstep again. I won't bother you anymore!" And she ran into the front room.

"Hey!" He went after her. The front door slammed shut behind her and within a few seconds he had it open again. She'd reached the gate.

"*Lettie! Don't go!*" he shouted.

She stopped and stared back at him, the rain pouring down her face. "What did you call me?"

"I—uh—"

"You called me Lettie." She stepped back onto the porch. "Why did you do that?"

"I—I don't know." He really didn't know. He knew her name was Jessie. His head started to hurt. Everything started to spin. "I don't feel right—"

"Chris!" he heard her shout, and then everything went black.


He opened his eyes.

She was looking down at him, her face lined with concern. But she wasn't Jessie anymore. Oh, sure, she was about the same age, and looked like Jessie, but she was different somehow. The hair—it was the hair. Jessie's hair was shoulder-length; now it was hanging down her back. And it wasn't raining anymore: the sun was shining and he could feel the sweat on his forehead and under his arms.

"Are you all right, Samuel?"

"I—" He struggled to get up to his knees, but the dizziness came back. He closed his eyes and took some deep breaths. He heard a horse clopping by and shook his head. The air was different somehow. Everything was the same but somehow different.

"Samuel, talk to me!"

"I don't know what came over me," he managed to say, opening his eyes and looking at her again.

"You scared me." Her voice was small, and shook with every word. He felt her lips press against his forehead. "Are you sure you are fine? Should I get you some water?"

"I'll be fine." He smiled at her, and she smiled back. God, he loved her. He thought about her every waking moment, and dreamed about her as well. The pretty face, the delicious figure, the sweetness in her eyes, the gentle way she molded her body into his when they kissed, the taste of her mouth, the swell of her breasts . . .

"Chris?"

He blinked a couple of times as he looked at her.

"Are you okay? Do you need me to get help?"

He sat up. The rain continued to pound down. A car went by. They sat there in the mud staring at each other, breathing hard.

"Let's get inside," he said.

"What happened to you just now?" Jessie asked, helping him stand.

"I—I don't know." He shook his head.

"You're white as a ghost."

"I feel a little dizzy, that's all."

She pressed her knuckles into her mouth and started shaking. "It's happening to you, too, isn't it?"

He walked away from her, up the steps and into the house. He sat down on the couch, mindless of how wet and muddy he was.

Jessie followed and knelt down on the floor in front of him. "Chris, talk to me. Tell me what happened."

He didn't answer. He couldn't. His mind was all jumbled. He looked at her and she was Jessie—the tangled wet black hair, the big brown eyes. "You"—he swallowed—"you weren't—"

"I wasn't what?"

"You weren't you." He swallowed. "You weren't *you* anymore." It sounded crazy, even to himself, but he couldn't think of any other way to say it.

Jessie looked at him intensely. "Was I *her*?"

"I—"

"Oh God." She got up and walked across the room.

"And I wasn't *me*, either." Chris took some deep breaths. *Calm down, everything's fine, deep calming breaths, in with the good air, out with the bad, get a hold of yourself, you're in control.* He looked over at Jessie. "Is this—is this what has happened to you?"

She nodded. "And it's happening more and more, Chris." She walked over and sat on the couch, taking his hand. "Now do you understand, Chris?"

He swallowed and nodded. "What—what is happening?"

"Isn't it obvious?" Jessie asked. "Lettie Hatch wants to live again."

# Chapter 5

"So what do you think of your new home?"

Sarah Jane stared at the white Victorian standing like some great lady on the beach. The wind was whipping her hair and a salty chill bore down at her from the crashing surf. There were hardly any houses nearby; the whole ride down to the end of the Cape had left her exhausted. This was truly the end of the world. Only yards from the house the land ended, crumbling into the sea. Sarah Jane had never known a place could feel so isolated.

"It's charming," she said, hoping her words didn't sound as false as she felt.

Horace offered her his arm. His pockmarked face was beaming, gaps in his walrus mustache exposing his yellowed and broken teeth. Sarah Jane took his arm and gave him her most gracious smile—the one she'd used on lawyers and judges to convince them of her sincerity. He swung her down from the automobile and she caught a whiff of his cologne and the slightly sour smell of whiskey it barely covered.

"Now, I know it's not what you were expecting after

*the house in Washington, my dear, but we have the
town house in Boston as well." Senator Hatch puffed
up his chest. "And it's very cozy and warm—especially
in the winter. Ellen—" He made a face, as he always
did on the rare occasions when his first wife's name
came out in conversation. "Ellen loved it here."*

Well, I'm not Ellen, *Sarah Jane wanted to say, but
she kept her smile plastered on her face as he escorted
her up the walk to the front door, jabbering all the way
about how long the house had been in the Hatch family. He'd been born here, his daughter was born here,
and he was hoping* their *children would be born here
as well.*

Have I died and gone to hell? *Sarah Jane wondered
as Horace opened the front door, bellowing for his
daughter and her governess. From upstairs came the
sounds of feet scurrying, and suddenly his daughter
descending the staircase, followed by a sour-looking
gray-haired older woman dressed completely in black.*

*"Papa!" The young girl practically leaped into his
arms, and he kissed her cheek and spun her around, finally setting her down.*

*"Lettie, this is your new mother, Sarah Jane."*

*The teenager turned to look at her. Lettie was pretty,
Sarah Jane thought. Not a knockout, not the kind of
woman men would serenade, who would inspire passionate poetry, or make men pine away for the love of,
but she was adequate. There would be any number of
eligible young men vying for her hand in marriage
someday—and the Hatch money wouldn't hurt either.*

*It was clear that Lettie didn't resemble her father in
the least. Her face was heart shaped, with a high
strong forehead that looked even larger with her hair
pulled back so severely, but her gray eyes were warm
~~and~~ intelligent, and her reddish lips were full and soft.
~~skin~~ was pale white, and her neck long and grace-*

*ful.* Her brown hair had glints of red that almost sparkled in the sunlight. She was shorter than Sarah Jane, but she had ample curves and the bosom of her white blouse was full.

The girl eagerly put out her hands. Sarah Jane took them, and the girl kissed each of her cheeks in turn. "Shall I call you Mother?" she asked, giving her a radiant smile.

Sarah Jane froze. The girl was older than her youngest sister. She tried to detect any hint of malice in the soft voice, but couldn't find any. "I—"

"Of course you should call her Mother," Horace said with a hearty laugh. "She's your mother now, girl!"

"Mother," Lettie said, smiling. But the smile didn't quite reach her eyes. "I am sure we will be great friends, Mother."

"Sister would be more appropriate." The older woman, still standing on the stairs, sniffed.

Horace's smile quickly faded from his face and he darted fury across the room. "And that would be none of your business, Ann Windham, and as long as I am paying for your keep, you'll keep a civil tongue in your head!" The senator's face reddened with rage. "I'll not be told how to govern my family by a servant!"

Ann Windham glared at Horace for a moment before turning to Sarah Jane. "I have tea ready in the kitchen, if you are so inclined, madame." Her eyes glinted malevolently. And her tone had gone up a notch when she'd said "madame," almost making a mockery of the term.

"That would be fine, Mrs. Windham," Sarah Jane said.

But she couldn't help but wonder: had she made a mistake by marrying Horace Hatch?

Karen sat up in bed and shivered. Lightning lit up the room, followed almost immediately by a crash of thunder so powerful she felt it in her bones. *What a strange dream*, she thought. *So vivid, so real.*

The room was dark, even though the alarm clock on her nightstand showed that it was after ten. She threw the covers off. *I can't believe I slept so late—what's wrong with me?*

She'd been having trouble falling asleep since she'd arrived. Sleep had never been a problem for her before. Her mother had once joked, "My Karen could sleep through nuclear war." But ever since her first night in the house, she had tossed and turned and found herself waking up at various times throughout the night.

She swung out of the bed and walked over to her desk, switching on her computer. *I've got to get a grip*, she decided. Philip had finally called, several times in fact, ingratiatingly apologetic for how busy he had been. She had kept her anxiety and fears to herself, and hadn't found the steel to ask him about Ivy's suicide, and when he had been planning on telling her. *He doesn't like confrontation. He'll think I'm weak, or complaining.* "That's my biggest turnoff," he'd told her, time and time again. "Nagging women."

Yet every time she hung up the phone, she cursed herself for wimping out.

But maybe she was being too hard on him. Maybe he hadn't told her because it was too painful. *Besides*, Karen thought, *it's not something we should talk about on the phone.* She'd wait until he was home to bring it up.

*But why didn't he tell me this was the old Hatch house?*

She walked into the bathroom and turned on the water spigot, staring at herself in the mirror. Dark circles were forming under her eyes from the lack of restful sleep. She washed her face, brushed her teeth, and headed back into the bedroom. Thunder crashed again, and through the window she could see whitecaps crashing in the bay. Everything outside was gray.

*Like my mood.*

Jessie still wouldn't speak to her. They ate meals in silence. When Jessie was finished she would bolt from the table and head back to her room. Then her door would slam. Karen had stopped trying to talk to her.

"I'm sorry she's so distant, Karen," Mrs. Winn had offered, and Karen had just sighed.

"She's just a girl, Karen, be patient with her," her mother had said on the phone last night. "And have a little sympathy for her." She clucked her tongue. "How horrible to have your mother kill herself—poor thing. Teenaged girls need their mothers, and you're going to have to be there for her."

*But I'm not her mother*, Karen wanted to say, and for the first time, she wished she hadn't married Philip, hadn't left Louisiana, hadn't moved up here to this weird house in this strange little village. Of course, she was instantly ashamed of herself.

*Stop being a baby and go get some coffee*, Karen scolded herself as she finished brushing her teeth. *You're always a complete bitch until you've had coffee.*

Alice Winn was in the kitchen reading the *Boston Globe* when Karen walked in. "There's coffee," Alice said without looking up. She had the paper open to the sports page. "Damn those Red Sox!" She looked over at Karen and smiled. "Sorry, after all these years you'd think I wouldn't get my hopes up, but—"

"I know," Karen commiserated. "My dad's the same way with the Saints." She filled a cup of coffee and spooned sugar into it, gratefully raising it to her lips. "What a miserable day! Where's Jessie? In her room?"

"She went out to meet a friend." Alice put the paper down. "Oh dear, are you not sleeping well?"

"Does it show?" Karen grimaced. "I don't know

what it is, Alice. It takes me forever to fall asleep, and
then I'm restless all night." She sat down at the table.

"I know what it is," Alice said, a sly smile playing
with her lips.

"What?"

"You're still a newlywed. You miss your husband."

Karen smiled. It was true. How wonderful it had
been for those few short weeks to fall asleep every
night in Philip's arms. Philip Kaye—her hero.

Their honeymoon had been spent in various hotels
in New Orleans, Washington, and New York, as Philip
fulfilled his publishing commitments, giving readings,
lectures, interviews. So it wasn't the romantic trip to
Hawaii she'd always imagined. But traveling with
Philip Kaye, getting into bed with the dashing success-
ful author every night—how much more romantic for a
fledgling writer was that?

Then it had been back to New Orleans, where Karen
got the Lexus and the directive to pack her things and
head north. Here. To Provincetown. To this house. And
Philip took off for Los Angeles. Then San Francisco.
Then Seattle, Chicago, St. Louis . . .

"Wait a minute," Karen said, her mind suddenly reg-
istering something. "Did you say Jessie went out to
meet a *friend*?"

"That's what she said." Alice shrugged. "That's all
she would say, actually, and I didn't press her. Would
you like some breakfast?"

"You don't have to—" Karen felt a little guilty that
Alice made all of their meals, but she'd insisted that
she didn't mind. *I'm just not used to having someone
wait on me, that's all.*

"Please, Karen. Allow me. Eggs and bacon?" When
Karen nodded, Alice took down a frying pan and
started cracking eggs into it. "Now, when I have trou-

ble sleeping, I have some red wine—that always puts
me straight to sleep."

"I'll have to try that." Karen yawned. "Maybe it's a
good sign, Jessie having a friend."

"I certainly hope so."

"Listen, Alice, I'm going to try to get some writing
done this morning. It's a perfect day, all stormy and
rainy, to really get into my story. But I have a contractor coming by to give me an estimate on the attic."

Philip hadn't been thrilled with the idea of her having a separate office at first, but she'd finally managed
to talk him into it. He'd agreed she needed to make the
house her own.

"A contractor? Who would that be?" Alice started
stirring the eggs. "Do you like them dry or runny?"

"Um, eggs dry, thank you. Bobbie Noble's the contractor." Karen picked up the paper and glanced at the
headlines. More bombings in the Middle East; another
lawsuit against the Catholic Church; another scandal
involving the Bush administration. Same old, same
old. She pushed the paper away.

"Bobbie Noble," Alice echoed as she scraped the
eggs out of the pan, then lined up some crispy slices of
bacon and set the plate down in front of Karen. "You
know he's a homosexual, don't you?"

"Yes, why do you ask?"

Alice just sat back down and picked up the paper
again without saying anything.

Karen felt herself getting a little angry. Could Alice
be homophobic? She took a deep breath. "I'm thinking
of making a work space for me in the attic . . . and he's
going to help me."

"That should be nice for you."

*It's my house now, too, you old witch.*

Where did that come from? Karen gulped down her

coffee. Alice Winn had been nothing but kind to her—more than kind—ever since she arrived. Where did that sudden surge of venom come from?

Alice put the paper down and smiled at her, her blue eyes twinkling. "Karen, I taught Bobbie when he was in high school. He grew up here on the Cape, down in Eastham. He was always a bit different, if you know what I mean, but—" She sighed. "I always liked him, and I remain fond of him of course—but I don't approve of his lifestyle."

"I see."

Alice picked up the paper again. "Live and let live, is what I say. It's none of my business or my concern. But that doesn't change the fact that it's a sin."

"Well, you're right," Karen said. "It's not your business." She wasn't hungry anymore. She stood, carrying the plate over to the sink.

"I'll do the dishes. Just leave it."

*And you're thinking Philip didn't marry me for my housekeeping skills, aren't you? I don't cook, I don't clean, I don't turn my hand to do anything around here. That's what you really think of me, don't you, you old bitch? You think I'm some talentless gold digger. . . .*

She shook her head. *What is wrong with me this morning? Just because Alice has some outdated notions about gay people doesn't mean she's thinking bad thoughts about me. . . .*

She tried to smile. "Bobbie said he'd be by around one to take a look at the space. Will you call me when he gets here?"

Alice nodded, and Karen went upstairs. She stared at her computer screen.

She wanted to go back downstairs and fire the old witch.

"Karen," she scolded herself. "Get a grip."

Alice was her friend; why was she thinking such terrible things about her? And it *was* kind of her to offer to do the cooking. It wasn't what she'd been hired to do, after all—and it took a lot of pressure off Karen.

*I guess she just caught me off guard with that comment about Bobbie—and I'm feeling guilty about the housework, that's all. I don't have the slightest idea of what to make for dinner or lunch or what anyone would want to eat anyway . . . so why am I so oversensitive this morning?*

*It was that dream—that's what this is all about. That dream about Lettie Hatch and her new stepmother. I've been obsessing about the whole Lettie Hatch thing the last few days. I was bound to dream about her.*

But the dream had seemed so real. Karen could remember the exact way Horace had smelled, the sound of the birds, everything—even the way the sun had felt on her skin as they'd come up the walk.

*You're imagining things again, dumb-shit. You've got a vivid imagination, that's why you want to be a writer—no, why you* are *a writer.*

"Okay, Vicky," she said aloud, pushing everything else out of her mind. "How are you going to get out of this one?"

She started typing, and before long she became completely immersed in what she was doing. The words started flowing out of her and she forgot everything else—the storm, Alice, Jessie, everything was gone. She was in Vicky's world, and Vicky had to get away. She hadn't been able to get the escape sequence to work—she'd erased several versions already, but today it worked. It all made sense, and she typed away.

She was so lost in her work that she didn't hear the doorbell ring, and when Alice knocked on her door she almost jumped out of her skin.

"I'm so sorry!" Alice wrung her hands. "I didn't mean to frighten you."

"It's okay." Her heart was pounding, and she took a couple of deep breaths. "I was concentrating and didn't hear you, that's all. It's fine."

"Bobbie's downstairs." Alice smiled. "He hasn't changed a bit." She shook her head. "The same terrible tease he always was. I showed him into the living room."

"Thanks, Alice." Karen gave her a smile. She saved her work and turned off the computer. The storm had passed, and the sun was out now. She walked into the big living room. Bobbie was standing on a chair, examining the crown moldings. He turned when he heard her and grinned.

"Hello, gorgeous," he said in his best Barbra Streisand imitation. He hopped down from the chair. "The woodwork in this place is exquisite."

Karen's jaw dropped. Out of drag, Bobbie was a very handsome man. He was short—which she'd known, since even in his heels and his towering wig his eyes had been about level with hers—but without the clothes and the makeup, there wasn't anything the least bit effeminate about him. His hair was dark and curly, his skin olive and tanned—and his eyes were so green they almost glowed. He was wearing a tight white ribbed tank top that showed powerfully muscled arms and a strong chest. He was wearing a pair of cargo shorts that clung to his strong legs like skin. His regular speaking voice was deep and melodious. He had a backpack draped over one shoulder.

"Wow," she said.

He laughed. "Quite a diff, huh?" He snapped his fingers. "It takes a lot of sweat and time to turn me into Zsa Zsa." His eyes twinkled.

She couldn't help herself. She stared at his chest. "How do you—um, how do you—"

"The boobs?"

"Yeah."

"Darlin', you'd be amazed at what you can do with tape, a push-up bra, and a nice pair of falsies." He shrugged. "I'm not transgendered—I'm not a woman in a man's body. Zsa Zsa is just something I do for fun. And a nice extra chunk of change to get me through the dark, cold, and very long Cape Cod winters."

"Well, I hope Philip and I are in Boston then. I've heard how isolating it gets out here—"

Actually, she hadn't. But it seemed as if she somehow knew it.

Or rather, that Sarah Jane knew it. . . .

Bobbie snapped his fingers again. "And I'm a perfectionist—if I'm going to do something, I'm going to do it right. That's why I'm the best drag queen *and* carpenter on the Cape. Now, let me get a look at this attic of yours."

She grinned. "I guess I just don't understand why anyone would subject themselves to high heels if they don't *have* to wear them. Come on, let's go on up."

She led him up the stairs. He whistled as he looked around. "What a waste of space!" He walked over to one of the windows and looked around. "So you're seeing this as an office, right?"

She nodded. "Yeah."

He pointed to the windows. "Back when this house was built, they understood the importance of natural light." He knelt down and felt the floor. "And this floor is nice and solid. It just needs to be sanded and finished." He stood up. "What did you have in mind?"

"What I'd really like is this corner over here." She led him to the corner farthest from the stairs. "I'd like some bookshelves built into the wall, if that's not too hard to do, and then I figured I could put my desk here."

He knelt down. "Okay, good thinking. There's a couple of outlets here—when they wired the house I guess they thought someone might use the attic for something other than storage." He began testing the floorboards. "Solid over here too—no signs of rot or anything." He stood up. "And we'll need to do some painting, obviously. Lucky for you, darlin', I come cheap. Ask anybody in town what a cheap floozy I am."

She laughed as he pulled out a tape measure and started marking off the walls and making notes. "You know, Bobbie, it's just so, so—"

"So hard to think Zsa Zsa and I are the same person?" He grinned at her and wiggled his eyebrows. "Girlfriend, that happens all the time." He started tapping on the walls. "Solid, solid—hey, what's this?" He tapped again, and this time she heard the difference. "Sounds hollow here. Weird. Do you have any tools handy?"

"I don't know." She looked around and spotted a rusty toolbox covered in dust. "What do you need?"

"A hammer, if you've got one."

She opened the toolbox and pulled one out and handed it to him. "Here you go."

He slipped the claw handle into a crack between the boards and started twisting. After a few moments of struggling, with a groan the board came loose. "Hello, what do we have here?"

Karen stepped over to the hole in the wall. There was a dark space behind it. "What's this?"

"A hiding place." Bobbie grinned at her. "Maybe there's a lost treasure in here."

She raised an eyebrow. "I don't think so."

"Hey, you never know. See—there's something in here." Bobbie reached in and pulled out a dusty book. "Looks like a ledger of some sort."

Karen grabbed it out of his hands and carried it over to the light. She opened it to the flyleaf.

*Property of Letitia Hatch, 1922.*

"Oh my God," she breathed, turning to the first page. "It's Lettie Hatch's diary."

*12 August 1922*

*He wants me to call her Mother! As though Mother never existed! I'd rather die!*

*I HATE HER!!!*

The last sentence was underlined three times.

"August twelfth, 1922," Bobbie read over her shoulder. "Almost to the day . . ."

"What do you mean?" Karen closed the book.

"Today's the sixteenth."

Karen nodded. "Which would mean . . . that I arrived here on exactly the same day Sarah Jane arrived here in 1922."

Bobbie hummed *The Twilight Zone* theme. "Weird . . ."

Karen sat down on a rusted old iron chair. "Wow. Lettie Hatch's diary. What do you think we should do with it?"

He shrugged. "Probably should take it over to the Historical Society, I would think. I imagine some historians would be really interested in it." He lowered his voice. "Do you think . . ." He paused, and theatrically looked over his shoulder. "That she talks about the murders in there?"

Karen flipped to the back of the book. The pages were brittle, yellowed with age, and the ends crumbled a bit as she touched them. "What was the date of the murders?"

"I don't know, offhand, but I think it was in December." He tapped his forehead with the index finger of his right hand. "I mean, it's not like we have a town holiday or anything on the anniversary."

"The last entry in here is dated December third."
She closed the book and clutched it to her chest.

*Lettie Hatch's diary—and no one has ever seen it
before.*

She let out a breath. Forget the Vicky mystery. This
was a gold mine! She could write a book about the
Hatch murders—and she would have access to information that no one else ever had before!

"What are you thinking?" Bobbie asked. "You look
like Lucy Ricardo when she's cooking up some scheme
to get into Ricky's show."

"Bobbie, think about it." She got up and started pacing, clutching the book tighter.

"I *am* thinking about it, honey, and you may be on to
something if you're thinking what I'm thinking."

"I *am.*" She beamed. "This is a *major* find. How
much interest do you think there'd be in this diary?"

"Oprah kind of interest, darlin', *Larry King Live.*"

"Yeah," she breathed. "Can you think of a better
hook for a book about the Hatch murders? I live in her
*house*! I have her diary—which no one has ever seen."

"Sweetie darling, you haven't even looked to see if
she writes about the murders yet. . . ."

"I know, I know. . . ." She began flipping through the
pages.

Bobbie laughed. "And to think—I knew you when."
He gave her a mock bow. "Please don't forget the little
people when you're world famous, Karen."

"I'm going to read this cover to cover."

"Okay, Ms. Soon-to-be Superstar, I'll get out of your
hair. I'll do an estimate on this and bring it back by
later. But you have to promise me one thing."

"What's that?"

He tapped the diary. "You have to tell me what that
thing says. After all, I found it for you."

"I will, but you can't breathe a word of this yet, Bobbie. You can't tell anyone. Swear?"

"I swear." He gave her a kiss on the cheek. "All right, all right, I'm going. I know when I'm not wanted or needed anymore. If you want me to find any more treasures in your walls, just holler." He bowed again at the top of the stairs, and then went down.

Karen opened the book again, her fingers trembling. She stared at the words on the first page again.

*Who were you, Lettie Hatch?*

She traced the underlined words with her finger.

*I HATE HER!!!*

She took a deep breath and turned the page.

*August 23*

*Mrs. Windham doesn't like her either. She hasn't said anything, but I can tell. She gets that sour look on her face whenever she says her name, the same one she uses when I don't get my lessons right—the one that looks like she's smelled something bad. She just sneers at her. She will not say anything bad to me about her—she knows her place—but I can tell she would just as soon slap her face than speak to her.*

*Oh! How could you, Father? How could you forget yourself, forget Mother—and marry this woman? I know that men have needs, and Mother has been gone for two years, but why this woman? How people in Washington must be laughing . . . just as the people in Boston and here in Province-town will be when they meet her. We will be the subject of so much malicious gossip—oh, it isn't to be borne!*

*And why did I know nothing of this until now?*

*The talk from Mother's death has finally seemed to die down . . . although the other youths in town still are cruel. Just two days ago that monster Abby Winston called me "ghost-girl" to my face . . . as God is my witness, someday she will pay for her slights and cruelties. But I know in my heart of hearts it is my fault—I should have simply kept my mouth shut and borne my burden alone rather than trying to get sympathy from the small-minded.*

*Dinner last night was horrible. Mrs. Windham made cold crab salad—Father's favorite—and I was polite, but it took all of my self-control not to throw my tea in her face. So smug, sitting there with her blond curls, acting like the lady of the house. She's from Pennsylvania—Philadelphia, she said—but her parents are dead and she has no other family. I would feel sorry for her—it's only Christian, and it must be terrible to be without any family—but there's just something about her, something that's not quite right. Why would such a pretty young woman marry a man Father's age? Surely there were many suitors for her—so why Father? I know it is terribly un-Christian of me to think this, but I cannot help myself. She must have married Father for his money and fame, that can be the only explanation for such a misalliance.*

*She says she worked for the suffragette cause, which also struck me as quite odd. She actually spent time in prison—and is proud of such a shameful thing! And Father just sat there, listening, smiling, and nodding his head. I cannot imagine Father marrying such a woman. How many times have I heard him rail about the suffragettes? "Women unsexing themselves, forgetting their God-given command to be subservient*

*to men." That's what he always believed. How has
such a silly filly turned his head?*

   *None of this makes any sense. Has she some-
how bewitched him? Father listened to her with a
smile on his face, nodding his head as she talked
about women's rights. He MUST be bewitched. I
remember how angry he was when I suggested
going to college—and he told me in no uncertain
terms how I was to be obedient to his wishes, and
there would be none of that for me. "A woman's
duty is to get married and have children and keep
house for her husband, my Lettie." Those are the
very words he used . . . but now he has married
this child, this girl, and his mind has changed?*

   *After dinner, they retired to their bedchamber
and Mrs. Windham also retired. I snuck out and
met S. If Father knew . . . but he must never find
out. He would kill me if he knew. No, he would
kill us both.*

   *It's late and I must get some rest. Lord, give me
the strength to deal with this.*


Karen closed the book, her mind racing.

S? Who was S?

A boy, of course. Who else would a teenaged girl
sneak out of the house to meet after everyone else had
gone to bed?

She stared out the window at the crashing sea. The
words rang in her head.

*But I know in my heart of hearts it is my fault—I
should have simply kept my mouth shut and borne my
burden alone rather than trying to get sympathy from
the small-minded.*

"What was your burden, Lettie?" she said aloud. It
had something to do with her mother's death.

Once again Karen felt a chill when she realized she had arrived at this house on the very day Sarah Jane had arrived here in 1922. The parallels in their stories were just too eerie. *Both of us were married to older men with stepdaughters the same age. And we live in the same house. And our predecessors—*

Did Ellen Hatch commit suicide too? Just like Ivy Kaye?

Maybe *that* was the burden Lettie carried—the same burden Jessie was now carrying.

Karen shivered. *That's just your imagination working overtime again, Karen. Get a grip. Tomorrow, you just march your butt down to the Provincetown Town Hall and see what you can find out about Ellen Hatch's death.*

For now, she had some reading to do.

*Oprah's Book Club—here I come!*

# Chapter 6

"Maybe this isn't such a good idea," Chris said, looking down at Jessie. "I mean, most of these people are fakes, aren't they?"

Jessie sighed. "Well, we have no way of knowing unless we go in and talk to her, do we?"

They were standing in front of a small cottage on Commercial Street, just behind an art gallery and a shop that sold sex toys. It was a one-story building painted a bright purple with yellow shutters. Wind chimes hung from the porch that ran the length of the house. A narrow flower garden fronted the porch. To the right of the front door hung a shingle that read: MADAME NADJA PSYCHIC READINGS. Stenciled beneath it was a big circle around a large palm with the fingers splayed out. Finally, below, in red letters, were the words NO APPOINTMENT NECESSARY—WALK-INS WELCOME.

Chris stared at the window for a minute. Now that the storm had passed, and the day had turned bright and sunny, he felt kind of silly. Sure, what happened back at the house had been spooky, but it could have just been some kind of—what was it called? *Collective delusion.* The characters in Philip Kaye's book talked about it—that was their rational explanation for what was happening at the boys' school. Of course, in the book there really *were* evil spirits in the school—but that was a book, not reality. With the sun beating down on him, it was easy to shake off the weird feelings he'd had.

*But you're not doing this for you*, he reminded himself. He looked down at Jessie. She was staring at the house, her eyes narrow. She ran a nervous hand through her tangled hair and swallowed. She looked up at him.

"Well?" One of her eyebrows went up, challenging him.

"Walk-ins welcome." He rolled his eyes. "You know, Jessie, somehow I doubt a real psychic would have that on her window. That's what beauty shops say."

"If you want to go home, Chris, be my guest." She opened the gate and stepped through. She took a few steps, then turned and glared at him. "Are you coming or not?"

"Oh, all right!" No sense in arguing with her.

*All I wanted was a girlfriend*, he thought glumly. Somehow he doubted other guys would go through all of this.

He stepped through the gate, hoping no one who knew Lois would see him. He could only imagine what she'd have to say about this. *A psychic?* Her voice mocked him in his brain. *Really, Chris. This isn't how I raised you, is it? To be a superstitious idiot? There's no such thing as psychics. They prey on people who can't face reality. It's just a holdover from an uneducated past.*

He shook his head, made up his mind, and stepped through the gate. They walked up the four wooden steps. After taking another deep breath, Jessie pressed the doorbell.

Whatever Chris was expecting, it wasn't the woman who opened the door. The best way to describe her was round. Her body and face had no angles. Barefoot with dirt under her toenails, she was barely five feet tall, with a short, squat body hidden inside a shapeless purple cotton housedress that exposed most of her shoulders and arms. Her shoulders sloped down, and her bare arms were thick, narrowing down to thin wrists and long fingers ending in purple-painted stubby fingernails. Her skin was so milky white he could see the bluish veins beneath. Her round moon face sat atop a short neck, with tendrils of wildly kinky black hair shooting out in all directions from the scalp, streaks of bright blue and orange scattered throughout without rhyme or reason. It looked as if some fluorescent paint cans had spilled onto her head. She had a small mouth with chapped pink lips barely covering unusually large teeth. Acne scars covered both cheeks, and a single black mole stood out on the left side of her crooked, flattened nose.

"Yeah?" she asked in a husky voice, surprisingly deep for such a short woman.

Jessie swallowed a few times, glanced over at Chris, and finally said, "I'd like to see Madame Nadja."

"Come in." The woman held the door open for them, and they stepped past her into a small, darkened living room. The thick curtains blocked out most of the sunlight. From every available surface candles burned. A white cat raised its head from where it had been sleeping on the arm of the dark sofa, yawned, and put its head back down.

The woman flicked a switch and the room filled up with light. Chris struggled not to cough from the heavy scent of incense in the air. Madame Nadja wasn't much of a housekeeper. Every surface was covered with a thin layer of dust and cat hair, cobwebs hung from the ceiling in the corners, and there was a faint odor of cat urine and stale smoke underneath the heavy incense. The room was cramped—*not enough room to swing a dead cat*, he thought, a sentiment he was sure wouldn't be appreciated in this house. Besides the white cat on the couch, a couple of gray kittens walked in from the kitchen, and an oversized tabby was curled sound asleep in a corner.

Chris turned around to make out the posters thumb-tacked to the walls: the Egyptian pyramids, what appeared to be Merlin, and the rings of Saturn. He gulped a couple of times. Every instinct told him to get out of there, fast.

"Sit down, kids." The woman moved to the couch, picked up the cat, and set it down on the floor. The animal stretched, yawned, glared at them all, then scurried off into the other room.

"Sit," the woman said again.

They obeyed. There wasn't enough room for Chris's long legs between the couch and the table. The woman reached over and pulled the table farther out to give him room.

"I'm Madame Nadja," she said, sitting down in a dark blue reclining chair, which groaned under her weight. "You kids want a reading? Palms? Tarot cards?" Her face was expressionless.

"I don't know," Jessie said, leaning forward. "I'm not really sure—"

Nadja's eyes narrowed. "Look, girl, either you want a reading or you're wasting my time, okay? *General Hospital* is coming on in a few minutes, so—"

*Oh, brother—that's enough of this stupidity.* Chris was sure that this crazy-looking woman was a phony and this was a complete waste of time. He stood up. "Come on, Jessie, let's get out of here. This is—"

Nadja cut him off. "You think I'm a fraud, don't you?" A faint smile played at her lips. "You know so much, don't you? Is that what they're teaching you at your school—what is it, Thomas Aquinas? Thomas More? Thomas Jefferson? Thomas something?—that your parents pay so much to send you to? So you can room with some spoiled blond boy who spends all of his time figuring out how to score more coke or how to get in some chick's pants?"

Chris stared at her, and sank back down on the couch. The hairs on his arms stood up. *Sure, she could have found out all of that stuff from gossip around town— everyone here probably knows all about my family, where I go to school, and she could have guessed about Josh . . . there's no such thing as psychic powers. But maybe . . . maybe it wouldn't hurt to hear what she has to say.*

"And you, girl." Nadja turned her eyes to Jessie. "You told everyone your mother was fine the morning she died, but that wasn't true, was it? You two argued that morning—you wanted a dog, or maybe a cat—and she said no, and like a spoiled little brat you threw a temper tantrum, and you've always wondered if that was why she did it." She leaned back in her recliner, folding her arms with a smug smile on her face, as though daring them to challenge her.

Jessie's mouth opened. "How—how did you know that?" she whispered.

"Maybe I'm really psychic." Nadja shrugged, staring into Chris's eyes until he looked away. "Or maybe it was just a lucky guess." She stubbed the cigarette out in a full ashtray and sighed. "Okay, that was harsh. I'm sorry, kids, I'm having a real shit-hole of a day, and I'm taking it out on you, and that's not very nice of me." She shrugged. "I get real tired of people coming here and acting like I'm a fake." She made a face and said in a squeaky falsetto, "'If you're really psychic, why don't you pick the lottery numbers? Why aren't you rich if you can see the future?'" She sighed. "It doesn't work that way, you know. I see things, okay? But I can't pick lottery numbers. I don't see my own future. Most people come in here and just want to know stupid shit, and I tell them." She lit another cigarette. "But you two—you two are different. You don't want to know if you're going to be Prom Queen or any of that stupid crap." She leaned forward, holding out her hands. "Give me your hands, girl."

The back of Chris's neck was tingling, his palms sweating. He wiped them on his shorts. *Don't do it, Jessie, this isn't a good idea, we should just get up and walk out of here—*

"Jessie. Call me Jessie." Jessie held her hands out, palms up. "We're here for me."

Nadja took her hands and closed her eyes.

Chris felt it, too. Something went through the air, almost like an electric charge, the way it felt when lightning struck nearby. There was a slight crackling sound. Time seemed to stand still for just that moment, and—

*—he struggled to keep his eyes open, even though everything in his body screamed at him to close them. Don't look, don't see, close your eyes until it goes away, and images flashed through his mind, the dunes at night, under a full moon and the waves gently lapping at the shore, the breeze in his hair, and he was waiting, and then he saw a knife, a huge bloody knife coming down, and the sound of bones snapping, a wet sound that he knew was blood splattering everywhere,*

*getting on everything. And he heard laughter. An evil sound, the sound of the pleasure taken from doing something wrong, something beyond the bounds of behavior, and it was a horrible sound, a sound that cut through everything else, something maniacal and dreadful and inhuman. That's it, it wasn't human at all, no human should be capable of making a sound like that, and then he opened his mouth to scream, to shout, and tried to reach his hands out to them, to break their handhold, he had to get them apart, it wasn't right, they shouldn't be doing this, this was* wrong, *most definitely wrong—*

Nadja's face drained of color. Her mouth opened wide, her eyes coming open wider than he would have thought possible. She looked like she was screaming, but there was no sound coming out. Chris turned his head. Jessie looked exactly the same, her face pale, her mouth so wide he could almost see down her throat—

And then Nadja pulled away, their hands coming apart.

The psychic fell back into her chair with enough force that the recliner opened, the footrest slamming into the table and almost turning it over. The ashtray slid off, dumping onto to the bare wood floor in between Chris's shoes.

Jessie fell back into the couch, the worn cushions giving beneath her weight, her entire body rigid for a minute.

Nadja sat there, breathing in loud, audible gasps. Her entire body shook. Chris's eyes kept moving back and forth, panicked, between her and Jessie. Jessie's eyes remained closed. Her breath was coming shallowly, her throat working.

"Jessie? Are you okay?" His heart was pounding, and he thought he smelled burnt ozone for just a moment.

She opened her eyes. Her color was coming back. She was trembling. She smiled weakly. "I—I think so." She sat upright.

"Sweet Jesus!" With trembling hands, Nadja shook another cigarette out of her crumpled pack and lit it with a candle. She closed her eyes and expelled smoke out through her nose. She repeated this a few times, until the room was filled with smoke lazily curling upward. She flicked the ash on the floor. She opened her eyes again, and they darted over to Chris, then back to Jessie.

Her voice shook when she finally spoke. "What the hell is going on with you?"

"That's why we came here," Chris heard himself saying. "To find out."

Nadja stood, with difficulty, and waddled over to a cabinet. Withdrawing a bottle of whiskey, she poured some into a glass, tossed it down quickly in one gulp, then poured herself some more. She sat down in the recliner again.

"You, Jessie," she said, "are in some serious shit."

*She's scared*, Chris thought, looking at her. *She's absolutely terrified. She won't be able to help Jessie.* His armpits went moist with cold sweat. *What the fuck is going on?* He glanced over at Jessie again. Her eyes had opened.

Jessie slipped her hand into Chris's and squeezed it reassuringly. Her palms were as sweaty as his.

Nadja took another sip of whiskey. "Okay, let me explain something to you. When I was a kid, I started seeing things, you know?" She set the glass down and leaned forward. "It scared people, so I stopped talking about it, but when I got older, I figured I might as well use this—well, this *ability* to make my living." She gave a harsh whelp of a laugh. "People come in here and want to know their futures, okay? I usually can see it, too. All I have to do is make physical contact, and I can see."

She refilled the glass and drained it again. "I don't tell them the bad things—they can't be changed—and sometimes the future is best left alone. The other day this college girl comes in here. All she wanted to know was whether she was going to get into a good grad school or not. So, I told her, sure, you're going to get into your second choice. I saw that. But I didn't tell her that she was going to die in a car crash right after she finished grad school."

"Why not?" Chris was horrified. He squeezed Jessie's hand again. It felt good there—it felt right, like it belonged there. "If you knew it about her, maybe you could've warned her."

"Don't judge me, boy. You think there's a code of ethics for psychics?" Nadja's eyes flashed, and she shook her head, tangled hair tossing around. "I could have told her, but what good would that have done?"

"Maybe she could've avoided it—"

"You can't avoid fate, kiddo."

"I understand." Jessie's voice was soft. "If you had told her, if she had known, it would have changed her life. She wouldn't have been able to change what was going to happen to her, but the time she had left she wouldn't have enjoyed. She'd think about it all the time, get depressed—"

"Exactly." Nadja nodded. "There was nothing I could do about it, so it was best not to tell her. She left here happy." She inhaled sharply. "But you—Jessie. Your future isn't clear. I can't see anything there."

"You saw *something*," Chris said. "I know you did. You saw something and it scared you." He remembered the knife, the dunes under the moon, the sound of the blood, and shivered. "I saw something, too."

Jessie didn't look at him. He might as well have not said anything.

"Are you saying I don't have a future?" she asked Nadja.

"That isn't it at all, Jessie. It merely means your future isn't clear—there's no definite path that you are heading for in this life, good or bad. That means your future is in your own hands. You have control over it, whereas most people don't."

"But you just said that we don't have control," Jessie retorted. "You just said—"

Nadja interrupted her. "Sometimes our fates are clear. Sometimes not."

She got up and walked across the room, her weight moving from side to side, gesturing with her hands. "Time is circular," she said. "Does that make any sense to you?"

They both shook their heads no.

"Okay, let me explain. The earth is round, and it revolves. That's how we measure hours and the day, right? And the earth revolves around the sun, which is how we measure years. Everything involving time in the universe is circular. Clocks, from the beginning of time when we started measuring it, were always round. But human minds can't grasp circular time—we think chronologically. Beginning, middle, end—everything in a straight line. Birth, life, death. But that isn't how it works."

Chris refrained from rolling his eyes. *This is such bullshit*, he thought, glancing over at Jessie again. But she was listening intently, her eyes focused on Nadja, occasionally nodding.

Nadja went on. "Have you ever noticed how TV shows eventually start recycling plots? Not just their own, but from other shows as well? That's because there are a finite number of stories—and the same is true of human life. They keep cycling around, in a circle. A circle opens, the same situation develops, and the same story plays out, over and over again until the circle finally closes, because the story is played to its eventual and correct finish."

"History repeating itself," Jessie said, nodding. "We hear about that all the time."

"Precisely. And this is where you are—the two of you." Nadja strained as she reached up into her bookshelf. "That's why I can't see your future—why it seems murky to me. You have the opportunity, right now, in this retelling of the story, to finally close the circle."

"Is that why I'm having these"—Jessie shivered—"these awful dreams?"

"Possibly." Nadja handed Chris the book. He turned it over in his hands. The front cover was purple, with a large golden circle against the background. In big black Old English lettering were the words *The Circle of Time*, and across the bottom, in the same style, was the name *Arthur Goodwin*. He turned the book to its back cover, which featured a photograph of a man who seemed to be in his midforties. His head was completely bald, and light reflected off it in places. He had strong features, large brown eyes, and a mustache and goatee. He was handsome in a vaguely satanic kind of way.

"Read that," Nadja said. "The book explains it all much better than I ever can."

Chris flipped through a few pages. "Is this about ghosts and stuff?"

"Ghosts are merely an echo across time." Nadja waved her hands again. "Ghosts are very real, and they can communicate with the living. Usually, this only happens when they are trying to *fix* things, to help the living finally close the circle. If it's a circle of violence and death, they cannot rest until the circle is closed."

"So the dreams . . . they're to help me."

"Yes, I think so. But, Jessie—" Nadja stood over them, her fat face twisting in thought. "Remember that if something was good in life, it's good in death, too. But if it wasn't good . . ."

Again Chris had the sensation of the knife. . . .

"Some of the echoes you're hearing," Nadja said, "aren't trying to help you. They may be trying to close the circle, too, but not in any way that's going to be good for the living. You're going to have to figure out the good echoes from the bad."

"So I can borrow this?" Chris asked, tapping the book.

Nadja made a face and took the book from him. "No, you can go buy your own copy off his Web site." She shrugged, giving him a cynical smirk. "You're going back to school in a couple of weeks—and too many people don't know the difference between the words *borrow* and *keep*, especially with books."

*Bitch*, Chris thought, opening to the back inside cover. The Web site was listed in the author's bio on the inner flap of the book jacket. It was easy enough to remember. *It can't hurt to read the book, even if Madame Nadja might be full of shit.* Still, something had happened when she touched Jessie. . . .

"You're not telling us everything," Chris insisted. "What did you see?"

"Violence and death." Nadja shuddered again. "The circle wants to close. But *how* it will close"—she looked from Chris back to Jessie—"remains to be seen."

"So that's it? That's all you can tell us?"

Nadja nodded. "That's right. Twenty dollars, please."

"Twenty dollars?"

Jessie squeezed his hand to keep him quiet. "I don't

care about money. I just want help. And I think there's something more you can do for us."

Nadja looked at her suspiciously.

"I want you to conduct a séance," Jessie said.

"Oh no. I don't do that. Séances are way beyond me. . . ."

"You've got to help! There's nobody else!"

"It's summer, girl! I want to have fun! I want to relax! I want to go to the beach!"

Chris made a face. He tried not to imagine Madame Nadja in a bathing suit.

"Please?" Jessie begged.

Nadja sighed. "It's not my specialty. And you have to remember—they can lie. You think just because you call them they're gonna tell you the truth?"

"Please," Jessie said again. "I need to find out what it all means. How else can I figure out the good echoes from the bad?"

"All right." Nadja folded her fleshy arms across her chest. "But it will cost."

"Fine," Jessie said.

Chris burned inside. What a rip-off this quack was. She knew Jessie was rich and would milk her for all she could. Maybe she had some ability, he'd give her that. But her greatest gift was for making money.

"It will be best to hold the séance where the echoes are strongest. They may not be able to speak to us here at my house."

Jessie bit her lip. "I'm not sure how I can manage a séance at my house. Not with my gold-digging new stepmother there all the time."

Nadja handed her a business card. "Well, if you can find a way to handle it, give me a call. Now off with you. I've already missed the first ten minutes of *General Hopsital*."

She walked them to the door. Jessie handed her a twenty-dollar bill.

"Be careful," Nadja called after them as they headed back out onto busy Commercial Street, all the festive summer tourists blithely going on their way, nightmares and echoes and séances the furthest things from their minds.

Chris suggested they get away from the madness of the crowds. They hopped on their bikes and headed out toward the dunes. They chained the bikes to the rack at the end of the road and pushed off into the sweeping mounds of sand, where the terrain took on the look of the Sahara Desert.

"You didn't really believe all that bullshit, did you?" Chris finally asked.

Jessie hadn't said two words since they left Madame Nadja's. They trudged through the sand the way you make your way through snow, your foot sinking deep and only with effort can you pull it out again. The sun had gone back behind the clouds, and without its warmth the wind smacking them in their faces was almost cool.

"Come on, Jessie, she was so full of shit it was coming out her ears."

Outside that cramped smelly house, it was easy to dismiss what he'd felt in that horrible moment when Jessie's hands had locked with Nadja's. *I expected to feel something, so I did, that's all it was.*

"You didn't experience what I did," Jessie said quietly. "It was"—she shuddered—"the most horrible thing I've ever felt, Chris. I'm not making it up."

"What did you feel?"

"Images. Thoughts." She paused. "Echoes," she said, using Nadja's word. "They were flashing through my head." She pushed farther ahead through the sand. They could see the water now. "I don't want to talk about it."

"Come on, Jessie—you owe me that much. Tell me what you felt." He sighed. She didn't answer, so he tried another tack. "Did you really believe all that shit about time and stuff?"

"It makes sense," Jessie replied stubbornly, not looking back at him. "It's the only explanation I've heard since all this began that does." She shrugged, pausing on the crest of a dune and looking off toward the sea. "Do I completely understand it? No, I don't. But I can't explain things any better."

Chris reached the crest and stood beside her. "Well, I'm going to order that book as soon as I get home. I mean—if you want me to." He stopped talking, his face flushed.

"Yes." She stole a sidelong glance at him. "I want you to."

They stood that way in silence for a while, just looking beyond them at the crashing surf. Then Jessie looked up at him. "Chris, thanks."

He smiled down at her. "For what?"

"For listening to me. For trying to help." She reached up and touched his face. "You have no idea how nice it is for me—" She choked a little. "She was for real, Chris, I know she was. She knew about my mother."

"Do you want to talk about it?" He could hear his mother saying the same words. It always annoyed him. Everything had to be talked about calmly and rationally. She called it "processing." *Now, Chris, nothing constructive ever comes out of emotional thinking. When you've calmed down we'll sit down and process your feelings. You have to examine everything—especially your emotions—so that we can understand where these feelings come from.* He hated "processing" more than anything.

But it had its time and place.

"Yeah," Jessie said. "I suppose it's time." She sat

down in the sand, and he plopped down beside her. She kept her eyes on the sea. "It was just a normal morning, like any other. Dad was gone—he's always gone, you know. Sometimes I feel like I don't even know him, really. We've never been close—even when he's home, he spends all of his time up in his office writing and can't be disturbed. So it was always just me and Mom, the two of us." She laughed bitterly. "You know, even now he doesn't talk to me. He calls *her* every day—sometimes twice—but he never asks to speak to me."

"That sucks."

"Yeah, well." She shrugged. "Well, one of my friends—back when I had friends—had a cat who'd just had kittens. And I wanted one, you know? I'd never had a pet, and I really wanted one. So, that morning over breakfast I asked if I could have one—and Mom said no."

It had quickly turned into an argument, Jessie explained. She couldn't understand why her mother was so unbending about the idea.

"I mean, she couldn't give me a good reason—like she was allergic or something, you know what I mean? It was just a flat no, and she wouldn't even consider it."

Their voices kept rising, Jessie remembered, her mother finally shouting back that unfair parents' mantra: "Because I said so!" Jessie had stared at her, frustration mounting, until she finally screamed in anger, "I hate you! You're so unfair!" She ran out of the house. She ran until her anger was mostly spent, until she was having trouble breathing, and she had to sit down for a while. She walked on the beach for a couple of hours, thinking about it, her anger coming back from time to time, until finally it was completely gone.

"I felt bad. I still thought it was unfair, but I shouldn't have yelled at her."

She walked back home, calling for her mom, "so I could apologize," but the house was still.

"Finally I went upstairs. She wasn't in her room, she wasn't anywhere, but the attic door was open, so I went up." Chris saw that she was crying softly. "And that's where I found her—hanging from the ceiling." She buried her face in her hands. "I started screaming— one of the neighbors heard me and called the police." She sobbed. "That's what they told me. I don't really remember much of what happened after I started screaming until I woke up a day later . . . and then they gave me something to 'keep me calm.' It's all a fog to me, Chris. I barely remember the funeral."

"It wasn't your fault." Chris put his arm around her and pulled her closer. "You know that, don't you?"

She nodded. "I mean—it wasn't the first time I'd screamed at her, or said I hated her. But something was wrong with her. I mean, it wasn't like her to just not give a reason for saying no—she was always really cool about that, so I should have known something was wrong, you know?"

"And you don't know what happened after you left, either." Chris kissed the top of her head.

"I just can't get it out of my head." Jessie sighed.

"How could you? She was your mom." He thought again about Lois, feeling just the tiniest twinge of guilt for always being so down on her.

"But now everything's far worse." Jessie shuddered. "You know Lettie Hatch's mom died, right?"

"Yeah. Lettie killed her."

"No, no, no. It was her stepmother she killed. Her father and her stepmother." Jessie closed her eyes. "Lettie Hatch's mother killed herself, too."

Chris just pulled her closer.

"The circle of time is open, Chris. Madame Nadja

was right; I feel it in my bones. I can't explain it any better than that. I just know somehow that she's right. It's all going to happen again. The circle is open." She started to cry.

"Well, this time we'll make sure it closes," Chris said, shifted his weight a little so he could bring her in even closer.

Having her so near to him, being able to smell her hair and feel her skin, was making him excited. *The last thing she needs right now is my raging hormones. But she smells so good, she's so close—*

"Will you kiss me?" Jessie turned her face up to him. She bit her lower lip. "I've—I've never kissed anyone before." Her face was eager, pleading.

He leaned down and they kissed.

# Chapter 7

Before Bobbie could start work on her office, Karen had to clean everything out of the attic. She knew it was going to be an onerous chore, one that would take her away from her writing—and more importantly, Lettie's journal—but the sooner she had her own space, the sooner she was certain that everything would fall into place. She was going to write the best damned book *ever.*

She hadn't told Philip about Lettie's diary. Just why, she wasn't quite sure—but she made sure to check with him that all the renovations could proceed as planned.

"Sure, do what you need, darling," he said. "I don't even know what's up there. I haven't been . . ." His voice trailed off for a moment. "In the attic for years."

"Well, I won't throw anything away that looks valuable," Karen replied. "There might be things of her mother's that Jessie might want."

"No," Philip said tersely. "I don't think so."

"Well," Karen said, realizing she was testing him, "maybe from the previous owners then?"

"The house was empty when we moved in." Philip

gave a sigh of exasperation. "Karen, I need to tell you something—"

"No need. I already know."

"About Lettie Hatch?"

"Yes, Philip. Alice Winn told me."

"I figured she would, or that someone in town . . ." He sighed again. "Darling, I'm sorry I didn't tell you about the house's history, but I really . . . well, I didn't want to prejudice you. I wanted you to love the place."

"I think I'm starting to," she said, glancing down at the diary in her lap.

"Good. Oh, damn, darling. I've got another call coming in. Will you give my love to Jessie?"

"She's in her room. Do you want to give it to her yourself?"

"I've really got to get this call, Karen. I love you, and I'll see you soon."

"I love you too," she replied automatically. She started to shut off the phone when she heard him say something else. "I'm sorry, Philip, what did you say?"

"Just don't throw out any boxes with papers in them— those might be important. I think Ivy"—she could hear the wince in his voice when he said her name—"might have stored some of my manuscripts up there." He laughed. "You know a writer should never throw away anything he's written." He clicked off without saying a further good-bye.

"Sweet dreams to you, too, Philip," she said, switching off the phone.

Why hadn't she told him about the diary? Bobbie was still the only person who knew about it.

*The diary*. Lettie Hatch's diary.

She held it in her hands and couldn't stop smiling. This diary was her ticket to fame and fortune. Philip always said you needed some kind of hook—and Lettie

Hatch's diary was better than any adventure she could come up with for Vicky Knight, Star Reporter.

Every night, before she went to bed, she read a few entries from the diary. She wasn't usually a patient person, and every night, she had to resist the urge to read through the entire thing in one sitting. But she wanted to savor it, to get the sense of the story that was unfolding, to see the kind of book she might write from it. Would it be an exposé of one of the great unsolved mysteries of our time, kind of like what Patricia Cornwell did with Jack the Ripper? Or would it be a nonfiction novel like what Truman Capote did with *In Cold Blood*? Or would she fictionalize it all, turning Lettie and the rest into a cast of characters she could manipulate and play with, controlling all their destinies?

During the day, she locked the diary in her desk drawer, waiting until the house was silent before getting it out. Then she would hold it in her hands, looking down at it, before walking over to her bed, sliding in under the covers, and opening to the last page she'd read.

*If I'm going to write about Lettie, I can't just rush through it. To do her justice, I have to read each entry slowly and carefully, to grasp everything that was going on in her head and her world.* It was all about character—Philip had told her that several times.

She sat now on the edge of the bed, the journal in her hands, and heard Philip saying, over dinner at Galatoire's one night when he'd flown in just to see her, "It's all about character, honey. You have to know everything about your characters. You have to completely understand them. Not just their eye color, or how they wear their hair, but whether they were popular in high school, what they want from life, what their hopes and

dreams are, as well as what's kept them from *getting*
their hopes and dreams. You need to know what kind of
people they're attracted to, what kind of friends they
have and why. I should be able to just throw a situation
at you, and you should be able to tell me exactly how
every single one of your characters would react in that
situation."

*Well, how better to get to know one of your charac-*
*ters than to read her diary?* Karen thought with a self-
satisfied smile, leaning back against her pillows and
opening the book, turning to the page she'd marked
with a grocery receipt.

*17 August 1922*

> *I really do not understand why I need to learn*
> *Latin; no one speaks it anymore, and the only use*
> *I see for it would be if I were going to go into*
> *medicine or law, which is certainly not a possibil-*
> *ity. Father insists, whenever I bring it up, that I*
> *am not going to college. "Women do not need to*
> *be educated," he always says. "A woman's place*
> *is to be a wife and mother, and to devote herself*
> *to making it possible for her husband to advance*
> *to the greatest of his abilities." Like Mother did?*
> *I want to scream every time he opens his mouth*
> *and preaches to me about a woman's place. But I*
> *hold my tongue. Maybe, someday, I will be able*
> *to really speak to him about Mother, and her un-*
> *happiness, but I bide my time. But that time will*
> *come someday, and it will be terrible . . . all the*
> *more terrible for him for the delay in the day of*
> *reckoning.*
>
> *I wonder how SHE feels about it—Father men-*
> *tioned something about my education again today,*
> *over dinner. I could tell by the look on HER face*

*that SHE doesn't agree with him, but neverthe-
less, SHE held HER devil's tongue. SHE is well
aware of which side HER bread is buttered on,
and will do nothing to provoke him. SHE is trying
to be my friend, I will give her credit for that—
despite the fact I am sure it is part of HER ploy to
stay in his good graces. Cannot have the daughter and the new wife not get along—what would
the voters think? More fool HER. I have nothing
to do with his politics—he does not trot me out
when he speaks publicly any more than he did
Mother. Has it not occurred to HER that we
stayed up here on the Cape while he was down in
the capital? Why hasn't that given HER pause?
He cares nothing for me—I am simply the child of
his disappointing first marriage, an onerous burden to his pocket which he hopes to one day get
rid of by marrying off to the first person to come
along—as long as it is politically advantageous
to him. Oh, yes, I am well aware I am nothing but
a pawn in his endgame. SHE hasn't learned yet
what a bad bargain SHE sold herself for.*

*But I have nothing to say to HER. There is
nothing I could say, nothing SHE would believe. I
see it in HER eyes—every time SHE calls him
Senator, I see the gleam come to her eyes. SHE
likes being the senator's wife. I try to look HER in
the face, to warn HER to get out while SHE can,
but my tongue is stilled. All I see whenever I look
at HER is Mother's face, all waxy and still in her
coffin, the last time I saw her, in her good black
velvet dress, her pearls at her throat, her mockery
of a wedding ring on her finger, lying in her ma-
hogany coffin in the living room. Mrs. Windham
makes no secret of her distaste for HER and is
barely civil. She always refers to her privately as*

"that woman," and when Daisy came in to clean the other day, SHE tried to give her instructions—and Mrs. Windham intervened. While I certainly do think that Mrs. Windham forgot herself and her place in our household, I was secretly happy that she spoke so sharply to HER. SHE doesn't belong here, and the sooner SHE realizes that, the better off we will all be. And the instructions given to Daisy—as if after all these years Daisy doesn't know how to scrub a pot! I fear SHE is even lower class than I originally suspected—SHE obviously has never had servants before and doesn't know how to speak to them.

Just this morning, as I was working my Latin in the kitchen, SHE came in and began to speak to me, knowing full well I was trying to finish my lessons. HER thoughtlessness knows no bounds—and SHE kept on until I was forced to give up and listen to HER. "I'm so pleased to see you working so hard on your lessons."

"Mrs. Windham would have it no other way," I replied, freezing HER with my tone. Yet unless you strike HER in the face, SHE pays no attention.

"You seem to be very bright."

I thanked HER, rather coolly, wondering what SHE wanted from me. There had to be something. And it didn't take her long to get to the point.

"You know, Lettie, I will support you if you want to go to college." This was the bait SHE dangled in front of me. Ah, how astute SHE is at getting what SHE wants! Father was no match for HER, of this I have no doubt. "Would you like that?"

"Father has already decided I am not to go to college."

"His mind can be changed." SHE gave me a

*knowing smile. There is no question that SHE can use her wiles to influence him, and for a moment I was tempted. This is undoubtedly how Satan wins souls, and one's heart must always be resolute not to fall into such a trap and risk eternal damnation. "I can help to change it."*

*I said nothing.*

*"Would you like to go to college?" this vile temptress went on as though I had not said a word about Father. "You'd like college, wouldn't you?"*

*"Why would you do such a thing?"*

*"Because I would like for us to be friends." SHE tried to take my hand, but I pulled mine away.*

*"That we shall never be," I said, looking her full in the face, "and I need to finish my lessons."*

*SHE walked out but first gave me such a look of vile hatred that I feared for my life. There is so much tension in the house! I couldn't finish my lessons. I had a headache, so Mrs. Windham gave me some powders for it, and allowed me to finish them tomorrow.*

*S. could not meet me this evening, so I am going to retire early.*

*What a little bitch*, Karen thought, closing the book and setting it on the nightstand. *Not even willing to give Sarah Jane a chance.*

*Just like Jessie.*

Jessie still resisted every attempt Karen made to even be civil, and she was getting a little tired of it. Karen tried talking to her about her lessons—nothing but a look. She asked her if she wanted to help go through the boxes in the attic, and Jessie said no. *What if some of your mother's things are up there? Don't you want to make sure?* Karen wanted to say, but she didn't.

She bit her lip and said nothing. *Poor Sarah Jane, having to deal with her own brat of a stepdaughter. And that crack about her being "of a lower class than I originally suspected"—snobby little bitch.* Her younger sister Kara had been like Jessie sometimes—distant and moody, monosyllabic answers, histrionic gestures, rolling her eyes, but *her* parents wouldn't stand for it.

"She's just spoiled," Mrs. Donovan would say, setting her mouth in a grim line. "Mother probably gave her everything she wanted—and with all that money!" She would shake her head. "She needs a firm hand, that's all."

*Oh yes, she's spoiled all right,* Karen decided, *everyone feels sorry for her because of her mother, so they let her get away with murder. When Philip comes home, I'll talk to him about it. This is going to change. Maybe it's time for the homeschooling to stop and little Miss Jessie to go back to public school. At least Alice talks to me, but she's got her hands full with the princess, too.*

Thank God for Bobbie! He was always able to make her laugh, to forget about the snotty girl dressed all in black scribbling away in her damned journal every day. The design plans he'd come up with for her office were fantastic; more than she could ever have dreamed of. He helped her pick out the right varnish for the floor and the paint for the walls, even made recommendations about curtains. He knew a seamstress who could make her whatever she wanted. At first, she worried about the expense, but whenever she mentioned her fears to Philip, he'd just laughed. "Baby, you can't bankrupt me unless you're having the whole room done in gold and diamonds." So she finally stopped worrying. It was a heady feeling. She could never remember a time when money wasn't a question. "Just don't cheat me, Bobbie," she said one afternoon as they went through cloth swatches for the curtains. "And don't make it tacky, please? I don't want . . ." She hesitated.

"You don't want Philip to laugh at you?" Bobbie asked gently.

She nodded, biting her lip.

He smiled at her, and touched her hand. "Well, don't worry, li'l Miss Cajun, it's going to be so comfortable and gorgeous the problem won't be whether he likes it or not—the problem will be he'll want it."

Bobbie came by every afternoon after he finished working on his current job. Alice always disappeared about half an hour before he showed up, and Karen had to make excuses. "She was such a great teacher—one of my favorites. She made high school *bearable* for me," Bobbie said once, "and I always felt bad I didn't stay in closer touch with her after graduation."

*If you only knew*, Karen thought, *what she really thought about you* . . . But she couldn't tell him, couldn't hurt him that way. He was so sweet and kind, taking such an interest in her—and she didn't have to worry about it being anything more than friendship. It just made her angry with Alice, but no matter how many times she tried to bring it up with Alice, she would just shake her head. It wasn't fair to be put in the middle of something this way—especially when it had nothing to do with her—but Alice simply wouldn't budge.

"It wouldn't hurt you to talk to him a little the next time he stops by," Karen had wheedled one morning in the kitchen. "He thinks the world of you, and I can tell it bothers him."

Alice didn't respond.

Karen sighed and gave up for good. When Bobbie arrived that afternoon, Alice was nowhere to be found. Karen worried Bobbie might catch on, but he was always in a good mood and after a while, he stopped mentioning Alice to her.

She turned on the bathroom light. *Maybe it would be best if we sent Jessie to a boarding school somewhere instead of to the public school,* Karen thought as she brushed her teeth. *That would solve both problems.* She made a face at herself in the mirror. *Homeschooled—throwing away good money just to spoil that little ingrate.*

She washed her face and walked back into the bedroom. Tomorrow Goodwill was coming to get the furniture out of the attic. She slid beneath the covers and reached for the diary. It couldn't hurt to read another entry.

*18 August 1922*

> They left for Boston today. SHE wants to buy new clothes, and of course, Father cannot deny her anything her acquisitive little heart desires. Of course, all of my clothes are from last year, and I haven't been to Boston since before Mother died, but that's no matter. It was never even a question of my going with them—SHE saw to that. This trip is all about HER. SHE will undoubtedly return with boxes of satins and silks and minks and ermines—and whatever jewelry SHE can use her wiles to get out of him.
>
> It's for the best, anyway. What do I need anything new for, after all? So I can go out and be called "ghost-girl" by the unwashed and unlearned trash in this town? And I would have had to spend the day in the city with them, and watch the entire disgraceful episode, been witness to my father fawning over a new wife young enough to

be his daughter while the salesclerks snigger behind their hands at the stupid old fool.

Father insisted that Mrs. Windham and I accompany them to the ferry. When I saw HER this morning, my heart almost stopped. I felt faint, and if not for Mrs. Windham's hand I would have undoubtedly staggered. He has given HER Mother's pearls! The pearls that she had promised to me! It almost made me retch to see the Chamberlain pearls at HER cheap neck. My grandmother undoubtedly was rolling in her grave . . . and the brazen hussy chose to wear them this morning, and she gave me a little smile when I saw her. "Are you sure you won't join us, Lettie?" SHE asked, fingering the pearls deliberately. I wanted to tear them from HER neck. I demurred, swallowing my anger and outrage. How like HER, to make such an offer to me when it was too late, to wear my mother's pearls, to flaunt them in my face that way.

How could he do it? Mother always promised the pearls would be mine . . . and now he's given them to HER. They were a gift from Mother's mother, and had belonged in the Chamberlain family since my great-great-grandfather bought them for his wife when he was ambassador to Spain. And now they are at HER cheap strumpet's throat. It is an outrage—not only the insult to me but the insult to my mother. If I had a gun with me, I would have shot them both dead on the spot. Mrs. Windham and I stayed until the ferry pulled away from the dock, and then she said, "The day of reckoning is coming, Lettie, never forget that. The wages of sin are always paid in blood."

*She frightens me a little sometimes, but she is always quoting the Bible and the minister to me about HER. She means to be comforting, but sometimes it's a very cold comfort.*

*S. says that I need to make more of an effort to be civil to HER. He thinks that if I'm not careful, SHE might convince him to send me away to school, and I couldn't bear to be separated from S. I'd rather die than be separated from him. As long as they don't find about him, I'm safe for now . . . we met tonight again at the dunes. It was such a beautiful night, and I don't want to worry about boarding schools or HER. I just want to go to sleep and dream sweet dreams of my beloved.*

Karen closed the book and swallowed. *I was just thinking the same thing about Jessie,* she thought, rubbing her eyes. Reading the spidery handwriting usually gave her a headache, and the faded ink wasn't always the clearest. She reached for the bottle of pain reliever on the desk and dry-swallowed a couple. *Maybe if Sarah Jane had sent Lettie away to school . . .* She turned off the light and slid under the covers, her heart pounding.

Finally, she fell into a dreamless sleep.

The Goodwill truck showed up around ten, just as she was finishing her breakfast. They were both young men, maybe in their early twenties, with deep dark tans and well-muscled bodies in their shorts and T-shirts. They were both blonds, and she fleetingly thought they kind of had that surfer look. She led them up to the attic. "All the furniture," she said, gesturing around the room. "There's quite a bit of it, obviously."

"Yes, ma'am," the taller one said, and she gave him a look. But there was no look of mockery in his face, just sincerity. She smiled and walked back down to her room. On the way, she glanced into Jessie's room. Alice had gone to get groceries, and Jessie was sitting at her desk, scribbling away in her journal. Karen cleared her throat. Jessie refused to acknowledge her presence.

"Do you want to be a writer, Jessie?" she asked, irritated, but trying to keep her voice friendly. *Try again, Karen. Be the bigger person.*

Jessie stiffened, and her pen stilled. She didn't turn around.

"That's what I want, too." Karen walked into the room. She could see the handwriting on the pages, but was too far away to read anything. *What is she writing about me in there? The same kind of nasty shit Lettie wrote about Sarah Jane?* "What do you write in there? Are you writing poetry? Short stories? A book?"

"Maybe a little of everything." The girl paused. "Or none the above."

Karen bit her lip. "Jessie, I know your dad kind of sprang me on you, but that's not my fault. I didn't know he hadn't told you we were getting married." She took a few steps closer. "I'd like for us to be friends."

"I don't have any friends. I don't want any friends."

"Jessie—" Karen sighed. "*Please* give me a chance." She fought her rising frustration. She wanted to just get up, walk over, and shake her until—she swallowed. *Not a good idea, Karen, not a good idea at all.*

Jessie just started writing again, as though Karen hadn't said a word.

*Okay, fine then.* Karen let out a big breath, got up, and walked back to her room. *She's just a little spoiled brat who needs a firm hand, or to be around other kids. Keeping her locked up and isolated in the house isn't doing her any good. It's been two fucking years since her mother died—she needs to get a goddamned grip and move on.*

She took a shower, letting the hot water flow over her, scrubbing her skin angrily until it turned red. She was meeting Bobbie for lunch at the Bradford House for her daily dose of sanity. *Thank God for Bobbie*, she thought again, as she saw him sitting at a corner table by the window.

"So how's the diary coming along?" Bobbie asked as she sat down.

She ordered a glass of iced tea and scanned the menu. "Lettie really hated her stepmother. Talk about history repeating itself." She made up her mind to have the clam chowder and a club sandwich, and slid the menu to the end of the table. "I tried talking to Jessie again today."

"And?"

She shrugged. "Same old, same old. I don't even know why I bother anymore. She's never going to come around."

"It's only been a little over a week. These things take time."

"Whatever." Karen smiled at the waiter as he put her iced tea down and they ordered. After he walked away, she said, "She's just spoiled. My parents would never have put up with this crap from me or any of my sisters. I'm going to talk to Philip about it." She drummed her fingers on the tablecloth. "I think she needs to go back to school—this homeschooling crap is just keeping her isolated. She needs to be around kids her own age." She looked at him. He wasn't listening, he was staring out the window. "Are you even listening to me?" She snapped her fingers in front of his face. "Hello? You there?"

"I'm listening." He gave her that impish grin again. "Maybe you're right—but then again maybe you're wrong."

"Bobbie, she needs to have friends her own age—"

He interrupted her and pointed out the window behind her. "Isn't that Jessie?"

She turned in her chair and stared. "Where?"

"Right there—see that really tall boy? The one in the blue sleeveless shirt and the tan cargo shorts? Sitting on the bench? Christ, Karen, are you *blind*?"

Karen narrowed her eyes and looked harder. A group of people directly in front of the window moved, and she saw them both clearly. They were sitting on a bench drinking out of plastic cups. The boy was good looking, a little on the skinny side, with longish brown hair and long legs. Jessie was smiling at him as they talked, and Karen gasped audibly. She'd never seen Jessie smile before, and the difference was phenomenal. *She looks like a completely different person, she's beautiful when she smiles, even in those damned black clothes and without makeup, the way she smiles at him . . .*

Jessie finished her drink and threw it into a garbage can. The boy said something and Jessie laughed, her head going back and her whole body shaking. She reached over and kissed the boy on the cheek, and then they both got up and started walking down the street back in the direction of the house. Karen whistled. "I'll be damned. If I hadn't seen that for myself, I would never have believed it in a million years."

"Looks like Jessie's got herself a boyfriend." Bobbie grinned. "Ah, young love. That explains a lot, don't you think?"

Karen frowned. "I don't see how." *No, it just complicates everything. I wonder if Alice knows about this— how could she not know? She's the only one Jessie tells where she's going. I wonder if she's sneaking out of the house at night—* She felt another headache coming on.

"Karen, it hasn't been that long since *you* were a teenager. It explains everything about her." Bobbie grabbed her hand. "Don't you remember what it was like when you had your first boyfriend? I know I do." He sighed and looked off into space. "All I did was think about him. I spent a lot of time daydreaming, and I'm sure my parents thought I was crazy. That's what's going on with her—she probably just sits and writes about him and how much she loves him. She thinks she's the first person to ever be in love, and nobody would understand. Teenaged hormones running out of control." He grinned at her.

*Great*, Karen thought, *now I have to worry about her getting pregnant. I wasn't like that, but then I didn't have any boyfriends in high school, all those boys were stupid and I didn't want anything to do with them, that was Vonda's territory, and look how she ended up. . . . It would be just my luck for her to get pregnant while Philip's away. How the hell would I explain that to him?* She thought back to when Vonda was a teen and still living at home, all the fights and arguments and screaming matches and slamming doors. *No, Vonda wasn't the same, she didn't hole up in her room and not talk to anyone, it was exactly the opposite, you couldn't shut her up about her boyfriends, and she didn't mope around and make everyone else feel bad, she was an unholy terror and Jessie, thank God, isn't like that. I think I would rather have the silent treatment than that . . . but I am going to have to talk to Alice about it, see what she knows. Jessie's my responsibility.* She was beginning to hate that word.

Bobbie kept a running commentary while they ate, filling her in on the progress he was making, and a new guy he was seeing. For the first time since Gary had left him last summer, he actually thought he could feel something for someone else. "He's so gorgeous, Karen, you should see him. He looks like he stepped right off the cover of an underwear box—not a spot of fat on him anywhere. And so nice! And sweet and funny and caring—he's from Boston, and has a week-end share here, I only wish I'd run into him sooner this summer—when I think about the time we've both wasted—but he's already invited me to come up to Boston and visit after the summer's over . . . this could be it. . . ." She paid attention just enough to make appropriate noises, but her mind was a million miles away. "I never thought I'd ever fall in love again . . . he's just so sweet . . . when I was performing the other night he brought me a dozen roses—no one's ever given me roses before . . . I can't wait for you to meet him . . . I wonder if I'll have to move to Boston or if he'll move here . . . I mean, he could live here on the weekends and commute . . . that makes more sense, I guess . . . I can't move my business to Boston and he can't just quit his job . . . he has a great job, very fast track to upper-level management . . . I've never met anyone like him before . . . and he's so much cuter than Gary! Gary would die if he ever saw me with this guy . . ."

"That's great, Bobbie." They finished lunch, settled the bill, and made plans to meet for lunch again in two days. Karen promised she'd have the attic cleaned out by then, and she headed home, her head still spinning.

Who was that boy? How and where had Jessie met him?

*I'm not very good at this mothering thing*, she thought as she unlocked her front door and headed back up to the attic to go through some more boxes.

It wasn't until she was digging through the third box that it occurred to her.

Lettie also had a secret boyfriend she only confided in her diary about.

# Chapter 8

*The full moon glowed in a cloudless sky as he paced through the sand. Out on the water, the lights of a ship heading for Boston floated as though on air. He glanced at his pocket watch again; she was over half an hour late. He kicked at the sand in frustration. He'd wait another ten minutes and then head back home.*

*The fisherman hadn't meant to fall in love with her. It just happened. He'd seen her walking down the street with her governess one hot afternoon, and he couldn't take his eyes away from her. The fishing boat for which he crewed had just arrived at the pier with a hold full of fish, and they were sliding the slippery, still flapping cod into ice buckets to take to the market. It was hard work; he'd been up since four and it was now midafternoon. He was looking forward to stopping at a grill for a roast beef sandwich and something cold to drink on his way back to his rooming house.*

*He had just finished handing a tub of fish over the side of the boat to one of the others when he happened to look up and see her. He froze, and time seemed to stand still. Everything else ceased to exist for that brief moment. She wasn't classically beautiful, her face set into strange angles and points, her lips a grim thin line. It was the face of a young woman who'd forgotten how to laugh. Her hair was tied back and away from her pale face. Her clothes were entirely made of black, as was the umbrella she carried in one hand. The collar of her blouse was high and the sleeves were long, despite the heat of the July afternoon. She kept her eyes down, avoiding the eyes of everyone she passed. The old woman with her was also dressed in black, her short, stooped stocky frame walking quickly to keep pace with her taller, younger companion.*

*"Who is that?" he asked Manuel, who owned the fishing boat he worked on.*

*Manuel, who always stank of fish and whiskey, looked up from the bucket he was filling with stinking fish and snorted. His balding head was red and peeling from long days spent in direct sunlight. "That's the good Senator Hatch's daughter. Best to stay away from that one."*

*"Why?"*

*"She's not right." Manuel tapped a rubber-gloved finger on his forehead. "They call her the 'ghost-girl.' She's not been right since her mother passed on."*

*"She's beautiful." He still hadn't stopped watching her slender form as it moved past, turning his head to follow her. "I've never seen anything like her before."*

*"Nothin' but trouble if you bark up that tree." Manuel shrugged. "The senator surely won't want the likes of you sniffing around his daughter." And with another snort, he turned back to the fish.*

*Now, waiting for her, the fisherman sat down on the worn blanket he'd spread out. Maybe she wasn't coming. Maybe she hadn't been able to slip out of the house—heaven forbid she'd been caught going out unescorted at this hour! Lettie's mind was quick, but he doubted she'd be able to think of any explanation that would be believed. Since her father and stepmother came home, it had gotten harder and harder for them to see each other. Her stepmother was watching her like a hawk, Lettie claimed. On the nights she couldn't make it, terrible, dreadful thoughts crept into his mind.* She's tiring of you, *an insidious voice whispered inside his head.* She's met someone in her class, someone acceptable to her family. She will never come again. *The fisherman hated having those thoughts. He hated doubting her, especially when he saw the naked joy on her face when she was able to meet him.*

*Of course, the senator would never allow him to court his daughter properly, and he certainly would never allow them to marry. He would never allow his daughter, his only child, to marry a poor orphan who catches fish for his daily bread. He didn't know the right utensils to use at a dinner table. He didn't have any clothing that was suitable. He always smelled of fish, no matter how much he washed. Lettie said she didn't mind, she liked the way he smelled, but it would be a lot different when the smell was in a parlor. Perhaps tonight she finally realized how hopeless the whole thing was, and stopped coming . . .*

*"Samuel?"*

*He jumped to his feet with a smile. "I was beginning to think you weren't going to make it." He held out his arms to her, and his heart leaped in his chest. It couldn't be wrong when it felt like this, he thought, it just couldn't.*

*She rushed into his arms, and they kissed deeply, hungrily. His hands crept up to her breasts, and for once she didn't push his hands away. Her arms went around his neck, holding his lips to hers. He could feel her heart beating faster, confirming that she did indeed feel the same as he. The kiss seemed to last an eternity, and he didn't want it to ever end. He wanted to hold her in his arms and kiss her until the end of time.*

*Finally, she pulled away from him. "Oh, Samuel, I do love you so." She sat down on the blanket. "I am going mad, Samuel. I can't stop thinking about you." She ran her hands through her hair, which hung loosely. She never tied back her hair when she met him at the dunes. He loved her hair, it was so long and thick and beautiful, the way it caught the moonlight and almost seemed to dance.*

*He sat down beside her and took her hand, pressing it to his lips. "You're all I think about, Lettie. All day, every day, out on the water, all I can think about is seeing you at night. I love you so much."*

*She kissed him again, and they lay back down on the blanket, their bodies entwined. He fumbled at the buttons on the front of her blouse, and this time she didn't stop him. He kissed her neck, her breath coming faster, shallower, and deeper.*

*"Oh yes, Samuel, I love you. . . ."*

Chris sat up in bed, his face flushed. The dream was fading from his consciousness even before his eyes opened; all he could remember of it was being on the beach at night with a girl and—

He swallowed. His curtains were open and the room was full of light. *Oh God*, raced through his mind as he realized his bedroom door was wide open. All he was wearing was a pair of white boxer briefs, so he pulled his comforter over his lower body. *The last thing I need is to have Lois walk in here with me like this.*

Lois was frank, embarrassingly so, about sex. He heard her saying again, "Now, Chris, an erection is perfectly natural. You're a teenager now, and your hormones are turning you into a man. It's just biology. You'll wake up with an erection in the morning. You may even have wet dreams. Do you know what a wet dream is?"

And then she had gone on to explain, in lurid detail, while he squirmed, wishing he was anywhere else in the world but sitting in the living room listening to his mother talk so casually and properly about sex. His father, Joe, on the other hand, never brought it up; apparently that was another area where Lois had decided she was the right parent to give the lecture. She never noticed how uncomfortable it made Chris, listening to her in her calm voice explaining just what exactly men and women did together, the variations, the way bodies functioned. *I bet I'm the only kid in the world whose mother explained masturbation to him.*

His erection was aching. He adjusted himself under the comforter, and reached down to the floor for the sweatpants he'd discarded the night before. He pulled them on under the covers, and got out of the bed and looked at himself in the mirror. No, you couldn't tell, the sweatpants were baggy enough to disguise it. He sighed in relief. He could hear Joe and Lois talking in the living room. The coast was clear, so to speak, so he slipped down the hallway to the bathroom, locking the door behind him.

Three days had passed since the visit to Madame Nadja. He hadn't seen Jessie since the following day, when he'd met her at their usual bench on Commercial Street near the library. That time, she'd been the most relaxed she'd ever been, and had even allowed him to walk her back almost all the way to the house. They hadn't talked about the visit, the dreams, or anything. He'd almost felt like they were a normal pair of teenagers on a date. She had kissed him when they'd parted, not on the cheek, but full on the lips, before breaking away and running up the street. Chris had walked home whistling, feeling the happiest he could remember. *Maybe now we can be normal, and go on dates, and kiss, and who knows?*

Even Lois had noticed his good spirits over dinner. He'd gone to bed looking forward to seeing Jessie the next day.

But the next day, he sat on the bench for almost two hours waiting for her before giving up and going home. He weeded the flower beds, did the laundry, and vacuumed the entire house, full of pent-up energy.

*Why didn't she come? Did the kiss scare her off? Was she just playing with me? Was this all just some big game for her?*

Maybe he would never see her again before he left. Ah, she was just crazy, he was right to begin with. Jessie was just a nutcase, of course she was, who else would want to be around him? Normal girls wanted normal guys, and now even *she* didn't want to be around him. *What's wrong with me?*

Chris didn't talk during dinner that night, just listened to Lois and Joe drone on about current events. Lois tried to draw him into the conversation, but he would just shrug and say, "I don't know." Usually that drove Lois to the edge—those were the three words she hated the most. But for some reason that night she let him alone, not badgering him. He didn't notice the glances Joe and Lois exchanged whenever he mumbled in response, keeping his eyes down on his plate, focusing on finishing his food and getting away from the table.

The next day, after working his frustrations out at the gym, Chris wandered down to the bench again and sat down. *Surely today she'll be here.* He watched the passing tourists in their bathing suits and flip-flops, smelling of body odor and sweat and sand and suntan lotion. He watched the street, hoping to spy Jessie emerge from the crowd. But after an hour of waiting, he finally got to his feet and walked up the street, standing across the street from her house.

But the house was still. The front door never

opened. Through one of the attic windows, Chris could make out someone moving around, but it wasn't Jessie. After about half an hour, he gave up and walked home.

*Probably better off without her anyway,* he thought as he brushed his teeth. *She probably doesn't like me that way, none of them ever do. Who could blame her? Big old stupid gangly Ichabod Crane. No girl would ever want me. She just wanted someone to listen to her crazy shit, and big dumb old Chris Muir was sucker enough to listen, to get the wrong idea, to think she actually might be interested.*

The kiss had been real, though. He couldn't deny that. *She's avoided me ever since. Guess that means I'm a lousy kisser—or she just doesn't like me that way. She probably just kissed me because I listened to her— it was a sympathy kiss, nothing more, and I read more into it because I liked her—stupid tall skinny loser that I am. Why would any girl want me?*

He spat toothpaste into the sink and washed his face.

*Look at you—long skinny neck, zits on your forehead, you're ugly. You must have been crazy to think she'd like you that way, no girl has before, no girl probably ever will. Stupid, stupid, stupid, you're a stupid fool, Chris Muir, forget about her.*

He plodded into the kitchen and filled a bowl with cereal. He drank a glass of orange juice while he waited for the milk to soften his Cheerios. One more week until Labor Day, and then it was back to school. He'd probably never see her again anyway, so what was the point? He'd be going to Boston, not Provincetown, on his school breaks, so the earliest he could ever see her again would be next summer—and that was only if Joe and Lois decided to spend another summer on the Cape.

*It wasn't meant to be, you've wasted the whole sum-*

*mer on some stupid girl with serious psychological
problems, just forget about her and be done with it.
Summer fling, don't mean a thing.*

The gym was crowded by the time he got there. He
stretched on a mat over by the mirrors, where several
people were doing crunches. *Forget about her,* he kept
repeating over and over as he started his biceps curls.
*Focus, Chris, focus on the weights, focus on working
your muscles, you've got to build yourself up if you
want to get on* Road Rules. *They're not going to take
some gawky, spindly dork from a private school.*

Maybe being a virgin would actually help him get
on the show, although the guys they had on there were
usually virgins by choice, deeply religious kids who
thought sex was a sin. Chris couldn't tell them he was a
virgin because no one ever wanted him. That would
make him sound like a loser and they didn't take losers.

He kept stretching between sets, between exercises,
because as long as he focused on how his muscles felt,
on the work he was doing, stray thoughts of Jessie
stayed out of his mind.

He was drenched in sweat when he walked out of
the gym a few hours later, every muscle in his body
tired, some of his muscles twitching a little bit from the
exertion. He hadn't worked that hard all summer, and
he knew he'd probably be sore later, but he didn't care.
He felt good, even though it had taken a lot longer to
get through his workout than usual. The gym had been
crowded with people, and he'd had to wait for some
machines. The town was getting more and more crowded
as Labor Day drew closer.

He stopped to put on his sunglasses and take a swig
from his bottle of water. Everyone on the street seemed
to be in a good mood, smiling and laughing and joking
with each other as they walked past him. He trudged
on through town.

He wasn't looking where he was going, and all at once he walked right into a short man in lycra shorts and a tank top. He stumbled back a few steps, almost dropping his bottle, automatically saying, "I'm sorry! Excuse me!"

The man smiled at him. "It's okay—I wasn't paying attention." He tilted his head to one side. "Don't I know you?"

Chris stared at him. "No, I don't think so."

The man was maybe five seven, with dark curly hair and a solidly muscled body. He stuck out his hand.

"I'm Bobbie," the man said. He seemed genuine and warm. "Maybe I've just seen you around town."

"I've been here all summer. My name's Chris." Chris shook his hand and gave him a polite smile. He looked at Bobbie. "I'm sorry, but you don't look familiar."

Bobbie laughed. "Well, there've been a lot of people passing through here all summer. I live here year-round. Just here for the summer, huh?"

Chris nodded. "Till Labor Day, and then I have to go back to school."

Bobbie nodded. "Hey, let me buy you a smoothie to make up for almost knocking you down. That be okay with you?"

*Don't talk to strangers,* Lois's voice echoed in his head. *But it's broad daylight, and I'm at least a foot taller than this guy—I think I can take care of myself.* "Sure, that'd be nice. But you don't have to . . ."

"I know. I want to. C'mon."

After getting their smoothies, they sat on the step in front of Spiritus Pizza and watched people walking by. Chris noticed that guys kept smiling at them both. "Why are they looking at me?" Chris asked. "Is it because I'm so tall?"

"Just take it as a compliment and forget about it." Bobbie shrugged. "Where do you go to school?"

"A compliment?" Chris tilted his head. "Being stared at is a compliment?"

"They look at you because you're good looking and have a nice body, even if you *are* jailbait." Bobbie laughed, sucking at his straw. "And most of them are probably wondering how I scored such a nice piece of chicken."

"Chicken?"

"It's gay slang for someone underage." Bobbie winked at him. "Don't worry—I'm not trying to get in your pants or anything. I don't go for twinks. I like older men."

"So," Chris asked, a light going off in his head, "you mean I get looked at in the gym—"

Bobbie smirked. "It's because they like you. They really, really like you."

"Oh." Chris leaned back against the step. "I mean, I knew there were a lot of gay people here and everything, but—"

"But what, dude? You don't think you're good looking enough to get cruised?"

Chris looked over at the man. *They actually think I look good?* He thought it would bother him, being looked at that way by gay guys, but it didn't: suddenly he did take it as a compliment. *They think I look good.*

*Then why do girls always look at me like I've got two heads?*

Chris changed the subject. "So you live here?"

"Cape Codder, born and raised." Bobbie shrugged. "But you didn't answer *my* question. Where do you go to school?"

"St. Thomas More Prep. In Connecticut. It's a boarding school. I'm from Boston, really." Chris bit his lower lip. "So you've *always* lived here?"

"Well, I spent a few years in New York. Learning the

tricks of the trade, so to speak. But, yeah. Most of my life has been spent here on this little spit of sand. Why?"

"Do you know Madame Nadja?"

"Oh, sure, I've known her for years, ever since she moved here." Bobbie grinned. "She's weird, but I like her. She's one of the characters of Provincetown. We've got a lot of those." Bobbie raised his eyebrows looking at him. "Why do you ask about Nadja?"

"I—uh—was just wondering if she's really psychic or if it's all an act."

Bobbie waved at a guy across the street. "Couldn't say." He shrugged. "I'm not sure if I believe in that stuff myself, and I've never gone to her for a reading or anything, so—" He held up his hands. "She's cool—but I think she drinks a little too much, to tell you the truth. Ever since Noreen left her a couple of years back."

"Noreen?" Chris swallowed. "Then she's a lesbian?"

"Yeah, she's a big ole dyke. That bother you?" Bobbie leaned back on the step, folding his arms.

"No, I was just . . ." His voice trailed off. Lois had sat him down once and explained homosexuality to him, before he'd left for school the first year. "Hey, it's the way you are. Doesn't make much difference to me. You like guys, I was born liking girls." He smiled to himself. *For all the good it does me.*

"And so the world goes round," Bobbie said, laughing.

Chris smiled back. "Lois—my mother—says that sexuality is the result of a complex set of circumstances of both nature and nurture, and that discrimination against gays is the result of ignorance and small-mindedness."

"Well, she's remarkably enlightened for a mother." Bobbie laughed. "Certainly more so than *my* mother was. *Is.* She keeps praying that I'll come to my senses—that

I just haven't met the right woman yet." He held up his hands. "Can you imagine that?"

"Well, for what it's worth my mom's a real pain in the ass, too," Chris heard himself say. He covered his mouth quickly, and flushed, feeling guilty. "I mean, she's a good enough mom, I guess, but sometimes she drives me crazy, you know?"

Bobbie laughed. "It's okay, Chris, really. Most teen-agers think that. I know I did." He tossed his empty cup into a trash can. "So you're here for about another week?"

Chris nodded. "Yup." He scanned the street for Jessie. *Give it up, Chris, she doesn't want to see you anymore.*

"How'd you like to make some extra money?" Bobbie asked. "You're a big strong kid, and I could use some help on a job I'm doing. You know, just helping me lug stuff and do some painting and things."

"What kind of job?" Chris turned his attention back to Bobbie.

Bobbie smiled at him. "I've been hired to turn an attic into an office space. I'll pay you fifty dollars a day."

*Fifty dollars a day?* Chris did the math in his head, and smiled. "Yeah, that would be great."

"Okay. You need to show up at this house tomorrow." He took a pen out of his backpack and wrote down the address. "Nine sharp, okay?" He stood up. "I've got to get running. See ya tomorrow."

Chris watched him walk away for a moment, and then looked down at the address. A grin spread across his face.

It was Jessie's house!

Of course, Lois didn't want him to do it.

"Your allowance is plenty of money," she argued,

looking to Joe for help. "Just enjoy the rest of your summer, Chris. You've only got a week. There's plenty of time for you to work when you grow up."

"But, Lois, please." He looked over at his father. "Joe?"

Joe shrugged. "If he wants to do it, Lois, I don't see a problem." His father smiled at him and gave him a wink. "I think it shows initiative."

"I've been bored all summer, Lois, please." He wasn't sure the guilt card would work. "I mean, all I've done all summer is go to the gym, do my chores, and read. I've done everything you wanted me to do without complaint all summer. Come on, Lois, be fair." *That should do the trick. Lois hates the thought of being unfair.*

His mother's face worked, her jaw clenching and unclenching. Then finally she just sighed. "Oh, all right." She threw her arms up in the air. "You finished your summer reading list, so I guess it's all right. I just hate the thought of you working when you don't have to, honey, you should be enjoying your youth while you can—"

"Thanks!" Chris bounded across the room, giving her a big hug and leaning down to kiss her cheek.

Lois smiled at him. "Oh, this came for you while you were out." She retrieved a box from the side table. "What is this?"

Chris smiled. "A book I ordered."

"What kind of book?" Her eyebrows went up.

"Philosophy." He tore open the box.

"Oh?" Joe slipped on his glasses. "What kind of philosophy?"

*Big mistake*, Chris thought as he pulled the book out and handed it to his father, holding his breath. Lois lost interest and walked out of the room. Philosophy was Joe's province.

"Oh, *The Circle of Time*." He hefted the book. "You know, I heard Dr. Goodwin speak last year at that conference in California. A very interesting man. I've always intended to read this, just never got around to it. May I borrow this when you're finished?"

"So, you know about this?" Chris sat down on the sofa. *Maybe that Madame Nadja isn't such a nutcase after all.*

"Well, I'm not sure if I agree with Dr. Goodwin's theory, but I do know he's studied many different religions, and he's culled this theory from some old Welsh myth. He claims to have found traces of it in other religions, and wrote this book based on his findings. He was a fascinating speaker, very charismatic." He handed the book over to Chris. "How did you come across this?"

"I was just surfing the Web one day and came across his site." Chris put the book under his arm and stood up. "It sounded interesting, so I went ahead and ordered it."

Joe looked pleased. "You're becoming interested in philosophy?"

"A little," Chris lied. He wanted to get away, get to his room so he could start reading, but he had to stay while his dad talked to him about philosophy.

"Maybe next summer I can give you some other books to read for your reading list." The list was always Lois's department; this was almost heresy in the Muir house.

"That'd be cool, Dad." He smiled awkwardly, hurrying down to his room, where he flopped down on the bed, the book in his hands.

*Tomorrow morning I'll be in their house, and if I read a lot of this, I'll have an excuse to talk to her. She'll have to talk to me about it, she said she wanted me to read it and tell her about it, she won't have a choice.*

Chris opened the book and started to read.

# Chapter 9

*The Cape wasn't nearly as hot as Washington in the summer, Sarah Jane thought as she made her way to the flower market. She had decided to fill the house with flowers. It had such a lifeless musty dead smell that was sickening to her. Even with the windows open and the bay breezes coming through, there was that horrible smell underneath the freshness of the breeze. She'd asked Horace about it, but he claimed to smell nothing—no wonder, with him smoking cigars almost constantly in his office, where he talked on the telephone all day while answering his voluminous correspondence.*

*The entire atmosphere of the house was stifling for Sarah Jane. It was bad enough to hear that old bitch Mrs. Windham using that condescending tone with her. But Lettie—Horace's dear little Lettie—continued to pretend that she didn't exist, and Horace let her get away with it. That's what vexed Sarah Jane the most.*

*Ever since they'd arrived in this godforsaken town, Horace had become a completely different person. Gone was the attentive, courteous, and well-mannered*

*Washington senator, and in his place was a boorish
beast who wanted everything just so—and screamed at
the top of his lungs if things didn't measure up to his
exacting standards.*

What have I done? Whom have I married? *Sarah
Jane shook her head as she headed into town, glad to
be out of the house even for a little while.*

*Senator Hatch had always been a fervent opponent
of the women's suffrage movement. Her old friend and
mentor Lizzie Standish called him "the worst of the
lot" and had urged her to not marry him. But Sarah
Jane wouldn't listen to anyone's counsel. She'd gone to
see him that first time to try to convince him that
women were not weak and foolish and that they deserved the right to vote. Senator Hatch carried a lot of
weight in New England, and if the amendment for
women's suffrage was going to get ratified by the necessary two-thirds of the states, they needed him on
their side.*

*When she was ushered into his office, she could tell
the newly widowed senator was not unaware of her
youthful feminine charms. They had a lively discussion,
and she knew her arguments were assisted in their
strength by the low neckline of her dress. After several
such meetings—sometimes over dinner—Senator Hatch
finally gave her his pledge to give up his active resistance. Sarah Jane considered it a major victory. That
night, as the carriage dropped her off at the women's
boardinghouse where she lived, she allowed him to
kiss her for the first time. The kiss did nothing for her,
of course. It left her cold, tasting of the bootleg gin he'd
slipped into his drink when no one was watching. Senator
Hatch was as firm a supporter of prohibition as he had
been an opponent of suffrage, yet it didn't seem to
apply to his own desire for spirits.*

*Still, they continued to see each other. Lizzie and her*

*other friends were scandalized, but Sarah Jane was not*
*about to let his support for women's votes wane. And it*
*would, she was certain, the moment she stopped seeing*
*him. She had to admit, too, that she enjoyed the access*
*to power she was suddenly granted after being so long*
*on the outside. Horace took her to all sorts of impor-*
*tant political and social receptions—even to dinner at*
*the White House one time, where she met the new pres-*
*ident, Warren Harding. Sarah Jane had immediately*
*disliked him. The rumors around town were that Harding*
*snuck mistresses in through the back doors of the exec-*
*utive mansion, and the way his eyes had lingered on*
*Sarah Jane's bosom left no doubt in her mind that, had*
*she been open to it, she could be one of those snuck in*
*underneath Mrs. Harding's nose.*

*When Horace finally proposed to her, Sarah Jane*
*hadn't even to think twice about accepting. She didn't*
*love him, of course, but she'd learned back home that*
*love meant nothing. Money and power, that was what*
*mattered, and she'd gone after it as soon as she'd ar-*
*rived in Washington. She'd become a suffragette be-*
*cause she was tired of being just a "pretty piece of*
*baggage" that men felt they were entitled to pinch and*
*kiss as they saw fit. As a senator's wife, she could do it*
*her way. She might even be able to run for office herself*
*once now that votes for women had been won. She*
*wanted to be a player in the games too long reserved*
*for men. She had tasted power and privilege, and found*
*the flavor very much to her liking.*

*She hadn't realized that marrying Horace would mean*
*spending time in this backwater on the Cape, bored out*
*of her mind. She hadn't realized it would mean dealing*
*with his spoiled daughter and her bitch of a governess.*

Well, at least we won't be up here much longer,
*Sarah Jane thought.* Once Congress is back in session,
we'll have to go back.

She smiled at the thought of presiding over dinners and parties as hostess, entertaining the most powerful men in the country and their dull wives. Quite a long way for the schoolmaster's daughter! The thought brought a smile to her face. If they could all see her now, she thought with a triumphant smile, all those bastards in Caddo Parrish who looked down their noses at her. Mrs. Senator Horace Hatch.

She'd gotten away from her hometown as soon as she could, taking the five hundred dollars that bastard Desmond Routledge had given her to get out of Louisiana—and as far away from his son as possible. Some day she'd make the high and mighty Routledges pay for the way they'd treated her. Oh yes, they'd all pay. The thought of returning to Shreveport as the wealthy and powerful wife of a prominent senator made her smile. And Louis Routledge—he was going to pay the highest price of all for his betrayal.

The flower market was exactly where Mrs. Windham said it would be—the old bitch hadn't sent her on a wild-goose chase after all—and Sarah Jane was placing sunflowers into her basket when she became aware of a young man staring at her. She blushed and lowered her eyes. He was very handsome, maybe twenty-two or twenty-three, wearing white trousers and a white shirt unfastened almost to his navel. His face was darkly tanned, as was his chest. The open shirt revealed a patch of thick black hair on his strong pectorals, and dried red paint was speckled through his thick black hair. An artist. She'd heard the town was full of them.

She turned to look at some irises and gladiola.

"You are the most exquisite flower in this place." The man had approached her boldly, and was holding a yellow rose out to her.

She knew she should tell him she was a married

*woman, cut him dead right in his tracks and turn away—
but she was all too well aware of how hard her heart
was beating, of the sudden surge in the blood racing
through her veins. The last time she'd felt this way
around a man—*

No, I won't think about that, *she told herself resolutely. That had resulted in disaster, and had almost
destroyed her in the process. No, she was now a re-
spectable married woman. A powerful, ambitious married woman.*

*"You are rather forward, sir,"* she said as coldly as
she could manage.

*"It is your beauty."* He bowed to her. *"My name is
Orville Axelrod, at your service."*

*"I am Mrs. Horace Hatch."*

*"Ah, then it's married you are."* He smiled, dimples
in his tanned cheeks. *"Then I shan't bother you anymore except to admire you from afar."*

*"See that you keep afar, Mr. Axelrod."*

Karen rubbed her forehead.

Axelrod. Why had that name suddenly come to her?

A dream. Had she dreamt about someone with that
name?

The man who was killed around the same time as
the Hatches?

"Are you listening to me?" Bobbie asked.

Her head hurt. Ever since she'd started working in
the attic, every morning she would awaken with a headache that no amount of aspirin seemed able to conquer.
The dreams she'd been having—she vaguely had some
sense that she was dreaming about Sarah Jane Hatch,
but her head hurt too much when she woke to remember much.

"It's brilliant, don't you think?"

Bobbie was grinned wickedly at her.

"He's leaving after Labor Day, so they'll get to spend that much more time together while he's here helping. And it'll be because of you. That's sure to make Jessie melt toward you. She'll be—"

"Absolutely mortified." Karen glanced at the door to make sure Jessie hadn't overheard what Bobbie had just told her. "God, Bobbie, hiring Jessie's boyfriend was the *worst* thing you could have done. I would have *killed* my parents if they did anything like this."

"But that's the beauty of it." Bobbie refilled his coffee cup. "My running into him on the street was a complete accident. I can honestly say it wasn't a setup. She'll see it as just a coincidence. Besides, she has no idea we know anything about them, right?" Bobbie was practically dancing with glee. "But you can suggest they have lunch together or something out on the deck. She'll be grateful when she sees she has your support."

*And what will Philip think?* Karen rubbed her head again. She hadn't told Philip that Jessie had a boyfriend—that wasn't something she wanted to do over the phone.

"I don't know, Bobbie. I wish you would've asked me first. Why do I feel like Ethel Mertz?"

Her head was throbbing again. She got up and shook more aspirin from the jar into her hand. "I've got the worst headache this morning. Nothing seems to be working." She swallowed the aspirin with a glass of water.

Bobbie looked concerned. "Oh, baby, why don't you go lie down for a while? I know what boxes you want to get rid of, and I'll have Chris carry them down when he gets here. I don't need you for anything today, sweetie, so you get some rest."

"Yeah, okay." They exchanged small smiles.

Climbing the stairs was torture. Karen closed the

blinds in the bedroom and lay down on the bed, closing her eyes. She heard the doorbell ring in the distance. That would be the boy—Chris, Bobbie said his name was. *What a lamebrained idea*, she thought, massaging her temples.

The pounding just seemed to be getting worse. *If this keeps up, I'm going to have to see a doctor.* The pain was almost blinding. *Maybe a cool damp rag will help.* She stood, staggering into the bathroom and running the cold water. Staring at herself in the mirror, she looked haggard. Dark circles under her eyes, sunken into her face. *Christ, I look like hell. What the hell is wrong with me?*

She couldn't sleep. She tossed and turned for about a half hour. *Axelrod. Why does that name keep popping into my mind?*

Finally she stood and headed back downstairs.

Chris Muir was a nice kid—unfailingly polite, friendly, and definitely a cutie. He worked hard, did everything Bobbie asked of him, and didn't talk much. Karen liked him almost immediately. He'd been here for the summer, he said, and would be heading back for school right after Labor Day.

Karen watched him, and she watched Jessie, who came down from her room, observed Chris with Bobbie, and said nothing. She just filled her sports-bottle with spring water and headed back upstairs to her room. Chris made no attempt to communicate with her either.

The next day was more of the same. Karen with her headache, watching the two teenagers ignore each other. Alice took Jessie's lunch up to her, and they did their lessons. Not a word passed passed between Jessie and Chris.

*Maybe they broke up, had a fight, something*, Karen thought, cursing Bobbie for making it worse rather than better. She imagined what it would be like when she was a teenager, sweeping out the beauty shop and answering the phones, if her mother had hired a boy she'd dated and was no longer interested in. She cringed inwardly. No, Bobbie just made everything worse.

And Jessie just went on ignoring her.

*That'll change when Philip comes home,* Karen kept telling herself. *He'll see how unpleasant his daughter is, and he'll step in. He'll have a talk with her. Things can't go on like this forever.*

Philip still called every afternoon, but it wasn't the same as having him here with her. She was lonely. Yeah, it was great living in this big house, and having more money than she'd ever dreamed of having, getting an office built for her up in the attic. But she missed Philip.

All she had was Lettie Hatch.

As she delved deeper into Lettie's diary, still measuring it out in two or three entries per night, she felt her own sympathies for Sarah Jane growing. When the noise from the construction work got to be too much, Karen ventured down to the Provincetown Library. She was surprised to find there were so few books about the Hatch murders. None of them could tell her anything she didn't already know from searching the Web. She wound a microfilm of old *Provincetown Advocate*s into the reader, located the contemporary accounts of the crime, and printed out copies for her growing file.

The more she read, the more convinced she was that Lettie Hatch got away with murder.

*And I'm going to be the one who finally reveals it to the world! Finally—a best seller for me!*

It would balance things out between her and Philip, Karen thought. Two best-selling, famous authors. What a great pair they'd make, invited to speak together at conferences and on television. Philip would be so proud of her. She'd justify his faith in her talent. She couldn't wait for him to get home so she could tell him of her find, to ask his advice on publishers and agents . . .

But first she needed to finish piecing the story together.

The biggest mystery, so far, was the identity of "S"— the mysterious man Lettie Hatch referred to meeting secretly in her diary. None of the books or newspaper accounts had shed any light on who he was.

She was a cagey one, that Lettie. In her diary, she never referred to her stepmother by name—only as SHE or HER, always capitalized.

*Dehumanizing her*, Karen wrote in her own notebook, *by not referring to her by her name, Lettie was convincing herself that Sarah Jane wasn't a person, was a thing, which eventually helped her to commit the crimes. Her stepmother wasn't human to her anymore. Classic sociopathic behavior.*

*But why kill her father, too?* Karen had pondered this mystery before writing out some thoughts. *Horace was definitely oppressive. He didn't want Lettie to go to college. But he was no different from many other men of the time. The fact that Lettie killed her father first, Sarah Jane second, doesn't make sense. Maybe by then Lettie was crazy, completely insane. Once she'd decided to get rid of Sarah Jane, there wasn't any reason not to kill her father too. Why not make herself completely free of both of them, free to live her life on her own?*

*Obviously she was in love with this "S" person, and she may have felt that her father was standing in the way of that. So—kill them both and be done with it.*

No one had ever discovered the fact that Lettie had a lover. If the prosecution had known that, their case would have been that much stronger. The jury hadn't wanted to believe that Lettie would have killed them both so brutally just for her inheritance—but if they knew she had a lover her father disapproved of, she would have been found guilty. And this diary definitely would have seen her hanged.

*And the references to* "the day of reckoning . . ." Karen would shiver when she read such passages in the diary. *She was planning on killing poor Sarah Jane almost from the day she arrived.*

It was the next day, when Bobbie and Chris were painting the walls and the fumes became too much for Karen, that she finally headed down to the town hall and asked to see Ellen Hatch's death certificate. She had a copy made for a three-dollar fee. When the clerk handed it over to her, Karen couldn't wait to check the cause of death.

*Unknown, probably heart failure.*

"What does this mean?" she asked.

The clerk, a tall, transsexual woman with tired eyes, simply sighed. "It means they didn't know what caused her death. Medicine has come a long way since then— ah, yes, see here?" She pointed to another entry. "The family refused an autopsy on religious grounds."

"That doesn't seem right," Karen replied.

*No autopsy? She died suddenly and there was no autopsy done? What if she'd been murdered, poisoned? She could easily have been Lettie's first victim!*

Karen racked her brain trying to remember the references in the diary to Ellen's death. Lettie hadn't written much about her mother, and when she did, it was usually in terms of how much she hated her stepmother for replacing her mother. And there had been that entry about the pearls . . .

"If there weren't any signs of violence," the clerk theorized, "and the family was against an autopsy, the doctor just put the cause of death as unknown and closed the case." She slipped on a pair of bifocals, examining the document closer. "Ah, Ellen Hatch." She gave a little laugh. "There you go. Nobody was going to cross old Senator Hatch, were they?"

"I guess not," Karen conceded.

The clerk nudged her glasses up her nose. "You trying to resurrect the Lettie Hatch case?"

Karen smiled. "I'm Karen Kaye."

"Oh, so you're the young Mrs. Kaye!" The clerk smiled. "And how do you like our little town thus far?"

Karen spent another ten minutes with her before finally managing to get away. All the way back to the house, she chewed on a new theory.

*What if Horace killed Ellen? Maybe that was why Lettie killed him first. But why wait two years for the "day of reckoning"? No, Horace couldn't have done it—if anyone killed her, it had to be Lettie.*

*I wish I had her earlier diaries, knew what they said about her mother's death. No one ever suspected that maybe Ellen was a victim too—of either Horace or Lettie. Horace was a powerful senator, nobody was going to look too closely at a sudden death in his family. Maybe that's what Lettie was counting on, and once she got away with killing her mother, it got easier to kill. Maybe she planned all along to kill her father— and the remarriage was just the icing on the cake for her.*

She couldn't make any sense of it. It was all theorizing, nothing concrete.

She was sitting at her desk, rubbing her forehead, staring at her notes. It was the Thursday before Labor Day.

Bobbie surprised her when he stuck his head into room and announced, "We're finished, believe it or not."

She nearly jumped out of her skin. "Jesus Christ, Bobbie, don't sneak up on me like that!" Her heart was pounding.

"Sorry, didn't mean to scare you. I just thought you'd want to come on up and take a look." He shrugged. "I knocked—you just didn't hear me."

"I thought you said it wouldn't be done for another couple of days." She rubbed her forehead.

"Yeah, well, my time estimate was based on doing all the work myself." He whistled. "That Chris kid is some worker." He did a little dance. "And now I can spend the whole weekend with David without feeling guilty."

"David?"

"My new beau. I can't wait for you to meet him."

Karen smiled. "Well, at least the room's done—that part of your plan worked out."

"Hey, you can lead a horse to water, but you can't make him drink."

"Whatever," she said. "Well, let's take a look."

The attic was completely transformed. Bobbie had banned her from the attic while the work was being done, and if she didn't know better she wouldn't have believed it was the same place. The floor was stained and varnished to a glassy sheen. Her desk was pushed snugly into an eave facing a window with a view of the bay. Bookcases lined one of the walls. Her books were on the shelves, the empty boxes they'd been in broken down in a corner and stacked on top of some of Philip's boxes of papers. A ceiling fan spun lazily overhead.

She whistled. "Wow, Bobbie, this is amazing." She looked around. "I can't get over what a great job you did!" She slid her chair in and mimicked typing on her laptop. She looked straight ahead out of a window and could see the bay shining in the afternoon sun. A feeling of calm came over her.

*I'll be able to write the best goddamned book in the world up here.*

She turned and gave Bobbie a big hug. "I love it!"

"I do good work, I told you." He smiled sadly. "I just feel bad about the Jessie thing. I really thought having him around—and then you and she—well, sorry about that." He sat down. "And he'll be gone by Tuesday."

"Just as well, I guess—one less thing for me to worry about." She walked around, grinning. "I can't get over this place! You're a miracle worker!"

He laughed. "Yeah, well, just be careful Philip doesn't decide to take this office and leave you downstairs."

"Over my dead body!"

But she didn't like the sound of that. The words left a bad taste in her mouth.

She grabbed his hand. "Come on, help me move my computer up here . . . let's get it all set up."

It didn't take long. There was just the laptop itself and her file folders and office supplies. When they were done, Bobbie insisted on taking her out to dinner to celebrate. She wanted to beg off—she wanted to get to work in her new space, but David wasn't due to arrive from Boston until the morning and Bobbie pleaded with her. "Come on, Karen . . . I don't want to have dinner alone with all these gorgeous men in town. I might be tempted."

"All right, all right."

They headed into town down Commercial Street, but her mind was a million miles away. Bobbie didn't seem to notice; he just chattered away. One of the things she most appreciated about Bobbie was that he was such a talker—all she had to do was pay nominal attention, and he'd just go on and on.

After dinner, Bobbie insisted they stop at the Central House lounge for a nightcap. One drink led to another, and finally, when she saw it was past eleven and Bobbie wanted to order her a fifth drink, Karen begged off.

"I'm plenty drunk already, Bobbie, and I'm tired."

She kissed him on the cheek. "Call me this weekend—I want to finally meet this David. We could have lunch or something."

Bobbie smiled. "Yeah. I'll do that. You sure you don't want just one more cocktail?"

"One more and you'd have to carry me home." She grinned at him. "And I'm not light as a feather."

She trudged on out into the night, sidestepping a couple of men in full leather walking hand in hand. The crowds were all heading in for a night of dancing and clubbing; she pushed through them in the opposite direction. She decided to walk home along the beach. The sea air cleared her head a bit. She wasn't weaving or anything, but she was definitely the worse for drink. *Why did I ever let Bobbie buy me that last one?* Finally, she saw the gate of the house ahead of her, and with a sigh of relief she started walking faster through the sand.

But just as she reached the gate, something out of the corner of her eye stopped her in her tracks. She turned her head and saw a figure moving through the shadows. *Jessie*, she thought. She stood watching as Jessie hurried the across the beach and then was lost in the darkness. *Where is she sneaking off to at this hour?*

The boyfriend, of course. *The sneaky little bitch! All this time, they were just ignoring each other and meeting at night, after I'd gone to bed! Well, I've caught you red-handed this time!*

Karen started to run, feeling glad she wore tennis shoes, and followed Jessie at a safe distance. The moon was full, and there were no clouds, so she could easily keep an eye on her. She was heading away from town, running along the edge of the surf. From the houses along the beach, Karen could hear laughter and music. All day long the ferries and planes coming in had been loaded with eager tourists, and the narrow streets had been clogged with cars packed down with luggage and people. The town was set to party, but Jessie was running in the opposite direction.

Karen watched as her stepdaughter suddenly crossed the beach and ran back toward the road, darting into the woods. Still making sure she kept to a safe distance, Karen followed. Why? She asked herself what reason she would have for spying on Jessie. It was late; she shouldn't be out at this time of night. But what good could following her possibly do? If Jessie saw her, it would just alienate her more.

But still Karen kept up the pursuit. She had the strangest sensation that somehow Jessie might lead her to "S."

Lettie Hatch's secret love.

Jessie emerged from the woods onto Route 6. Karen watched as the girl looked in both directions, then made a mad dash across the highway into the dunes.

Karen did the same. On the other side, she slipped off her socks and shoes and shoved them into her purse. Following Jessie's footprints in the sand, lit by the moonlight, Karen moved slowly, not sure where Jessie was and not wanting to surprise her and Chris—

*No, I want to catch her in the act. Wait till her father hears about this! It's off to an all-girls school for you, you spoiled little brat!*

Karen stopped, surprised at her venom. Was it the alcohol? What made her so nasty all of a sudden? She didn't want Jessie sent away. She wanted to make friends with her. She wanted them all to be a family, she and Horace and—

*Philip.* Of course she meant Philip. Why did she think Horace? She must be more drunk than she thought.

She made her way through the dunes. She could hear the waves crashing from the beach somewhere off in the darkness. *Where are they?* she wondered, pausing and listening.

From off to her right, she heard the sound of whispered voices. She climbed the small dune rising in front of her and she saw the sea. The moonlight suddenly revealed two figures on the beach.

Chris and Jessie were lying on a blanket, their naked bodies clearly obvious in the moonlight. Chris was in between her legs . . .

*. . . but it didn't seem right.*
*Something was wrong.*
*"Lettie!" she screamed.*
*The two figures stopped moving and sprang apart. She could see Lettie's naked breasts as she scrambled for her clothes.*
*She lifted her skirt and ran, her shoes sinking into the sand.*
*"You little whore!" she screamed, slapping her face. "Wait until I tell your father about this!"*
*The boy was running away across the sand, carrying his clothes. She grabbed Lettie by the arm. "Your father is going to love hearing about this, you little slut!" she screamed, as Lettie struggled to break free of her grasp . . .*

She shook her head.
There was no one there.
She tried to catch her breath. She blinked a few times, and stared. *Am I going completely insane? I heard them.* Goose bumps rose on her arms.
Something was very wrong.
*I'm not that drunk—*
Karen bent over and took a couple of deep breaths. Her head was spinning. A pinpoint of pain flared be-

tween her eyes and slowly began to spread through her brain. *No, not another headache, please . . .*

She felt her stomach churning. *Just breathe,* Karen commanded herself, *deep breaths, come on, you aren't that drunk, you're not imagining things, you can't be, you saw her, you followed her down here, she's here somewhere.* She stood up and looked again.

The beach was empty.

"What are you doing here?"

She looked up. Standing in front of her was Lettie— No, it was *Jessie . . .*

There was no sign of Chris anywhere.

"I could ask you the same thing," Karen replied, taking some more deep breaths.

Jessie's face was flushed with anger and embarrassment. "I just wanted to go for a walk. So you're spying on me?" She turned her back and started to walk away.

Karen grabbed her arm. "Wait, Jessie!" She spun the girl around.

*But what looked at her through Jessie's eyes wasn't Jessie.*

It was the dead eyes of Lettie Hatch.

Karen took a few steps back, her heart pounding.

*Oh my God, oh, sweet Jesus, I'm losing my mind. It's the drinks, that's it, it's Jessie all right, it can't be Lettie, it's the drink, sweet Jesus, what the hell is going on, what am I doing here . . . ?*

Jessie tore her arm away and with a cry, ran off through the dunes.

Karen's stomach clenched. She bent over from the waist as she threw up, then fell down hard to her knees in the sand. Her stomach kept on, until there was nothing left to come up, and she gagged, shivering, the cool night breeze from the sea blowing over her hot face.

She staggered to her feet, still nauseated, her head pounding.

And she heard laughter behind her.

She turned around. There was nothing there.

She started to run, barefooted, the road tearing at her feet as she dashed across the highway and through the woods, ending up once more on Commercial Street. She ran past people out strolling for the night air, who stared after her as she ran, one more crazy drunken tourist. Karen didn't stop running until she was back home.

*What the hell is going on? Am I losing my mind?*

She crept up the stairs.

Jessie's door was open. She was in bed, her eyes closed, breathing evenly.

Karen walked in, careful not to make any noise. When she reached the bed, she looked down into Jessie's face. Her breathing was even, her face peaceful.

*There's no way she could have gotten back here so fast, fallen asleep, and be breathing that evenly.*

*That wasn't Jessie I followed out to the beach.*

Her entire body shaking, she walked to her own room, splashing cold water in her face, staring at herself in the mirror.

"I'm not crazy," she said aloud to her reflection. "I know what I saw. It was Lettie. I saw Lettie Hatch."

Karen slid to the floor and started to cry.

# Book Two

# ECHOES ACROSS TIME

# Chapter 10

"Shouldn't you be home with your husband?" Bobbie dumped a couple of packets of sugar into his coffee and stirred it. "The last thing I figured you'd want to do today was meet me for coffee." He gave her a sly wink. "I figured you'd both have some catching up to do, if you know what I mean."

Karen shook her head. "Well, that's what I would have thought, too." Her disappointment was plain. She shrugged. "He's worn out and wanted to sleep." She looked out the coffee shop window at a woman walking a small bundle of white fur on a leash. "I just can't seem to focus today." *Or any day, really.*

"So, did you get a chance to talk to him about"— Bobbie lowered his voice—"the diary?"

"I haven't talked to Philip about anything." Karen sipped her coffee. It was hot and strong, and she added another packet of sugar, stirring it in absently. "I haven't had a chance to talk to him at all." She rubbed her forehead. She was getting yet another headache. *If this keeps up, I'm going to have to go to the doctor.*

Labor Day had come and gone, and Provincetown

had become a different place. The weather hadn't really changed—the days were still long, warm, and sunny. It did seem chillier to her after dark than it had been, and she'd taken advantage of the sales on Commercial Street to stock up on sweaters. Tourists still flooded in on the weekends, but there was a different feel to them. They didn't stay as long, for one thing, and they didn't seem to be as pressured to have a good time the way the summer people had been.

The village was definitely heading into a mind-set of autumn. Vacancy signs were hung in the windows of the inns; others closed for the season, dragging in their patio furniture and boarding up their windows. The lines in front of restaurants vanished as if they had never existed. A calm dropped over the end of the Cape.

*It's kind of like the weekend after Mardi Gras*, Karen thought, *when New Orleans just kind of holds its breath and relaxes again for a while. Only this stillness is going to last until next summer.* For the first time it hit Karen just how far out they were, at the very end of the long slender finger of Cape Cod, surrounded on three sides by water. How isolating this place must be in the winter.

*Godforsaken* was the word that suddenly came to her mind.

She hadn't really noticed the noise before—she'd thought Provincetown rather quiet all along, in fact—but now, with the vast majority of the tourists gone, she realized there had always been a low buzz: people talking and laughing as they passed her house, the music from boom boxes on the beach. Now: nothing during the long quiet weekdays except the occasional shriek of a seagull cutting a swath through the blue September sky.

Karen understood silence. Her big white house at the end of Commercial Street was almost always silent.

Occasionally the telephone rang, or a buzzer in the kitchen would go off, breaking the stillness. Such sounds startled her now. Whenever she was on the phone, she found herself talking in a low whisper. The quiet was intimidating, as if it were something that needed to be maintained. *It's almost like the house is dead*, Karen thought morbidly one morning, *and you mustn't disturb the dead.*

Her old apartment in the Quarter had never really been quiet; no place in the Quarter was. There was always some sort of noise in the Quarter: a car driving by on the street, a walking tour with a loud guide describing a house's architecture to a crowd of tourists, tinny music bursting forward from the bars, a loud car stereo with the bass turned up so loud all that could be heard—and felt—was its steady thump, thump, thump.

Even the little house where she'd grown up in Chalmette was always alive with noise during the day—the television, conversations, a stereo, *something.* So it wasn't surprising that the silence of this house, broken only by the steady, monotonous crash of the surf, was enough to set her teeth on edge. Karen found herself closing doors slowly, so the only sound was the doorknob catching. She padded around in her socks, never placing her entire weight down on her feet so tired boards wouldn't groan beneath her.

Yet as unnerving as the silence was to her, Karen no longer tried to initiate conversation with Jessie. *You can only take so much, can only try so hard before you have to stop*, she reasoned the morning she gave up on her stepdaughter. *If she doesn't want anything to do with me, that's fine. Two can play that game, little miss. There's no law that says we have to be friends, have to be close, have to have anything other than a civil polite relationship—although that would be a step up from what we have.*

She'd also long since run out of things to say to Alice. The early friendliness Alice had shown her had degenerated into an icy politeness, limited to short discussions on meals and groceries. Any time Alice seemed interested in talking, Karen couldn't forget—or forgive—Alice's bigotry. *She thinks Bobbie's a sinner. Well, then I want nothing to do with her.* Alice seemed to look at Karen with more contempt now, too, as if she no longer approved of Mr. Kaye's new young wife.

Karen found herself stealing glances at Alice sometimes. She still looked like the nice, kindly older woman Karen had first met, the epitome of everyone's favorite high school English teacher. It just didn't make sense that underneath that sweet exterior was a bigoted mind twisted by hatred. They had stopped speaking long before Philip got home.

All that had come to matter to Karen was reading Lettie's diary, which she still did, every night, limiting herself to just two entries at a time, to keep the sense of story she wanted to recapture in her own book.

She still had no idea of who "S" was, or possibly could be. Karen had visited the Provincetown Heritage Museum up at the monument, perusing personal letters from the Hatches that the society had collected. But there were no clues, no gossip, about Lettie and a young man. The local women who wrote letters to friends and sisters loved to gossip about their neighbors—to the point where Karen sometimes wondered what *her* neighbors knew about her—but other than catty references to the second Mrs. Hatch's age, there wasn't much of anything there to help her.

Even the letters after the crimes—and during the trial—weren't much help. Most of the townspeople were certain that Lettie had killed both Horace and Sarah Jane—but none of them had anything concrete to offer in the way of proof. And Orville Axelrod—the poor artist whose murder was overshadowed by those of the Hatches—it was almost as if he'd never really existed until he was killed.

Karen was certain the crimes were connected, but there was no proof. Some writers, in articles about the Hatch murders, had speculated about a connection—but there was never any evidence to offer other than wild speculation. No one seemed to know much about Axelrod.

From what little Karen had been able to find out, Axelrod had been in his late twenties and originally hailed from New York. He was a painter but had not yet made a name for himself as an artist at the time he was killed. His body had never been claimed; eventually it was buried in a pauper's grave. None of his work had apparently survived; he hadn't exhibited any paintings in group shows. He'd lived in a boardinghouse with other artists; but he was a loner, and no one knew where his money came from.

The mysteries were driving her crazy. She knew she'd have to solve them—all of them—if she was to make a splash with this book. Every day, she kept hoping she'd find clues, the definitive break that would help her get moving on her theories. But no. Her chief piece of evidence was the diary, which, she fervently hoped, would reveal everything she was looking for by the time she reached its last page. But would it? Lettie was frustratingly obtuse. She was writing to herself, after all, so she didn't write about things she knew or that were obvious to her. She didn't reveal much about Mrs. Windham, for example, and "S" remained nothing more than an initial. What happened to "S" after the murders? Why did he drop out of Lettie's life so completely?

And then Philip had come home, and Karen's life had changed completely.

"You're glad he's home?" Bobbie asked. "Aren't you?"

"Of course I am."

Philip had taken the red-eye flight from Seattle to Boston, and then had to wait several hours before the next Cape Air flight into Provincetown. He was cranky and groggy when he walked into the little terminal building where Karen sat waiting for him. He'd spilled coffee on his white shirt at some point, and his hair was disheveled. His suit was wrinkled, and his laptop was slung over his shoulder in its case, the strap twisted in fifty different directions.

"Karen." He put his arms around her and gave her a quick kiss. "Jesus, I'm tired."

His mouth tasted of stale coffee. "I'm so glad you're home, Philip." His arms felt good around her—it'd been such a long time.

He let his head fall back briefly, looking up at the sky. His handsome face needed a shave. "All I want to do is go to bed and sleep till tomorrow," he said. "The flight last night was one of the worst. I couldn't sleep because there was constant turbulence and this crying brat behind me kept kicking my seat. You'd think in first class they'd take care of such things."

He went on grumbling as they waited for his suitcases to be brought in. Karen took a deep breath and listened with only half of her mind as her husband went on and on about glitches on his tour—hotel rooms that had to be changed because they weren't adequate, bookstore owners who hadn't done enough promotion for his appearance, bad reviews in shit-rag local papers.

Philip's droning continued, even after they'd retrieved his bags and loaded them into the SUV. Not once did he mention Jessie—or for that matter, ask Karen anything about herself, how she liked Provincetown, what she'd been doing since she arrived. Just a never-ending stream of complaints. Karen drummed her fingertips on the steering wheel as she maneuvered through the narrow streets, a smile plastered on her face. Apparently, all her husband required was that she smile and nod every once in a while.

*Not a word about my work, or what's been going on since I got here, or Jessie, or anything*, she thought as she pulled the SUV into the driveway. *This is the husband I've been missing all these weeks?*

Philip had walked ahead of her into the house. "Jessie! I'm home!" he shouted as he flopped down into a reclining chair in the living room. "Babe," he said to Karen, "will you get me something to drink? A soda or something? I'm so damned dehydrated."

Karen heard Jessie's footsteps on the stairs as she retrieved a can of Coke out of the refrigerator. Alice was sitting at the table, reading the paper, and didn't look up until the refrigerator door shut. Their eyes met, Alice giving her a tight little grimace and a slight shrug before looking back down at the paper.

*She's used to him, more used to him than I am*, Karen thought, closing the refrigerator door.

When Karen walked back into the living room, Jessie was sitting on the sofa opposite her father, chewing on one of her fingernails. She was wearing a black sweatshirt and black jeans, her feet bare. Karen glanced at her as she handed Philip his soda. "Thanks, babe," he said, taking a long gulp.

"So did you miss me, cupcake?" he asked finally. Karen wasn't sure whom he was talking to, but she noticed his eyes were on Jessie.

"Sure," the girl said, not making eye contact with her father.

Karen sat down on the far side of the couch from Jessie. Philip looked from one to the other. "You two are getting along great, right?"

"Just fine," Jessie mumbled.

Philip beamed over at Karen. "I knew you'd hit it off."

*Oh yes, we hit it right off, we're thick as thieves. Can't you tell? Are you so clueless you have no idea what goes on in your house? She won't talk to me, she won't acknowledge me—I might as well not even be here as far as she's concerned. She might as well be a total stranger to me.*

"Can I go?" Jessie asked, standing up, brushing imaginary crumbs off her black jeans. She didn't look at Karen once. "I'm working on something Alice assigned me."

Philip nodded. "Sure, sweetheart, we'll catch up later. Brought you a few things. They're in my bags somewhere."

The teenager clomped back up the stairs.

Philip closed his eyes and sighed. "Damn, I'm tired." He stretched. "I think I'm going to try to nap for a while."

"Philip, I was hoping I could bring you up to date on a few things," Karen said.

"Can't it wait, hon?" He stood from the chair, standing over her. "My mind is so scrambled right now—I just need some sleep."

"But—"

"I know—I've missed you, too." He cupped her chin with his hand. "But after my nap I'll be better able to focus. Can it wait?"

She smiled tightly. "Fine. Sure. Get some sleep."

He winked at her, walking out of the room. He never even acknowledged Mrs. Winn.

As she watched her husband head up the stairs, Karen's head started to ache again. She took some aspirin, then called Bobbie. That's when they decided to meet at Spiritus.

\* \* \*

*Thank God for Bobbie*, she thought again, taking another sip of her coffee. "Christ, my head hurts."

"You should really see a doctor, Karen." Bobbie gave her a look of concern. "I mean, it's not normal to get as many headaches as you get. There might be something wrong, Karen."

"Really, it's nothing." She waved her hand. "My mother used to get headaches all the time. I guess it's what I always feared." She gave him a weak smile. "I'm becoming my mother."

"Yeah, well, it's even worse for me, with all my hammers and wrenches. I'm becoming my *father*. For a gay man, that's a problem, honey. Next thing you know, my ass will be four feet wide and I'll be drinking Budweiser watching *Bowling for Dollars*."

She laughed. "I should probably get back home so that I'm there when His Majesty wakes up."

Bobbie reached over and took her hand. "Karen, you're still a newlywed. You shouldn't be talking this way."

"He was just tired, that's all. I'd be cranky too if I had been away that long. He just needs time to adjust."

"Philip Kaye's bad temper isn't exactly a secret in this town," Bobbie told her.

"He's just tired," Karen repeated.

Bobbie let go of her hand. "Okay, baby. But I'm here if you need to talk. And David, too. He loved you, by the way. He wants us both to come up to Boston to see him. Getting out of P-town for a day would be good for you."

Karen agreed it might. The town felt so confining now that the summer was over. But it would be different now that Philip was home. She was certain of it. She had her husband back. They'd take walks along the beach, they'd make love under the stars, they'd talk about writing . . .

But why was she so reluctant to tell him about Lettie Hatch's diary?

She walked out onto the sidewalk.

Because it was gone. Whatever spark she had seen in Philip's eyes in New Orleans was gone now. Why had he married her? He had barely kissed her at the airport. Bobbie was right: *we're still newlyweds! Why aren't we acting like ones?*

*What am I doing here?* Karen asked herself as she trudged back home, the heavy weight of depression settling around her. *This whole marriage was a mistake. If I was smart I'd just pack my stuff and buy a one-way ticket home.*

The sun shone as she passed the wharf, and she stopped at a stand specializing in sausages and corn dogs to buy a fresh lemonade. The coffee had been a mistake; it felt as if she had battery acid sloshing around in her stomach. She sipped the lemonade and walked out to the end of the wharf. A line of people were waiting for the Boston ferry, suitcases piled unevenly all around them. Yes, she'd like to go to Boston. Get away. Get away from all of this . . .

The wind off the bay was cold and biting, despite the warmth of the sun. Karen sat down on a bench and looked out across the water. The bay was calm, small rippled waves scattering over its blue surface. A chill went through her and she hugged herself for more warmth.

No, she couldn't leave.

Lettie Hatch and the mysteries had entered her soul.

*Orville Axelrod couldn't have just appeared from nowhere. He's connected to the Hatches, somehow, and his murder—did Lettie kill him, too? And why?*

The only picture she'd found of Axelrod—the one they used in the papers with all of the write-ups—had shown him to be a handsome man, but there'd been something sly about his eyes she hadn't cared for, as though he knew something. He'd been in his late twenties. Some of the articles had speculated he might have been a criminal—or had some kind of underworld connections. It wasn't hard to imagine from his picture. There was something about the way he held his head, in the slant to his eyes and the curling of his lips, that was not only sly but smug, as though he were playing a massive joke on everyone.

Where did his money come from? He claimed he was an "artist," but never sold any of his paintings, never displayed them in any of the local galleries. So how was he supporting himself? No one was ever able to figure out his source of income. Back then, being in a different state was literally like being in a different country. Karen closed her eyes. Okay, a man with no verifiable source of income, in 1922. What was going on in 1922? She'd done enough reading in the last few weeks to know. Women had just gotten the right to vote, Warren Harding was in the White House, the Teapot Dome scandal was about to erupt, Europe was still recovering from the Great War, people were making fortunes on Wall Street. She opened her eyes. Maybe Axelrod was a speculator?

No, that didn't make any sense either. Provincetown was too remote, too far from New York. Sure, there were telephones and telegraphs back then, but not everyone had access to one. He couldn't have lived here and conducted that kind of business in New York. *Maybe he made a small fortune, pulled his money out, and moved up here to be an artist—but if he was just an artist, why would anyone kill him in such a brutal way? What connection was there to Lettie Hatch?*

*I'll probably never know.* With a sigh, Karen tossed her empty cup into a trash barrel and walked back to the house.

She could hear Alice and Jessie talking upstairs—probably going over schoolwork. Her head was still hurting—the aspirin she'd taken had done nothing. She rubbed her temples again, walking into the kitchen to get more. She shook out four, popped open the top of a can of Coke, and washed them down.

Upstairs, Philip was snoring, fully dressed, on their bed. She watched him for a few moments—Jessie and Alice had fallen silent down the hall—and then turned to the attic stairs. There she sat at her desk staring out the window before finally reaching into her top drawer and retrieving the diary. She opened it to the book-marked page. She stared at the faded writing.

She turned the page, scanning the next entry. Nothing about "S" or Orville.

*Come on, Lettie, give me something to go on already!*

She turned another page. Still nothing. She almost screamed in frustration. It shouldn't be this hard to trace someone. Somehow, she knew that he was the key to unlocking the puzzle of the past.

She set the diary down and opened her notebook, flipping through the pages to where she kept her notes on Sarah Jane. The second Mrs. Hatch was another cipher. Some writers claimed she was from Philadelphia, others Albany, and one had even claimed she was originally from Baltimore. How had she met Senator Hatch? Why had she married him? From the photographs, it was patently obvious why *he* had married *her*—she was quite beautiful, with her long curling blond hair, pert chin, and flashing eyes. Karen had gotten a copy of the death certificate from the town archives, but no place of birth was listed—and cause of death, multiple stab wounds.

Out of everyone in the tragedy, she felt the closest to Sarah Jane. They had so much in common—marrying an older, famous man, moving up here to the Cape, having to deal with a stepdaughter from hell the same age as Karen's.

*Who were you, Sarah Jane? What were your thoughts? Did you find this house as oppressive as I do? What did you want from your life—why did you marry a man old enough to be your father? Did you love him?*

She clicked on her laptop and opened a new document. She stared at the screen for a moment, and then started typing.

> *It was a hot August afternoon. The horses' hooves threw up clouds of dust. Sarah Jane longed for something to drink to ease her dry throat. The carriage headed down Commercial Street, her husband acknowledging the waves and shouts from some of the citizenry as they passed. From her face Sarah Jane pushed an errant blond curl. Her stomach was in knots. She felt a sense of foreboding, as though she were heading for her doom. . . .*

"Too melodramatic," Karen decided after a moment, deleting what she'd written. She buried her face in her hands.

*I could write it as fiction, I don't know how to do nonfiction, I could get things wrong. It would be easier to write it as fiction; then I could just make things up that I don't understand, and I could put my theories together and write it that way without the evidence. . . .*

But that would be cheating—the easy way out.

*The one thing you can never, ever do, is cheat your readers,* Philip's voice echoed in her head. *They'll forgive a lot of things—but cheating, they never forgive that. You can't have a character suddenly start acting in a way that doesn't work with what you've already established for them just because you* need *the character*

*to do something. That's why you have to know every-
thing about your characters before you start writing
about them. You have to catch that kind of thing. You
can't count on your editor being that thorough. Remember, you aren't the only author they're working with,
and they're under a lot of pressure to get their work
done, so they often just skim. It's* your *work, it's* your
*name on the spine. No reader's going to think,* Boy, the
editor really fucked this up. *They'll blame you. . . .*

She sighed. *Maybe I should just go back to Vicky
and forget about this.*

The printout of the first two hundred pages of the
Vicky book sat on the corner of her desk. She picked it
up and started reading through it again. After about
five minutes, she put it down. Her headache was coming back—it seemed like every time she tried to work
on Vicky, the headache came back.

This time it got worse, worse than it had ever been
before. A throb went through her head that made her
eyes go black and water.

*It's not normal to get as many headaches as you get.
There might be something wrong, Karen.*

She put her hands on her forehead and pressed in on
the pressure points of her temples. No relief. She felt a
wave of nausea. Karen closed the laptop and stood up,
almost stumbling. She staggered over to the stairs,
clutching the handrails with both hands as she carefully felt her way down them. Another wave of nausea,
and the coffee in her stomach churned. She choked
down the acrid vomit and gasped for breath. She felt
her way down the hall, pushed open the bedroom door,
and collapsed onto the bed next to Philip. She closed
her eyes, willing the pain to stop, to go away. She
began taking deep breaths, and the pain began to ease a
little bit.

* * *

*She was sitting in the kitchen, sipping a cup of hot tea. Her heart was pounding, and she felt sick to her stomach. She could hear movement upstairs, voices shouting at each other. Horace was furious with Lettie— she wasn't really sure what the girl had done, but whatever it was, it had brought out Horace's blinding rage. She'd gone into Lettie's room, seen the girl cowering in a corner, her face ashen, eyes wide, obviously terrified, and despite her own resentment of the girl, her heart had gone out to her. She'd tried to intervene, but Horace had briefly turned his anger to her, screaming at her, spittle flying into her face. He'd raised his hand to her, as though he was going to strike her, and she'd fled the room, down the stairs, and with shaking hands she had boiled some water for a calming cup of tea.*

*What kind of monster have I married?* she wondered again. *What could Lettie have possibly done to make him so angry? Horace liked things his way—and he brooked no arguments. He was always right, everyone else always wrong, and his anger—so far, it hadn't been directed at her, but it was only a matter of time. And then, once his rage was spent, he calmed down and acted as though nothing had ever happened.*

*There was a knock on the back door. Sarah Jane forced herself to stand and opened the door. It was the man from the flower market, smiling insolently at her. His shirt was open, and she caught a glimpse of tanned skin, hard muscles, and curling black hair. He stood with his legs apart, hands on hips, and his eyes were on the open neckline of her dress.*

*"May I help you?"* she asked stiffly, feeling her own temper starting to slip away from her.

*"Just making a delivery, Mrs. Hatch."* He picked up a wooden crate and carried it into the kitchen.

*"We didn't order anything."*

He set the box down next to the counter and gave her that lazy grin again. *"Just your friendly neighborhood bootlegger, Mrs. Hatch. I've a standing order from your husband."* His hands went back to his hips, his eyes glancing down at her bosom again. The grin grew wider, into almost a leer.

Bootlegger? Sarah Jane's eyes glanced over at the crate, then back to the stranger. He bowed at the waist, doffing an imaginary hat in mock deference. *"Orville Axelrod at your service, ma'am."*

She bristled. How dare he look at her in that fashion! She wasn't some trashy wench, she was a lady, the wife of a United States Senator, and she deserved to be treated with a little more respect. He was mocking her, and she was just about to put him in his proper place when a loud shout came from upstairs, followed by a door slamming so hard that the entire house shook.

Axelrod raised an eyebrow. *"Have I come at a bad time?"*

Sarah Jane glanced up at the ceiling. *"Um, I—"*

Horace stomped into the kitchen, swearing under his breath. *"I have a good mind to put that girl in a convent!"* Then he noticed Axelrod standing there. *"Orville! What have you got for me today?"*

*"Some of the finest whiskey to make its way onto the Cape in many months, Senator."* To her disgust, Axelrod's manner turned obsequious and deferential. *"You will certainly enjoy it, sir."*

*"That last batch was more suited to thinning paint, Axelrod."* Horace took out his wallet and handed over a sheaf of bills. *"If this batch is more of the same, I'll be needing to find another supplier."*

*"Ah, but you're a hard man to please, Senator. Such a discriminating palate."*

*"I just know the difference between liquor and tur-pentine."*

*Sarah Jane felt ill. She walked out of the room, turning back at the door. Her eyes met Axelrod's, and he gave her a wink. Her face flushed, her heart beating a little faster. How dare he—and right in front of her husband! She turned her head and walked over to the stairs.*

*But he was rather handsome. . . .*


"Karen?"

She opened her eyes. The sun was going down, shadows creeping across the room. Philip was staring down at her, a smile on his face. Had he been watching her sleeping?

"What time is it?" She sat up, yawning. The headache was gone, thankfully, and she stretched, arching her back until it cracked. She scooted up to the headboard and wrapped her arms around her knees. She smiled back at her husband.

"It's a little after eight." He shrugged. "I was going to wake you up earlier, but you looked so peaceful. You were smiling in your sleep. It was the cutest thing."

She'd slept for almost six hours, wasted almost the entire day, but she was still a little tired and groggy. Her stomach growled. She hadn't eaten since breakfast—and then she'd only had a little toast. "I'm hungry," she said.

"So am I," he purred. "It's been so long." He sat down next to her on the bed and kissed her neck. "You're so beautiful. I've missed you so much, Karen. Every night on the road, when I was so alone, all I could think about was you, and how much I wished you were there with me."

Karen wanted to believe what she was hearing. But why was there still a gnawing suspicion that Philip wasn't always so alone on the road . . . ?

"I've been waiting for this so long." His mouth moved from her neck to her lips.

Karen closed her eyes.

# Chapter 11

Chris tossed his backpack onto the floor of his dorm room. Josh, his roommate, wasn't there. The room smelled of teenaged boys—sour socks and underwear, sweat and cologne. It was a typical dorm room at More Prep—just big enough for two single beds shoved up against opposing walls, two desks, a large shared closet, and a small refrigerator with a telephone resting on top. Chris's side of the room was neat. He made his bed every morning and stuffed his dirty clothes into his laundry basket. Josh's bed was unmade, and the floor around it was buried in dirty clothes.

The wall over Chris's bed was bare, just the sickly beige color all the rooms were painted. He'd thumb-tacked a calendar—*Castles of Europe*—to the wall over his desk, his sole effort at decoration. Josh's wall by contrast was hung with posters of women in bikinis, nipples hard, posing seductively. Some of the posters were hung crookedly, and in places their corners over-lapped.

Josh was different this year. The last two years, he'd been a full-blown jock—football, wrestling, and baseball—which meant he never got back to their room until almost dinnertime. Josh would change out of his uniform into something more comfortable, go down to eat, then hang out with his other jock buddies until lights out. But this year, Josh wasn't playing football, nor was he hanging with his usual friends. He still wasn't around right after school—he might not be on the team (for whatever reason, Chris had yet to find out), but he still went to work out after his last class every day.

Josh and Chris had always gotten along—tolerating each other more than anything else, which was better than a lot of the kids who were forced to room together. Every week or so there was a fight between room-mates—sometimes violent, with yelling and screaming and punches flying, things getting broken, until the house proctor managed to break it up and reshuffle room assignments. Josh seemed quieter this semester—and when they were both in the room at the same time, he seemed more open to talking to Chris than he ever had been before.

Chris didn't waste a lot of time trying to figure Josh out. His course load, hand-selected by Lois, was too heavy for much psychoanalyzing; every night he had several hours' worth of work to do. Lois would not settle for anything less than straight As. Chris had gotten a B in math once in junior high and he thought his mother was going to have a stroke. It was easier to study hard than go through that mess again.

*You're smarter than this, Chris, you are, and you have to understand that everything in life is hard work—after high school, college is even harder, and then graduate school is even harder, and then the real world is even worse than you can imagine. This is the time of your life when you set up the success of your later life, when you develop the good work ethic and study habits that will eventually pay off with you being a success later in life. You simply cannot get grades like this; this means other people are better than you, more success-ful than you, and you've got to just work harder. I know math isn't an easy subject—I always had trouble with it myself when I was your age, but I just buckled down and worked harder. Maybe we can get you a tutor or something to help you understand math better.*

He had just sat there and listened to her as she went on and on, not bothering to explain to her the reason he hadn't been able to focus on math as hard as he proba-bly should have was that his teacher, Ms. Blaylock, was in her late twenties and beautiful, and always wore low-cut clinging silk dresses to class, dresses that hugged every inch of her body and showed off her long sleek legs. Rather than listening to her explain how to work the problems on the board, he was lost in fantasies of kissing her, what she looked like naked. No, Chris re-membered with a laugh, he could *never* tell Lois that.

He logged onto the Internet and checked his e-mail. Nothing from Jessie. He swore under his breath and closed the laptop. He lay down on his bed and stared at a water spot on the ceiling. He hadn't started the re-search paper for his ethics class that was due in two weeks, and hadn't even thought about what topic to write about, but he wasn't in the mood. There was plenty of homework to do—all of the teachers at More Prep subscribed to the theory that keeping their stu-dents occupied with hours of homework every day would keep them out of trouble, but he wanted to relax for just a bit. He wanted to close his eyes and picture Jessie Kaye.

He loosened his tie and unbuttoned the collar. In the two weeks since he'd returned to school, every day when he got out of class there was always an e-mail from her waiting for him. It would automatically bring a smile to his face, even though her e-mails were usually brief. Still, she always ended by telling him she missed him.

Chris suspected he missed her much more than she did him. He'd gotten to the point where he watched the clock in his last class, waiting for the bell to ring just so he could run back to his room and read her latest e-mail. He stared overt at his computer, willing it to ring and say, *You've got mail*.

He glanced up at his calendar. *Oh yeah, her dad was coming home today*, he remembered. *That's why she hasn't written. She probably has other things on her mind. It's not like I'm ever this huge priority for her anyway*.

Chris sighed. The week he'd spent helping Bobbie renovate the attic had been tough. Jessie had been adamant.

"No way can they have *any* idea we know each other," she'd said when he'd told her about the job.

They'd met at the dunes, and were sitting on a blanket he'd stuffed into his backpack. That first day had been torture for him. He enjoyed the work, it was mindless, and pretty much required him only to carry things and move things. It was good, hard, muscle-straining work, so he didn't miss his morning workouts. His back and legs were a little sore, and he knew when he woke up the next morning they'd be even stiffer. But the work hadn't been what was hard. Not exchanging looks with Jessie was the difficult part. Jessie had ignored him that whole week, staying in her room.

"Why?" It didn't make any sense to him. "Are you ashamed of me?" he asked her when they met in the dunes.

He didn't understand why they couldn't act like other teenagers. He saw the town kids walking around in couples, holding hands, stealing kisses when they thought no one was paying attention, laughing, and having a good time.

"They'll get the wrong idea," Jessie said, looking out at the waves, the wind blowing her hair.

"What do you mean?"

"They didn't like it when Lettie Hatch had a boyfriend either."

Chris had just sighed. There it was again: her weird theory that time was echoing, that bad shit was going to happen, that she was part of some kind of murderous cycle that lived in that house.

Or was it simply that she didn't like him enough to let people think he was her boyfriend?

He didn't say anything to her. He kept his hurt to himself. Maybe all girls were like this at first. He had no basis of comparison, other than what he heard the other boys say at school, and he suspected that was all bullshit. Even if it wasn't, Jessie wasn't like other girls. There was pain there—he could see that she had built up walls to keep other people out. Just meeting him every day, talking to him, was an effort for her, and she was trying. Usually that was good enough for him, but sometimes her reticence and secrecy wounded him. Every night, before he went to bed, he prayed that tomorrow would be the day she'd relax and loosen up, be willing to bring him to the house and introduce him as her boyfriend.

In those last days before he'd left for school, things had finally shifted somewhat. Jessie wasn't having the dreams anymore—and neither was he, which was a relief.

"Maybe it was just some weird coincidence," he offered.

She made a face. "Believe what you need to believe."

"Listen, Jessie, I read that book Madame Nadja told us about."

She lifted an eyebrow at him in response.

He told her about it, how Dr. Goodwin had made a lot more sense to him than Madame Nadja's cracked interpretations of his theories. For one thing, Dr. Goodwin didn't believe in ghosts—but he did believe that sometimes it was possible to receive messages from the dead. Chris fumbled through his backpack to find the book. He had underlined a passage and read it out loud to her:

*"Ghosts and hauntings are not what are commonly supposed—a spirit trapped in a house and unable to pass over, which is one of the most frequently used explanations for what is known as 'haunting.' Rather, with all time being in simultaneous existence but merely on a different plane, sometimes the circles come very close to each other, and what is heard, seen, or felt is merely an echo across time.*

*"There are many locations on Earth where the veil between the planes is very thin—and just as Person A in the 'present' day experiences the echo, in the other plane Person B experiences the echo as well. When these kinds of occurrences happen, it frightens people because they don't understand, cannot comprehend, what is going on, and anything out of the ordinary is frightening. They do not understand that it is merely a harmless echo through the planes, and that any 'ghost' they might encounter is just as frightened as they are. Because a ghost is merely a human being existing on another plane, and no matter how thin the veil might be, they are incapable of causing any physical harm.*

*"These are 'messages from the dead' simply in the sense that in linear time, in our plane, these humans have already died, yet in their plane they are very much alive. Likewise, those who claim to 'see the future' aren't really seeing the future— they simply are more sensitive to the veils, and are catching glimpses of a plane that, in our linear way of thinking, has not yet come into existence, has not happened yet."*

"So he doesn't think Lettie can cause us harm." Jessie chewed on a fingernail. "But Madame Nadja—"

"Madame Nadja is a fake," Chris replied. "None of that stuff she talked about is in this book—none of it."

"She wasn't faking that day, Chris." Jessie had slipped a hand into his. "You were there. You felt it, I know you did. *And you saw something too*—you can't deny it."

He didn't respond. Her hand felt so right in his, he'd just squeezed it and said nothing.

Now, lying on his bed in his dorm room, Chris thought about that day, the reading, and remembered what he'd experienced—the sound of the knife slashing, the splattering of the blood, and that horrible laughter. He shuddered.

*No, I didn't really experience anything except a collective hallucination, that's all it was. Jessie wanted to believe it was happening so badly that I believed it too. At first. Of course I would. All that Lettie Hatch stuff was so fresh in my mind. Is it any wonder that I thought I heard what I heard?*

*And the dreams I'd been having—that was part of it too—I was thinking about everything so much my subconscious mind made me dream about it. And that day at my house, in the rain, when I called her "Lettie" and thought she was someone else—just a trick of the mind, that's all it was, nothing more, nothing less. Just my subconscious mind at work.*

*Why can't Jessie see that? Her obsession with Lettie Hatch—that's what's causing everything. Sure, it's a coincidence that the situations are the same, but Jessie's not a killer, she could never do what Lettie Hatch did— why can't she see that? There's no such thing as a ghost—and if she doesn't let up, Jessie is going to make herself crazy.*

He hopped off his bed and checked his e-mail again—still nothing. He dug his history textbook out of his backpack. Might as well start some homework. He grabbed a yellow highlighter from his desk and flopped back down on the bed, opening the book to the chapter on the eighteenth century.

All at once his door flung open, smacking against the opposite wall. Chris almost jumped out of his skin.

"Hey, dude, did I scare ya?"

It was Josh. His dirty blond hair was damp from his after-workout shower, and his school uniform had been hastily thrown back on. His white shirt was partially untucked, the mandatory undershirt nowhere in evidence, and he wasn't wearing socks. His tie was tied around his forehead, the limp ends hanging down past the right side of his face.

Chris sat up. "No prob. I was looking for an excuse not to read anymore."

Josh threw his gym bag onto the floor and fell onto his bed. "Man, I'm fucking beat." He yawned. "You wanna blow off dinner and grab something in town? Tonight's special in the cafeteria is fucking stew."

Josh hated the food in the residence halls, and took every chance he could get to skip out. The food wasn't that bad, but the stew was disgusting. No one ate it if they could get out of it. Everything that was left over from previous dinners was just tossed into the big pots and boiled all day over a low flame. You never knew what you were going to find in the stew.

Josh had never invited him before to go on any of his excursions into town. Josh was wealthy; he had his own car on campus. "We won't miss curfew?" Chris asked. Curfew at the school was 10:00 p.m.

"Live a little, Muir. Don't you ever do anything you're not supposed to?" Josh grinned over at him. His teeth were completely even and perfectly white.

Only this semester had the campus found out that Josh's father was the action-adventure movie superstar Kyle Benton, whose films cost sixty million dollars to produce and were filled with explosions, car crashes, and gratuitous sex. The administration had agreed previously not to tell the student body so that Josh would be treated like any other kid. But word had leaked; how does one really keep such a secret so long? Given their friendly but casual, nodding acquaintance, Chris wasn't surprised that Josh had never said anything. He'd known his roommate was from Los Angeles, but had no idea Josh's Bentons were *those* Bentons. Funny how the semester everybody found out that Josh was the son of a movie star was also the semester he dropped out of sports and started hanging around the room more.

Of course, Lois hated Kyle Benton movies and banned them from their house. "They promote violence, degradation of women, and appeal to everything that's wrong in men," she'd said when Chris had told her who his roomie was. Leave it to Lois to suck the life out of his exciting news.

Josh was the kind of guy Chris wished he was. Good looking, with a strong resemblance to his father. He had the same mouth, the same nose, the same cheekbones—why hadn't Chris seen it before? It was because Kyle Benton was dark, Chris figured, and Josh's blue eyes and blond hair must have come from his mother. Josh was tall—not as tall as Chris, of course, but no one at More Prep was *that* tall. Josh was normal tall, good tall: just under six feet with one hundred eighty pounds stacked pretty solidly on his frame.

He claimed he'd lost his virginity to one of his father's fans on a movie set when he was just thirteen, one more reason for Chris to be envious. "My dad's fans are nutcases," Josh told him the other night, "and they'll do pretty much anything to get close to him." Chris figured most of the "stud" talk the other students indulged in was just that—talk—but he believed Josh. He'd seen how girls blushed and giggled when Josh just smiled at them from across the room, how they always flirted with him when he talked to them.

"So," Josh said now, grinning lazily at him, "where do you want to eat?"

"Is there a McDonald's in town?" Lois hated fast food, so they never ate it. No pizzas, no drive-through windows for the Muir family. It was like forbidden fruit, and so Chris ate at McDonald's every chance he got.

"There's a McDonald's everywhere," Josh said.

*Not in Provincetown*, Chris thought, his thoughts wandering back to Jessie out there on that strip of sand.

Josh dropped his pants, grabbing a pair of baggy jeans out of the pile of clothes on the floor around his bed. "I could go for a Quarter Pounder myself. But if you're coming into town with me—" He pointed at Chris's uniform. "You've gotta get out of that monkey suit."

A half hour later they were in Josh's Porsche convertible flying along the county road leading into town, the top down, rap music blaring out of the stereo. The leaves in the trees were changing: violent explosions of reds, yellows, and oranges on the branches. Those already fallen along the side of the road flew up into the air as the car zoomed past.

The McDonald's was right on the edge of the highway. Josh flirted with the stocky teenaged brunette girl working the window while they waited for their food. They ate in the car, the music so loud they couldn't talk, and Chris savored the experience. He hadn't eaten at McDonald's in months, and it was every bit as good as he remembered.

After they were finished, Josh revved the engine and peeled out of the parking lot, a big grin on his face as they headed down the main street of the little town. "Man, they just fucking roll up the sidewalks in this burg at five," Josh shouted over at Chris. He reached down and turned down the stereo.

When they reached the end of the road, Josh pulled in a quiet, well-manicured cemetery. He stopped the car, reached into his backpack, and lit up a joint.

"Want some?"

Lois's voice, in his head again. *Your father and I smoked pot a bit in college, son, and we don't think there's anything wrong with it, other than that it's illegal. You can go to jail for smoking pot, Chris, and that would destroy your future—that will follow you everywhere you go. I know you're going to be curious about it, but with the drug laws the way they are now, with this ridiculous so-called war on drugs—which we are losing, I might add—I absolutely forbid you to buy it or keep it in our house. If the police find anything like that, we'll lose everything—they can seize our house, freeze our bank accounts, and we'd lose our jobs. Is a little experimentation worth losing everything over?*

Hesitating for just a moment, Chris took the joint and breathed in, coughing and choking, finally grabbing his super-sized Coke and drinking to relieve the burn in his throat. A blissful feeling came over him, even as he coughed and gagged. They kept passing it back and forth until there was nothing left but a bit, which Josh pinched out and put in the ashtray.

Chris was pleasantly stoned as he looked up into the fading light of the sky.

"You like being stoned?" Josh winked over at him. "I kind of like being a bad influence on you. Can I ask you something?"

Chris made a sound of agreement in his throat.

"Why are you always so uptight?" Josh looked at him intensely. "I mean, you seem like a pretty cool guy. I always thought so, but you never talk—and you keep everything so neat and tidy and in its place. It's fucking wild, man. Everyone else in this place is a fucking slob, myself included. It trips me out."

Chris shrugged. "My mom's a complete anal-retentive control freak. It's just easier to be neat than to listen to her bitch."

"Man, that must suck." He leaned back against the car seat. "I've always had people picking up after me, you know? It's wild, you know? This summer I realized—I had to sign all these papers like I always do, and it just hit me—my parents have lined up so much shit for me—I mean, a lot of it's tax dodges and stuff, trust funds, putting property and stuff in my name—but I realized I'm set for life." He gestured with his hands. "I never have to fucking work a day if I don't want to, so what's the point of going to college? If I'm smart, I'll never have to do anything except enjoy myself, so that's what I'm gonna do, ya know? What was the point of playing football and all that shit?"

"Yeah, well, I don't have that luxury."

Josh was looking at him a bit strangely. "So, what was your summer like, roomie?"

Chris started talking, and before he even realized what he was saying, he was telling Josh all about Jessie. All of it. The strange dreams, the encounter with Madame Nadja, the theory of time echoing from the past and the present. . .

"Dude—" Josh shook his head. "That's some fucking crazy shit. I remember all those crazy 'Lettie Hatchet' stories. Isn't there even like some weird alternative rock band named after her?"

"Probably, she's quite a legend."

"Lettie Hatch took a knife . . . how does that go?"

Chris tried to recite the rhyme, but his tongue wouldn't work right. "All I know is, Jessie thinks she's possessed by her sometimes."

"Crazy shit, man. Crazy!"

"Yeah, well, once I even called her *Lettie*. I mean it was like she was really her."

"That is so whacked." Josh's voice turned solemn. "You know, I believe in that stuff."

"You do?"

"Oh, hell yeah. When my dad was filming *No Left Turns*, we stayed at this old castle in England. I used to see and hear shit all the time—that place was haunted. This one time, I heard a woman crying, and so I kept following the sound, and every time I'd think I'd found the room it was coming from, there'd be nothing there." He shivered, closing his eyes. "And then I'd hear it coming from somewhere else. Supposedly, she was a daughter of a duke or something that got pregnant, and he'd walled her up somewhere in the house." He opened his eyes and looked over at Chris. "So, what're you gonna do about it?"

Chris shrugged. "Do about it? What's there to do about it?"

"You can't just leave her down there to fight this all alone."

"What am I gonna say to my parents? Sorry I can't go to school because my girlfriend is possessed by a ghost?"

Girlfriend. He'd called Jessie his girlfriend.

"Well, dude, if she was my girlfriend, I'd try to do something." He started up the ignition and backed the car screeching out of the cemetery. "If you ever need any help, let me know. I believe in this shit, dude. I really do."

Chris was asleep almost as soon as they staggered back into their room, just a few minutes before curfew. He hit his pillow hard and fell into a deep, dreamless slumber.

The breaking of the storm woke him around three in the morning. Chris sat up, wiping his eyes. His computer screen glowed in the dark room. Over the rain hitting the window, he could hear Josh snoring gently. In the gloom he saw Josh lying on his side, his covers tangled all around him. Chris got out of the bed, realizing he was still dressed, and sat down at his desk. He checked his e-mail. A broad grin crossed his face when he saw there was a message from Jessie in his in-box. It had been sent at midnight.

*Chris—*

*Dad came home today, but nothing's different. I don't know what I was hoping—you'd think by now I'd know better—but he barely even spoke to me. Some things never change. There's something weird going on with him and Karen, too. She's finally given up on talking to me—thank God—but she's acting weird. Alice told me tonight before she went to bed that Karen has gotten really rude to her and she doesn't know why. Something's come over her. Alice doesn't think she and my dad*

*will be married much longer, but she wouldn't tell
me what she meant by that. Alice has gotten a little strange, too. Or maybe it's just me. As usual.*

*But you know what? The weirdness—my
dreams, everything—didn't start until Dad married Karen. That hit me the other day. I looked in
my journal and found the date of my first nightmare. I found out today from Dad that's when he
and Karen got married in New Orleans. So
maybe if SHE goes away, the weirdness will stop.*

*But until that time it's not over.*


*Miss you,*
*Jessie*


*She misses me*, Chris thought, a big smile creeping
over his face. He quickly typed a response, that everything was going to be okay, that he was going to try to
find a way to get out there to see her, that he missed her
too. Then clicked Send.

He got undressed and lay back down in his bed, staring at the ceiling, a goofy smile on his face, until finally, he fell asleep again.

# Chapter 12

Sophie Pilkowski woke up with a mouthful of cat fur. "Goddamn it!" she howled, tossing Lance, her big furry white cat, off her chest.

She sat up in the bed and moaned. Her head was throbbing—every movement sent a bolt of pain through her skull. Even the weight of her hair seemed to be hurting her scalp. Her head felt like a dead weight on her neck, pressing down on her spine. The room was completely dark, even though her alarm showed it was past ten. She got up, wincing. She scratched her hip, fumbling her way through the gloom to the windows. She yanked the cord for the blinds too hard, forgetting they were loose until it was too late. The blinds came out of their holder and fell to the floor with a loud crash that almost made her scream.

Fortunately, the day was gloomy, clouds covering the sun—bright sunlight would be too much for her to handle. Sophie sighed, reaching down and picking up the blinds and setting them on top of the dresser before walking into the bathroom. She downed some aspirins and brushed her teeth. She turned on the shower. Shower-

ing usually helped with her morning headaches. Usually
the headaches were an aftermath of the vodka she'd
drunk the night before, but since Labor Day they'd gotten worse. Now she was getting them whether she drank
or not.

*Probably a brain tumor*, she thought as she stepped
into the hot spray of water, *which would be just my
luck.*

After all, on her soaps, wasn't that how brain tumors
always started? With headaches? The heroine would
start getting headaches and wham—within a week she
was in surgery. *I wish someone could remove the part
of my brain that hurts every day*, Sophie thought, rubbing her body vigorously with soap.

She toweled off and put on her robe, heading into
the kitchen and almost tripping on Lance, who hissed
at her and shot down the hallway. "Fucking cat!" she
shouted after him and winced.

The aspirins were starting to work their magic, but
her head was still throbbing. *The whole fucking house
is gloomy*, she thought as she flicked on the kitchen
lights and turned on the coffeemaker. She always prepared the coffee the night before so all she had to do
was turn it on in the morning. The caffeine would help
wake her up, and she retrieved the bottle of Bailey's out
of the refrigerator.

She groaned when she saw that some good fairy had
not filled her refrigerator with food miraculously over-
night. She heaved a brown, soggy head of lettuce into
the garbage can. Par for the course. She was always
buying lettuce and vegetables, determined to eat health-
ier, and then just letting them rot in the refrigerator
while she lived on hot dogs, frozen dinners, and chips.
All that was left in the fridge was a half gallon of milk
turning into curds, well past its expiration date.

*You're really losing it, sister*, Sophie thought as she

filled a cup with coffee and added the creamy liqueur. *You've got to get over this funk. Maybe taking better care of yourself would help—eat better, go on a healthy diet, take some of this extra weight off, get some exercise.*

Yeah, right. She'd joined the gym over a year ago, gone three times, and never set foot in the place again. Still, every damn month her checking account was deducted the seventy dollars to pay for it.

Her empty stomach growled as she swallowed some coffee. *Look at yourself*, she thought, taking another sip, *almost forty and living like a slob. And still alone.* She ran a finger along the kitchen table and looked at the dirt on her fingertip. *Christ, Sophie, you need to take some control over your life.*

Relationships had never worked for her. When she'd hit puberty, her sense that she wasn't like the other kids at her public school in Queens became even stronger. Somehow, she'd always known she was different. Other kids never knew what was in their Christmas presents before they opened them. Other kids didn't know when there was a pop quiz coming. Other kids didn't seem to hear what other people were thinking if they concentrated hard enough.

It had gotten worse when she became, in her mother's words, "a woman." Other girls got cramps and had mood swings; Sophie would have welcomed such discomfort. Instead, she found herself hearing what people were thinking around her without even trying. And other things too—things that scared her.

The little two-story three-bedroom house the Pilkowski family called home in the Whitestone neighborhood of Queens was always immaculately clean. Her mother took being a housewife completely seriously. Every morning, Ruth Pilkowski rose at five and started her day by scouring the kitchen clean before making breakfast for her husband and kids and sending them off on their days. She packed lunches for all of them and labeled the brown paper sacks with their names. It was always the same: two sandwiches, a small bag of some sort of chips, napkins, and two quarters to buy a carton of milk.

Once the kids were out of the house and she was alone, Ruth spent the morning vacuuming, dusting, doing the laundry, and making sure the house smelled antiseptic. Her afternoons were spent running errands in her battered old blue Volkswagen Beetle. She was always home by three to start dinner. Not once in Sophie's entire childhood did she remember a time when her mother wasn't in the kitchen when she got home from school.

Sophie had been the quiet child, never fighting with either of her older brothers. Benjamin and Judah were also quiet, never boisterous like other boys at school, and very serious. They looked enough alike to frequently be taken for twins, even though there was almost exactly a year between their birth dates. They had the same thick dark hair, the same round wire-framed glasses, the same solemn round brown eyes. Every afternoon the three kids walked home from school together, their lunch bags neatly folded up in their pockets, carrying their books and not stopping anywhere, not talking to anyone. Ruth was always terrified someone would carry her children off; she constantly drilled them about not taking candy from strangers or talking to an adult they didn't know. She told them horrible stories of what happened to children who did just that—how they were found in ditches with their throats slit, or just disappeared completely.

Sophie never argued with her mother, even though somehow she knew she and her brothers were safe from such a dreadful fate. Somehow, she just knew both of her brothers were going to grow up and get degrees from NYU, marry women similar to their mother, and buy houses in Whitestone not far from where they grew up. She didn't know what her future held for her, but she knew she wasn't going to be kidnapped. Still, she could sense the fear and terror in her mother when she told her children her tales of what happened to children who didn't do what they were told, and if it made her mother feel better, *safer*, to obey her rules, well, it wasn't much too ask.

The kidnapping of her children was her mother's biggest fear—but there were other fears lurking inside Ruth's head as well. Sophie knew her mother worried about cancer, and car accidents, and criminals, and Communists. In the back of her mind, all day, Mrs. Pilkowski was figuratively holding her breath until her children were safely home—and then relaxed completely when her husband walked through the front door and kissed her on the cheek before sitting down to dinner.

Sophie knew all this. She could just could look at her mother and know what she was thinking, know that her mother lived her entire life in a sense of terror— terror that her husband was going to have an affair, or be killed, or get some horrible disease and die, leaving her alone. That was Mrs. Pilkowski's biggest fear— being left alone to fend for herself in a cold world that scared her to death.

Sophie was in junior high when her "visitor" first came. When it finally arrived, she felt a sense of relief. She'd known for several days that things were going to be different in her life from then on, that things were about to change. She sometimes felt, as she walked from class to class, this weird sort of tingling in her skin. In her English class, as Mrs. Gibbens wrote the assignment on the blackboard, her back to her students, thoughts came into Sophie's mind.

*I don't even know why I bother with this half of them won't even bother to do the assignment and the ones who do will get it mostly wrong they don't pay attention my back hurts and I hate these shoes and we have that goddamned staff meeting this afternoon which means I won't even get home until after six and then I've got all these damned papers to grade and I know Joe will be even later does he think I'm stupid enough to not know what's going on I wish he just had the fucking balls to tell me he's cheating . . .*

After the bell rang and the other students had fled, hesitantly Sophie walked up to Mrs. Gibbens, who was erasing the board to get it ready for her next class.

"Mrs. Gibbens?"

Her teacher turned around, still holding the eraser. "Yes, Sophie, did you have a question about the homework?"

Sophie stared at her. She'd never really noticed before how tired Mrs. Gibbens always looked. She shook her head. "No, ma'am." She bit her lower lip. "Um, I just wanted to tell you—"

"What?" Mrs. Gibbens pushed her glasses up impatiently.

"Joe's not cheating."

Mrs. Gibbens reared back as though she'd been struck. Her jaw dropped. *"What?"*

Immediately Sophie regretted saying anything. Instead of being relieved, Mrs. Gibbens was more upset. And Sophie could feel something emanating from the teacher—waves of fear. *I'm scaring her,* Sophie thought, but she plunged on. "He's working overtime. To pay for diamond earrings. A birthday surprise."

Mrs. Gibbens went white, and she backed away

from Sophie until her back was against the chalkboard. "How—what—how—" she croaked out.

And Sophie, seeing her good intentions paving her way to hell, just ran out of the classroom.

Sometimes she thought it would drive her crazy, this knowing without understanding where it all came from. She would be sitting in class, taking notes, and something would just pop into her brain. One day, in her math class, she thought she heard the girl across the aisle from her crying. Sophie looked over at her. The girl, Judy Nader, was frowning as she concentrated on what the teacher was saying, a pencil gripped in her teeth, her white-blond shoulder-length hair sprayed firmly into place. Judy was a quiet girl, a straight-A student who didn't really have many friends, who always had her homework done on time and always knew the answers. Sophie stared at her, until Judy turned and looked at her, giving her a puzzled frown, and then it was more than just crying.

*Judy was crying because she was being held down on the bed by an older man, her nightgown pulled up over her head, her panties in his hand, and he was inside her, doing something that Judy didn't want him to do, something that made her feel dirty and awful, that God and the preacher thought was a sin, but she couldn't do anything, there wasn't anything she could do to stop him, no one would believe her, and besides it was all her fault, she made him this way, he said so, even though she tried to be good, she was bad, she was evil, she made things go wrong.*

Judy smiled, and Sophie turned around and stared at the teacher.

She'd gone to the school counselor, Mr. Abrams, and told him about Judy. He took off his glasses and rubbed them with a tissue. "Judy told you this?"

"Um, no."

"Then how do you know?" Mr. Abrams slipped his glasses back on his nose and peered at her. "I mean, Sophie, these are *serious* allegations."

"I just know." She had to make him believe her. Judy needed her, she had to save her. "Mr. Abrams, I know about Judy just like I know about your wife."

He visibly stiffened. "My wife?" He laughed. "Now, Sophie, what could you possibly know about my wife?"

"You think . . ." She hesitated. She knew it was going to make him angry, but she had to keep going. For Judy. "You think she's got a boyfriend, some guy she works with, that she's going to leave you. She *is* going to leave you, Mr. Abrams, very soon, she's only waiting for the right time to tell you."

His face went red. "Young lady, you need to stop this right now!" He wagged his index finger in her face. "Now, shouldn't you get to class and stop wasting my time?"

"But, Mr. Abrams—"

"You heard me! Go!"

She ran out of his office, tears in her eyes. She stopped at her locker and wiped at her eyes. *Why me, God? Why did you curse me like this?*

Two days later Judy wasn't in school. Sophie knew, without having to be told, that Judy had done it, after the man had left her and gone back to his own bed, she'd gone into the bathroom and filled the tub with water. She undressed and gotten into the warm water and drawn the razor blades up the veins in her arms, and closed her eyes and let her life be drawn away into the water. Later that day, a hall monitor got Sophie out of geography class and led her to Mr. Abrams's office.

His eyes were red, like he'd been crying, when she timidly walked into his office. "Sit down, Sophie. You've heard about Judy Nader?"

She nodded, biting her lips.

"And my wife left me last night." He took his glasses off and rubbed his eyes. "How did you know, Sophie? How could you have known?"

"I don't know," she'd whispered. "I just—know."

He'd looked at her, his eyes sad. "God help you, Sophie."

Lance rubbed against her legs, meowing, bringing her back to the present.

She stood with difficulty—damn all this weight—and filled the cat's bowl. She sat back and scratched her head, reaching for her dream journal. She opened it and turned to a new page, writing in the date and sitting back in her chair. She'd started keeping track of her dreams when she was in high school. After the experiences with Mrs. Gibbens, Mr. Abrams, and Judy, she knew she could never, ever talk about what she saw, what she felt and heard. Always quiet, she withdrew further into herself, and what few friends she had drifted away from her. She didn't want friends, because she always knew without trying what they were thinking and feeling. She scared people. And so she became a witch: she put on weight, she never smiled, she filled her house full of cats.

She started writing.

*September 23*

*Last night was the same dream. The same one I've had at least twice a week since that girl Jessie and her boyfriend came here. About death, but whose I don't know. Why it won't come clear to me, I don't know. It's cold and snowy, the ground is all covered with snow, the windows in the house are all fogged up, and it's dark—the whole house is dark and cold, like the power is off or something. It seems relatively early, and it's really windy* and the snow is coming down really hard. Even though it's really cold I don't feel anything, and I'm barefoot and in the Pooh T-shirt I always sleep in, but still I can't feel the snow under my feet. Then I get to the front door—I don't recognize the house even though it's familiar, like I've seen it before, and then I open the door and I walk in, and I hear this horrible laughter, maniacal laughter that's almost not even human.

I start climbing the stairs, and when I get to the top a long hallway opens out before me, and there's a door at the end of the hall, and I know that's where I need to go. I walk down the hallway and as I get closer, this feeling of dread comes over me, and all I want to do is get out of there, everything inside me is screaming to get out, but I can't, I keep walking forward, and then I see there's blood all over the walls, running down, horrible splashes of blood everywhere, and it's on the floor and it's on my feet and it's sticky. But I keep walking forward. I can hear the sounds coming from the bedroom—that horrible laughter, even louder now than it was before—and I can hear this horrible squishy sound, and I know it's a knife. It's the sound of a knife cutting into flesh with tremendous force. The cracking sound I hear is bones breaking under the force of the blows.

I reach for the doorknob, which is also covered with blood, and just as I start to turn the knob I wake up. I didn't start having this dream until the girl and her boyfriend came to me, with their talk of ghosts and possession and Lettie Hatch. I don't know if what I'm dreaming is something that happened in the past—maybe I'm projecting my dream self through the circle of time into the Hatch house

*the night of the murders—or am I seeing what's*
*going to happen? I couldn't see the girl's future*
*when she was here—it was all murky and liquid*
*and not fluid—but I know the circle is open, I*
*could sense that—and I should.*

"Fuck!" Sophie threw her pen away in frustration.
*You know what you have to do, Sophie. You have to*
*see that girl again. Why are you putting it off, what are*
*you so afraid of? The dreams started when she came*
*here—you know in your heart you're supposed to help*
*her somehow. It all has something to do with her. You*
*might be able to stop what's going to happen. You can't*
*just do nothing, like you did with—*
"Stop it," Sophie said to herself.
She'd promised herself she would never think about
that again. The guilt was too much. She hadn't been
strong enough to close that circle; what did she think
she could do now? It's not like she was any stronger
now than she'd been then, and back then she hadn't
weighed two hundred pounds or drunk so many gal-
lons of vodka or smoked kilo after kilo of pot all in an
attempt to kill off the brain cells in that part of her
brain that was open to other people.
*I'm not as strong as I was back then, and look how*
*that turned out—people dead and suffering, their souls*
*doomed to replay the whole thing again in another*
*time. And who knows if I even helped them at all? I*
*might have made things worse for them the next time*
*the circle opens—*
The doorbell rang, startling her back into the present. *Who can that be?*
Now that the summer was over, she had taken the
WALK-INS WELCOME sign off her gate. She only saw
people by appointment—a few regulars who depended

on her to tell them everything was going to be okay. She rose from her chair and tottered out into the living room and opened the door.

"Morning, Nadja." Bobbie grinned at her, holding up a box of donuts. "You got coffee?"

"Don't call me that," she groused, letting him in. Bobbie was one of the few people in town who knew her real name, and it bugged her when he called her Nadja. Nadja was the professional name she'd taken when she moved to Provincetown eight years earlier. It sounded gypsylike, and it was all about the marketing, after all—who would come to a fat Polish psychic named Madame Sophie?

"Coffee's in the kitchen," she grunted. She followed him in, sitting back down hard in her chair and grabbing a glazed donut from of the box. Bobbie helped himself to coffee and sat across from her.

"You look like hell," he told her, strawberry jelly leaking out of his donut.

"Top of the morning to you too."

He gave her that lazy, impudent grin. "Sorry. What's wrong?"

She shook her head. "Same fucking dream."

"Still can't get through that door, huh?"

She sighed. "Those damned kids."

"Kids?"

She grabbed another donut. She never talked about her clients, but her head was still aching, and Bobbie was a good listener. They'd met when she'd bought the house and needed some shelving put in. They'd hit it off, and she always tried to keep her mind closed to anything that was going on in his head, to keep her eyes away from his future. It wasn't good to learn your friends' secrets without them telling you first.

"Talk to me, Sophie," Bobbie said. "What kids are you talking about?"

So she told him all about Jessie and the echoes of the past.

Bobbie whistled. "You don't mean Jessie Kaye, do you?"

"I don't know her last name."

"Dressed all in black, about fifteen? The boyfriend was really tall and pretty hunky?"

She nodded. "Yeah, that's them. I take it you know them?"

He gave her a strange look. "Yeah, I know them. Jessie's Philip Kaye's daughter. I know her stepmother pretty well." He scratched his head. "Maybe you should talk to her about this."

Sophie raised an eyebrow. "I can't tell anybody about the session, you know that. I shouldn't even be telling you. They came to me in confidence." She snorted. "Besides, she wouldn't believe me anyway. They never do."

"But you need to get this off your chest, honey," Bobbie said. "If there's something you psychically sense about Jessie, well, then I think Karen would want to know." He paused. "See, she's been having some dreams, too. . . ."

"The stepmother? She's been having visions too?"

"Something strange is going on," Bobbie admitted. "Tell ya what—I'll get Karen to come by." He winked at her. "You can figure out what to say to her." He stood up.

"Don't let on that I saw Jessie."

"I promise."

"Maybe it's a good idea. I mean, if the stepmother is having dreams too . . ."

She didn't finish. Bobbie wouldn't understand. But if what she suspected was true . . .

The echoes from the past were getting very loud.

And very dangerous.

She walked Bobbie to the door. "Thanks for the donuts."

"Don't eat the whole box in one day."

"One day? They'll be gone by noon."

She stood there watching him go down her walk, and suddenly an image flashed into her brain.

*The ground, covered with snow. The wind howling through the bare trees, bending them in half, the wind cold, oh so cold, that penetrating cold that only a strong wind off the Atlantic can have, the kind that knifes through the clothing, no matter how thick, and gets into the bones and makes the joints ache. Darkness, despite the glow of the moon reflected off the layer of white on the ground. Someone, walking, completely bundled up, a thick down jacket and a stocking cap fitted over the head, over jeans and boots that made a scrunching sound on the hard-packed snow on the ground. Sophie couldn't tell if it was a man or a woman, but whoever it was, whatever it was, it was walking as slowly and silently as it could.*

*And suddenly hate raged through her—a blinding, consuming hatred, the hatred that comes from being betrayed, from being wronged. All Sophie could feel was hate, cold emotionless hate.* Die. You deserve to die.

*And she raised the knife suddenly high, slashing it through the air back down into the back of the figure walking through the snow. She pulled it out again, the knife making a hideous sucking sound. The figure staggered to its knees, gasping in shock, but did not scream— and Sophie raised the knife back up again, feeling an exhilaration she'd never experienced before. Justice was going to be done, finally, justice was finally being served! The knife came down again, and blood sprayed out onto the snow.*

*She kept stabbing, stabbing, her arm hurting, her*

*muscles giving out, but still she stabbed, feeling a joy-
ous laughter bubbling up inside her. It felt so good, it
felt so wonderful, what a rush, what a release to finally
give in to the hate and just let it go . . . and the blood
kept spattering, staining the snow with red, and the
moon went behind a cloud, and she heard something—
someone was coming. She tucked the knife back inside
her coat and ran across the snow.*

*Her work was done.*

Pain exploded through Sophie's head, staggering
her. Her legs gave out from under her and she sat down
with a bone-jarring thud on the floor. Another bolt of
lightning shot through her skull, and she shouted out.
Lance backed into a corner, his back arched and his fur
fluffed out, his mouth open in a terrified hiss. Sophie
slid down until her hot face was pressed against the
cold tiles of the floor. She lay there, breathing heavily
in and out, expecting each new breath to be her last.

# Chapter 13

"Karen?"

Hearing footsteps coming up the stairs, Karen quickly closed the diary and shoved it into her top desk drawer. Her notebook, too, went inside, and then she locked the drawer with a key.

Her heart was racing. Turning back to her computer, she closed every document on her screen and opened the last chapter she'd completed on Vicky. Just in time, too: as she turned in her chair and smiled, Philip's head poked through the doorway.

"Hey, honey."

He hadn't been up to her office since he'd gotten back. Other than at night, in fact, when he crawled into bed beside her and started kissing her neck, expecting his "husbandly right," Philip paid no attention to Karen at all. He hadn't asked about her work, how she liked the town, how she felt about the house—anything. It was as if she were just an appendage, another person in the house to be shut out while he worked on his new novel.

*Is this how you treated Ivy?* she'd wondered more

than once, passing by the door and seeing him hunched over his computer. *Small wonder she came up here and put a rope around her neck.*

Philip whistled as he peered into the attic. "Wow, this is great!" he said. "Bobbie sure did a fine job."

Karen watched him as he walked over to one of the eave windows, glancing down at the bay. He looked as handsome as ever, so tall, so dark. How many other girls on his book tour had thought the same exact thing?

"This is better than my office," he said, grinning. "No wonder you wanted your own." He shrugged, pushing his hands down into his pockets and smiling his dimpled grin, the one that made Karen melt. It still worked, but she found herself trying to resist his spell. "It's probably a better idea for you to have your own space, anyway," he said. "I'm not that easy to be around when I'm working."

He walked over and kissed the top of her head. He was wearing gray fleece sweatpants and a maroon Harvard sweatshirt. His feet were bare. He pulled a chair over to the side of her desk and sat down.

"I came up here to apologize to you."

She stiffened a bit before forcing herself to relax. "Apologize?" She smiled. "For?"

"The way I've been acting since I got home." Philip sighed, rubbing his eyes. "It takes me a while to decompress from a tour, you know? People don't realize how much work it is to go out and do public appearances. You always have to be cheerful, up, and friendly— no matter what. You can't afford to piss off anyone, bookstore staff, and God forbid if you're ever snotty to a fan."

"Oh, sure, Philip, I suppose it's hard . . ."

He grinned sheepishly. "Especially now with the Internet. Back in the day, you piss off some fan in some

Podunk town and it doesn't mean anything. Nowadays, with chat rooms and list serves and all those online booksellers letting people post so-called reviews, you piss someone off and the next thing you know everyone in cyberspace knows you're a prick." He grinned again, his dimples deepening. "So, I'm sorry if I've been acting like a selfish jerk lately. This deadline—"

"Deadline?"

Philip sighed again, turning back to look out the window. "Yeah. I knew when they planned this huge tour for me it was going to cause problems with finishing my novel. I don't know why I didn't ask for more time."

She was melting; there was no doubt about it. Philip looked so forlorn standing there in the sunlight, like a tired little boy. All she wanted to do was to put her arms around him.

"Can't you get Bill to tell your editor you need an extension?" Karen asked. Bill was Philip's agent, a short, dumpy, unkempt man she'd met once and hadn't much cared for. He was one of the best in the business though; he'd helped make Philip a huge star and a rich man. But Karen did not appreciate the way he spoke to her breasts instead of her face.

Philip lifted his strong muscled arms to place both hands behind his head. "I've never had to ask for more time before. That was part of Philip Kaye's reputation. On time, every time. But I'm getting so stressed I suppose I'm going to have to swallow my pride and ask for it."

"Is the writing not going well?" Karen glanced at her computer screen. She hadn't exactly been writing up a storm either. All she'd been doing was reading that diary, so obsessed with it that she'd increased the number of entries she allowed herself per day from two to three.

Philip was shaking his head. "No, it isn't going well. I'm way behind—and I keep blaming it on the tour, but . . ."

His voice trailed off. He stood up and walked back to the window, looking out over the bay. Even from up here you could hear the steady crash of the surf.

"But what, Philip?" Karen asked.

"I reread what I've already written and it's just not any good. I'm going to have to start over." He covered his face with his hands. "It's just crap, Karen, crap. I haven't written such crap in years, since I was in college. I keep forcing myself to sit down and work, but all I'm producing is garbage nobody will want to read. I don't understand." He removed his hands to look her straight in the eyes. "Maybe I'm tapped out."

Suddenly she felt horrible for being so impatient with him, for doubting him, for all the bad thoughts she'd allowed herself since Philip came home. She loved him. She loved him more than anything. She stood, rushing over to him and reaching up, massaging his shoulders. Hard knots of tension thrust forward under his skin. "Philip, sweetheart," she said. "I hate to see you like this. Is there anything I can do?"

"Just having you here makes things better." He gave her his most winning smile—the one she hadn't seen since their wedding night. They kissed. How good his kiss felt. Soft, real—so unlike the hard, urgent kisses of their lovemaking the past few nights.

They stood looking into each other's eyes.

Philip cupped her chin in hand. "How's *your* work coming?"

"Well . . ."

Karen hesitated. *Tell him about the diary*, she urged herself. *He's not going to try to take it away from you. He'll be happy and excited for you.*

She opened her mouth, then closed it again as another voice raised an objection in her mind—a voice she didn't like, but was hers nonetheless. A voice that had been intruding into her thoughts more and more these last few weeks, a voice that was jealous, hateful. First against Alice Winn, now Philip. A voice that told her: *Don't be stupid. His own work is going badly. Of course he'll take it away from you. He doesn't care about you, he never did. He'll just see dollar signs if you tell him about the diary—an easy way out of his own dilemma. Keep your stupid mouth shut.*

"Well?" he asked.

"I guess . . . not so well, either." She shrugged. "I don't know, Philip. I've been, well, really distracted since I got here."

"That's understandable. You've had to adjust to a lot of things the last few months." He smiled. "Being married, moving a thousand miles away from your family, your friends, and your life—of course you're going to be distracted until you've completely settled in here."

The sympathy in his voice made her feel guilty once again, and she moved away from him.

"What's wrong, darling?" he asked. "What's on your mind?"

She turned to face him again. "Philip, why didn't you tell me the truth about Ivy? I mean, I felt like an absolute idiot when Alice told me what happened to her." Karen wrapped her arms around herself. *It's always so cold up here, I'm going to have to get a space heater. Is this what the winter will be like? So cold? And that eternal wind blowing off the bay?*

Philip seemed stung by her words. "I'm sorry, Karen. I . . ." His voice faded. What did she see on his face? Grief? Anger? "I should have told you, I know, but—" He started pacing. "How do you tell your new wife that your first wife committed suicide?"

She felt defiant. "Maybe with those exact words?"

He stopped at one of the bookcases. He reached over, touching the spine of one of his books.

"I feel guilty about Ivy," Philip said, his eyes averted. "I guess I figured if I blocked it all out of my mind, the guilt would go away."

"Why do you feel guilty?"

He sighed, walking back to her and taking her hands in his. Karen felt the moistness of his palms.

"I met Ivy when we were both in college, in a writing course. She was a brilliant poet—really gifted. But she wasn't—" He frowned. "She wasn't really *stable*, you know? She was prone to depression and mood swings. But I fell in love with her, and after we graduated, we got married."

"You were very young."

"It was a mistake, Karen, a really big mistake. But I didn't know that at the time. She was getting published in literary journals—but poets don't make much money. She was planning on grad school, to teach writing and literature, but she couldn't handle the course load. She loved writing poems, but they took so much out of her. It would take her a month to write a poem, and when Ivy was writing nothing else mattered. She was a real artist. Really, I think she was."

A stab of jealousy shot through Karen.

"I was teaching English at a high school, trying to write my book at night," Philip continued. "Ivy was hard at work on a series of poems. Now, when she was working on a poem, she wouldn't eat, she wouldn't sleep. She wouldn't do anything—cook, clean, even bathe. It was like, for her, the world stopped turning. All that mattered was that damned poem." Philip's face was tight with the memory. "It was up to me to keep everything going, you know? I had to do the laundry, the shopping, the cooking, and the cleaning, all while working full-time and trying to get my book done. It was so hard—and I resented her for being so selfish. I kept thinking about leaving her—and then she got pregnant, and I thought maybe being a mother would help. You know, help to get her focused."

Karen couldn't think of anything to say, so she made a sympathetic noise in her throat. She hoped it sounded sincere.

Philip went on. "Neither one of us was prepared for what happened when my first book was published. I mean, I thought it was a good book, and I dreamed it would be a success, but it's a crap shoot. Who knows what makes one book take off and other, equally worthy ones, vanish without a trace? *Snowblind*—" He gave her that adorable crooked grin of his. "It took off, became wildly successful. And Ivy had a miscarriage. It was horrible. Being pregnant had helped her. She was determined to be the best wife and mother. Then she lost the baby just as the book came out. I was going on tour, and I insisted that Ivy come with me. A huge mistake."

"Why?" Karen asked.

"I thought it would help her, you know? I thought getting away from our house, away from the nursery she'd decorated, would help her see that we did have a future. We could have other children. But it was terrible. We fought. It was very bad between us."

"Is that why you didn't want me to come with you on your tour?" Karen watched his face. "You were afraid the same thing would happen?"

He didn't seem to hear her question. "I was so full of myself, and so preoccupied, I didn't even notice Ivy was breaking down." He buried his face in his hands. "Finally, in Seattle, she refused to come to the signing with me. She said she was tired, so I left her at the hotel. When I got back that night, she wasn't there. She'd left her purse, everything. I called the police.

They found her, wandering in the rain, with no idea of who she was or where she was going. When I got to the police station, she didn't recognize me. She was admitted to the psychiatric ward of a local hospital. I canceled the rest of the tour. In a few days she was better, so we came home, and I got her to see a psychiatrist. He put her on some antidepressants. When she took the pills, she was fine—but she didn't always take them."

Karen had reached over to stroke his cheek.

Philip closed his eyes. "She was in and out of hospitals for several years."

"It must have been awful for you." The pain in his face was too much for her. She wanted to hold him, bring him to her—

*But he should feel guilty—he was her husband, for God's sake. Who else was going to notice she was in trouble?*

She quashed that thought and shook her head. *What the hell is wrong with me? He's my husband now and he's pouring out his heart to me. Why is it so hard to be compassionate?*

"Ivy always liked Provincetown," Philip said. "She always seemed to be better here, so I figured if we bought a house, moved here, that might help." He made a gesture. "So I bought this house and here we were. And she did get better. I could write without worrying about her. And then she got pregnant—I don't know, it scared me a little. But then Jessie was born."

At first, Karen learned as she listened to her husband, being a mother seemed to cure Ivy of whatever demons haunted her mind. But then, when he was on a book tour a few years later, he got a phone call at his hotel in Chicago. Ivy had gone off the deep end again, and had to be hospitalized. This time, she stayed in the hospital for almost a year.

"I felt so guilty, like such a failure, but I had my

work to get me through. Marrying her had been such a mistake . . . but now there was Jessie to think about. So I bought the town house in Boston, and began spending more and more time there. I found I couldn't work here in Provincetown anymore, always worrying about Ivy, what she might do next. She'd get out of the hospital, would be fine for a while, and then would start to break down again. I couldn't live like that anymore, so finally I just moved to Boston for good. She didn't seem to care that I was leaving. We were separated for two years. I'd come out here to see Jessie on weekends, and everything seemed fine. Then, I found out Ivy was having an affair."

He got up and walked over to the bookcases again. "I mean, it was stupid, so damned stupid. Our marriage was over, so why did I care? But I reacted badly. I filed for divorce. The day she was served"—his voice broke— "was the day she did it."

Karen sat there for a moment, just staring at his back. Finally she stood and reached up, sliding her arms around him.

"Philip, you can't blame yourself. You can't. You said yourself she was ill."

"That's why I didn't tell you, Karen. I wanted to— but was afraid if you knew, you wouldn't marry me."

*Why did you marry me?*

Karen stiffened. Where did that voice keep coming from? She felt another headache lurking somewhere behind her eyes. She turned quickly, walking back to her desk and shaking a couple of aspirins from the bottle she always kept close at hand. She tossed them in her mouth and swallowed them dry. Philip was watching her curiously.

"Philip, I love you," she heard herself saying. "That hasn't changed, and knowing all this about you and Ivy wouldn't have stopped me from marrying you."

*Of course not. Because he's a famous author who can help me in my own career.*

She shook her head as Philip came back to her and took her into his arms. She allowed herself to relax into the embrace, and when he started kissing her neck, she didn't pull away. He smiled at her. "Let's go down to our room, shall we?"

She started to protest that she had to work to do, but she saw the look in his eyes, the naked pleading, and knew she couldn't refuse him. She allowed herself to be led down the stairs and into the bedroom. Philip peeled her T-shirt up over her head, and Karen didn't resist, even though she wanted to. She allowed him to gently push her down on the bed. She closed her eyes.

*"What have I done?" she asked herself as Horace turned off the lamps and undressed. He stank, as he always did, of sour whiskey and cigars. He'd started drinking the very night they arrived, and Orville the bootlegger had made his regular weekly visit. It was quite queer. Sarah Jane found herself drawn to Orville. He was everything Horace was not. Handsome, young, and virile—Sarah Jane found herself watching the clock every Tuesday night until it was time for the delivery. She always managed to be in the kitchen when he knocked on the back door. She liked the way he always looked her over, as though he were imagining what she looked like without her clothing. And she found herself wondering what he looked like without his, what his lips would taste like, what his body smelled like, what it would feel like to be in his arms.*

*She almost hated Horace, his clumsy lovemaking, the way he ignored her opinions on politics. Before they were married, he had asked her opinions and lis-*

*tened to what she had to say with interest. He'd always seemed so pleased.*

*"You have such an intellect," he told her one night when she'd given her opinion on why it was so vital for the United States to join the League of Nations. "You have a better, more sound mind than most of my colleagues! If someone had spoken so eloquently when it was time to ratify the treaty, there's no doubt it would have passed resoundingly."*

*Sarah Jane had glowed from his words of praise, for seeing her as something more than a round body and a pretty face, like so many other men did. He encouraged her to read the newspapers, to keep abreast of current events, even invited her to come sit in the gallery as his guest to watch the debates on the floor. Afterward, he would ask her opinion on what she'd witnessed. She found herself speaking out more at dinner parties they attended, and chafed against the tradition of the women retiring to another room for sherry while the men headed to a different room for brandy and cigars. That's where the real discussions occurred, Sarah Jane knew, where the deals regarding legislation were made, cemented over a snifter and a handshake.*

*"Let me join you in there," she demanded, more than once.*

*Horace had looked amused. "Women just got the right to vote, precious. It's going to take some time before women's opinions are going to be taken seriously— rightly or wrongly. Not every woman is as sharp and intelligent as you are."*

*Yet now that they were married, it was as if he seemed to think her mind had ceased to work—as though by becoming his wife, she had surrendered her right to think, her right to do anything other than service him on the nights when his lust overwhelmed him. This house was like a prison, and that horrible Mrs. Windham watched her with those lizardlike eyes—always searching for something, anything, to report back to the warden, or his miserable little hateful daughter.*

*Oh, how Sarah Jane hated Mrs. Windham, her palms always itching to slap that wrinkled, smug face. Mrs. Windham ignored her instructions, did as she pleased, contradicted her with Daisy, the cleaning girl, and just smiled when Sarah Jane complained. "It's how things have always been done since the time of the first Mrs. Hatch," she'd say in that infuriating, condescending manner that made Sarah Jane want to scream until the windows shook.*

*Horace wouldn't hear of firing her. "Lettie is fond of her, and where else am I going to find someone to teach Lettie how to be a proper wife?"*

*Lettie, for her part, continued to ignore her, only speaking when spoken to, spurning Sarah Jane's offers of friendship. Lettie was so bright, it was a pity that Horace wouldn't send her to college. It was a natural opportunity for an alliance between Sarah Jane and her stepdaughter, but Lettie wouldn't budge. She glared at Sarah Jane with such hateful eyes that Sarah Jane sometimes felt frightened. So much hate there—so much hate that she thought Lettie might be capable of physically attacking her.*

*Even killing her.*

*So she watched the girl. She didn't dare take her eyes off her. Lettie thought she was so smart, but Sarah Jane knew she was sneaking out of the house late at night. After Horace satisfied his lusts he always almost immediately rolled over and fell sleep, leaving Sarah Jane feeling used and dirty. She would sneak up to the dusty attic to smoke cigarettes until she could shake off the unpleasant memory of what had transpired in her marriage bed. It made her feel cheap, like a whore. And she hadn't felt that way in years—*

*Several nights, sitting in one of the attic eaves, smoking her cigarette with the window open, she'd seen Lettie sneaking out the back gate, heading in the direction of the dunes. One night, Sarah Jane decided, she was going to follow her. Maybe if she had something to hold over her stepdaughter's head, she could balance out their positions. Sarah Jane didn't like feeling powerless. It was not what she had worked and struggled and scraped and fought so hard for all her life.*

*Horace finished his business and rolled off of her. "Maybe this time will be the time," he said drowsily, his breath still coming in gasps, his hair matted with sweat.*

*"The time?" she asked, wishing he would just fall asleep so she could go wash his smell off and sneak up for a cigarette.*

*"The time you become pregnant," he murmured as his eyes closed. "It would be wonderful if you were to give me a son."*

*She stared at him in horror as his mouth dropped open and he started to snore. Pregnant?*

*She got out of the bed and walked into the washroom. She looked at herself in the mirror.*

*As though she would want to bear his child, even if she could. . . .*

"I love you." Philip nuzzled on her neck.

"I love you," Karen replied automatically.

He sat up, yawning and stretching like a cat. "Sorry to take you away from your work, but it *was* worth it, wasn't it?"

"Oh yes," Karen said, without thinking about it.

"I think I'm going to take a nap," he said, lying back down. "Why don't you bring your manuscript down and leave it on my desk? I'll look it over when I wake up."

*Such noblesse oblige*, she thought, standing and pulling her panties back on.

"Why don't you nap with me?" Philip asked, patting the place on the bed she'd just vacated.

"I've got some errands to run." Karen was aware of how cold her voice sounded as she pulled her T-shirt back over her head. "I'll be back in a little while."

He tried to catch her eye, but she avoided it.

She hurried back upstairs, withdrawing the last print-out of the Vicky manuscript from the bottom drawer of her desk, where she'd relegated it. She hadn't looked at it in weeks. She read the first paragraph again.

*It's not that bad. I'm much too hard on myself. I should just forget about all this Hatch stuff and focus on Vicky. It's so close to being done—a good push and I could probably finish the whole thing in a couple of weeks. And then Philip will show it to Bill.*

She walked back down the stairs and glanced into the bedroom. Her husband was already asleep, snoring lightly. She placed the manuscript on his desk chair, pulling on her tennis shoes and grabbing a windbreaker from the closet. She leaned over and kissed his cheek.

*I do love you*, she thought. *I really do.*

*So why does this other voice keep popping into my head?*

A cold wind was blowing off the bay as she stepped outside. Karen shivered, zipping the jacket up. *This is just the beginning*, she thought as she hurried down Commercial Street. *By the time winter hits, I'm not going to want to leave the house.*

Late September in New Orleans was always warm and sunny. A burst of homesickness swept over her.

She didn't miss waiting tables, that was for sure, but there were other things she did miss. Like hopping on the streetcar and riding up St. Charles, getting off at Washington, and walking down to the Garden District Bookshop. The bookstores in Provincetown were nice— and the people who worked there very friendly. But she suspected they were nice because she was Mrs. Philip Kaye. In New Orleans, people were nice to her because she was Karen. Just Karen.

*I'm still her*, she thought as she headed toward the library. *Still Karen.*

*Except—*

A shiver passed through her.

*Except not always.*

What an odd thought to have. But thoughts of poor Sarah Jane never seemed to leave her. And here she was, heading back to the library to find out still more.

Olive Zelinski, the research librarian, waved as Karen walked through the front doors. Olive was in her early fifties, with reddish hair shot through with gray that she wore piled on top of her head. She always wore somber clothes, dressed to her knees in dark colors over sensible rubber-soled shoes.

"Mrs. Kaye," Olive called. "I found something for you."

"Really?"

From under the counter Olive produced a dusty-looking hardcover, wrapped in that clear cellophane libraries use to protect book covers. She handed it over to Karen.

"I found this way back in the stacks. Thought it might be of use to you." Olive smiled. "There's a local connection as well. The author and her husband bought a house in Truro. They were here this past summer."

Karen looked down at the book. *Suffragette Writings: The Earliest Feminists*, edited by Lois Bancroft-Muir.

The front cover was a black-and-white photograph of a parade of women in turn-of-the-century clothes carrying picket signs. Turning the book over, Karen gazed at the author photo on the back cover. Pretty in a scholarly way, Lois Bancroft-Muir was wearing a dark sweater with glasses hanging on a chain from around her neck.

"I'm sure it's interesting," Karen said, "but what does this have to do with—"

"The Hatches?" Olive's eyes danced with excitement. "Open to the table of contents."

Karen opened the book and glanced down the list. There it was, and she almost shouted. *On the Rights of Women*, by Sarah Jane McConnell. She pulled her library card out of her wallet. "Thanks, Olive."

"I knew you'd be thrilled." Olive processed the book and handed it back over to her. "Let me know if there's any other way I can help."

"Well, I have a feeling you just have. Tremendously."

Karen hurried out of the library, the book burning in her hand. Heading down Commercial Street was easy now: with the tourists largely gone, there were fewer bikes to avoid, fewer gaggles of drag queens to scoot around. Her destination was Lagniappe Café, a little hole-in-the-wall place with great coffee, and the name made her think of New Orleans. She took a small table in the corner, ordered a mocha cappuccino, and flipped the book open to the chapter on Sarah Jane.

*Sarah Jane*, she thought. *I have been dying to meet you. . . .*

She read the words that began the short biographical essay that preceded Sarah Jane's treatise on woman suffrage.

> *Sarah Jane McConnell was one of the later suffragettes, appearing on the scene only towards*

*the end of the movement. Not much is known of
her before she arrived in Washington at the age of
twenty in 1919; Caroline Cargill mentions her in
a letter to Mary Warren as being from Louisiana,
some small town in the northeast section of the
state whose name she couldn't remember.*

Karen stopped reading. The parallels were uncanny,
with Sarah Jane being from Louisiana, too. . . . She resumed the story.

*Sarah Jane impressed Cargill as being very in-
telligent and devoted to the cause. Cargill's exact
words were: "The future of the movement, dear
Mary, is certainly assured if we can continue to
recruit women of the intellectual level that Miss
McConnell presents. There's a fire in her when she
talks about the cause, and her logic and thinking
have left many men scratching their heads in
utter defeat once she has presented her arguments. I have tried to find out more about her, but
she adamantly refuses to discuss her past or her
family. I get the sense that she ran away from a
particularly oppressive environment—which is
why she is so passionate. The other day, she said
to me, 'Mrs. Cargill, our work is not for ourselves, but for the future generations of women,
so that they are not forced to endure the things
that we have in our lifetimes. We have to educate
women, from the moment they are girls, and convince them that they are just as capable as any
man.'"*

Karen smiled. She liked Sarah Jane more all the
time.

*Unfortunately, Sarah Jane McConnell is best known, not for the work she did, but for the tragic circumstances of her death. She married Senator Horace Hatch in 1922, retiring to his home in Provincetown. That December, she and the senator were murdered in one of the most violent unsolved murders in Massachusetts history. Her stepdaughter, Letitia Hatch, was tried for the murders and found not guilty. The murders remain unsolved to this day.*

*Yet Sarah Jane's writings prove that she was not only a great writer, but possessed of a brilliant, analytical mind. In this essay, she takes to task not only "male-dominated society" but also Christianity, for subjugating women and making them little more than "brood mares" and slaves to their husbands. This was radical thinking, particularly for the time. Even today, many feminists are afraid to take on the church, but Sarah had no such compunctions, despite the fact she could have been ostracized from polite society for taking the church to task. What might have come from her pen had her life not been cut so tragically short? We will never know.—L.B-M., editor.*

Karen stared out the window. The sun was starting to set, the days already growing shorter. She closed the book carefully.

*You already know everything you need to know*, a voice in her head told her.

Karen smiled.

She thought about Horace back home, sound asleep, and Lettie out there, somewhere, sneaking off to see her beau . . .

She slipped the book into her purse and headed home.

# Chapter 14

She found herself leaving the house every afternoon, hoping to see him.

Sarah Jane passed a woman hauling a stinking basket of fish. She nodded pleasantly to her, but she made no attempt to speak. She'd tried talking about women's rights to some of the townswomen—thick, stocky, hardy Portuguese wives of fishermen and whalers—but it was like talking to brick walls. They were too brainwashed already, mired in their lives and their church. This was the life their mothers had lived, the lives of their grandmothers, and it would be the life they passed on to their own daughters.

"The endless cycle of enslavement," Sarah Jane had called it in her last essay. Horace had forbidden her to continue writing, of course, and she'd agreed, early on, because she thought he'd relent, that she could change his mind. Then she'd have him right where she wanted him. Oh, what change she could affect with a supportive, progressive husband in the Senate!

But it hadn't quite worked out that way. Horace remained as conservative as ever, and Sarah Jane found

*herself writing in secret, the only way she could keep
her sanity in this cold, dark place at the end of the
world. She'd write an essay, sending it off to a journal
under a false name. It bothered her that it had come to
this, that she had become what she had worked so hard
against all her life: an enslaved woman. And now, shut
away here in this backwater town, far away from the
corridors of power—what good was being Mrs. Senator
Hatch now? She had hoped for access to power, to
change—but now, if she dared speak out, Horace wasn't
above striking her. And what recourse did she have?
Men were allowed to beat their wives like animals.*

*A gull soared above her, letting out a long cry. The
village was beautiful, she had to admit that. The sunlight reflecting off the water was striking—she'd never
seen anything like it before. No wonder the painters set
up their easels on the beach and tried to capture the
light with their oils. It was all so different from Cooper
Road, that horrible hellish place where she'd grown
up. There was nothing beautiful about Cooper Road—
everything was dingy and shabby, suffused with an ugliness down to its very core. The roads were dirty and
dusty when it was dry, rivers of mud when it rained.
Rotting wooden planks served as sidewalks, and nobody owned automobiles. What was the point when
they'd just get stuck in the mud if it suddenly rained?*

*Oh, how she'd hated Cooper Road, hated the back-
breaking work on the little farm just outside the town
limits, hated the way the snobby merchants looked
down on her and her bare feet, her faded clothes. Her
father was a drunk and completely useless—and if that
weren't shameful enough, everyone knew it. Sometimes
when he was drunk he'd stagger into town on their only
mule and make a complete fool of himself, sometimes
getting arrested and having to spend the night in the
small jail. All the work fell on Sarah Jane and her*

*brothers, their mother having died when she was just a little girl, worn out from the life on the farm. It was a wonder she lasted as long as she did.*

*Sarah Jane had vowed, standing in the little cemetery as her mother was laid to rest, that she wouldn't end up the same way—worn out and beaten down by life, a husk of the woman she had once been. She was going to get out of Cooper Road, out of Louisiana, away from the shame, away from the townspeople with their contemptuous eyes, away from anyone who knew her as white trash. She was going to be different—she was going to have a better life than the one she'd been born into.*

*And then she met Earl, and everything changed.*

*She headed into the fish market, closing the door on her mind. Louisiana and, most of all, Earl were in the past. They were gone. Her predicament now might be unpleasant, but it paled in comparison to the past.*

*The smell of the fish hit her with an almost physical force. She looked, hoping that among the men gathered around with their pipes, she might spot Orville. But he was nowhere to be seen.*

*"Ah, Mrs. Hatch, good day to you," said Pedro, one of the fishermen who supplied the market. He was gutting a large fish, wiping his hands on his bloody apron to give her a smile. Men always smiled at her. "Anything in particular you're looking for today?"*

*She smiled back at him. "No, Pedro, I don't really need anything, I just needed to get out of the house for a bit." She winked at him. "And say hello to people."*

*"And how's the senator?"*

*"I just got a letter from him today." She kept the smile on her face, although her eyes hardened. "Business as usual in the capital."*

*Horace had left her behind when he returned to Washington. She'd been furious when he told her she wasn't returning with him. "Washington is no place for a woman," he'd said.*

*"You* met *me in Washington." She felt her temper rising. Horace didn't know she had a temper; she'd kept it reined in almost from the moment they met. "Once you admired me for having something to say!"*

*"But now you are my wife, and so you must keep my house."*

*"The other senators bring their wives." Her dreams of dancing at balls at the White House, of attending the theater and the opera, and—of course—working behind the scenes for women's rights seemed long gone.*

*Horace gave her a smile. "The other senators aren't married to the most beautiful woman in the country."*

*She knew the compliment was supposed to make her simper and smile, and forget everything. But that day she couldn't play the game. She was too angry.*

*"Are you sure this has nothing to do with Eliza Washburn?"*

*She watched as Horace flinched. He thought she didn't know about that woman, the fool. Everyone in Washington knew that blowsy woman was his whore, and had been for years.*

*"Eliza Washburn is no concern of yours," Horace said gruffly.*

*"I would think where my husband spends his nights is very much my concern!" Sarah Jane shouted, losing her temper. "You think you can leave me here while you go down there and make a laughingstock of yourself with that painted whore? You think people don't know? Everyone knows, Horace, and they laugh—they laugh at you." She spat the words at him, shaking uncontrollably, knowing losing her temper was stupid, certainly not the correct way to win this battle.*

*Her husband's face reddened, and he crossed the room much faster than she would have thought possi-*

*ble for a man of his girth. He slapped her across the face so hard he knocked her down. She fell to the floor, her forehead barely missing the bedpost. She lay there, on the floor, her head pounding, rage filling her. He screamed at her, "You'll do as you're told, woman, as your betters did before you!"*

*"My betters?" She sat up, rubbing the stinging place on her cheek. "How dare you!"*

*"You think I don't know what you are?" He smirked at her. "Do you think I married you without checking into you? You think I believed that ridiculous story?"*

*He got close enough to her so she could smell his breath.*

*"Your father is still very much alive, still trying to eke a living out of that farm when he isn't too drunk to stand up, missy. I'm sure he'd love to know where his daughter is. Oh yes, I know all about you, Miss McConnell! You left that town with your head hung in shame, everyone knew what kind of a woman you were! You're no better than Eliza Washburn. At least she did her duty, married a man and bore him sons—which is more than you can say!"*

*Her eyes widened. She felt rage and hatred bubbling up within her. She grabbed onto the bedpost.* Get control, Sarah Jane, get control, don't let the rage take over again, that's not how to win, it just makes things worse, control your temper . . .

*It took every ounce of self-control she possessed not to get up and throw something at Horace, to dig her fingernails into his eyes, to claw his face until the blood ran. But while that might be momentarily satisfying, it wouldn't solve anything, and it would only make matters worse. He was bigger and stronger than she was . . . but someday he'd regret hitting her.*

*He had slammed his trunk shut. "I'll be back in December." He grabbed a fistful of her hair and pressed his lips against hers. He gave her an ugly smirk. "You may put on airs, my dear wife, but I know you're nothing but white trash."*

*"Why, Mrs. Hatch, I believe."*
*The voice came from behind her and left her startled, bringing her out of her reverie. Sarah Jane turned. A broad smile spread across her face.*
*"Why, Mr. Axelrod, what a pleasant surprise! I wasn't expecting to see you. . . ."*

October brought another temperature drop.

The house always seemed to be cold to Karen. The days were getting shorter, darkness falling like a cloak over the town earlier every day. The silence in the house was even more unnerving than it had been before Philip came home. Jessie stayed in her room, not talking much even to Philip, but then again he was so focused on his book he barely noticed anyone else.

When Karen broached putting Jessie back in public school, Philip flatly refused to consider it. "No," he said, turning back to his computer. How quickly he had changed from that day he bared his soul to her. How quickly he had returned to being distant and cold. "Please, Karen, I can't write with you hovering like that."

*Or is it me who's changed? Why can I look at him— my husband—and feel nothing? Feel almost as if—I hate him . . . ?*

*I do. I do hate him. And that sneaky daughter of his, too . . .*

*Why won't you send her to college, Horace? She deserves an education. . . .*

As if she cared anymore about the girl's education. She just wanted the little bitch out of the house.

Karen shivered. *What am I thinking? How can there be there so much rage inside me?*

The Vicky Knight manuscript sat on the edge of her desk, where it had sat since Philip gave it back to her. Every page was covered with red pencil marks, with multicolored sticky notes jutting out from the pile. She knew what he had written on them. Even if he didn't use the exact words, what he meant was: *You suck, Karen, you're never going to be a writer, you're just a loser!*

She hadn't touched the manuscript since he'd brought it up to her.

*And every word you type is just a pearl of genius, isn't it, Mr. New York Times Best-seller List?* Karen looked over at her husband and seethed. *Which is why the critics just love you, right? That explains all those writing awards on your shelf, right? Oh yeah, I'm sorry, you've never won anything, have you, Philip? The critics think you're a hack who appeals to the lowest common denominator in your readers. You pander. But I guess being a best seller makes you a literary genius, right? Guess that gives you the authority to critique my manuscript.*

*Just wait, Philip. You'll pay for that slap. You'll pay when I publish the best-selling account of Lettie Hatch. . . .*

The wind howled, rattling the window in front of her desk, and she shivered again. She was dressed in layers, T-shirt, flannel pullover, sweater, but she was still cold. Philip wouldn't let her turn the heat up. He said he worked better when it was cold.

*And it's all about you, isn't it, Mr. Best Seller? Nobody else matters, not your daughter, not me, certainly not your first wife. She didn't matter either, did she? She had some problems and you bailed on her—God forbid anything interfere with your holy work. Yeah, no fucking wonder Ivy killed herself. She should have just let you divorce her and taken everything you had, you pompous, arrogant asshole.*

For the last several mornings Karen had wakened to the sound of his fingers punching keys. He stayed there all day, typing away. Her anger had grown, stewing within her. Dinners were an unbearable exercise in tension. The four of them sat around the table, the only sound the utensils scraping on the plates. Jessie didn't talk, just kept her eyes on her plate until she was finished and could escape. Alice might try to say something, but Karen just froze her with a look.

*I should just pack my stuff and leave, take the SUV and drive back to Louisiana, move back in with Mom and Dad until the divorce is settled. I bet I could get enough money out of him to live on so I wouldn't have to wait tables anymore. That would show his pompous ass, wouldn't it? Then I could write a book about a hack writer who treats his wife like shit until she finally has enough and walks out the door, but that wouldn't be satisfying, would it? No, he needs to be punished worse than that, much worse than that.*

The headache was coming again. Karen pressed her fingers into her temples.

*What is happening to me? Why am I so angry all of the time? Why do I think such things—*

*Such things? It's perfectly appropriate to be angry at your husband, that callous male supremicist. He wants to keep you down. He wants to stifle your voice.*

*He called you white trash!*

"No," Karen said to herself, struggling to get a grip on her thoughts. "No, Philip never called me that."

She needed to talk to Bobbie. She needed a friend badly. But Bobbie had been gone so often lately. Every weekend he was off to Boston to be with David. Karen was alone. She'd called her mother a couple of times, just to hear a friendly voice, and sometimes her mother's thick accent brought tears to her eyes, but she couldn't bring herself to open up to her, to tell her she'd made a mistake and wanted to come home.

*I should just leave him,* she thought as she stared out into the dark night. *Just pack my things and load up the damned SUV and get on the road, and just go, keep going, I don't need this.*

"But I love him," she whispered to herself. "I do!"

*You don't love him! You never did! You married him because he offered you access to power . . . a chance to make things happen . . .*

"I married . . . him . . . because . . . he seemed interested in me. I thought I could . . . change him . . ."

*And he has changed, hasn't he? But not the way you hoped . . .*

"He's not the man I married anymore."

Karen pressed her fingers into her temples again and forced herself to remember the night Philip proposed. Between his signing in St. Louis and Chicago, he'd flown down to New Orleans to take her out for dinner. He'd booked a room at the Ritz Carlton on Canal Street—he didn't like her apartment, and she couldn't blame him there, the place embarrassed her—and he'd taken her to dinner at Galatoire's. Afterward, they'd held hands and walked down to the river. On the Moon Walk, with the moon and a sky full of stars over her head and the big muddy river at her feet, he'd gotten down on his knees and asked her to marry him. She was so overwhelmed she'd started crying right there, not caring if anyone saw her, and she blubbered, "Yes." Then he'd slid the beautiful diamond ring on her finger, and sworn he'd always make her happy.

She stared down at the ring now and twisted it on her finger.

*Make me happy? By bringing me here, to the end of the world?*

Karen slowly pulled open the top drawer on her desk. She reached in and carefully removed the diary, caressing it, holding it to her chest.

No, she couldn't leave here. Not before she had learned how that evil Lettie Hatch had slaughtered poor Sarah Jane.

She opened the diary to the page she'd marked.

*24 October 1922*

> *SHE knows.*
> *I don't know how, but she knows. I catch her looking at me, when she thinks I am unaware, and a small sly smile plays on her lips. Why, oh why, did Father marry that she-devil? I cannot conceive of how she could have found out—no one knows, we've been so careful—but somehow she knows. Mostly she ignores me, which is a welcome blessing, but every so often, at the table as we eat, she will say something that might mean nothing, but it strikes me to the heart. Perhaps S is right, and it's only my guilty conscience giving her words meanings she didn't intend, but he does not see her face when she says them. She has the meanest eyes—as if she knows the torment I am going through and is enjoying it. She is evil, I think, the most purely selfish creature I have ever encountered. She doesn't care anything about anyone except herself—why did Father marry her? Why? Was he so blinded by her beauty that he couldn't see her rotted soul?*
> *I don't think she has said anything to Father— his letters to me would surely mention it—nay, if he knew about me and S he wouldn't confine himself to letters, he would come back and there would be hell to pay. No, she is keeping her own counsel*

*on this . . . trying to decide how best to use the
knowledge to her own benefit. There will be a day
of reckoning, of that I have no doubt.*

*S thinks we should run away, and I am begin-
ning to think he is right. But where would we go?
We cannot live on love, and where could we go
where we couldn't be found? I love him so, but I
have to be realistic. He's only a fisherman, it's the
only skill he knows, so where could we go where
we could escape Father's wrath? S doesn't understand any of this—he's convinced that as long as
we are together and love each other, everything
will work out in the end. For a man, he really
doesn't understand how this world works.*

*Oh, Mother, why did you leave us? Why? You
would understand, and Father was afraid of you.
I need you so badly, why did you leave? Why?*

Karen closed the book and held it to her breast.
*Poor S*, she thought. *I wonder if he finally woke up
to the fact that Lettie cared more about money and social standing than him. "He's only a fisherman!" Nice
thing to think about the love of your life.*

Karen felt certain this would turn out to be the reason Lettie killed Horace and Sarah Jane—because her
stepmother had found out about S. *Maybe Sarah told
Horace when he came home—and there was a scene.
And of course that bitch Mrs. Windham covered up for
Lettie.* She was getting close to cracking the motive for
the murder. She felt certain of that.

She knew in that moment that she had to tell the
story from Sarah's perspective. The poor rural farm
girl from Louisiana who'd gone to Washington to fight
for women's rights, who'd had her head turned by a
wealthy and powerful senator and married him, only to
meet her fate at the hands of her spoiled, selfish slut of

a stepdaughter. It was a great story. Karen felt a kin-
ship with Sarah Jane and it went beyond the similarities
in their lives. It seemed to stretch across the decades,
connecting their souls . . .

"I won't let you be forgotten, Sarah Jane," she vowed
out loud.

If only it were fiction . . . How much she'd prefer to
have Sarah Jane escape from the murderous Lettie.

She sat down at her computer and stared at the screen.
She had started. In the last few days she had banged
out several pages in Sarah Jane's voice. She liked what
she had written. It was so much more real, so much
more alive, than anything she'd written about Vicky.
Sarah Jane lived again in these pages.

"Lettie Hatchet took a knife," Karen sang under her
breath as she printed out what she had written. She
grinned. Maybe that would be the title.

She decided she'd show it to Philip. It was time. She
knew now that it was going to be bigger than anything
he'd ever done. She was going to be more famous than
he was. All the talk shows would want her—Katie,
Oprah, Ellen, all of them—and it would skyrocket up
the best-seller lists and be made into a huge hit movie.
She'd write the screenplay herself and win an Oscar,
and she'd buy a really cool beach house in Malibu and
move there. She'd become a player. Philip would be
sorry he'd been such a jerk to her, and Jessie would regret being such a little bi—

"Karen?"

Philip was on the stairs.

She quickly closed the document and shut her laptop, sliding the diary back into its drawer. "Yes?"

"Karen, you've hardly come out of the attic for days."
He stood in the doorway looking painfully at her. "Is
everything okay?"

"I've been writing."

He approached her. "You've been distant. Irritable . . ."

She gave him a look. "As you were. Am I not allowed? I'm a writer, too, Philip, and writers sometimes—"

"Of course you're a writer, darling. I'm sorry." He tried to smile, but she turned away from his dimples. "I was thinking we need some time together."

She arched an eyebrow at him.

"Would you like to go to Boston this weekend?" He stood over her, trying to catch her eyes. She kept looking at her computer screen. "A treat? We could stay at the Ritz Carlton, maybe take in a play, go to some great restaurants—do the town up right. I mean, you've never even been to Boston yet. What do you think?"

She finally gave in and looked up at him. His eyes—of course he loved her. Why had she been so hard on him? Why—

He had knelt down beside her. "I want things to be right between us."

"Things are right," she said awkwardly, ashamed of the feelings she'd been having. It was as if they weren't her feelings. It was as if that other voice in her head wasn't her own. . . .

He smiled. "There's a party on Friday night. You might enjoy it. Joe Butler is giving it for Mary Ann Fletcher, and I thought it might be fun to take you up and show you around the city. . . ."

She recognized the names. Joe Butler was a best-selling horror writer—Philip's main competition, actually—and Mary Ann Fletcher wrote best-selling fantasy novels. Karen relaxed and smiled. "That would be fun, Philip."

"And I have this for you." He winked at her, pulling a small velvet case from behind his back and handing it to her. "Will you ever forgive your wayward husband for his bad behavior?"

She opened it and gasped. On a satin matting rested a double-strand pearl necklace with a diamond clasp. "Philip!" She picked it up and stared at it. "It's—it's beautiful."

He took it from her and fastened it around her neck. "Almost as beautiful as you."

She shut off her computer, took his hand, and walked downstairs to bed with him.

They passed Jessie's door on the way. She was sitting on her bed, headphones over her ears, hunched into a ball. "Good night, Jess," Philip called in to her, loudly enough to be heard over the music.

The girl looked up and grunted.

"Jess," Philip said, still holding Karen's hand. "We're going up to Boston on Friday for the weekend. You'll be okay here with Mrs. Winn, right?"

She nodded, seeming annoyed at being disturbed.

Karen had an idea. "Jessie," she said. The girl looked darkly over at her, and a shudder of fear passed through Karen's body. It was rare that either of them ever addressed each other, but Karen persevered. "Why don't you come with us? We can all see Boston together. . . ."

Philip made an uncomfortable little laugh. "Karen, I don't think . . . I mean, Jess would be bored by the party. . . ."

"Yeah," Jessie said. "I'm sure I would be."

"Well, I just thought that maybe it would finally give us a chance to, you know, do something as a family. . . ."

Karen noticed Jessie's eyes had hardened on her. She felt another chill.

*She looks as if she could kill me.*

"What's that you're wearing?" Jessie asked huskily, removing the headphones from her ears.

Karen fingered the necklace. "Your father . . . he gave it to me. . . ."

The girl's face went pale. "He gave—he gave you *that*?"

"Yes. Isn't it beautiful?"

Jessie glared at her father. Philip said nothing. Then she got up off her bed and slammed the door in their faces.

"What—" Karen stuttered.

"Jesus Christ, that kid isn't right. She just isn't right." Philip dropped Karen's hand and staggered on into the bedroom on his own.

Karen walked slowly over to the hallway mirror. She stared at the pearls draped around her throat. She stroked them lovingly. *They really are beautiful*, she thought, as she turned to join Horace in the bedroom.

# Chapter 15

It had been days since Chris had last heard from Jessie. Once again his doubts resurfaced. *She's forgotten about me, I didn't mean anything to her. I might as well forget about her and move on.*

Josh was sympathetic. "Maybe this weekend we can head into town and meet some townie girls," he said, winking. "That girl's just a big cock tease, Chris, my man. Trust me, you can do better than that. These townie girls like us prep school boys."

But nothing could stop Chris from thinking about her every night, after they'd turned off the lights and gone to bed. He stared up at the ceiling as Josh fell asleep. He wondered if Jessie was okay, how she was doing, remembering the feel of her lips when she kissed him, the way he'd felt an electric charge whenever she'd slip her little hand into his.

She had to be okay. All those weird dreams and premonitions . . . if she had a sense that they were returning, that anything creepy was happening, she'd have e-mailed him. He was the only one she trusted about that stuff. She'd contact him if things got weird. He knew she would.

Well, he hoped so anyway.

He'd had a crappy day. He'd gotten a B on a paper for political science, a project he'd worked his ass off on, and he heard Lois's voice in his head as he stared at the big blue B on the paper. *B means other people are doing better than you, Chris, and you know what that means, you can't ever do substandard work, your research must have been sloppy, or your conclusions. You're going to have to work harder.*

He threw his book bag against the wall, furious.

"What's up, dude?" Josh said from his desk, looking up from his geology textbook.

"Aw, nothing."

"Hmmm—sounds like you need to spark up."

"Yeah, whatever." *Might as well check my fucking e-mail,* Chris thought, sitting down at his desk and signing online. And there it was.

A note from Jessie!

> *Chris:*
> *Is there any way you can get up here this week-end? They're going to be in Boston, and I'll be here alone with Alice. I really need to talk to you.*
> *Jessie*

"Well, fuck." He smacked the side of his computer in frustration. It was already Thursday, and there was no way he could get the requisite permission from his parents. *Not that they would do it anyway,* he thought. *They'd want me to come home. They'd never let me go see Jessie.*

"Dude, what's wrong?" Josh looked up from the joint he was rolling. He'd already stuffed a towel under the door and opened the windows.

"That damned Jessie." Chris ran his hands through his hair. "No word from her in days and then all of a sudden she wants me to get away this weekend and come see her." Chris banged his hand against the computer again. "Like my parents would let me out of here—and besides, I'd have no way to get all the way out to P-town."

Josh licked the joint and handed it over to Chris with a lighter, a huge grin on his face. "Easier than you think, homie."

Chris lit the joint and sucked in the smoke, holding it the way Josh had taught him, then blowing it out the window. "What do you mean?"

"Trust me." Josh winked and got out his cell phone. He pressed a button and held it up to his ear. "Hey, Rod, it's Josh. How are you? I'm fine? How's Dad? The shoot's going well? Cool, look, I need a favor. Can you call the headmaster and get me permission to leave campus this weekend? Me and a friend?"

Chris watched in amazement. Could this really be happening?

"Hang on a sec, Rod—Chris, write your parents' phone number down. Okay, thanks. Rod, can you call a Mr. Joe Muir at this number"—he read the number off—"and tell him that Dad's invited us to New York? They'll need to call the headmaster too. . . . Cool, thanks a million, Rod, I owe you one."

He hung up the phone and grinned. "Consider it done."

Chris stared at him. "What do you mean, done? I don't want to go to New York. I want to go to Provincetown. And my parents—"

"New York's the cover story, dumb-ass. You really don't know much about breaking rules, do you?" Josh rolled his eyes. "All we need is permission to leave campus for the weekend, and Rod'll take care of it all."

"But my parents—"

"Look, bud, I know your mom's a women's lib teacher—"

"Women's studies," he corrected.

"—and a control freak, whatever, but you'll see. Anyway, I've found that whenever a movie star calls, people jump. You'll see. People are fucking awed by celebrity. They never say fucking no." He cocked his index finger at Chris, and clicked his tongue as he flexed the thumb. "Besides, virgin boy, you definitely need to get laid."

"It's not like that." He took the joint again.

Josh just smiled. "It's *always* like that, homes."

Josh was as good as his word. On Friday afternoon they were packing for the weekend. Lois had, amazingly, given her consent. Was she really so easily swayed by celebrity?

"Now, Chris, I want you to behave yourself in New York and not be any trouble to Mr. Benton," she'd said breathlessly. "And make sure you stop by the Met. Tell me, Chris. Do you think Mr. Benton would be interested in being the guest of honor for a fund-raiser I'm putting together this February?"

Chris laughed as he hung up the phone. *So much for Kyle Benton being a fascist macho male pig whose movies appeal to the lowest common denominator and exploit women.*

They threw their bags in the Porsche and headed off campus. Josh drove fast—Chris was afraid to look at the speedometer—and they shared a joint as the car hurtled through the countryside, the stereo blaring. The green backwoods of Connecticut gave way to the stark asphalt of I-95. They passed through Providence, then out along the coast of southeast Massachusetts. As they crossed the Bourne Bridge, Chris's heart leaped as he saw the message hewn into the shrubbery: *Welcome to*

*Cape Cod*. It had been almost two months since he'd seen Jessie. He couldn't wait.

One hour later, the Porsche pulled up in front of the Muir house in Truro. The windows had been boarded up, the phone disconnected, but Chris knew the power was still on. He was out of the car in a flash but noticed Josh had left the car running. "Aren't you coming?" he asked.

Josh handed him a baggie with a couple of joints in it. "Nah. Me and my fake ID are spending the weekend in Boston. I've got some friends up there." He grinned. "Women friends, if you catch my drift. I'll pick you up at two on Sunday."

Chris didn't know what to say. "You drove me all the way here? Boston is another two hours back."

"Hey, what's a couple hours among friends?"

Chris was touched. "You rock, dude."

Josh winked, and tore out of the driveway in his car.

Chris spent the evening trying to study, but kept looking at his watch every few minutes. What if Jessie didn't come? What if her parents changed their minds and didn't go? What if he had come all the way up here for nothing?

He smoked another joint to calm himself down. He was sitting in the living room, reading by candlelight. Even with the windows boarded up, he didn't want to risk turning on a light, alerting the neighbors who might then alert his parents there was a prowler in the house.

Finally, a hesitant knock on the front door. Chris bolted over to it and pulled it open. A huge grin spread across his face.

"Oh, thank God you're here." Jessie threw her arms around him. She was trembling. "I was so afraid you wouldn't come, that something would go wrong."

"I told you I'd come," he said, smelling her hair. "I'll

always come when you need me." She felt so good there in his arms, and her hair smelled so good . . .

She stiffened in his arms, and pulled away from him. Her face was white. "Why—why did you say that?"

He stared at her. "Because I meant it, Jessie. What's wrong?"

She shook her head. "Nothing. It was just—"

"It's not nothing. You look like you've seen a ghost."

"It was just—" She shivered. "I've heard that before. It was just déjà vu, I guess. But—I don't know, I'm such a fucking nutcase. I don't know why you put up with me."

*Because I love you, haven't you figured that out yet?* He put his arms around her again. "It's okay, Jess. I'm here now. What's wrong? Are you having the dreams again?"

She shook her head. "No, Chris, I'm not. Not since August." She pulled away from him and walked over to the couch, removing her coat. "And that scares me even more than having the dreams."

"You're not making any sense." He sat down next to her, stretching his legs out under the coffee table. "Come on, Jess. The dreams scared the pants off you, so why should you be scared that you *aren't* having them?"

"It's still going on, Chris. I don't have the dreams— it's almost as if I don't need to have them anymore. It's like it's happening whether I'm asleep or awake. That it's always going on."

"I don't follow."

"The circle is still open, I know it." She looked at him. "You don't know what it's like, Chris. To have your mind suddenly seem as if it's not your own. That someone else is doing the thinking for you. That the feelings you're having aren't yours . . . that they belong to someone else."

He took her hands. He wanted her to curl up with him, cuddle next to him, and kiss him again.

"I told you, Jessie, Madame Nadja was full of shit. I read the book, remember? *The Circle of Time*? And none of that crap about ghosts was in there. It's just a theory, anyway. Dr. Goodwin himself says so, in the introduction. Look. In Nadja's whacked-out brain, she came up with some bullshit to explain what you were feeling and you bought it—the whole thing. It just doesn't make sense."

"You were there, Chris. You know what happened. You saw it." Jessie turned away from him, staring into the candle flame. "And you've felt it, too—I know you have."

He shook his head. He didn't want to argue with her. "So what's got you so freaked out?"

"They went to Boston for the weekend." She laughed bitterly. "And she's acting weird, anyway. She has been for the last couple of weeks. Alice Winn says she's gotten so sharp with her. Mean. Nasty. And I catch her looking at me, her eyes so filled with hate . . ."

"She sounds like the classic wicked stepmother, Jess."

"I think she's up to something." Her eyes filled with tears. "And to add insult to injury—he gave her my mother's pearls." She slammed her fists down on the coffee table, making the bric-a-brac jump. "Can you believe it? Those are *mine*! He thinks I don't remember, but I do . . . I remember when he gave them to her. It was when he sold the film rights to *Dusty Death*, and he bought her those pearls, even though she hated pearls. She always did. She called them old ladies' jewels. She would never wear them, but she told me I could have them and now he's given them to *her*. . . ." Jessie started to cry, covering her face with her hands. "They're *mine*, Chris. They were my *mom's*!"

"Hey." He pulled her close, putting his arms around her and squeezing. "It's okay, Jessie, just cry it all out, you let go, okay? Don't hold it in anymore." He held her while she cried, and finally she managed to get a hold of herself. She wiped her face and gave him a weak smile.

"I'm sorry." Her voice still shook a bit. "I've just missed you so much. You're the only person I can talk to about anything."

"I've missed you, too. I've thought about you every day. I've been going crazy missing you." He kissed her forehead. "The days you didn't send an e-mail—man, I thought I'd lose it. I'd think you didn't care anymore."

"Of course I care, Chris." She wiped at her eyes. "I'll always care."

He kissed her forehead. "Me too."

*Oh, Jessie, I'll never doubt you again, never again, you're the best thing that ever happened to me, and I will always come when you need me, all you have to do is call and I'll be on my way if I have to move heaven and earth to be here with you.*

"How'd you manage to get up here?" She grabbed a Kleenex and blew her nose.

"Remember me telling out about my roommate, Josh Benton?" He grinned, and explained to her how he and Josh had become friends. She laughed out loud when he mimicked his mother's phone call. "Can you believe it? She's probably bragging to all her snotty colleagues about how her kid is friends with Kyle Benton's son."

They both started laughing, and leaned back into the couch. Chris pulled her to him, and they kissed again, on the mouth this time, and they looked into each other's eyes. They kissed again—

\* \* \*

*—and Samuel pulled back from her. He sat up, his head cocked, listening.*

*"What is it, Samuel?" Lettie whispered, worried. She was reclining on her back, resting on her elbows. Her blouse was open, and he could see the curve of her bare breasts inside. Her skin was milky white and smooth, and soft to the touch.*

*"I thought I heard something, but I guess I was wrong."*

*He peered through the gloom. There was no moon, although the sky was filled with clouds. It was a bit chilly, but Indian summer had lasted much longer than anyone could ever remember it lasting before. It seemed as though God and nature were conspiring together to allow them to continue being together. Soon enough the weather would turn cold, too cold for them to continue meeting in the dunes. Where would they rendezvous then? They hadn't talked about that. They'd cross that bridge when they came to it, Samuel thought again.*

*He was squinting, trying to see. The sound still troubled him. Might it have just been an animal? Sometimes deer made their way out onto the dunes.*

*It was no deer.*

*He couldn't help but feel someone, or something, was out there, watching and waiting.* That's ridiculous, he told himself. No one knows we're here, no one even knows we know each other. If anyone comes along, it would just be a coincidence.

*Lettie sat up, pulling her blouse closed. "You're scaring me, Samuel." She looked out into the darkness. "Maybe we should be going. Someone might just wander along out here and—"*

*"I'm sorry." He smiled down at her. She was so pretty, he thought again, and he was so blessed to have found her. "I love you, Lettie."*

*"Do you, Samuel?" Tears filled her eyes. "You make*

*me so happy, Samuel, you give me a reason to wake up in the morning. I get so scared—" She started to cry.*

*"Shhh, Lettie," he whispered. "I'll always take care of you. I'll always come for you, you know that."*

*She pressed her lips against his again, and they slid back down on the blanket. He kissed her neck, then moved his lips down her throat and began kissing her breasts. She moaned a little, arching her back so that her breasts pressed against his lips even harder than before.*

*"Make love to me, Samuel, please."*

—and Jessie slid her sweatshirt over her head. She smiled at him as she reached behind her and unhooked her bra.

The flickering candlelight danced shadows over her white skin. His breath came faster. He kissed her again, placing his hands on her breasts. They were firm yet soft, and he lowered his mouth and kissed her throat. She moaned, yanking his sweatshirt up. His arms got caught momentarily in the sleeves, and she laughed. Then his arms were free, and they came together again, her breasts in their bra pressed up against his bare chest. It felt so good, so right, like this was their destiny, they were meant to be together—

*"Why are you crying?"*

*Samuel reached down and touched the moisture on Lettie's cheeks. "Are you ashamed? Have I hurt you in some way? I didn't mean to!"*

*"No, Samuel." She smiled at him. "I'm crying because I'm so happy. I never dreamed I could ever be this happy."*

*He crossed his heart with his fingers. "I swear to*

*you, with God as my witness, Lettie, I will do every-*
*thing I can for the rest of my life to make you happy."*
*He smiled at her tenderly. She was so much more beau-*
*tiful in her nakedness than anything he could ever have*
*imagined.* What does she see in me? *Samuel wondered*
*again for perhaps the thousandth time since they'd first*
*started meeting at the dunes.* What does she see in a
*gangly, awkward fisherman?*

*"You—your body is so beautiful," Lettie said, fin-*
*gering the scar on his chest where a fishing hook had*
*caught him, tearing into his skin, ripping up his flesh*
*and spattering blood everywhere. He had always been*
*ashamed of the scar, ashamed of its angry puckered*
*red ugliness, but she thought it was beautiful, and he*
*thanked God again for bringing them together.*

*"I love you so, Lettie Hatch," Samuel murmured.*
*"It's you that's beautiful. I wish I were a poet so I could*
*write a poem about how beautiful you are."*

*"Samuel—" She reached for him, and he leaned*
*down and kissed her again.*

*A twig snapped behind them.*

—yes, meant to be together, and in that moment
Chris knew all the locker room talk about sex had just
been talk.

There was no way any of those boys could ever have
made love to a woman, he thought as he moved over
Jessie's naked body. This was just too incredible, too
amazing; nothing in his life had ever prepared him for
this. There was just no way. If they had, they wouldn't
talk about it in the crude ways they did, making jokes
and boasting about how good they were. It was beautiful, this coming together of two bodies, coming together in love, and he vowed he would never tell anyone
about this. He would never boast about her. Now he

understood what kept Joe and Lois together, understood the little looks they gave each other every once in a while when they thought he wasn't watching them. This was what they wrote songs about, poetry, books, and movies. This was love, and he loved her, he would never stop loving her, he would do anything for her. She had gasped a little when he entered her the first time, and he'd stopped, looking down at the tears in her eyes. "It hurts a little," she whispered, "but don't stop, please, Chris, I love you, I want to be close to you, just be gentle."

And even though his mind, his body, everything was urging him to go fast, to keep the feeling going, he slowed and tried to keep breathing. Nothing had ever felt this good. He'd never known anything could feel like this. He looked down and smiled at her, and she smiled back, even though tears were sliding down her cheeks, and she reached up and touched the side of his face—

And the front door opened.

*Lettie screamed, grabbing for her clothes, pressing them up against her nakedness as a man stepped into view from behind a dune.*

*"Well, isn't this just a pretty picture?" the man said, lighting a cigar and smiling at them both.*

*She recognized him and her entire body went rigid with terror. It was Axelrod—Orville Axelrod, her father's bootlegger—a man who broke the law at every opportunity and therefore couldn't be trusted. And worse: he was a friend of Sarah Jane's. Lettie had seen them talking to each other. Now he would tell Sarah Jane, and she would tell Lettie's father—and her father would kill Samuel. Tears welled up in her eyes.*

*"The senator's daughter and boat trash!" Axelrod*

*threw back his head and laughed. "If I hadn't seen this
with my own eyes, I'd never have believed it myself."
He winked at Lettie, who pressed her clothes tighter
against her, her face flushed with color.*

*"Will you excuse us, sir?" Samuel pulled his shirt on,
standing there, naked from the waist down. He seemed
to fumble for words. "Please allow us to cover ourselves."*

*Axelrod looked down at Lettie, and leered at her.
"None of my concern, now, is it, how the two of you
pleasure yourselves?" He turned his back to them and
started walking away, then turned and looked back.
"Though you might want to consider finding a more
private place than this. For shame, Miss Hatch." He
walked away, his mocking laugh echoing back to them.*

*"Oh, sweet Jesus, he's going to tell." Lettie scram-
bled to her feet. She began dressing hurriedly. "Oh my
God, what are we going to do?"*

*Samuel stopped her by putting his hands on her
shoulders. "Let's run away together, Lettie, tonight. We
can go so far away from here that no one will ever be
able to find us. We can go to California, find work
there, get married—"*

*Lettie choked back a sob. "You don't understand,
Samuel. My father would never stop looking for us.
Never." She buttoned her blouse with trembling fingers.
"Never." She grabbed her shoes and ran.*

*"Lettie!" he shouted after her, but she didn't turn back.
She just kept running, her head down. "Lettie! Come
back! Please!" Samuel sank to his knees in the sand
and started to shake, his entire body convulsing with
sobs. "Please come back. . . ."*

*And somehow, he knew he'd never see her again.*

"Jesus, Mary, and Joseph, what the hell is going on
here?"

Bobbie Noble flicked on the light switch. When he noticed the teenagers on the couch, their limbs intertwined, he immediately averted his eyes.

"Jessie? Chris? What the hell?"

Bobbie. Chris had forgotten about Bobbie. Joe and Lois had hired him to watch the property for them during the winter. He was probably making a regular check—

*Shit!*

Chris fumbled for his underwear, pulling it on. *Oh, Christ, this is bad, this is horrible, this is the worst thing that could ever have happened, the only thing worse would be if Lois showed up, oh God, why is this happening to me?*

Jessie didn't bother with her bra or underwear. She pulled on her sweatshirt and her jeans. "Why are you spying on us?" she demanded, standing to face him. "Did *she* send you?"

"I'm not spying," Bobbie said indignantly. "I'm doing my job. I came by and saw the candlelight. You're lucky I didn't call the cops—which was my first thought."

Chris slid his sweatshirt back on. "Bobbie, I'm so sorry—"

Jessie whirled around. "What are you apologizing for? He's the one who should be apologizing!"

He gaped at her. Her eyes were blazing. "Jessie—"

He didn't recognize her. Her eyes were black, filled with rage.

She looked like—someone else.

*You don't know what it's like, Chris. To have your mind suddenly seem as if it's not your own.*

Bobbie still had his back turned. "Everyone decent? You better be, sugarplums, cuz I'm turning around."

Jessie drew closer to him, her eyes shooting daggers.

"You're going to tell her, aren't you?" Jessie spat the words out venomously. "Aren't you?"

Bobbie took a deep breath. "Tell who?"

"Her! My stepmother!"

"I—I don't know what I'll tell her—"

"Oh, you'll tell her all right. You probably can't wait to tell her, can you? Dirty little man!" She grabbed her shoes and shoved past Bobbie, out into the night. The door slammed behind her.

Chris ran to the door in just his underwear. "Jessie!" he shouted after her as she ran off down the dark street. "Jessie, come back!" He sank to his knees, and tears filled his eyes. He knew he couldn't run after her. Not now. Not with Bobbie here. He looked up at the older man. "You've ruined *everything*."

Bobbie crossed his arms over his chest. "Don't get me wrong, kid. I'm all for young love, but somehow I don't think your parents know you're here, do they? Aren't you supposed to be like in Connecticut or somewhere? Going to school?"

Chris got to his feet and sank down onto the couch. He'd go after Jessie, take the shuttle into Provincetown and find her. But he had to convince Bobbie not to tell what he'd seen to Lois and Joe—and, more importantly, to Jessie's stepmother.

"Jessie asked me to come up. I've missed her. I wanted—"

Bobbie sighed. "Okay, I'm going to come clean here, okay? I probably should have in the first place."

"Huh?"

"Chris, I've known about you and Jessie for quite a while. Karen knows, too."

"Karen?"

"Jessie's stepmother. She's cool. Jessie won't give her a chance, but she's cool. She'd be very supportive of the two of you seeing each other." He grinned. "Though I don't think she knows you've gone this far—I certainly didn't." He leaned over and tossed Chris's jeans to him. "Put your pants on, please."

"Her stepmother knows?" Chris stared at him, struggling into his jeans. "All this time—*she knew*? And didn't say anything? Why?"

"We saw you two one day on the street." Bobbie shrugged. "It was pretty obvious what was going on. Karen was worried about Jessie, and when we saw you two on the street that day—well, I thought it would be a good idea to hire you to help me do the work on the house. I mean, it would give you two an opportunity to be around each other . . ." His voice trailed off. "I guess I shouldn't have. Good thing I don't have any kids of my own."

"You can't tell Mrs. Kaye about this," Chris pleaded. "You can't, Bobbie, please."

"I kind of have to, Chris. You're both minors—"

"You don't understand, Bobbie."

Bobbie sat down opposite him in a chair. "Okay, explain it to me so I can."

Chris did the best he could. He started at the beginning, about how he'd first spotted Jessie on the street back in June, how he made up his mind to meet her. He talked, and talked, and Bobbie just sat there listening, nodding from time to time. "This was the first time we . . ." Chris stuttered. "The first time we actually tried . . . well, you know."

"Yeah, I know," Bobbie said. "And I don't see any condom wrapper on the floor."

Chris's face burned.

"Safe sex. Baby-making. Need I say more?"

"I hear you, I hear you."

"But why was she so scared?" Bobbie asked. "You

said she was freaking about stuff. That's why she asked
you to come down? What's she so scared of?"

Chris took a deep breath and told him the rest of it.
The dreams. The visions. The circle of time. The sense
that sometimes . . . they felt they were different people.

"Even tonight," Chris said. "As I was making love to
her. It was strange. But I had the feeling we weren't in
the house. I thought we were outside. In the sand . . ."

Bobbie raised an eyebrow. "So you believe all this?"

"I don't know what to believe, Bobbie. I just know I
was fine when I was away from here, back at school.
But as soon as I came back, it was like that day I called
Jessie 'Lettie.' Jessie says it's still happening. . . ." He
remembered the look in her eyes right before she left.
"I think I'm starting to believe her, yeah."

Bobbie let out a long sigh. "Chris, you know I have
to tell Karen. I have to. I don't have a choice."

"You can't!"

"If Jessie is having these delusions about being possessed by Lettie Hatch, I have to tell Karen. She's my
friend and Jessie is her stepdaughter, and Jessie needs
help. You have to see that. I mean, you do care about
her, don't you?"

"I love her," Chris said simply. "And what about
me? Do I need therapy, too?"

Bobbie just shrugged.

"So are you going to tell my parents, too?"

"Tell ya what, Chris—get your stuff. You're staying
at my place this weekend. No, no arguments. If you
don't, the first thing I'm doing when I get home is calling your mother, okay?" Bobbie stood up and smiled.
"Don't forget, I know your mother. I know exactly
what will happen if she finds out about this. You're a
good kid, Chris, and if you and Jessie want to—you
know"—he waved at the couch—"we're not going to

be able to stop you. But I want us to go talk to Sophie tomorrow. She's a friend of mine."

"Sophie?"

Bobbie opened the door, and stood aside for Chris to pass. "You know her as Madame Nadja." He clapped Chris on the back. "And she's not a fake—just so you know. If she confirms your story—"

"You won't tell?"

"I can't promise that, Chris, much as I'd like to." Bobbie locked the door behind him. "But maybe we can figure out something."

# Chapter 16

The girl was going to kill her.

*Stop it*, Karen scolded herself. It was just this old house that was making her edgy and nervous. This creepy, smelly, musty old house, and the storm blowing in off the sea. Karen had never experienced a storm quite like this, sitting in a one-hundred-year-old house built on a sand spit, with waves crashing at the back door. She half expected the house's foundation—just wooden pilings, after all—to crumble, and the sea to flow in at them, carrying them out in the surf.

"It's not what you expected, is it, Karen?" the girl asked her.

Jessie had come home from wherever she went at night. She had seemed surprised to discover Karen at home. Karen had hastily explained that due to the storm she wouldn't be joining Philip in Boston until tomorrow morning instead of tonight. She expected Jessie to shrug and head upstairs to her room as she usually did. But instead she had held Karen's gaze, walking into the living room and sitting opposite her. The girl's demeanor left Karen unnerved. Alice Winn was out for the night. It was just she and Jessie, alone in the house.

That's when the lights went out. *Another power outage here at the end of the world*, Karen thought. They sat facing each other in the dark. Only a flicker of candlelight played against the girl's thin, bony face.

"I'd say it's quite romantic, quite the adventure."

Karen stood, ignoring the meaning inherent in the girl's words, leaving her to glower in the dark. "Your father told me that when storms hit the Cape, it's like being on a ship. You feel every surge of wind, every rocking of the sea."

Lightning crashed, filling the room with a terrible white light.

"My father loved being here with my mother," the girl said, once the room had returned to darkness. "Why do you think he has been here so infrequently this summer?"

"He's had a lot of commitments," Karen said, but she said it without any conviction behind her words.

She had reached the wall of glass that looked out from the house onto the roiling, whitecapped sea. The rain battered against the windows; the waves pounded the casements below. She really did feel as if she were on a ship—trapped—lost at sea. Karen wanted to get out of this house. No, it wasn't what she expected. Not at all.

"You'll love it on the Cape, darling," Philip had promised. "We'll be there, out on the deck, admiring the uncanny light. You and I and Jessie . . ."

*She is going to kill me.*

Just like Lettie Hatch killed her stepmother, eighty-odd years ago.

In this very house.

This very room.

And Lettie had been Jessie's age, too. Just sixteen, going on eighty-seven. And just as withdrawn and moody and eccentric. The villagers had called Lettie Hatch "ghost-girl" because she rarely ever left this house. The kids around town called Jessie "Spook" for precisely the same reason.

Even on the most glorious day this summer, Jessie had stayed indoors, sitting at the old rolltop desk overlooking the bay, writing in her leather-bound journal with her small, cramped penmanship. Her fingers and the sides of her hands were permanently stained with blue ink.

"Are you hungry?" Karen asked, turning around now to look at the girl. "I can make us some sandwiches—"

But Jessie was gone.

Up to her room. Karen could hear her footsteps now, above her head, across the ceiling.

*She's getting the knife.*

"Stop it," Karen scolded herself again.

*She's getting the knife and will be back here soon.*

"Stop!" she nearly shouted.

But she couldn't deny the terror. It had been building ever since she'd found Lettie Hatch's journal, sealed up in the wall. The articles had revealed that the senator and Sarah Jane had been stabbed to death right here, in this very room. Blood was everywhere, the newspapers had reported. Whoever had done such a vile deed had evidently enjoyed their task, smearing the blood all over the walls, drawing flowers and stars and happy faces with it.

That was a little detail she'd just learned, having obtained the original police report from the Provincetown Police Department.

The entry Karen had read this morning had sent her blood running cold. Lettie had written a poem.

*The moonlight beckons*
*And blood is spilled*

*As the sea keeps time
With unceasing fury*

Karen shivered. Involuntarily she began to hum the old, familiar jingle: *"Lettie Hatchet took a butcher knife, and with it took her father's life. To put an end to all her strife, she used it then on her father's wife."*

God, she needed Bobbie. And wouldn't you know it? The one weekend he was here in town, she was leaving for Boston first thing on a Cape Air flight.

"I'm getting weirded out, more all the time," she had told Bobbie when he stopped by yesterday. How good it was to see him. She'd missed him. They'd sat out on the deck drinking margaritas. "I mean, the more I read in this diary . . . and then compare to my own life . . . You have to admit the parallels are pretty creepy."

Bobbie was pouring them margaritas straight out of the blender. "Yeah, and the creepiest of them all is that little Spook you've got in the house. I can't believe it's been all these months and you two still have barely said a word to each other."

Karen had looked up then to see Bobbie gaze off toward the house. Behind the glass Jessie was inside, hunched over her rolltop desk, writing furiously in her journal. One more parallel between their story and Lettie Hatch's. Karen already knew the twisted thoughts Lettie had written. What might her strange stepdaughter be recording in *her* journal?

"I thought it was going to be so different, coming here," Karen said wistfully. "Philip and me sitting out here, admiring the sea."

"And instead you got me, the drag queen from hell," Bobbie said, laughing, settling down with his margarita. "So have you told Philip yet about the diary?"

Her face told him the answer.

"Okay, sweetums, if you're going to go it alone,

you've got to get yourself an agent." He shook his head at her. "You are sitting on a goddamned gold mine. You can tell Lettie's story while setting it against your own. *Is it happening again? Is the past about to repeat it-self?* It will be brilliant!"

"You are freaking me out," Karen had said, holding out her glass for a refill. Bobbie complied.

God, she wished he was here now.

Another crash of lightning lit up the house, and Karen thought she heard a noise.

Where was Jessie? Had she come back downstairs?

*I surprised her in the dark*, Lettie had written. The words from the musty old journal had burned them-selves into Karen's brain. Lettie described a night not unlike this one—a foreshadowing of the night she would commit murder. *It was a stormy night and the sea was wild. She was wandering in the dark, alone and scared. She turned just in time to see me—I saw the fear in her eyes! How delicious to hear her scream! How I laughed as I ran back upstairs.*

Not far from her, Karen heard the distinct creak of a floorboard.

"Jessie?" she called.

No answer.

"Jessie, where are you?"

Another creak. Karen was sure she heard another creak, even beneath the hard, driving rain upon the glass and the incessant crash of the sea against the wooden foundation of the house.

"Jessie!" she called. "*Answer me!*"

"Why do you call me by such a name?"

The voice was so plain, so real, so terrible, coming out from the darkness. Karen stood in utter stillness, unable to move, frozen by her terror.

The meager candlelight from the table picked out the vague shape of a girl, in a long dress, with hair falling past her shoulders, moving toward her through the shadows.

"Jessie?" Karen rasped.

"Come now, Sarah Jane. You know my name. You know who I am."

"No," said Karen, shaking horribly now.

"Say my name, Sarah Jane. *Tell me who I am!*"

"No!" Karen screamed, falling to her knees.

Lightning flashed. She saw the glint of a knife in the girl's hands, raised up over her head.

"No!" she screamed again. "No!"

More light. But not lightning this time. Harsh, blinding white light, shone directly into her eyes.

"What's wrong with you?" came another voice.

She recognized it as Jessie's. Beyond the brilliant glare Karen could see the girl approaching, a flashlight in her hand. She wore blue jeans and her hair tied back in a ponytail.

"What are you screaming about?" Jessie asked her contemptuously, standing over her now.

Karen got to her feet, her heart still shuddering in her chest and her ears. "I thought I . . . I . . ."

"Saw a ghost?" Jessie laughed, a brittle little sound. "Lettie Hatch, maybe?"

Karen glared at the girl.

"Really, Karen, I thought you weren't afraid of such things," Jessie said. "Didn't Daddy tell you not to listen to the legends that the locals will tell you? Or has that transvestite you've been hanging around with been filling your pretty little head with ghost stories? Really, now. My big brave stepmother, cowering on the floor."

Karen had to grip the edge of a table to balance herself. She counted her breaths, willing herself calm. She leveled her eyes with her stepdaughter's.

"First of all," she managed to say, "Bobbie isn't a transvestite. He's a performer. Second . . ." Her voice trailed off. What *was* her second point? *No, I haven't been listening to the tales of the locals. I've read it all, firsthand. In Lettie Hatch's own journal!*

No, she couldn't tell Jessie that.

"Second," Karen said, finding her voice, "I had a momentary hallucination. That's all. I'm over it now."

Jessie was shaking her head, smirking. "Won't Daddy find that amusing?"

"He'll think it a silly trick of the lightning, which is all it was." Karen was fumbling in the dark at the cupboard, trying to pull out a drawer. She finally managed, withdrawing a candle. "We just need more light around here until the power comes back."

She struck a match and lit the candle. Holding it up in her hands, she observed Jessie in the back-glow. The girl's face was pinched and bitter, an old woman despite her mere sixteen years. She was small but strong, with big hands like a man's.

*She's to be pitied, not feared*, Karen thought, looking at her now. Jessie had no friends, no hobbies, no interests other than writing in her journal. And that boy she'd been seeing—what was his name? He'd gone back to school, leaving Jessie all alone.

As alone as Karen was.

Her heart was still racing from the hallucination. Finding Lettie Hatch's journal had been both a blessing and a curse. A blessing because, as Bobbie was always pointing out to her, it could be her ticket to success. A curse because it made her jump at every sound, to see things that weren't really there, and to suspect all sorts of crazy things about Jessie. And about herself. And the voices in her head . . .

*There once was another lonely, unhappy girl in this house*, Karen thought. *A girl who hated a new young stepmother who dared to take her father away.*

A girl who wrote strange poetry in her journal.

Poetry of death and rage . . .

Karen walked up behind Jessie, carrying the candle. The girl was staring out into the storm, watching it as if mesmerized as the waves crashed against the house.

"Jessie, let's have something to eat," Karen suggested. "Maybe we can even pull on our raincoats, brave the storm, venture into town . . ."

The girl turned slowly to look at her. Something in her eyes made Karen pull back. There was a darkness there, darker than usual. Jessie looked straight at her, but wasn't really looking at her. It was as if she were looking at something else . . .

"Brave . . . the storm?" the girl said dreamily.

"Yes." Karen smiled. "What do you say?"

Jessie moved her eyes back to the ferocious sea. "An unceasing fury," she whispered.

Karen felt the fear rise again in her throat. "What did you say?"

"The sea keeps time," the girl replied, her voice far away, "with unceasing fury."

It wasn't possible. Lettie Hatch's journal hadn't left Karen's possession since she found it. Even now it was locked in her desk upstairs, and Karen had the only key. There was no way Jessie could have read it.

*So how would she know the words to Lettie's poem? Dear God!*

Karen stared over at her stepdaughter.

*They call it possession, don't they? The spirit of the dead taking hold of the living . . .*

"No," Karen murmured, moving away from the strange silent girl staring out into the storm.

*It's not possible, it's all just a coincidence, or else it's not Lettie's poem at all, it's a poem I'm not familiar with, a poem they teach in schools, so that Jessie would know it, and this stupid silly idea about possession would be—*

The lights suddenly flickered back into life.

"Oh!" Karen shouted, startled.

Bright yellow light filled the room. Voices boomed out of the television set, which came on in the middle of some inane sitcom, the laugh track crackling loudly and absurdly.

But Jessie didn't move from her position staring out the window at the roiling sea.

"*Finally*," Karen said, aware of how much her voice was trembling. "Let's just hope the power doesn't go out again. . . ."

Her eyes were drawn by something across the room. Something on the floor. She took a few steps toward it, blinking, her eyesight still unaccustomed to the light. It was the very spot on the floor where moments before she had cowered, convinced the ghost of Lettie Hatch stood over her, holding a knife over her head.

The spot where she had looked up, only to see it was really Jessie.

Karen gasped.

On the place where she had fallen, the place where she had braced herself against the dead girl's upraised knife, there was blood.

A puddle of bright red blood.

And with it, drawn with a hasty finger, were flowers and happy faces.

Karen screamed—

—and sat up in bed, gasping, her heart pounding in her throat.

Philip snored beside her, and outside the glass doors of the balcony, the lights of Boston spread out before her like stars.

How much of it had been a dream? She couldn't tell anymore. Dreams, real life . . . her voice, someone else's . . . it all blurred together in her mind. She slid out of bed and walked shakily to the bathroom. Yes, she had met Philip here in Boston only this morning, her plan to drive up on Friday night changed because of the storm. Yes, Jessie had come home, acting strange. Yes, the power had gone out—but had she seen the blood? Had that been real? Had Jessie seen it too?

She ran the tap, filling a glass with cold water. She splashed some on her face before drinking. She stared at herself in the mirror. She looked terrible. She was still a little groggy from the wine she'd drunk at the party.

Why couldn't she remember? There was a whole chunk of time she couldn't remember at all. From the moment the lights came back on in the house to the moment she stepped off the Cape Air flight onto the tarmac of Logan Airport. Philip had been waiting for her outside the gate. "Welcome to Boston," he said, and Karen felt as if she'd just woken up from a dream.

A nightmare.

The party tonight had been fun—her first public appearance as Philip's wife. Everyone had wanted to meet her, and everyone had been friendly and nice. She'd gotten tons of compliments on the pearls, on the little black silk dress she'd bought that afternoon at Nieman-Marcus. Philip had been beaming, obviously proud of her. He introduced her to everyone as "a greatly talented writer who's going to make everyone forget about me." It embarrassed her, and shamed her for the terrible thoughts she had been thinking. Here in Boston that strange, bitter, angry voice was gone from her head. And she hadn't had a headache all day.

*I do love Philip, and he loves me. Why was I being so petty and insecure?*

Holding on to his arm, gliding about the room, was a dream come true for Karen. *So this is what literary parties are like*, she thought as she circulated, a wine-glass in her hand. Maybe she'd drunk more than she should, but Philip was downing scotch like it was going out of style, so why not indulge? She slowed down enough so she didn't get drunk—God forbid she get drunk and do something stupid, like spill wine or become incoherent and sloppy, but the whole night turned out to be magic. Mary Ann Fletcher asked her what she was writing, and Karen had almost slipped and told her about the diary. But she recovered quickly enough and gushed about Vicky Knight, Reporter. "I can't wait to read your book," Mary Ann had said. "It sounds splendid."

Karen glowed the rest of the night from the kind words. *Mary Ann Fletcher wants to read my book!*

"Are you having fun, darling?" Philip had whispered to her when they ran into each other at the bar.

"I'm having the best time ever." She leaned over and kissed his cheek. "Thank you so much for this, Philip."

"All I want to do is make you happy." Philip touched her chin. "I know I'm an ass when I'm working, and I swear I'm going to make it up to you."

"I love you," she whispered as the bartender refilled her glass, and he kissed her again before walking back off into the crowd.

"What was that dream?" she asked her reflection in the mirror, sipping her water in the harsh bathroom light. But it was fading quickly enough as she walked back out into the bedroom again. The lights of Boston beckoned from outside. She quietly slid the glass doors open, slipping out onto the hotel balcony. Wrapping her arms around herself against the cold, she sat down in one of the chairs and crossed her legs.

*I can't keep the diary a secret from Philip any longer. It's wrong. He won't try to take it from me. He wouldn't do that. His own book is coming along well now. I need to tell him. He's my husband and he loves me.*

The lights of the Tobin Bridge sparkled in the purple night. *And I've got to get a grip. Why can't my head be as clear in Provincetown as it is sitting here on this balcony? Jessie isn't Lettie Hatch. There's no such thing as ghosts. I've been obsessed for weeks about the Hatches. Of course I'm going to dream about them.*

*Then again, maybe I was going crazy.*

She took another drink of water from the glass. Here, in Boston, away from Provincetown, everything seemed so clear. Philip wasn't perfect, and he should have told her about the history of the house, and about Ivy. But he didn't. And he apologized. *Time to move on, Karen.* She'd allowed those fears to color everything. She'd stopped trusting Philip. And their marriage would fall apart without trust.

*When we get back, I'm going to do better*, she decided. *I'm going to show him the diary and all the research I've done, and explain to him how I want to do the book. And I'm going to make more of an effort with Jessie, too. It's ridiculous that I've been such an immature bitch about her . . . she's just little more than a child, and she's had a major trauma—imagine what it would have been like to find your mother hanging from the rafters. And if Ivy was unbalanced, what must Jessie's life have been like when she was alive? She was there in the house with her all the time—that couldn't have been easy for her.*

She felt a surge of compassion rise in her chest for her stepdaughter.

*All this is probably why I've been having all those headaches—stress and tension.*

But had she seen the blood? Was there really blood on the floor? Those hideous flowers and faces drawn everywhere to mock her?

She shivered again. No, she wasn't going to surrender to such nonsense anymore. She loved her husband, and it was time to come clean with him, start afresh. Yes, that's what she was going to do. She toasted the city lights with her glass, and finished it off. She walked back into the bedroom, shut the door behind her, and slid under the covers up next to Philip's warmth. She closed her eyes.

Everything was going to be just fine.

# Chapter 17

"All right, all right, I said I'm *fucking coming*!"

Sophie's head hurt. She'd drunk too much the previous night, hoping to have a dreamless sleep. She was tired of dreaming about death, blood, and knives. But the scotch hadn't worked. The dreams had still come. She swung the door open and groaned.

"Bobbie! What the *hell* are you doing pounding on my door at this hour? Don't you have anything better to do than make my life a living hell?"

Bobbie held up a box of donuts and grinned. "I brought you breakfast. And a guest." He gestured, and the tall, skinny boy who'd been with the girl who'd started the whole mess in her head stepped onto the porch. He shuffled his feet nervously.

"You," Sophie said sourly. *Fucking great.*

"Hello," the kid said quietly.

"Aren't you going to invite us in?" Bobbie winked at her. He held the donuts up enticingly.

*Damn him.* Bobbie was too sweet to stay mad at long. Besides, she could never stay mad at anyone who brought her donuts. She held the door open and waved them in. "All right, already. Get your asses in here. I'll make coffee."

She led them into the kitchen and started coffee. Bobbie and the kid took their seats at the table, a cracked Formica relic from the '70s Sophie had bought at a yard sale for twenty dollars. It sagged a little in the middle and was probably going to collapse one day, but until it did, it worked just fine. She nudged her cat out of the way and lumbered over to the table to snatch a glazed donut.

"So what is this morning visit about?" She licked icing off her fingers. Her head still hurt, but the donut was helping.

"Well," Bobbie explained, helping himself to some coffee, "Chris here tells me you, um, *consulted* with Jessie Kaye back in August."

*Consulted.* That was one way of putting it. "I'd rather not think about that, thank you very much. Pour me some coffee."

Bobbie obliged, taking down two more cups. "Chris?"

The tall kid just shook his head, his hair getting in his face. Sophie looked at him. He looked mutinous. *Don't have to be a psychic to tell he doesn't want to be here*, she thought. She looked back over at Bobbie, who was liberally dosing her coffee with sugar. He handed it to her and she held it, letting the heat from the cup warm her hands. She examined the tall kid's face.

He was good looking, in that way teenagers have—soft skin, a little bit of acne here and there, and that fresh, innocent look. He was maybe a bit too skinny, but there was a tension about him like a coiled spring. He was probably a lot stronger than he looked—he looked as though a strong wind would carry him away like a scarecrow. His neck was long, and he had a prominent Adam's apple that bobbed every time he swallowed. His brown eyes were almond shaped, and there was a spark of intelligence there. He was wearing an orange sweatshirt that hung off him, but wasn't quite long enough to reach the waistband of his baggy carpenter's jeans, showing a ribbon of tanned, smooth hairless skin. He ran his long fingers through his shoulder-length brown hair, messing it up. It was already wind-blown, stray hairs standing up at weird angles. His mouth was set in a straight line, and a vein pulsed in his neck. He didn't have enough facial hair to require a daily shave yet, but the hairs above his lip were darkening. His thick eyebrows were knitted together, his forehead wrinkled and scrunched in a scowl.

*He'd probably be cute if he smiled once in a while,* Sophie thought. When he noticed she was looking at him, he looked back at her, matching her cool apprais-ing gaze. *Probably thinks I'm a hideous old witch—which is what I look like most of the time anyway.*

Bobbie sat back down at the table. "Okay, since no-body else around here seems to be willing to talk, I'll start." He leaned forward. "Sophie, Chris is here under duress."

"Du-uh." She rolled her eyes. "Okay, let's get to the point, Bobs. I ain't got all day."

Bobbie arched an eyebrow. "Oh?" He grinned again, damn him. "Busy social schedule?"

"Fuck you." She looked at Chris. "I guess it's safe to assume this has something to do with your little girl-friend?"

Chris reddened. "You're the psychic. You tell us."

*Okay, smart-ass.* She closed her eyes and leaned back in her chair, tried to focus her mind through the ache, reached out with her mind, and concentrated. Images started coming to her, not as clear as usual—*damn that scotch, anyway*—but while they were a little on the fuzzy side, it was pretty clear what she was seeing. She opened her eyes, a smile spreading over her face. She looked at Bobbie. "You caught them?" She couldn't help herself. She started to laugh. "Coitus interruptus?"

Chris stared at her, his face filling with color. "You told her, didn't you?" he whispered, turning his head back to Bobbie, his eyes blazing.

"He didn't tell me anything." Sophie picked her donut back up and took another bite. "I'm psychic, remember?" She finished the donut off and resisted taking another. "Last night. Your parents' place. They don't know you're here. They think you're in—oh, fuck, I couldn't see that part—but they think you're off somewhere with your roommate. Instead you snuck up here to meet your girlfriend. Jessie. Bobbie walked in on you." She pressed her fingers to her forehead. The ache was still there, getting stronger. "It was the first time for both of you, wasn't it?"

Chris just gaped at her.

"You see?" Bobbie was asking him. "I told you she was good."

"So," Sophie said, keeping her eyes on Chris. "Is the situation we discussed last time you were here getting any better?"

"She hasn't—" Chris broke off.

Sophie nodded. "The dreams have stopped, haven't they?"

Chris nodded.

*And I know why*, Sophie thought. *She passed them on to me. Somehow when we connected that day, the veil of time shifted, and that's why I've been having these horrible dreams about knives and blood and killing, why I've had to drink myself into a stupor every night so I won't dream, why I've woken up with a bitch of a hangover every morning for the last few months. Thank you very much, Miss Jessie Kaye.*

"Is it true, Sophie?" Bobbie asked. "Is it true what Jessie thinks? That the past is haunting her—that the spirit of Lettie Hatch has returned to live inside her? I trust you, Sophie. What did you sense when she was here?"

"You're asking me, really, if Jessie is delusional." Sophie leaned back. She closed her eyes again and took deep breaths. The pain was fading a little, but the throb was still there. "You want to know if this is real or if it's just a fucked-up kid who needs a shrink. Look, I've been going through hell since that day, okay? She is not delusional. I sensed the past haunting the present."

"It's just so fantasic, so hard to believe," Bobbie said.

"Do I know what the hell is going on? No, I really don't. But I can guess." Sophie shrugged. "The Hatch murders—look at the setup from eighty years ago. It's been replicated today, almost exactly. A famous widowed man with a teenaged daughter. A new wife, not much older than the daughter. There's even a live-in tutor, just like there was eighty years ago." She shrugged. "The boy here, Chris? He's a part of it somehow. It's a circle of time."

"That's bullshit," Chris burst out, glaring at her. "I read that book. There wasn't anything in it about ghosts and hauntings. It was about—" He fumbled for the right words. "Metaphysics. Time. It didn't say anything about the stuff you told us. That was all bullshit."

"The book simply explains, in scientific terms, how time really works. I told you to read it so you'd have a basis for understanding what's happening." She frowned, looking at him. "You don't want to believe. It goes against everything your mother has programmed into you—it's not rational, not logical. Ghosts? The past haunting the present? The past replaying itself until it gets things right? That can't be explained away, wrapped up, and neatly put into a box, so your mind rejects it."

The kid had shut up. He was listening to her.

She leaned across the table and looked into his eyes. "You've had the dreams, too—but you refuse to believe. You've sensed someone other than yourself sharing your mind, but you won't accept the truth. You think it's your subconscious mind or collective hysteria or the power of suggestion. But it's not, buddy. There's something Mommy doesn't know."

Chris's mouth opened, then closed. His eyes had widened as she'd spoken, the redness draining out of his face. "I—I—" He closed his mouth and looked away from her.

"Didn't you feel it last night, when you were with her?" Sophie felt tired. *I just wish they'd go away and leave me alone, let me go back to bed and forget all of this, forget I ever saw them, forget I talked to them.* "Not to be crude, but when you were on top of her, didn't you feel it had happened before?"

Chris didn't answer. His fingers fidgeted, and he kept his eyes firmly focused on his hands.

She softened toward him. "It's okay to be afraid, Chris. It's okay."

"Yes!" he shouted, so suddenly that Sophie fell back against her chair, which rocked on its back legs before slamming back down to the floor. Down Sophie went— all of her. Bobbie flinched, and the cat shot out of the room as if a firecracker were tied to his tail.

"Are you all right?" Bobbie jumped up, standing over her, trying to help her stand.

"Yeah, yeah," Sophie huffed. "I've got enough padding on me to cushion a fall." She took Bobbie's hand and gripped the table and got to her feet. She looked over at the kid. His eyes had welled up with tears.

"It's true," he said. "Every time I'm with Jessie I

feel like it's all happened before. Even before I met her, I was so drawn to her—now I know why. We say things, and it's like—it's like we remember saying them before. Last night—" He choked.

Bobbie put a hand on his arm reassuringly. "Go on, Chris, get it all out."

He flushed red again. "I kept thinking—I kept thinking—we weren't at my parents' at all, we were out by the dunes, and it was night, and—"

"And what, Chris?" Sophie prodded.

*"We got caught! A man came along and caught us! And right when he did, Bobbie walked through the front door!"* He put his head down on the table and started crying.

Sophie walked around the table. She was about to rest her hand on the poor kid's back when she stopped.

*Don't do it, Sophie, it's dangerous. If you touch him you'll open yourself up to more of what you've been suffering with. It's the worst thing you could do. You swore you would never do this again. It hurts too much, don't do it—*

She placed both hands on his shaking shoulders—

*—and everything faded, and she was no longer in her kitchen, but instead floating along the beach, through the dunes. She could hear the waves gently lapping at the shore. There was no moon, the sky was gray and cloudy, but she could see clearly. She could hear sounds coming from around the dune up in front of her, she could hear the sounds of two people who were making love, whispering to each other as their bodies came together. She was aware of another presence as well, someone who had dark thoughts in his mind. She tried to focus, to clear her mind and get a read on him, but the harder she tried, the less she*

seemed to sense him. So she reached out to the love-making couple again, and felt an overwhelming sense of love, pure love. They truly loved each other. They were so happy to be together, even though the joy of being together was always followed by the almost unbearable pain of being apart.

Then suddenly the other was there again, she could sense him, and his thoughts weren't pure, his thoughts were amused in an ugly way. His soul was dark. He had chosen a selfish dark path early in life until it blackened his mood and his soul, and he had a plan, a plan that involved the young couple, a plan that spelled death and doom and blood, and then Sophie wasn't on the beach anymore. She was inside a house, a darkened house in the middle of a bad snowstorm, the wind was howling and the snowflakes were coming down so hard and fast that it was almost as blinding as a hard rain. The house was cold and she could feel the presence of evil there—not evil in the biblical sense of Satan or demons, nothing like that, but the evil of a mind poisoned with hate and envy. A mind that was twisted. In the darkness Sophie could hear blood splattering, the horrible sound of a knife coming down through the air and slicing into flesh with enough force to splinter bone. She heard maniacal laughter. It was the most chilling sound she'd ever heard in her life.

And then suddenly she sensed purity, goodness, again—love. It came from another part of the house, and she knew the love was supposed to conquer the evil that was taking place, but it was going to be thwarted. That was the worst part of it. The love, the light, was not going to be able to fulfill its destiny, unable to cleanse the house the way it had been ordained. The play wasn't going right in this circle, the circle wasn't going to close—

She let go of Chris and staggered backward. Even though the contact was broken she could still feel the waves of evil. It was infecting her in that insidious way that evil has, and she backed deliriously into the wall. She heard a crash as something fell, and then there were the voices of both Bobbie and Chris, saying things she couldn't understand. Then finally there was merciful darkness.

When she opened her eyes she was sitting on the floor, her back against the wall. Bobbie and Chris were looking down at her.

"Are you okay, babe?" Bobbie asked.

"The circle has to be closed," she managed to say.

Bobbie held out a glass of water to her, and she gratefully drank from it. She looked up at Chris. "What did you feel?"

"Bad stuff." He shuddered and hugged himself. "I felt—real bad shit going down."

"You should be afraid." She felt tired, drained the way she always did after using her power to its fullest extent. "The circle has to be closed."

"How?" Bobbie was shaking.

"The stepmother. What's her name? Karen. I need to see her. Bobbie, you know her. Get her over here to see me." With help from both Bobbie and Chris, Sophie slowly managed to get to her feet. "I—I'm really tired and I need to lie down for a while."

"What about Jessie?" Chris asked.

Sophie turned to him, and opened herself just a bit. He loved the girl, she could feel that quite readily. He was worried about her. He was willing to do whatever it took to help her.

Sophie forced a smile on her face. "It'll be okay, Chris. Do you understand what I'm trying to say? It wasn't meant to happen the way it did the last time—to the Hatches. And we're not going to let it happen to the

Kayes." Even as she said the words, however, doubts began to cloud her mind.

*Oh, sure, Sophie, you're going to be strong enough to stop the evil, strong enough to close the circle. You weren't able to stop it the other time—*

She closed her eyes. *Stop it*, she admonished herself. *You can do it.*

*Tired, so tired.*

She didn't hear them leave, didn't hear the door shut behind them as they walked out of her house, but she knew they were gone. She staggered back over to the couch with what strength she had left, and sank back down into its softness. Two cats immediately jumped up on her and curled into balls among the folds of her flesh. Sophie closed her eyes and everything went dark again.

The rest of the day passed in a daze. Everything she did was out of habit, the mechanical moving of her body in response to biological imperatives to eat, drink, and relieve herself. She had no energy, her mind was unable to focus, and she gratefully allowed her brain to not function. It was just like the other time. The last time, when things had gone so horribly wrong, when she had tried to close the circle and couldn't, she had felt just like this. Lethargic, confused. The memory of that time still pained her. She hadn't been able to stop the chain of events that had already been set into motion.

The next day, Sunday, she spent in the same fugue state, moving through the day mechanically, her mind unable to focus on anything. But Monday morning she was herself again. She woke at ten, feeling fully rested and alive again, her brain turned back on, which was, she realized, a good thing.

*She's coming.*

She lit the candles in the living room, made herself a

pot of coffee, and made an omelette to eat. Afterward, she sat back down on the couch to wait. The stepmother.

*I can do this, I can, I can close the circle. I can help these people. Isn't that why God gave me this gift, so I could help? It's what I have to do, it's why I'm here, it's all preordained, I can do it.*

At eleven o'clock, there was a knock on the door. She opened it.

"Hello." The woman who stood there was pretty, maybe twenty-three, twenty-four years old. Sophie couldn't get an exact read on that. The woman had shoulder-length black hair and wide green eyes. Underneath the heavy trench coat she was wearing it was obvious she had a slender figure. *One of those lucky bitches who can eat whatever they want and never gain a pound,* Sophie thought, plastering a welcoming smile on her face.

"My name is Karen Kaye." She fidgeted with the belt of the coat, clearly uncomfortable. "I really don't know why I'm here. Bobbie—"

"Bobbie is a master at talking people into doing things they don't want to do," Sophie said, motioning for Karen to come inside. "Please, have a seat. My name's Sophie. Can I get you anything to drink?"

Karen shook her head. "No, thank you."

Sophie sat down in her reclining chair. Karen didn't remove her coat, just sat on the edge of the couch.

"Mrs, Kaye, I asked Bobbie to send you here for a reason."

Karen gave her a faint smile.

"I won't beat around the bush, then. I'm sure you have other things to do than humor some total stranger."

"Any friend of Bobbie's . . ." Karen laughed hollowly.

Sophie kept her eyes open, focusing her mind on Karen. *Creative, intelligent, but insecure. The husband doesn't help in that regard. She has doubts about the marriage. She's from New Orleans, and gets homesick more than she wants to admit, because to admit it would mean she's not happy here, and she wants everyone to think she's happy.*

"Mrs. Kaye, have you noticed anything strange in the last few months? Have you been reacting to things in different ways than you usually do?"

"I don't know what you mean." Karen stiffened.

*Bull's-eye.* "You know the history of your house."

"Yes." She gave another short laugh. "Everyone knows the history of the house."

"Doesn't it strike you as an odd coincidence that the living situation in your house is the same as the situation was eighty years ago?"

Karen bit her lip. "Yes, that has occurred to me."

"Have you been having strange dreams, by any chance?"

"No stranger than usual."

*She's lying.* "Mrs. Kaye—"

"Karen."

"Karen. I'm trying to help you, so please." Sophie closed her eyes. "You've been dreaming about Sarah Jane Hatch, haven't you?"

The green eyes widened. "Look, Bobbie told me that Jessie's been to see you. I came here because I'm concerned about her. . . ."

"But you've been having dreams, too, haven't you? You've felt some kind of connection with Sarah Jane?"

"Well, yes, I suppose—"

"And it's made you think in strange ways. Made you doubt your husband, your marriage. You feel angry much of the time, resentful . . ."

She noticed the paleness creeping across Karen's face as she recognized Sophie's words. *Slow down, you're scaring her.*

"Karen," Sophie said, "I'm a psychic. I know things. And I'm worried about the situation in your home."

She launched into the speech prepared in her head. Sophie explained about the circle of time, about the theory of unfinished business of the past shadowing the present. Karen just stared at her as she talked, not interrupting, but she was listening. That was the important thing. Some of what Sophie was saying was sinking in.

When she finished, Karen sat there in silence for several seconds. Then she let out a long breath. "So you think Jessie might be . . ." Her voice trailed off. "Possessed?"

"Not all the time. And not in a Linda Blair *Exorcist* kind of way. Think of the past and kind of like a radio station that sometimes comes in strongly, crowding out another station next to it. And sometimes it fades out, depending on conditions, and the other station comes through full blast."

"Then Jessie is in danger. . . ."

"Sweetie," Sophie said. "It's not just Jessie."

She reached over and took Karen's hand firmly—

*—and she was in a small room, with a crucifix the only adornment on the whitewashed walls, and there was a woman on the bed, pregnant and screaming. She was in pain. She was giving birth. A nun was sponging off her forehead, murmuring gently to her that she was doing fine, that everything was going to be just fine. All she needed to do was simply focus on a spot on the wall and concentrate on pushing. The woman's blond hair was hanging wet in her face, and sweat was rolling off her in waves. She was in pain, but she was also angry, angry and bitter. How could he have done this to her? He said he loved her, but he had only used*

*her, and now look at this mess she was in. She wouldn't
ever be able to return home. She wouldn't be able to
hold her head up in that godforsaken hellhole. Once
this was over she was going away. She was leaving, she
was going to start over somewhere else and never
come back to Louisiana. She was meant for better than
this, better than all of them in this godforsaken backwater. She was destined for greatness.*

Karen pulled away from her, rubbing her hand, her
eyes wide, her face white. "What . . . what just happened?"

Sophie's head rang with pain from the vision. "The
bloodline," she muttered. "That's the key, the key to
everything, it's the *bloodline, oh, dear God*—" She pressed
her hands to her forehead.

"Are you okay?" Karen rose, her face concerned.
"Maybe I should go get help?"

"No, I'm fine." Sophie staggered to her feet, hearing
herself babbling, unable to stop. "I'll be fine. The
bloodline—"

"You had the same vision I did?" Karen asked.
"About the woman giving birth?"

Sophie nodded, rubbing her temples.

"What do you mean by the bloodline?"

The pain ratcheted up to another level. "Look, Karen,
I know I asked you to come here, but this headache—
I've had them before—it's not going away any time
fast. I just—I just need to lie down for a while." She
gave Karen a weak smile. "We'll talk more, I promise."

"But the vision—and what you told me—about
Jessie—" She hugged herself. "About me!"

Sophie knew that she shouldn't let Karen go, that it
wasn't fair to spring all this on her, then kick her out.
But the pain was too much, and getting worse. She

needed to lie down, she needed to close her eyes, she had to rest, she was barely conscious, her mind hadn't overloaded like this—

*—since the last time she tried to close a circle. She wasn't strong enough then, and she wasn't strong enough now. . . .*

"Please, Karen, I'm sorry," Sophie said. "I can't tell you any more today. Just be careful. Just . . ." She could barely speak. "We'll talk again."

"If you thought you were helping me," Karen told her, "all you've done is frighten me."

"I'm sorry . . . I . . ." Sophie couldn't force any other words from her lips. *I'm sorry I failed you. . . .*

She leaned back into the recliner, her breath coming in gasps, her mind still racing and jumping around, unable to focus, unable to think clearly. As though from a million miles away, she heard the door shut behind Karen and she knew she'd failed. All she'd done was scare her. That wouldn't do any good—

—then merciful darkness descended and her eyes closed.

But even in her sleep she knew she was not alone.

Someone—something—had come forward from the past, and now it was in the house with her.

Sophie had no idea how long she'd been in the recliner. She had no sense of time. She tried to open her eyes, but didn't have the strength to do even that. There was someone—*something*—watching her. She could sense it—she tried to reach out with her mind, but nothing came to her. Finally she forced her eyes open, but they didn't focus. She was still too drained, too tired. Her mind was still short-circuited. It had all been too much for her.

*Smoke.*

*The house is on fire.*

She summoned all her strength and focused her

eyes. The curtains were on fire, the other wall—the candles, oh God, the candles . . .

She pushed herself up, but her legs gave out underneath her, and she fell to the floor in a heap.

*I'm not alone.*

She opened her eyes again. The room was full of smoke. The heat—the heat! She could feel her skin starting to smart as her body woke up to the danger, adrenaline pumping through her heart and veins. The front door was engulfed in flames. She looked back at the kitchen. It, too, was a raging inferno.

She started crawling to the front door.

But there was someone, something, that didn't want her to escape.

Over the crackle of the flames Sophie heard laughter.

Maniacal laughter. The same she'd heard before.

She gagged suddenly from smoke. Her caftan was on fire. She reached down and tried to put out the flames, jumping up her clothes like little imps. Her hands burned but she got the flames out. But then above her, she heard a terrible cracking sound, as the timbers fell from the ceiling, blocking the front door—

She heard the laughter again. Sophie choked, trying to remember everything she'd heard about fires. Stay close to the floor, the air's better down there, it's the smoke that kills people, not the flames—

She heard Lance howling in the kitchen. The cats were screaming. She looked up.

"Oh God, oh God," Sophie croaked out.

Through the smoke, she could still make out a figure standing in front of her, blocking the way into the kitchen.

Her eyes widened in horror. In that instant, she knew she'd been wrong, wrong about everything. She wasn't going to get out. She was going to die here in the flames, and she'd been wrong, so unbelievably fucking wrong about everything, but now she understood, finally she understood. The circle of time—it was more than that. The enemy they faced was far more powerful than she had realized, and the power it held was not going to allow the circle to be closed. How could she have been so, so blind, so wrong? She'd thought it had all been coincidence, the circle opening again as the players went into place—but there was a reason why the veil between the planes had come so close, why it had opened, here, now, in this way—

*I'm going to die, this can't be happening to me, how could I have been so wrong? Oh, dear Lord, they are all going to die. I've got to get out of here, I've got to warn them, I've got to . . .*

The figure just stood there watching her in the flames.

With a superhuman bolt Sophie managed to grab hold of the telephone cord on the table ahead of her. She yanked on it, knocking the phone off the table, the cordless headset falling from its cradle and clattering to the floor. The heat was growing stronger, and she coughed as she tried to reach forward enough to grasp the phone.

That laughter again. *That horrible laughter!*

It was the same laughter, the same mania, she'd heard in her dreams.

Her eyes tearing, she punched in speed-dial three. She heard the phone ringing, and then the answering machine clicked on.

"Howdy, boys and girls! You've reached Bobbie! Can't get to the phone right now, and you know what to do, so do it now, babe, or forever hold your peace!" *Beeeep!*

"Bobbie," Sophie croaked out. "Bobbie, I was wrong, wrong about everything. . . . There's a reason it's happening now. And it's strong, Bobbie, stronger than I knew. It's the bloodline . . . the bloodline . . . you've got to tell them . . ."

Her throat filled with smoke. In an instant she couldn't speak, couldn't even think. As she lost consciousness, the phone fell from her hand.

And the last thing Sophie heard before she died was the hideous laughter that had haunted her dreams.

# Chapter 18

Karen staggered on the sidewalk, almost bumping into a guy on a bicycle. She muttered an apology and kept walking, her head held down against the wind. It was so cold, so unbelievably cold. She walked along the storefronts, so many closed now, with signs reading THANKS FOR A GREAT SEASON, SEE YOU NEXT SPRING. The few that were still open had strung miniature plastic Halloween pumpkins around their doors, but the upcoming holiday meant nothing to Karen. She felt lost, oblivious. She didn't see the people she passed on the street. She wasn't aware of the cars that honked at her to move so they could get around her on the narrow street. She felt sick to her stomach, and another one of her headaches was coming on.

*It had been so good in Boston. And now I'm back. And it's starting all over again.*

*Why did I listen to Bobbie?* Karen's mind raced as she walked aimlessly. *Why did I let Bobbie talk me into going to see to that crazy woman?*

Madame Nadja—or Sophie, whatever her name was— was definitely crazy. A flake. Karen shuddered, hoping she was okay. She had seemed pretty disoriented when she left. *She's a drunk*, Karen told herself. Bobbie might trust her, but he admitted she drank a lot. And there had been a number of empty bottles of scotch on the floor.

*Why couldn't we have stayed in Boston? Why did we have to come back?*

They'd returned late last night. The weekend had been great. Karen had never felt so close to Philip before, not even during those first few glorious days in New Orleans. Philip loved her. Somehow this great, big, wonderful, famous writer had fallen in love with her and she was happy. They'd toured the city hand in hand: Bunker Hill, the Old North Church, all the places she'd memorized in American history but had never really given much thought. Boston was a beautiful city, and she'd fallen under its spell. It wasn't New Orleans, of course, but nothing was. Boston would hold a place in her heart; it had given her a much-needed second honeymoon with the man she loved.

She'd fallen asleep in the car on the way back, as they wound up the long slender arm of Cape Cod. Philip kept stroking her hair with his right hand as he steered with his left. The house was quiet and still when they got home, Jessie's door closed. They'd tumbled into bed, falling asleep in each other's arms, and Karen had awoken this morning determined to put a fresh new face on everything.

It all seemed to be working. She had a pleasant chat with Alice over coffee. She told her all about Boston and Alice agreed it was a lovely city. Karen felt herself warming to the woman again. Her feelings about Bobbie, after all, were just part of who she was, part of her generation, part of the way she was raised.

Jessie, of course, hadn't come down for breakfast, but Karen was determined to befriend her stepdaughter.

*I can charm her. I'll just talk to her every day, make a point of finding something to talk about. Pretty soon she'll realize I'm not her enemy.*

Whistling happily, she'd carried a thermos of coffee up to her office. It was cold up there as always, and it was going to get colder. Alice had told her that there was a major cold front coming down from Canada, with talk of snow. Karen shuddered. Did it always snow this early? She was assured it did not, but that the forecast for this winter was bleak. *The Farmer's Almanack* predicted this could be the coldest winter in years.

*Stop bitching about the cold weather*, Karen told herself just that morning as she had settled down in front of her computer. *You knew it was going to be cold up here when you married Philip and agreed to come here to live. Stop being such a spoiled whiny brat.*

She'd set the thermos down, turned on her computer, and whistled happily while she waited for it to boot up. She unlocked the top drawer and pulled out Lettie's diary.

*Tonight I'll tell Philip about this, get it all out in the open. Then everything will be just fine—no more secrets between us. It was ridiculous to think he'd try to take it away from me, keep it for himself. He's a big enough name already. He's already a star, everyone knows who he is. He'll be just as happy and excited for me as Bobbie was.*

As though thinking of him made him show up, Bobbie had climbed the stairs a few moments later. "Hey, snookums."

"Bobbie!"

"Alice let me in." He pulled a chair over and sat on it backwards. "So how was Boston? I want all the details."

So she gave them. Including how she had resolved to be happy and glad and give everything a new start.

"I've got a whole new lease on life." She grinned at him. "Everything is going to be just fine. I didn't even wake up with a headache this morning. Can you believe it? I feel like a new person—a better one."

"That's great." He was smiling, but the tone in his voice was wrong.

Karen looked over at him, her smile fading. "Bobbie. What's up? Did something happen with David?"

"David?" He looked startled. "Oh, no, no, sugarplum. Everything's fine with David. Couldn't be better."

"But something's wrong."

He swallowed. "Um, I need you to do me a *huge* favor."

"Okay." She searched his face. Something was definitely wrong. The sparkle that was usually in his eyes wasn't there. "Spill."

"I want you to go talk to a friend of mine. Her name's Sophie. Sophie Pilkowski."

"Why?"

"I need you to go over there now."

"*Now*?" She frowned. "Bobbie—what's going on?"

"You promise you won't think I'm crazy?"

"You're scaring me." She shivered. She glanced out the window. The wind was picking up. The waves out on the bay were rough, choppy, whitecapped—

*—just like they were in that crazy dream Friday night, when I dreamed that Jessie was going to kill me—*

She shook her head. No, no more of that, it was just a dream, that's all it was, and things were wrong in the dream. *I don't believe in prescience.* "Bobbie—"

"I can't—I can't explain, Karen, I wish I could. Sophie can explain better than I can." He hesitated. "She's a psychic."

Karen laughed. "Oh, please, Bobbie, I'm not interested in what some fortune-teller has to say."

He grabbed her hands, gripping them tightly. "Please,

Karen. I don't want to spoil your mood, or ruin your resolutions, or turn back your fresh start on things. But the weirdness you've described . . . well, I think there's something to it."

"What's happened that's made you say this?"

"Jessie went to see her, hon. A few months back. And Sophie told Jessie some things . . ."

"What things?"

"Things that might explain what's been happening to you. To both of you. I know it sounds whacked. Maybe it is. But Chris—Jessie's boyfriend. He was here this weekend. They were together and both of them are afraid."

"Afraid of what?" Karen tried to steady her racing heart. Part of her was angry with Bobbie for bringing all this up again, just when she thought she had put it all in the past—

*The past.* Why did simply thinking those two words frighten her?

"I spent part of yesterday with them. Jessie came to my house." He hesitated, then continued. "Don't worry, Karen. Nothing went on. Nothing that was inappropriate, nothing you would feel you'd tell Philip about. It was just really wonderful watching the two of them together. Young love. Jessie could really blossom being around Chris."

"Well, that *is* good. But you said they're afraid."

Bobbie nodded. "I trust Sophie. She's a good psychic. Authentic. And if she saw something troubling about them, I believe her. I wouldn't be sticking my neck out like this if I didn't think it was important." He gripped Karen's hands. "I really think you should go see her. As soon as possible."

"All right." Karen pulled her hands away from him. "If you think it's that important, Bobbie, I'll go."

She had never seen him like this. But why now?

*Why—when everything is going well and I've put all
the nonsense behind me? Bobbie's been my rock. He's
helped keep me sane all this time. Don't go crazy on
me, Bobbie, please.* "All right," Karen said. "Let me
get my coat."

Bobbie had walked her to Sophie's house, but left
her at the gate. "She knows you're coming—she's expecting you." He kissed her cheek. "I don't know what
I believe— but I do know Sophie's real. Trust me on
this—she is for *real*."

Then he turned and walked away.

Karen had taken a deep breath and walked up to the
front door.

*Why did I go in? I should have just walked away,
said no. Sophie's a crazy woman. All her rantings about
circles of time and history repeating itself. It was all
just looney tunes. What's clear is that Jessie has serious
problems—surely lingering from finding her mother dead.
But she's not going to kill me or Philip or anyone else.
She's not Lettie Hatch. That's just the rantings of some
crazy psycho who somehow managed to convince Bobbie
there was danger. Who knew Bobbie believed in this
kind of nonsense?*

But Karen couldn't deny what she'd felt when the
woman had taken her hand. She couldn't deny having
that strange vision of the woman giving birth.

It had felt like it had that time when she was little,
wandering around her uncle's farm out in Placquemines
Parish. She hadn't been watching where she was going
and had walked straight into the small electric wire that
kept the cows in the field. A strange humming noise
and a tiny volt of electricity had rushed through her entire body. She could feel the hairs on her arms standing
up, and she'd wanted to scream but couldn't. She couldn't
get enough air into her lungs. That's exactly the way

she felt now, trying to breathe as she walked against the wind.

All she wanted to do was run, get away, put as much distance as she could between her and this nutcase woman. But the images began to rush through her head.

*Hate. So much hatred. Blood, a knife clattering to the floor, blood splattered everywhere, and she could see the body in the bed. It was Horace Hatch, his gray hair clotted and matted with blood. She could feel the scream starting in her lungs. This couldn't be real, she couldn't be seeing this. The candles flickered and it was cold, oh so fucking cold, she couldn't stand it. She turned and suddenly there was a figure standing there. She knew it was Lettie. Oh, what a horrible smile stretched across her face. She just stood there without saying anything, murder in her eyes, hatred radiating from her like heat from a radiator.*

*She knew in that moment that Lettie was going to kill her, there would be no escape, and still the scream wouldn't come. She tried to run, tried to get around her, but Lettie kept moving and getting in her way. Then Lettie reached out and grabbed her wrists. The girl was so strong. No matter how much she struggled she couldn't break her grip. She was going to die, no, she couldn't die, it wasn't meant to end like this, there was so much she wanted to do, wanted to accomplish, and if she could just get away—*

"Excuse me, but can you watch where you're going?"

It was an old woman. Karen had nearly plowed right into her as she staggered past the post office.

"I'm—I'm sorry," she managed to say.

*I need to get home. Lie down.* Her head was throbbing.

But she knew she couldn't make it. Not yet. She

needed to rest. She found her way into Lagniappe. The woman behind the counter recognized her.

"H'lo, Mrs. Kaye. What can I do you for?"

"Um, I guess, um—a hot chocolate, please."

"Coming up. Sure is getting cold, isn't it?"

Karen nodded, hugging herself.

She sat in the corner, her palms taking warmth from the mug of chocolate. What had Bobbie been thinking, sending her to see that madwoman? He said he was concerned. But all he had done was bring it all back. She tried to calm the pounding of her heart.

She was startled out of her thoughts by the sound of sirens. Loud, insistent. The woman behind the counter stepped forward to peer out the window. "They sound close by," she observed.

Karen stood. The sirens troubled her. She walked outside and saw two large yellow fire trucks at the far end of Commercial Street. Suddenly above the white clapboard of the houses she saw black smoke billowing into the gray sky. People were running in that direction. "A fire!" someone shouted from the street. "Fire!"

She found herself following, drawn to the flames like a moth, hoping it was some summer person's home, some place boarded up for the season, with no one inside in risk of being hurt. But as she reached the fire trucks she realized the smoke came from Sophie's block, and Karen started walking faster.

She spied three firefighters in orange rubber suits holding a long, pulsing hose that was shooting water into the flames. To her horror, she realized it was Sophie's house.

*Oh God, I should have called the paramedics, she was having trouble breathing, all those candles and she couldn't stand, she must have knocked one of them over and it started the fire, oh my God, this is all my fault—*

"Karen!"

She turned and saw Bobbie running toward her. He didn't have on a jacket or anything, and he was shivering in the cold wind.

He grabbed her by the shoulders. "Thank God, Karen! It's Sophie's house! I thought you might still be inside!"

"Is she—is she okay?"

Tears were coming down his cheeks. "I don't know. I think she's still in there."

"Oh, Bobbie!"

She fell into his arms. They watched as flames shot up through the roof of the house. A loud crack was heard, and part of the roof caved in.

"I can't watch this," Karen cried.

"Did you talk to her?" Bobbie gripped her arm, not letting her go.

"No," Karen lied. "I—I was on my way when I heard the fire engines."

*Why am I lying to him? It's not my fault what's happened.* But somehow it seemed the right thing to do.

"What did you think she'd tell me, Bobbie?"

"I don't want to talk about it right now." He turned back to watch the fire, his entire body rigid.

"Do you think . . . this fire is somehow connected?"

"I don't know," he said. "All I'm praying for now is that Sophie is safe."

"Yes," Karen said, stepping away from him a little. "I'm praying for that, too."

The crowd surged. Police had arrived on the scene, and they pushed the onlookers back. Bobbie managed to sneak around to the backyard of a house. Karen watched him go. What could he do? She sensed it was too late for poor Sophie.

Too late for all of them.

Everyone else in town seemed to be rushing in the

direction of the fire, but Karen slowly headed the other way. She needed Philip. She needed him to hold her, to kiss her, maybe even to make love to her—to make it all right, to make it like it was in Boston. Smoke and soot floated over her head as she made her way back to the east end.

She pushed through the front door. Alice was gone. She'd probably heard about the fire; news spreads fast about things like this. She was probably down there, too, with everyone else. Karen wasn't sure where Jessie was, whether she was home or not. Her door was closed, but the tiny buzz of her headphones weren't heard through the door.

She was about to open the bedroom door, hoping Philip wouldn't mind the interruption of his work, but she paused, her hand on the knob, when she heard his voice through the door. He was talking on the phone.

"Well, of course she's got no talent, Bill."

*His agent. He's talking to his agent.*

"Yeah, yeah, I know, I know. You should read this manuscript she's working on. It's the worst piece of crap I've ever read . . . *amateurish* would be a step up. Yeah, I know I'm going to have to tell her at some point, but I keep hoping she'll listen to me, to do what I tell her, take my advice. Maybe then something could be salvaged. Look, she's a great girl, but she's never going to be a writer. . . ."

Her entire body went numb.

She stepped back, her hand dropping from the knob. Tears formed in her eyes.

It was as if reality shifted. Her entire body went stiff and numb, and it was as if she wasn't really standing there. She was watching from a great distance. Her fingers and toes started to tingle.

*Worst piece of crap I've ever read . . .*

A blinding pain shot through Karen's head, staggering her, forcing her to hold on to the wall for support. She took a deep breath, focusing on her breathing as the pain faded to a dull throb.

She turned and saw Jessie standing there in the hallway behind her. The girl's face was grim.

*She's going to kill me.*

*She's going to stab me to death and then draw flowers and faces in my blood.*

Karen pushed past her. She focused on the stairs. She needed to get to the attic, to her office, and shut the door behind her. She thought she heard Jessie ask if she was okay, but she wasn't sure. All she could hear was this dull roar in her head. If she could just get up the stairs, everything would be all right. *There's another step, Karen, pick up your foot, just get up these stairs and everything will be okay, you'll see.* No way was she going to let that little bitch see her cry, see how badly she was hurt . . .

She made it. She got to her office. She locked the door behind her. She was safe.

For now.

She moved numbly over to her desk and sat down. Her computer was still on.

*He thinks I have no talent . . . he's been lying to me all this time . . . just like he lied about Ivy, lied about everything . . .*

She put her head down on her hands and cried. . . .


*What is this letter?*

*She held it out in front of her. Horace had just arrived home, and she was helping him unpack. The letter from Eliza Washburn was there, as though he'd wanted her to find it. She read only a snippet of it, but she saw what that horrible woman had written. "Thank you, my darling Horace, for bringing me to meet the president and his wife. In time, we can roll back the nineteenth amendment. I feel certain we can, together, if we can influence enough people."*

"You—you are working to overturn a woman's right to vote!"

Horace smiled at her. "Some women don't want to be men, my dear," he said, gently taking the letter from her hands.

"She is a traitor! A traitor to her sex!" Sarah Jane felt the anger flush her cheeks, overpowering any fear she might have for her husband. "And you, a traitor to your wife!"

"Spare me the melodrama, Sarah Jane." Horace unbuttoned his overcoat, hanging it on the rack. "Many women would be very happy with the kind of life I've given you."

"I'm going back to Washington."

"You are my wife. Your place is here, in our home, where a woman belongs."

Fury rose in her. "Maybe the next time you come back, I won't be here."

Horace laughed at her. "And where would you go? Back to Louisiana? Back to Cooper Road?"

All the blood drained out of her face.

He laughed, malevolence in his eyes. "That's why I can't take you back to Washington with me. You may have fooled me into marrying you, my dear, but now that I know the truth about you, I can't have you there. As it is, my political enemies could find out what you really are—so it's best to keep you hidden here, where no one will think about you, or think about striking at me through you."

He approached her, grabbing her arm and pulling her to him. "Can't have anyone finding out that the good senator's wife is nothing but a whore!"

*"Let go of me!"* She tried to pull away, but he was too strong for her.

He tore the front of her dress. *"Isn't this all you're good for? Once a whore—"*

She screamed as he threw her onto the bed, closing her eyes as he forced himself on her. Afterward, when it was over, her body burning with fire, Sarah Jane lay there in silence, listening to the monstrous breathing of her husband beside her.

I've got to get out here, *she told herself.* I've got to escape.

She stood, every muscle in her body aching. Her lips were bruised, as were her breasts and arms and legs. She limped into the washroom, staring at herself in the mirror. The numbness began to fade.

*Replaced, once more, by fury.*

*"You'll pay, Horace,"* she whispered. *"You'll pay. . . ."*


Karen stared out at the ocean as she reached into the drawer for the diary. She didn't need to look at what she was doing. She could find it by habit. She clutched the musty old leather-bound book to her chest.

*Okay, Philip, you win this round, I'll play your game, I'll be the devoted wife . . .*

*But you will pay.*

Karen smiled.

*Yes, Horace, you will pay.*

# Book Three

# CLOSING THE CIRCLE

# Chapter 19

Later, Bobbie was unable to pinpoint the exact time when he noticed the change in Karen. It was so gradual—little things here and there, things most people wouldn't have thought about even if they'd been paying attention. *And*, he was able to rationalize, *I was too busy thinking about David, why our relationship had suddenly gone south, to be paying as much attention to her as maybe I should have.*

But there was no question that Karen had changed. She'd stopped complaining about both Philip and Jessie. Even more unusual, she stopped talking about her writing. She stopped giving him updates about what was happening in Lettie Hatch's diary. She stopped talking about her dreams of glory and success, but Bobbie didn't notice right away. His mind was on autopilot while she was talking, just waiting until it was his turn to talk about David.

So when she dropped the bomb on him about the cooking class he couldn't do anything more than just stare at her, his mouth open. *A cooking class? What on earth is going on here?* He stared at her, watching her face, trying to detect some clue as to what was going on in her head, but there was nothing he could latch on to definitively. And it was in that moment that he started wondering what was going on with her writing, what happened to her dreams, and what was going on in that house.

"Don't look so shocked!" Karen smiled at him, smearing butter on a toasted poppy seed bagel. "Sheesh—the look on your face! It's not like I'm going to the moon or anything like that, Bobbie." Her eyes lit up. "Here's a crazy thought—why don't you sign up with me? It'll be fun! We could try out recipes on each other . . ." She continued on in this vein for a while, about cookbooks she'd ordered, the new pots and pans she'd bought at the Cape Cod Mall in Hyannis, as she ate her bagel and took sips from her coffee.

*Oh . . . my . . . God*, Bobbie thought, narrowing his eyes and really looking at her, as though for the first time in months. The dark circles under her eyes that he'd been so worried about were almost gone, and she'd lost a little weight. Her face was thinner, the little pudge of baby fat under her chin gone completely, and he had to admit it looked better on her. Her shoulder-length light brown hair was longer, too, hanging down her back now. Her bangs were pulled back from her face and tied up in a ribbon at the back of her head. She had transformed right in front of his eyes.

When he first met Karen, she usually wore just a little lipstick and maybe the tiniest bit of mascara. But now her entire face was completely made up, rouge and mascara and eye shadow and liner. Her skin was practically glowing. In fact, now that he thought about, all of her hair was in place and shone more than it had when he'd first met her. Back then, there were always stray strands in disarray; she was always pushing her hair out of her face. He'd kind of liked the way she always looked a little disheveled, in a way that seemed to tell anyone who looked at her that her appearance wasn't the most important thing she had on her mind.

"I'm—just a little surprised, is all," he finally managed to say, putting a weak smile on his face. "I mean, *cooking*? I thought you hated to cook—and what about your writing? Won't the class take up a lot of your time? I mean if you're going to experiment and all."

"Pish. I have plenty of time for that." She rolled her eyes and patted his hand. Her nails were longer than he remembered and perfectly manicured. *Didn't she used to bite her nails?* Karen shrugged. "Trust me—I have *plenty* of time. Besides, I need to fill up my days. I think that was part of my problem—why I was so obsessive. I mean, I just didn't have enough to *do*." She searched his face, her brows furrowed together as she gave him a slight, concerned frown. "Is everything okay with you, Bobbie? I know your friend's death was hard on you. . . ."

Yeah, it was hard all right. Sophie's death was an emotional sucker punch right to the solar plexis. Bobbie's only prior experience with the death of someone that close to him had been his father. His father had died of cancer, but his death had been a lingering one, lasting several years, with many operations, chemotherapy, and the endless emotional roller coaster of hope and despair. By the time Dad finally died, he'd wasted away to a shell of his former self, no longer the man Bobbie had loved so much.

For weeks after his father's funeral, Bobbie still found himself expecting to see Dad in his usual haunts—the barbershop, the corner diner, the bench in front of the town hall—but Bobbie had been thankful his suffering was over. Sophie's death had been a completely different story. He hadn't been prepared for it. She was only in her midthirties, and despite her being overweight, her smoking and other bad habits—like the scotch she was overly fond of—Bobbie still figured she had a lot of time left. Her grisly end, charred to a crisp on her living room floor, made death suddenly very real and personal for him.

*It could happen to me, too—in a car or a fire or anything. There's no rhyme or reason to it. Lives are suddenly over without warning.* Bobbie had cried staring out the window of the train coming back from Sophie's funeral in New York City. *And what a terrible way to die.*

Try as he might, he couldn't get the memory out of his mind for days afterward, reliving the sirens in his head, the billowing black smoke just a few blocks away. Somehow, he had known it was going to be Sophie's house. He ran over there, and then seeing the reality, he'd felt a burning sensation of his own, the terrible knowledge in his gut that Sophie was inside, burning to death, her skin melting from the heat. He watched the firefighters desperately trying to douse the flames, the whole time praying that he was wrong, that Sophie wasn't in there, that she'd gone for a walk or to the store—anything that would mean she wasn't in there. He kept watching the faces of the crowd, hoping that he'd see her. He didn't, of course. She was inside, and her last call had been to him.

He'd liked Sophie almost from the first time he'd met her. She'd hired him to do some work on the house when she'd bought it, tearing out a wall and making the cramped little living room bigger. It hadn't seemed to help much. She just crowded so much furniture back in there it still seemed cramped, with piles of books and magazines everywhere. She was such a lousy housekeeper that he'd teased her about it.

"You don't need to buy spray-on cobwebs and dust to get a spooky ambience for your clients," he'd say, laughingly dodging whatever she threw at him. "You actually live like an old witch!"

"Take it up the wazoo, Noble!"

He liked Sophie's blunt way of talking, without regard to hurting anyone's feelings. There was nothing phony about Sophie—she wouldn't say polite things that people just wanted to hear. She spoke her mind, and if that hurt your feelings, well, she was sorry but she wasn't about to lie.

"As it is," she'd say, "I have to tailor my damned readings to just saying only good things, so I'll be damned if I'll tailor the rest of my life just to make other people feel better. Besides—" She'd shrug in that way she had. "Nobody ever seems to try to spare *my* fucking feelings."

Bobbie liked that Sophie called him on his bullshit, whenever he'd come by to whine about his latest relationship going down the drain. And even though he'd go weeks sometimes without seeing her or talking to her, he knew he'd get a smile on her face whenever he'd show up without warning with a box of glazed donuts, her favorite sugar high. She'd offered to do readings for him, gratis, more than once, but he'd always declined. "I like not knowing what the future holds," he'd insist. "I like being surprised. That would just take all the suspense out of life, and who needs or wants that?"

"You'd be surprised," she'd say grimly, reaching for the scotch bottle and another cigarette, "at how many people are afraid of the uncertainty."

He wondered if she'd seen her own death, if she had known it was coming, known it was inevitable and there was nothing she could do about it. *That would be horrible*, he thought with a shiver.

Just what was she calling him about in those last few agonizing moments? What was she trying to say?

"Yoo-hoo, Bobbie." Karen's singsongy voice cut through his reverie. "Are you listening to me?"

"Oh, sure, sweetums. You were talking about your class. . . ."

"Yes. Talking about getting you to come. It might help take your mind off all those unpleasant things." She grinned from ear to ear. "Come on, Bobbie—it'll be fun."

He looked at her again. *She's changed*, he thought. *She's not the same person she was during the summer— and it's not just the superficial things like the hair and makeup. It's other things too—like her voice and her facial expressions, the way she holds her head—it's all different.*

"No, thanks, Karen," he said slowly, "it's not for me. I appreciate the thought though. But why are you doing it? Just a few months ago you had no interest in cooking."

She shrugged. "Well, it's really not fair to Alice to make her feed us all the time, you know? Her job is to be Jessie's teacher, not our housekeeper, and I've been taking advantage of her all this time—because she doesn't seem to mind, but it's still not cool." She gave him a sly wink. "I've even started doing some of the housework, if you can imagine that."

"A regular Stepford wife." For a brief moment, he had an image of her, in a skirt and blouse and high heels, pearls at her throat and an apron tied around her waist as she vacuumed. Rather than making him laugh, it seemed, well, kind of scary.

"Bobbie!" She laughingly slapped his hand. "That's so unfair!" She popped the last bit of her bagel in her mouth. "I just finally realized one morning that I was being a spoiled brat, you know? So Jessie wouldn't talk to me, so my marriage wasn't everything I dreamed it would be—what marriage ever is? And I just kept expecting everyone else to change, to adapt, without making any effort myself to change or compromise—

and that's a sure trip to the divorce attorney, don't you think?"

"You've been watching Dr. Phil, haven't you?" He was sorry the instant he said the words without thinking, and she didn't miss the sarcastic, joking tone. Her face immediately darkened into a frown.

"Don't make fun of me, Bobbie." Her lower lip quivered. "Please. My marriage is important to me—and I want to make it work."

*My God, who is this woman, prattling on about her husband and her marriage like June Cleaver or some stupid soap opera heroine who spends most of her time crying?*

Suddenly he just wanted to get away from her. He glanced at his watch. "Look at the time!" He stood up, leaning over to give Karen a kiss on the cheek. "I've got to hurry to a job. Doing some electrical work." He pulled on his jacket and stocking cap. "I hope the class works out, Karen, I really do." He left her there, with a slight hurt look on her face, her lower lip trembling.

He walked out into the cold wind, shivering as he put his collar up. He didn't really have a job—he just didn't think he could sit there and listen to it anymore. He hurried back to his house near the corner of Franklin and Bradford, letting himself in and tossing his coat on the couch. It was a raw day, cold and damp, with a chill wind blowing in off the bay. Rubbing his hands together for warmth, he jacked up the heat. For the cold to be bothering Bobbie, it had to be *really* cold, since he generally liked the winter. He liked wearing sweaters and coats. He liked the snow and the isolation Provincetown developed in the wintertime, the way the snow covered everything and the town was so deserted. It was his town then, no tourists, just him and the few diehards, foraging to make their little nests, huddled around the fire with a good bottle of brandy.

It wasn't that he didn't enjoy the summer, by any means. The summer was fun, with the hordes of gay tourists with whom he could flirt. He enjoyed the way the faces of the town changed every week as a new crop arrived by car or ferry or plane, but he wasn't sure he could handle the town if life was like that year-round. Winter was necessary. *A season of rest*, he thought as he checked his answering machine. No messages. He swore under his breath and made himself a cup of hot chocolate.

Things were cooling off with David, as he feared they would once the season ended and David stopped coming up on the weekends. Bobbie had gone up to Boston a few times, but he sensed the distance growing. David had seemed fidgety and nervous, as if he could read the writing on the wall but didn't have the heart to admit it. *Summer fling, don't mean a thing*, Bobbie thought as he sat down on his couch. *Why don't you ever learn? The tourists aren't a good source of boyfriend material. How many summers are you going to repeat this goddamned pattern? It's time to forget about him and move on, even if there's no one around to help me get over him.*

That was one of the things so special about Sophie— she'd always been around to listen. He had hoped he'd found a new friend in Karen—he always found women better friends than men—but now he wasn't sure. He had hoped to talk to her about David, but all she wanted to gab on and on about was her latest facial and her newfound consideration of Botox and—Bobbie still couldn't get over it—her goddamned cooking class! He'd never had a chance to bring up David.

*Maybe I'm overreacting. Maybe he will call. Stop being such a clingy fucking high school girl and start thinking like an adult and stop expecting the worst.*

*Maybe David isn't like the others. Maybe he'll still turn out to be the one.*

They'd met "cute," as he liked to think of it, one morning at the gym. It was chest and back day for Bobbie, one of his favorite programs—he always felt his chest and his back were his best assets, so he never had to talk himself into getting there on those days, like he did when it was leg day—a workout he loathed. He'd been deep in thought, reaching for the same pair of dumbbells as another guy at the same time—and their hands had touched. "Oh, I'm sorry," Bobbie said quickly, pulling his hands back. Despite the fact that most of the tourists were gay, you could never be sure—even at the gym.

"I'm not," the other guy responded with a smile. "David Weston." He stuck out a strong hand.

David was taller than he was, maybe five eleven, with close-cropped dark hair and big round brown eyes. His nose was strong, and he had deep dimples in both cheeks. He hadn't shaved that morning, so there was a ghost of a shadow on his chin and cheeks. He was wearing a tight-fitting tank top that hugged every inch of his torso, and a pair of loose-fitting basketball shorts that reached his knees. The calves exposed between the bottom of the shorts and the top of his white ankle socks were equally tanned and smooth.

"Bobbie Noble," he managed to say, offering his own hand. That was that, but when Bobbie was finally finished, David was waiting for him outside, and invited him to go for a smoothie. And that, as they say, started a beautiful summer together.

*Maybe I'm just a lousy boyfriend*, Bobbie thought, kicking off his shoes and lying back against the sofa cushions. He picked up the remote and turned on the television, flipping through the channels until he found an old movie he'd seen a thousand times—*The Philadelphia Story*—and left it there. *Maybe that's why I'm still single, still living alone at thirty-two.* He kicked himself for thinking, once again, that David might have been the one.

There had been plenty of Davids in Bobbie's life, none of them ever lasting more than a few months at best. When Bobbie reached thirty, he'd decided that love just wasn't in the cards for him anymore—not an option for him. He sighed. His circle of friends, never particularly large, just seemed to be getting smaller. Sophie was dead, Karen acting weird—what to do now? He got up and walked over to his junk drawer and pulled out the tape from his answering machine with Sophie's final message on it.

The horror of the fire had driven everything else from his mind, and the strange message had been too horrific for him to deal with when he got home that afternoon. He'd listened to it, not understanding what she was trying to tell him, listening to the sound of the fire in the background, those poor cats screeching, her own coughs interfering with her words. After getting back from the funeral, he hadn't really wanted to listen to it, relive that afternoon again. Besides, it didn't make any sense to him.

*Maybe it's time to figure out what she was talking about,* he thought as he put the tape into his system and hit Play. He shivered as Sophie's final words played back through the speakers.

"Bobbie . . . Bobbie, I was wrong . . . wrong about everything . . . it's the bloodline . . . the bloodline . . . you've got to tell them . . ."

"What did you mean, Sophie?" He ran his fingers through his hair. "What was so damned important, honey?"

Across the room Jimmy Stewart was asking Katharine Hepburn to marry him.

"Tell *who*? You meant Chris and Jessie, didn't you, baby? But what *bloodline*?" He tapped his fingers on the stereo, thinking. Nothing came to him, so he hit Rewind and listened to it again, despite the tears coming to his face as he listened to Sophie's last moments once again.

*The cats' screaming is the worst. I could handle it if it weren't for that. I didn't like that lazy fur ball, but neither one of them deserved to go like that.*

The last time he'd seen Sophie was that morning he'd gone by with Chris. He remembered, as he played the tape a third time, the electric charge when she had grabbed Chris's hand, the energy that had flowed through the room. The memory gave him a sour feeling in his stomach. He hit Stop and ejected the tape, putting it back into the drawer.

If only Karen had gotten over there in time to see her. What might she have told Karen?

Letting out a long sigh, he scuffed into his bedroom and flicked on his computer. Chris had been e-mailing him pretty regularly since that weekend, mostly pleading with him to get Jessie to respond to him. She had shut down again, cutting off communication. He didn't know what Chris expected him to do. He liked the kid, but getting any further involved in the drama of a teenage romance wasn't a good idea.

Bobbie knew he should have told Karen what Jessie had been up to while she and Philip were in Boston. The girl needed help. How sweet the two of them had been later that weekend, sitting here together—but then, on Sunday, just as Chris was getting ready to leave, she had turned icy again, and Bobbie could almost swear her voice sounded different. An octave higher. Shrill.

Part of him worried that Jessie was well on the same path her mother had taken, and she needed to get to a good therapist.

But another part of him thought—well, he wasn't sure what he thought. But the weirdness that Chris had been talking about—the weirdness he'd experienced firsthand that day at Sophie's—well, maybe there was something to it all.

Now talking to Karen seemed impossible. *Maybe I should talk to Jessie myself first, and then decide what to do.*

"It's what Sophie was asking me to do," Bobbie said out loud, realizing the truth.

*Sophie was talking about Chris and Jessie in that last message,* he reasoned, knowing he'd been dancing around the issue because he didn't want to deal with it. *Sophie knew something was seriously wrong in that house, but what on earth did she mean in her message? Does it have something to do with Karen, maybe— maybe that's part of the reason why Karen is acting so strange?*

But how well did he know Karen? Maybe this *was* the real Karen. All Bobbie knew was that the Karen he'd met last summer was much more likable than this perky sweet version.

*It's the bloodline . . . the bloodline . . . you've got to tell them . . .*

"What did you mean, Sophie? What the hell did you mean?"

What bloodline could she have meant? Lettie was the last of the Hatches. There *was* no bloodline as far as that was concerned. Did she mean Jessie's blood-line, maybe? Or Chris's? No, it was that house she was so worried about.

*Maybe I should talk to Chris about it, let him know what Sophie said. If she* was *talking about the two of them—and who else?—then I owe it to all of them to let them know. It was so important to Sophie that she had called me with her house burning down around her ears.*

He couldn't make sense of any of it, though, no matter how hard he tried.

He wondered again what Karen had been reading in Lettie Hatch's dairy. Had she gotten to the murder yet? How had Lettie accomplished it? Were there any clues that might explain some of the weirdness going on? Why had Karen just stopped talking about it—and her dreams of glory the diary might bring?

Checking his in-box, Bobbie found no e-mail from David. Not that he expected there to be anything, but he couldn't help feeling a little let down anyway. *Oh well, so I've become an old irrelevant supporting player in the soap opera of life. Like the old actors on* All My Children *or* Guiding Light *who fade into the background, kept on the payroll only to stand around and offer advice to the young upstarts.*

"Teenage drama, here I come," Bobbie said with a sigh, and clicked on a new e-mail to send to Chris Muir.

# Chapter 20

The change in Karen was even more obvious to Jessie.

Her stepmother's initial attempts at friendliness had been easy enough for her to brush aside with a mono-syllabic answer or an unfriendly grunt. As Jessie confided, on more than one occasion, to her diary, *It's not like I have a reason to dislike her—mostly I feel sorry for her. She has no idea of what she is in for being married to Dad.*

But ever since the night Karen had been given the pearls, Jessie had seen a new look in her stepmother's eyes.

*Of course she couldn't know the pearls were my mother's—certainly Dad didn't tell her, like he didn't tell her anything about Mom at all,* Jessie wrote in her diary that night. *But I got the sense somehow that she knew those pearls would upset me (which they did), and she was GLAD—she was happy to know I was hurt.*

*And that wasn't like her.*

As much as she had avoided Karen, Jessie still had

sensed that her new stepmother wasn't a bad person. She had never fully understood the intensity of her dis- like—it just was—but ever since the night with the pearls, there seemed to be real malice in Karen's eyes. When she'd first come to Provincetown, those big brown eyes always had tried to offer sympathy to Jessie—but not anymore. It was as if something had changed her—the pearls? This house?

No, Jessie knew what had changed her. The same thing that had been playing with everyone's mind.

It was the past. The echoes of the past.

Even now, she couldn't hate Karen. There was no way this young girl from Louisiana could have had any idea, any concept, of what she'd gotten herself into, what a huge mistake she'd made by marrying Philip Kaye. Jessie knew why her father had married Karen. She was young, she was pretty, and most importantly, she was one of his *fans*. Philip's ego was so huge he had to have someone around all the time who adored him without question, and Karen certainly fit the bill. Philip would suck her dry, drain all the life out of her before she even knew what hit her, and then she would be gone.

Jessie knew all too well what life was like for Mrs. Philip Kaye.

She tried, sometimes, late at night in her room with the door closed and the rest of the house silent, to re- member a time when her parents had gotten along. No matter how hard she tried, no happy memories would come to her. No birthdays, no happy holidays, none of those happy family times she saw in movies ever hap- pened in her house. Oh, sure, at Christmas time there'd be a big fresh tree in the living room, but she and her mother decorated it while Philip stayed up in his office working. He never even had the decency to compli- ment the tree, if he even noticed it. Jessie knew the presents, ostensibly from him, were really bought by her mother. She despised her father. She longed for the days when he would pack his bags and leave on a trip—whether it was a tour, or research, or just to meet with his agent or editor or whatever the hell it was he did when he went to New York.

How different her mother had been. Ivy Kaye, when alone with her daughter, was a kind, soft-spoken, loving person—contrasted more sharply by the screaming shrew she became when Philip was in the house. *That* Ivy Kaye threw things, screamed at the top of her lungs without a care as to whether passersby on the street could hear, and cried almost constantly. The battles were followed by an icy silence that was unbearable to Jessie.

Not that Ivy was always the best of mothers. Jessie sometimes felt guilty for thinking that, but she knew she was right. Mom was almost always preoccupied, off in her own little world, lost in thought or thinking about something. She loved her daughter, but she loved her poetry even more. That was the most important thing to her in the world, and if she had to choose between them, Jessie was pretty certain she would have chosen the poetry. If she was cooking and a line came to her for a poem, for example, she would walk out of the kitchen with the stove still on, sometimes with a pan on the flame, and write it down, agonizing over whether it should go into a poem she was already working on or if it was the genesis of a new one. Before long, whatever she was cooking would burn. Jessie was around eight when she realized that she needed to be in the kitchen as a safeguard whenever her mother was cooking.

During the "dark spells," Ivy became another person—one her daughter almost didn't recognize. Gone was the loving, if somewhat preoccupied mother, replaced by someone with no interest in anything, her eyes glassy. She wouldn't bathe, wouldn't get out of bed for days at a time. Jessie became very adept at recognizing when one of the spells was coming. Mom's speech would start to become more and more slurred, her eyes would become less focused, and glassy in appearance, she moved in slow motion. During these times—which lasted as long as a week, or as little as a few hours, there was no way of telling how long it would last—Jessie would have to get herself up for school, make sure she had breakfast and lunch money so that no one outside the house would know anything was wrong. Her biggest fear was that someone would find out what was going on in their big white house near the end of Commercial Street.

Jessie withdrew even further from her classmates, further into herself. Her classmates began to tease and make fun of her. They started calling her Spook, singing that damned Lettie Hatch jingle. She hated them all. Sometimes at night she prayed that the earth would open up at recess one day and swallow her tormentors all whole. She hated the teachers just as much as she hated the other kids, hated them for the way they ignored the harassment she suffered. She'd remembered the time someone wrote on her hall locker in Magic Marker: *Lettie Hatchet took a butcher knife*. She'd told her teacher, but the teacher didn't do anything.

Even the other outsider kids made her their target— the nerdy kids, the effeminate boys, and the tomboy girls, even Johnny Richards, who always had a booger in his nose and used to eat paste in first grade—they were just as mean to her as the rest of the kids. Jessie hated those kids the most, because they should have *understood*, they should have been her friends and stuck up for her, but they didn't.

That was one of the reasons she liked Chris so

much. He wasn't from here. He had never seen how
mistreated at school she'd been. He'd actually found
her pretty—her! Jessie Kaye, the Spook! She'd noticed
him watching her at the beginning of last summer—he
was so tall, he was hard to miss. At first, she'd dismissed
it as more cruelty—*he's making fun of me, wondering why
I'm so weird, following me around to stare at the town
freak; well, fuck you, buddy, I'm not going to talk to you,
not now, not ever; if you just get your kicks by following
me around, have a good time—you're the freak, not me!*
But still, one night she wrote in her diary about him:

> *He's so cute, and he always is around when-*
> *ever I leave the house. It can't be coincidence, it*
> *happens too often for it to be that, it's like he's al-*
> *ways looking for me. I know it's stupid to hope,*
> *but maybe he thinks I'm pretty? Maybe he wants*
> *to be my friend, maybe he's not like the other*
> *kids, maybe he doesn't think I'm a freak, maybe,*
> *just maybe I'm not a freak, if he can look at me*
> *the way he does . . . maybe someday when I get*
> *done with school and I'm older, I can get out of*
> *this godforsaken town and have a life somewhere,*
> *somewhere far, far away where nobody knows*
> *me, doesn't know that I'm a freak of nature, and*
> *maybe have some sense of being normal, even*
> *though I'm not. . . .*

And thinking about him had been a welcome distraction from what had been worrying her all summer.
   She described it in her diary as "shadowing." She
couldn't exactly pinpoint when she'd begun to feel that
way. Sometime in early July she started having the
weird dreams. Dreams of blood, and murder, and rage;
dreams about the house eighty years earlier, in a time
when she knew the Hatches lived here. There were

times, alone in her room, when she sensed she wasn't alone. Sometimes it was as if there was someone just outside her peripheral vision, but when she turned her head to look, there was nothing there.

*Is this how the "dark spells" started for Mom? Is this how it all starts? Just when there's a chance someone out there doesn't think I'm a freak, I have to be like Mom and start to go crazy? Is it hereditary?*

It got worse after her father called to tell her he had remarried.

"You've got a new mom, sweetie," her father said cheerfully over the telephone, completely oblivious of her feelings as always. "Her name is Karen, and she's going to be moving up there soon. You're going to just love her, Jessie girl—she's smart and funny and sweet. Isn't that great? I'm sure you two will be great friends."

She'd hung up the phone and walked back to her room. Once in her room, she'd sat down at her desk and stared at her diary, conflicting emotions at war in her mind. And as she sat there, trying to determine how she felt about this big new change in her life, everything had faded away. . . .

*"Can you believe this?"*

*Lettie handed the letter over to Mrs. Windham.*

*"He's married again, and this is how he chooses to tell me—in a letter, after the fact! And he says we're going to be great friends!"*

*Mrs. Windham read the letter quickly, then folded it and set it down on the kitchen table. "He's entitled to marry again, my dear," she said softly. "Nor does he require your permission to do so."*

*"I won't accept her! Ever!"*

*Mrs. Windham reached across the table and took her hands. "There's nothing to be done about it. You shall simply have to make the best of the situation. Surely you had to know at some point he'd marry again. Men have needs, and only a woman can satisfy them."*

Lettie pulled her hands away, standing and walking over to the window. The sea outside was restless. *"Of course, I know he's a man and has need of a wife, Mrs. Windham. But why keep it a secret from me until it's done? And Mother in her grave just over two years. Why so hurried? Why no big Washington wedding? Is there something about this new wife he's ashamed of?"*

Lettie shivered and hugged herself, remembering the day she'd found her mother in the attic, and tears filled her eyes again. *Why, Mother? Why did you leave me alone here with HIM?*

*"Don't, Lettie,"* Mrs. Windham said mildly, reading her mind as always. *"Don't think about that now. Your mother loved you so very much. She wasn't well, what happened was no one's fault. . . ."*

But Lettie couldn't help herself. She remembered climbing the stairs to the attic, remembered pushing open the door, and there was her mother hanging from a rafter, her face blackening, the tongue and the eyes protruding, and Lettie had let out a scream that had brought Mrs. Windham running, and it was Mrs. Windham who had led a hysterical Lettie back down to her bedroom and to her bed, who had gone for the doctor, who had arranged everything so that no one knew Ellen Hatch had killed herself, covered it all up, while Lettie sobbed quietly.

Jessie had come back to herself horrified.

*Is this how it feels to lose your grip on reality? Or am I really seeing the past in my mind?*

As the days passed, she soon realized it was much more than her sanity. She didn't tell Alice—dear, sweet

Alice, who made it possible for her to stay home rather
than return to school—what was going on. Instead, she
spent more and more time writing in her journal, trying
to understand what was happening to her.

*I'm not losing my mind. This is really happening.*
*Lettie Hatch is reaching through the years to talk to*
*me, to take control of me somehow. . . .*

Chris was the first person she'd talked to about it—
the first person she'd felt comfortable opening up to.
She wasn't sure why, maybe it was the kindness in his
eyes when he'd approached her that first day. When she'd
blurted out her fears, she was sure he'd never want to
talk to her again. She'd been wrong, and he'd even gone
with her to see Madame Nadja, who seemed to understand, who seemed as if she might be able to help. For
the first time Jessie had actually felt some hope—but
now her hope was dead. Burned to a crisp. Snuffed out.

And on top of that, she'd lost Chris for good.

Not that he wasn't trying to stay in her life. She
might not answer his e-mails, but she read them. That
last weekend—how wonderful it was. Making love,
and afterward, holding hands, just sitting together, safe
at Bobbie Noble's house . . .

But it was wrong. She knew it. Oh, not the sex—she
had no patience for moralists. It was wrong because
they weren't themselves. It wasn't the two of them,
Jessie Kaye and Chris Muir, making love in his parents' house. It was Lettie Hatch and some unknown
lover, some person named Samuel, making love on the
beach. That's who they had been—not themselves.
Jessie had realized sitting there next to Chris the horrible truth: that so long as she was with him, so long as
she allowed herself to love him, she would lose her
self, her very soul. She would become Lettie Hatch.

Karen said nothing to her. Maybe Bobbie hadn't told

her. Jessie was dying to know what he did or didn't say, but she was too embarrassed to seek Bobbie out.

Now everything was happening fast. Karen's change—it terrified Jessie. It had started that night before she went to Boston. The fear that had been etched on Karen's face—what had she seen on the floor? Why had she screamed? How Jessie had taunted her for her fear—but it wasn't Jessie! It was Lettie! It was Lettie taunting Sarah Jane!

*I've got to fight it. I've got to prove stronger!*

She had to—because she didn't think Karen would turn out to be strong enough to fight off the echoes of the past.

She had been convinced of that fact a few weeks ago, that night when Jessie had come out of her room and found her stepmother standing outside her father's door, listening to him within, talking on the telephone to his agent. What a horrible, pitiful look on Karen's face . . . Jessie had shivered. The last time she'd seen a look like that on anyone's face was with her mother, in the days before she killed herself. So that cycle was starting over again. She had wanted to scream: *Run, Karen! Get out of this house as fast as you can!*

But instead she just asked her stepmother if she was all right. Karen just gave her a terrible look, a look of pain and confusion—

And for one panicked moment, what looked back at her through Karen's eyes *wasn't* Karen. Jessie had taken a step backward from it. *Oh my God, what's wrong with her? That's not Karen. . . .*

"I'm fine, my dear," her stepmother had replied, a smile stretching across her face that had chilled Jessie's blood. Then Karen simply turned away and resolutely climbed the stairs to the attic, shutting the door behind her.

That night Jessie locked her bedroom door for the first time.

Since then, Karen had been nothing but sweetness and light—but there was something different about her. It was in the way she held her head, the inflections in her voice when she spoke. It was still Karen's voice, but it wasn't, somehow. She was always so upbeat and cheerful, always smiling, but the smile never quite reached her eyes. Her eyes were cold, calculating, watching to see how Jessie reacted to whatever it was she was saying.

"Jessie?"

The girl jumped back in her seat. He heart was still thudding as she asked, "Yes, what is it, Alice?"

Mrs. Winn walked into her room and shut the door behind her, sitting on the edge of the bed. She looked terribly uncomfortable. "Can we talk?"

Jessie closed her journal and swiveled around in her chair. "Okay. What about? Schoolwork? I'm getting to it, I promise. . . ."

"No, not schoolwork, dear." Alice struggled for words. "I've not said anything for a while, but something has been weighing on my mind. This isn't going to sound normal, but please just hear me out, okay?" She fidgeted with a cameo on her blouse. "Something is going on in this house that isn't quite normal."

Jessie said nothing, just stared at her.

"And it's not—" Alice seemed to notice she was playing with the cameo, and let her hand drop into her lap. "Okay, I'll just say it plain. I think this house is haunted."

Jessie eyed her. "But the town has said that for years."

"Back then it was a lot of nonsense."

"Not anymore?"

"Not since Karen came. Things started changing

then. This house—whatever it is—oh, Jessie, sweetheart, I'm a good Christian woman, but the things I've felt. Surely you must have too. I've seen the way this place has affected you, and then it started affecting Karen, and now—" She shuddered. "It's affecting me."

Jessie struggled to keep her voice steady. "What do you mean, Alice?"

"I was just down in the kitchen, and—" Jessie noticed that Alice's hands were shaking. "And it was like I *wasn't* in the kitchen. I mean, it was still there, of course, but it wasn't the *same* kitchen. The stove wasn't electric but gas, and I wasn't wearing the same clothes, and—someone else came into the kitchen, and I called her Mrs. Hatch."

Jessie's voice cracked. "Mrs. Hatch?"

"And it's not the first time this has happened." Alice rubbed her forehead. "Sometimes I think I'm losing my mind."

"Then we all are," Jessie said.

"I can't talk to her. Karen. She's so hot and cold. Sometimes she's so sweet and nice and other times it's as if she's someone else. Lately I don't recognize her at all." She seemed near tears. "And here I am, talking such foolishness to a teenage girl, someone I'm supposed to be teaching, setting an example for . . ."

"Alice," Jessie said, grabbing her hands. "Bad things are happening. I've tried to stop them, but I don't know what else to do."

So she told her everything. At first the words came slowly, but as she watched Alice's face, and saw the comprehension and fear dawning there, the whole story came pouring out of her—the way she'd felt since the summer, the visions she'd been having, the sense that she was in tune with Lettie Hatch. Part of her worried she was going too far—after all, Alice worked for her father, and it was her responsibility to tell him what was going on with Jessie. But she couldn't stop talking. Everything was spilling out of her, everything about Chris and Madame Nadja and Bobbie. When everything was out, Jessie just sat there, her heart pounding, her eyes staring at Alice's face, waiting for her to respond.

Alice said not a word.

Jessie began to cry. For the first time in a long time, she let herself really cry.

Alice got up and put her arms around her. "You poor darling." Alice started stroking Jessie's hair. "My poor, sweet darling Lettie."

It took both of them a full minute to realize what she had said.

"You see?" Jessie said, gently pulling out of her embrace and looking up into the older woman's eyes.

"You . . . you say Bobbie Noble knows about this?"

Jessie nodded.

"Then perhaps," Alice Winn said, "he is our only hope."

# Chapter 21

The first snow of the season fell the following weekend, and the sun disappeared behind the clouds, giving the daytime a strange gray feeling. The wind from the bay was strong and cold, and those still in town shivered, turning up their thermostats and digging electric blankets out of closets where they'd been relegated the previous spring. The days were getting shorter, the sun setting just a little after four now. Even though Bobbie usually kept his house colder than most, the Saturday of their gathering he turned the temperature up to seventy and brought in plenty of wood for the fireplace.

He still couldn't believe Alice Winn had showed up on his door, asking him to invite Chris up so they could have, in her words, "a powwow." He wasn't quite sure what she expected them to figure out, but he'd been happy to e-mail Chris—although he made a point of telling him to ask for his parents' permission this time.

*Don't want Lois Muir to land on me like a ton of bricks*, Bobbie thought after he sent the e-mail. *That's one woman whose bad side I don't ever want to be on.*

Chris had immediately e-mailed back, deliriously

happy at the chance to see Jessie again. His roommate Josh would drive him up again, and yes, he assured Bobbie that his parents knew he was coming. Bobbie somehow doubted that, but decided to just take him at his word.

He wasn't sure what Alice or Jessie hoped to accomplish by getting them all together. He felt Karen should have been included, but they had insisted she shouldn't be. Jessie had made the strange observation that it was "too late" for Karen. Bobbie hadn't pressed, but in truth, he hadn't seen Karen since their coffee date the other day. He'd seen her once though, at the big supermarket in New Orleans, all done up in makeup and high heels, pushing her basket up and down the aisles, smiling eerily, as if she wasn't really there picking out cantaloupes, but a million miles away planning to overthrow a country. There had been such *intent* on her face. Such malice, despite the smile. Bobbie was just grateful she hadn't seen him, and ducked out fast.

He was in the kitchen when the first knock came on his door, followed by a steady pounding. *That's got to be Chris, impatient as always.*

Bobbie set out a plate of crackers on his coffee table and walked over to the door. "All right! I'm coming already! Sheesh!" He opened the door and grinned up at Chris. "Do you think I'm such an old auntie that I'm going deaf?"

Chris shrugged as he walked into the living room, unbuttoning his long gray trench coat. He took it off and tossed it over the blue reclining chair, brushing snow from his hair.

"You sure Jessie's going to be here?" he asked, grabbing a handful of chips and cramming them into his mouth.

"Leave something for the rest of them," Bobbie

scolded. "Yes, she'll be here. Now would you mind building a fire? You've done it before, haven't you?"

"Sure." Chris walked over to the fireplace and piled newspapers and wood expertly, then struck a long match and touched it to the paper. "Sometimes I think I'm the only person in my family who knows how."

Bobbie watched him pile the wood with a bemused smile. Chris looked bigger than he had before, but it could just be the baggy sweater and jeans. Still, Bobbie figured a compliment might go a long way. "You've kept up your workouts, haven't you? Nice job."

Chris grinned up at him. "Yeah—pretty much every day. Does it show?" He held up his arms and flexed, but Bobbie couldn't tell anything through the thick wool, though he whistled appreciatively. Chris blushed and turned away.

"So school's going okay?" Bobbie asked.

"No. Not really. I haven't been able to focus. All I think about is what's happening here . . . and Jessie. Has she said why she won't answer my e-mails?"

Bobbie sighed. "I haven't talked to her. I told you, this is all Mrs. Winn's idea." He couldn't stop calling her that, even though she'd insisted he call her Alice now. She would always be Mrs. Winn to him in his mind. *Old habits die hard, after all*, he thought. In his mind she'd always be his high school English teacher; he doubted he'd ever be comfortable enough to call her Alice.

"So what is this powwow for? Has something happened?"

Bobbie glanced out the window to see if they were coming up the walk yet. No sign of them. "I have no idea. I'm still not convinced this is a good idea." He walked into the kitchen and emerged with a plate of cheese, setting it down on the coffee table. "But I suppose getting all our cards on the table is a good thing."

"It can't hurt," Chris said. He popped a cube of cheese in his mouth. "You have anything to drink?"

"There's soda in the fridge—help yourself." Chris disappeared into the kitchen, and Bobbie sat down in the recliner, helping himself to a pretzel. *Maybe this isn't such a great idea*, he thought again, *but I suppose it can't hurt for all of this to come out in the open. That's exactly what Sophie was trying to do, why she wanted to see Karen. I just hope Chris and Jessie*—

He swallowed, glancing into the kitchen, where he could hear Chris rummaging through the refrigerator. *They're just kids. If something really freaky is going on, something bigger and beyond anything they can understand, their parents are going to have to be brought into this.*

The doorbell rang. Bobbie stood, took a deep breath, and hurried over to open it.

Jessie stood there with a sullen look on her face, but Mrs. Winn—*Alice*, he amended—offered him a tight smile.

"Hello, Bobbie," she said. "Thank you for doing this."

"The pleasure is mine, Mrs. W— I mean, Alice." He gestured for them to enter, taking their coats and hanging them on the rack. Jessie avoided his eyes, looking down at her hands and ignoring the food spread out on the coffee table.

*Oh, this is going to go just great*, Bobbie thought, heading back to his reclining chair. Alice politely helped herself to some cheese and crackers. Everyone was ignoring the bubbling cheese fondue. *Not a fondue crowd*, Bobbie thought. *I guess I'll be eating melted cheese all week.*

Chris walked into the room carrying a can of Coke. His eyes sought out Jessie, but she quickly looked away. Bobbie watched the boy's smile fade.

"Okay, everyone, so here we are," Bobbie said, breaking the ice. He clapped his hands together, and three pairs of eyes turned to him. He'd agonized over what he was going to say, how to say it, what was appropriate and what was not, before finally just giving up and deciding to spell out the facts.

He cleared his throat nervously. "All right, then. I guess the thing to do is bring you all up to speed. We're all here because, at one point or another in the last few months, we've all felt something, well, strange is going on." He looked over at Jessie, who looked away. "Some of us more so than others. My own personal experience with everything is mostly secondhand, so, when I'm giving the particulars, please feel free to interrupt and correct me if I've gotten something wrong." He noticed that Chris sat down on the couch next to Jessie, and almost unnoticeably, she inched a bit away from him. "I guess the first thing I need to get clear is that I knew Ivy Kaye fairly well."

*That* made Jessie look up and take notice. "You knew my mother?" she asked. "Then why did I never meet you?"

"I met her one day when I was still in high school, at a café where I was working as a busboy." Bobbie shared the story with them. Ivy had been writing in a little spiral notebook at her table when he came by to clear the next table. He had been watching her; she would write for a moment, put her pencil in her mouth and frown at the page, then erase and write again. She never touched her perspiring glass of iced tea. When she noticed him watching her, she smiled and invited him over.

"She was so nice, so friendly," Bobbie said. "I really liked her—and then she started coming in every day and talking to me, letting me read some of her poetry. She was really good, and she was always encouraging me to do something creative."

Whenever they saw each other around town, they always stopped to chat. As the years passed, Bobbie grew quite fond of her. "But that was all there was to it," he said. "We didn't call each other on the phone and chat, hang out together, anything like that. But I could tell, each time I saw her, that something was wrong—something was going on with her that she didn't want to talk about. And then—" He bit his lip. "Then she . . ."

"Killed herself," Jessie said.

Bobbie made a face in compassion.

"I asked Bobbie to bring up your mother, dear," Alice Winn said. "I knew they had been acquaintances. And I think we can only understand what's happening in that house if we can understand what happened to your poor mother."

"She wasn't well," Jessie said quietly, not looking at anyone. She started gnawing on a fingernail. "She had, um, she had breakdowns. Once she had to go away, to a hospital. Dad had to cancel a book tour or something and come stay with me. He wasn't happy about it."

"Do you think Mrs. Kaye had anything to do with what's going on?" Chris asked. It was the first time he'd said a word, and Jessie didn't look at him. "I mean, Jessie told me that she died over two years ago. I don't see how that could have anything to do with what's going on now."

"Well . . ." Bobbie hesitated again. "Like I said to Alice, as I began thinking about it, the first Mrs. Hatch also died two years before the murders. Coincidence?"

Jessie's lower lip trembled. "Ellen Hatch killed herself—she hung herself in the attic, just like my mom."

"How do you know that?" Bobbie asked, looking intently at her. "I mean, I've spent the last few days cruising the Internet, even went down to Town Hall, but there's no cause of death listed anywhere for her." He remembered Karen telling him about the death certificate, how confusing it was.

Jessie's head tilted up, her jaw set defiantly. "I—I just know. You'll have to take my word for it. You're going to have to take my word for a lot of things." Her lips thinned. "Unless you think I'm crazy."

"Nobody thinks you're crazy, honey," Bobbie said. "We're all here because we're convinced there's weirdness going on we can't explain."

He stood and walked over to the white marker board he'd bought that afternoon, taking the cap off of a blue marker. In big letters wrote ELLEN HATCH/IVY KAYE in the center of the board. He then wrote HORACE HATCH/ PHILIP KAYE to the left, and then drew a line connecting the names.

"Horace Hatch was pretty well known in his time. He was a powerful and influential senator. Philip Kaye is one of the biggest-selling authors of our time. I think it's fairly safe to say we can make some comparison between Philip and old Horace."

Nobody said anything one way or the other, which he took for agreement. Next to the name of Horace Hatch, he now wrote SARAH JANE HATCH/KAREN KAYE.

"There is also a parallel between the second wives. Both the same age, both much younger than their husband. Both from Louisiana."

He drew a line downward from HORACE/PHILIP and wrote LETTIE HATCH/JESSIE KAYE.

"Again, parallels. Two girls, the same age, living in the house primarily with their stepmother while the father is off traveling or working or whatever it is he does."

"They called Lettie *Ghost-Girl*," Jessie said, hugging herself. Her face was chalk-white, and she seemed to struggle with the words. "They call me *Spook*."

Bobbie looked at her sympathetically, then resumed drawing on the board, making a line off to the side leading from Lettie/Jessie. He wrote the word CHRIS and next to it the letter S. "Jessie has a young male friend named Chris. According to information I've received, Lettie had a similar male friend whose name began with S."

"Samuel," Chris said automatically. They all looked at him, even Jessie. "His name was Samuel," Chris continued. "I don't know his last name. It's come to me. I've been Samuel. He's been inside me."

"Oh dear," Mrs. Winn said, trembling.

"I know it sounds crazy," Chris said.

"No," Jessie said without emotion. "It doesn't sound crazy."

Mrs. Winn was looking at Bobbie. "How did you receive that information about 'S'?"

"I'll get to that eventually," Bobbie promised. He wrote AMUEL after the S. Finally he drew a line off to the other side of LETTIE/JESSIE and wrote in ANN WINDHAM/ALICE WINN. "Both girls have a live-in teacher—and look at the similarity in the names."

"Oh dear," Mrs. Winn said again, pulling her glasses out of her purse and peering in at the board.

"So there we have it," Bobbie said. "As near as I can figure—"

Jessie was looking at him with cold eyes. "You've forgotten yourself."

Bobbie laughed. "Sweetie, I'm just the facilitator here. . . ."

"No, you're more than that." She kept staring at him. "I've seen you. When I've been Lettie. When I've felt her inside me. I've seen your own echo, Bobbie. I didn't realize it until this moment, but I've definitely seen you."

Bobbie felt a chill drop down his spine. "What do you mean?"

"Orville Axelrod," Jessie said. "He was Sarah Jane's lover."

Bobbie didn't know what to say. Finally, slowly, he turned and wrote his own name on the board, along with that of Orville Axelrod. His hand was shaking.

"Then I'll bet," Chris said, rubbing his chin as he thought, "that Axelrod knew the first Mrs. Hatch, too. If Bobbie knew your mom, Jessie. You get what I mean?"

She nodded.

Bobbie stared at all of them. *I thought I was just helping out here. But it seems I'm as much involved in this madness as anyone else.* He felt frightened, terribly frightened, and after taking a long breath, sat back down in his chair.

"I just don't understand how we can feel like someone else," Mrs. Winn said. "How I can suddenly be seeing out of someone else's eyes, feeling their emotions—emotions I can't comprehend the reasons for."

Bobbie looked over at Jessie, then at Chris. "Both of you have said there have been times that you 'just know' things. Can either of you explain this?"

Haltingly, without looking at anyone other than Bobbie, Jessie started to talk. "I call it 'shadowing,' because that's the only word I can think of that makes any sense. It started earlier this summer." Her voice was soft and quiet, barely audible over the crackling of the wood in the fireplace.

"Go on, Jessie," Chris encouraged her.

"It's really weird," she went on, her voice starting to get louder and stronger, as though she were drawing confidence from finally talking about it. "It's like there's always this— this thing in the corner of my mind—you know how you see things out of the corner of your eye? You can't see what it is, but you know there's something there? Well, it's like that, only in my mind. And then sometimes, I get flashes from the past, something from 1922, things I shouldn't know. Like how Lettie's lover was named Samuel. And sometimes, when something is going on right now in the present, I feel like it's happened before. Sometimes, when it's really strong, it's like they're both happening at the same time, and I can see both."

Alice's face had gone pale and she'd taken her glasses off.

"The time it was the strongest . . ." She hesitated, looking down at her lap. "It was the night Bobbie caught us at Chris's place. I had the sense we were some place else, down by the dunes, and I wasn't with Chris but with *Samuel*, and I wasn't *me*, I was *her*. And the guy who caught us back then, in 1922—" She swallowed. "He was Orville Axelrod, which is why I'm convinced that *you're* the Orville of this time, Bobbie."

"I felt the same way," Chris said quietly, his eyes on Jessie, even though her eyes remained downcast. "If only Madame Nadja didn't die . . . she was going to help us."

Finally Jessie looked over at him. "So you believe her now?"

"Chris and I went back to see her, Jessie," Bobbie explained. "Two days before she died. We didn't tell you because we weren't sure it was the right thing to do unless we'd talked to Karen or your father. Sophie— that's Madame Nadja—wanted to see Karen. She wanted me to get Karen to go see her."

"Did she go?" Jessie sat forward, her eyes wide open. "What did Madame Nadja say to her?"

"I tried to get her to go on the day of the fire." Bobbie shivered, stood up, and walked over to the window. He stared out at the falling snow, at the white blanket covering the ground, the flakes melting against the window. "The day Karen and your father got back from Boston, I convinced her to go see Sophie. Or at least I thought I did. After the fire, Karen claimed she didn't go—she'd chickened out, but—"

Bobbie sighed, looking out into the night. The snow was coming down harder, and a thin layer had accumulated on the ground.

"But what, Bobbie?" Jessie insisted.

"I didn't believe her then, and I still don't believe her now."

"It's too late for Karen," Jessie said. "She's become Sarah Jane. You've seen it, haven't you, Bobbie?"

"We'll get to Karen later, okay?" No matter how Karen had changed, she was still his friend, and Bobbie felt guilty talking about her behind her back. "There's something else I need you to listen to." From his drawer he retrieved the answering machine tape and popped it into his stereo. "As soon as I heard the fire engines, I went over to Sophie's house, but by the time I got there the fire was out of control."

His voice broke. *Oh, Sophie.* He took a deep breath and regained control.

"When I got home, this was waiting for me on my answering machine." He hesitated for a moment before hitting Play.

The roar of the fire, the shrieking of the cats. "Bobbie . . . Bobbie, I was wrong, wrong about everything . . . it's the bloodline . . . the bloodline . . . you've got to tell them . . ."

The tape hissed, and he turned it off.

Alice Winn was shuddering. "Dear God, that's horrible. That poor woman—"

"The bloodline?" Chris asked. "What the hell does that mean?"

"I haven't been able to make any sense of it." Bobbie shrugged. "Sophie and I were friends—for a long time—and we never talked about anything like this. I knew she had psychic abilities—I'd seen proof of them, when she'd talk to friends. But I wouldn't let her 'read' me. I'd rather not know what the future is, if you know what I mean."

"Then what do you make of her message?" Chris asked.

Bobbie looked over at the young man. "I just have this strong sense that it has something to do with you and Jessie—and Karen."

"I think you might be right about her going to see Sophie," Mrs. Winn said.

"How do you know?"

"It was a strange day. I wasn't myself. I felt hostile toward her. It's terrible, it really is, because I have nothing against her. But sometimes I feel—"

"Like Ann Windham," Jessie said, completing her sentence. "Ann Windham despised Sarah Jane."

Mrs. Winn sighed. "Yes. I suppose that's whose emotions I was feeling. Anyway, I thought I should follow her when she left the house. As if I was spying on her. As if I had reason to be suspicious about something. And I followed her almost to Sophie's house. She went down her block anyway. That's when someone spoke to me and I snapped out of it, became myself again."

Bobbie scratched his head. "But why would Karen lie about going to see Sophie? What could Sophie have told her—what could she have seen?" He sat back down. "Since Karen got back from Boston, she's been acting different—not like herself."

"I've noticed that," Alice offered. "Jessie's noticed, too. But, Bobbie, it's been going on longer than that. When Karen first came here, she was very friendly to me. We used to chat every morning over breakfast— and then that changed."

"Here's what I believe." Bobbie looked around the

room. *Well, here goes nothing.* "Somehow, what happened in 1922 is replaying itself now."

"That's exactly it," Chris said. "There's this book. Madame Nadja—Sophie—told me to read it. It's about the nature of time . . ."

"She called what's happening to us 'echoes,'" Jessie added. "It's like there are echoes from the past and we're responding to them."

Bobbie shook his head. "All well and good. But what did Sophie mean that she was wrong? That it was about the bloodline? I've checked—Lettie was the last of the Hatches. There is no bloodline. So it doesn't make any sense."

"But what about Sarah Jane Hatch?" Alice took off her glasses and rubbed her eyes. "Maybe it was Sarah Jane's bloodline that Sophie was talking about. I mean, nobody really seems to know much about her. She just kind of appeared."

"Sarah Jane didn't have any children." Bobbie shrugged. "The Hatches were childless. I think old Horace was past his prime."

"But she could have had relatives," Jessie said. "Maybe one of the McConnells—"

"Wait a minute," Chris said, seeming to consider something. "You're saying Mrs. Hatch's maiden name was McConnell?"

"Yes," Jessie said. "Sarah Jane McConnell."

"*Sarah McConnell?*" Chris jumped to his feet. " Are you fucking—excuse me, Mrs. Winn—are you kidding me? Sarah Jane Hatch was Sarah Jane McConnell?"

"That's what they're telling you, bro," Bobbie replied, staring at him.

Chris started pacing in front of the fireplace. "Oh my God. Sarah Jane McConnell? Was she a suffragette? She died in December 1922?" He kept pacing. "Oh my God. I never knew they were the same person!"

"Chris," Bobbie asked, "what are you talking about?"

"A couple of years ago, my mom paid me to help her with a book on the suffragette movement. One of the things I had to do was organize all her notes. It's weird how it's all still in my head. But I remember very clearly that one of the ladies she was writing about was Sarah Jane McConnell, who was from a little town called Cooper Road, Louisiana. My mom's an expert on her!"

"Well, looks like you're the man to find some info on good ol' Sarah Jane for us. See what your mom can tell us," Bobbie replied.

Chris smiled wryly. "It'll be weird bringing it up with Lois. She'll wonder why I'm suddenly so interested in her work. I can say it's for a school project. I'll figure out some way." He sighed, looking over at Jessie. "If there's a way to fight back these echoes, I'll do everything I can."

Alice cleared her throat again. "Jessie explained this 'circle of time' theory to me. Is it possible that the past is reaching through to us now—and not trying to hurt us, but to actually help us? To help us break this cycle?"

"Look," Jessie said, standing and walking over to the window. "We can believe all we want. We can hope for the best. But we all know how this is supposed to end."

"No," Bobbie said. "We don't know—"

"Sure we do. Lettie Hatch killed her father and her stepmother. She probably killed Orville Axelrod too. Everyone knew she did it. The jury was just too scared to convict a woman in those days and sentence her to death."

"So what you're saying is . . ."

She seemed almost angry as she spun on them. "What I'm saying is—we know what this echo is leading to!" She slammed her hand onto Bobbie's board.

"Look how it's assembled all of us, brought us all together, lined us up just as it was in the past! And all that's left is for me to play my part. All that's left is for me to kill Karen—and my father—and you, too, Bobbie!"

He jumped in his seat. Jessie faced all of them. No one said a word. Then the girl started to cry.

"I don't want to hurt anyone!"

Chris leaped to his feet and put his arms around her. "It's not going to happen that way, Jessie. It's not!"

She pulled out of his embrace and walked back to the window. "What makes you so sure?"

He looked from Jessie back over to Bobbie and Mrs. Winn. "You know, when I have my—*my flashes*, I never get a sense of anything *evil* coming from Lettie. All I ever get is . . ." His voice trailed off. "It's going to sound stupid."

"No, it won't," Bobbie replied. "We have to tell each other everything. Part of the problem is that we've all been going at this in different directions."

Chris swallowed. "I just get this feeling—of this horrible sorrow." His own eyes teared up. "It feels so awful, you can't imagine—this yearning, this grief . . ."

"Do you mean," Alice said, leaning in to look at him, "you don't think Lettie was the one to kill her father and stepmother?"

"No," Chris said confidently. "I don't."

Alice Winn sighed. "If only there was some way we could know for sure."

"There is," Bobbie said. "Karen found Lettie's diary."

Three sets of eyes, wide open, turned to him in shock.

"She keeps it in her desk." Again he felt guilty for telling Karen's secret, but it was pointless to keep it from them. Besides, he'd just told Chris not to hold back on them. So he gave them a quick explanation, telling them how it had turned up when he was looking over the attic for the renovations, how Karen was using it to write her own book.

"She was reading only a few entries per day," he said. "It was to keep the suspense, help her figure how to structure her book. She used to give me updates, but now . . ." His voice trailed off. "She hasn't mentioned it in a while."

"But what had it revealed so far?" Chris asked.

Bobbie shrugged. "That Lettie was a really spoiled little bitch who hated her stepmother. Karen claimed it seemed obvious that's where it was heading."

"I've got to read it," Jessie said, her eyes far off. "I've got to read Lettie's words . . . see for myself."

"There's one other thing," Alice said, her voice grim. "You all must be aware of this. The anniversary of the murders is in three weeks. December eighteenth, the week before Christmas. If the past is indeed replaying itself—"

"We'll come up with a plan of some sort," Bobbie said, his heart almost breaking when he saw the look of horror and fear on Jessie's face.

They planned to meet again in a couple of days, at least the four of them who lived in town. Chris thought he could get Josh to bring him down again next week sometime. Josh was apparently seeing a girl in Boston and was glad to get off campus as much as possible. They promised to stay in touch by e-mail.

"But what about Mr. Kaye?" Alice Winn suddenly asked. "He must be having these same experiences, don't you think?"

"It would make sense," Bobbie agreed. "Have you seen any evidence that he thinks he's Horace Hatch?"

"I can't say I have," Mrs. Winn told him.

"My father is in his own world. If he's experiencing anything odd, he won't let us know. He might tell his agent, but that's about it." She grunted. "Not until he's totally tipped over into Horace Hatch insanity would we know about it. Maybe he already is."

"That's possible," Bobbie suggested. "He hasn't seemed to notice a difference in Karen, has he?"

Jessie smirked. "He pays no attention to us peons. We could start wearing leopard-print pants and paint our faces green and he wouldn't notice."

"Still, I suppose we should keep an eye on him," Alice Winn said.

"As for Karen," Bobbie added, "I haven't given up on her. If we can find a way to break the circle, to stop the echoes, whatever you want to call it—then I believe she'll come back to herself. But I'm going to try to connect with her just the same."

"We shouldn't mention we met, should we?" Alice asked, pulling on her coat.

"No. Not yet. And, Jessie, if you're going to try to read the diary—"

She eyed him. "Don't you think I should?"

He nodded. "Yes, I do. I think one of us should. But you've got to be careful. If Karen isn't herself, and she finds out I've told you about it . . ." He hesitated. He realized he didn't know what this was doing to their minds. He hadn't felt the echoes the way the others had—yet. But what kind of emotional damage was this doing to their psyches? Suddenly his heart ached for Karen, that fun, spirited girl he'd met that night at the A House. What was this madness doing to her?

Jessie promised to keep mum and move with caution. Bobbie showed them all to the door. He watched as Alice moved off down the street alone, leaving Jessie and Chris under the streetlight, the snow still coming down. He shut the door to give them some privacy.

He walked over to the marker board and stared at it. *Orville Axelrod. They think I'm the modern-day ver-*

*sion of some guy named Orville Axelrod. But I haven't
felt shadowed. I haven't felt anything like what they described. I wonder why that is.*

He stood staring at the board. *Because Orville was
Sarah's lover and I'm gay? Maybe if I wasn't gay, and
Karen and I—*

*But even Alice said she was receiving echoes from
Mrs. Windham. Why am I the only one who hasn't? It
doesn't make any sense.*

He sat down on the brick lip of the fireplace and
stared into the flames. Sophie had once taught him that
he could put himself into a trance if he looked into the
flames and concentrated, cleared his mind. It seemed a
lark to try, but he had nothing else to do, the snow was
coming down, and he'd just had the weirdest conversation of his life, so what the hell?

*Are you there, Orville? Will you talk to me? Please?*

He waited.

*Orville?*

The heat from the fireplace finally snapped him out
of it and he laughed. *Nothing, I felt nothing, except this
need to get out of here. I feel claustrophobic. I should
go out and take a walk in the snow. That'll clear my
head, help me think better.*

He grabbed his coat and pulled on a stocking cap
and his gloves. The snow was still falling heavily, big
thick wet flakes, and the ground by now was covered
with a thick blanket of white. He decided to walk out
along the beach. The beach was beautiful in the snow,
the way the snowflakes evaporated over the ocean, cre-
ating a mist of white smoke.

*I wish Sophie was still here. None of us know
enough about ghosts and spirits and this whole circle
of time stuff.*

He heard a voice. He turned around, but the blowing

of the wind and the crashing of the surf below obscured any sound. He saw no one through the mist.

"Hello?" he called.

Nothing. *Probably just another crazy townie like me, walking on the beach in a snowstorm.*

Then he heard the voice again. What was it saying? Was it man or woman?

Still he saw no one. His palms began to sweat, and he curled his hands, shoving them into the pockets of his coat.

*There was no voice, it's just my imagination. All this talk of ghosts and murder, is it any wonder?*

He heard it again.

*I'm not alone out here.*

His scalp began to crawl, and he could feel a chill going down his spine, adrenaline starting to race through his blood. He looked again all around him. Nothing, as far as the eye could see.

*You're scaring yourself, baby chile*, he said to himself as he started walking again. *What's got you so jumpy? Just head back home and stoke that fire some more and put on a pot of hot tea and you'll be just—*

Bobbie never saw the knife as it sliced through the air and plunged into his back.

# Chapter 22

Jessie looked up at Alice. "I'll see you at the house, okay?"

Alice Winn smiled, then turned and walked hurriedly up the street, her head bent down against the wind.

Standing behind Jessie in the glow of the streetlight, Chris waited. His head was bare. Wet snowflakes frosted his hair, and he wouldn't meet her eye. He was such an abject picture of misery, she could barely stand to look at him. *I've made him feel like this by avoiding him.*

Jessie stood up on the balls of her feet and touched the side of his face. "Chris, I'm so, so sorry," she said softly. "I've missed you too."

His eyes found hers. *You're my only friend,* she thought, *the only person who cared and understood from the very beginning.*

"Then why wouldn't you answer my e-mails?" The torment, the hurt in his voice was almost more than Jessie could stand. There were tears in his big brown eyes.

She looked up the deserted street, the snow falling

heavier. She shifted her weight from one foot to the other.

"Chris, I truly believe . . ."

"What, Jessie?" He grabbed her shoulders. "What do you believe?"

*What can I say to you? What is there to say? I don't know if I can give you what you want, my dear sweet Chris.*

"I don't know if there's a future for us. I'm sorry, you deserve better than that. You deserve a better explanation, but I don't know what more to say."

"I wrote you e-mail after e-mail, telling you I wanted to be at your side, that I believed you finally, that I would fight this to the end with you!"

"Yes, I know. I read all of your e-mails. They were very sweet—more sweet than maybe I deserved." She looked down at her feet and started brushing snow off the sidewalk with her foot. "I like you, Chris. I like you a lot. But—"

She couldn't finish. *What do you want me to say, Chris? That I love you? I can't, I can't until all of this is over and done with, and what happened that night is something I can't explain, I can't make you understand without hurting you more. How can I tell you that I never intended for that to happen, never meant for it to, had no idea it was going to? That what I felt that night I'm not sure I was really feeling? That I don't know if what I feel anymore are actually my feelings—that they're really mine, coming from me—or Lettie's feelings? I don't know, I can't say for sure, I know how Lettie felt for Samuel, it's so strong, it comes through more than anything else, and maybe I wasn't thinking about you that night. Maybe I was thinking about Samuel—and if you were thinking about me and not Lettie, oh, I couldn't bear it, I couldn't bear it if your feelings weren't really yours, and I can't, I just can't take that chance, it would kill me, I would shrivel up and die inside. . . .*

"When I'm with you, Chris, it's . . ." She steadied herself to keep from crying. "The more I'm with you, the more likely I am to be Lettie."

Chris reached over and took her mitten-clad hand. "So that's what you're afraid of. That together . . . you and I . . . we become other people. So the feelings we have for each other. You're afraid they aren't really our own?"

"I'm not sure what I feel anymore, Chris." Against her will, her eyes started to tear up. "I don't know if what I feel for you is real, or if it's just what *she* felt. And I don't even want to take the chance that what you feel isn't really you. I don't think I could handle that on top of everything else, Chris."

"I understand, Jessie—more than you think."

"I'm afraid I might hurt you, Chris." This was her worst fear, and speaking it out loud made her feel sick. "You heard what I said in Bobbie's house. There was never any word of a man in Lettie's life after the murders. So what happened to Samuel? Did she kill him too? If there's a chance I might try to harm my father and Karen, then maybe there's a chance I'm going to harm you, too."

"I don't believe that, Jessie."

"But we don't know!"

"No, we don't." He pulled her hand up to his mouth and kissed her mitten, giving her a shy smile. "We don't know a lot of things. Maybe it was the circle of time that brought us together just so we can play out Lettie's and Samuel's story. But maybe it's our story as well."

"I don't know . . ."

"Neither do I. But if and when this is all over, can we try to find out? Will you give me that much?"

She opened her mouth to answer, but a car came around the corner off Commercial Street, its headlights almost blinding her. A loud bass beat thumped inside the car loud enough for her to feel it in her bones. The car pulled up alongside them, the passenger-side window rolling down, and she could make out the music—it was Destiny's Child.

"Hey, Chris, bud, you ready to head back? The snow's coming down pretty hard, so we gotta hustle." A handsome blond boy leaned through the open window with a wide grin on his face. He gave Jessie the once-over. "You must be the famous Jessie." He winked. "I've heard a lot about you."

She looked from him back to Chris, who gave her a faint smile. "Jessie, this is my roommate at school, Josh Benton."

"Hi—nice to meet you." She looked from him back to Chris. "I guess you need to go, huh?"

"Are you okay?" His lower lip trembled. "I can try to skip classes and stay—"

She shrugged. "I'm all right. For now."

Chris kissed her softly on the lips. She didn't respond. Sighing, he made his way through the snow and opened the passenger-side car door. Just before he got in, he gave a little wave, a sad smile on his face. She waved back. Then the car roared off, leaving her standing there looking after it until the taillights faded in the distance.

Now she let the tears come, wiping at them with her mittens.

*"Lettie, you have to know how much I love you."*

*Lettie started crying, hating herself for doing so. "Oh, Samuel, I don't know what to do." She put her hands to her face and sobbed into them. Everything was going* wrong. Why had she allowed herself to even hold out the tiniest bit of hope that it would somehow work out for her, for them, in the end?

"Come with me, Lettie. Come away with me. Tonight. I've got enough money put aside—if we can get to Boston we can take the train out to California." His big brown eyes were open wide. He gently pulled her hands away from her face and clutched them tightly in his own.

She looked into his eyes and wished that she had the courage to run, to get away, to start over somewhere else with him. She loved him so much it ached inside when they were apart. But ever since that night in the dunes, she had stayed away, no matter how much it hurt.

And it did hurt, it affected everything she did. In the mornings, it took a special effort for her to get out of bed. It took all of her strength to smile and politely converse with Sarah Jane over meals, all the while wondering if she knew, if that horrible Axelrod had told her what he had seen. Lettie was unable to focus on her lessons until Mrs. Windham gave up in despair, leaving her alone to lie on her bed and stare at the ceiling.

Even sleep wasn't kind to her. Every night, she dreamed such horrible dreams. She dreamed of Samuel getting tired of waiting for her, rejecting her, laughing at her, and leaving her once and for all. Sometimes she wondered if she was going mad—the way her mother had at the end, which was something she never told Samuel. She told no one about that, but every day she looked at herself in the mirror and wondered if she'd inherited the seed of madness from her mother, if she would pass it on to her own innocent children.

Every once in a while, she would notice Sarah Jane watching her silently, a sly smile playing across her lips, her eyes cold and calculating. Had she already written to Father? Jessie wondered. Or was she keeping the information close, to figure out how to effectively use it for her own gain?

Sarah Jane seemed distracted, almost agitated, all afternoon, and had retired early. Something was bothering her, but Lettie couldn't worry about Sarah Jane now. Samuel was all she cared about. That and her father's temper. She recalled the time that poor yardman had tried to flirt with her two summers ago, and Senator Hatch had taken his buggy whip to him, even though Lettie had begged and screamed for him to stop. He'd kept whipping the poor man, and as long as Lettie lived she would never forget the sound of the whip cutting through the man's shirt, the blood spurting from his wounds, and the grim look in her father's eyes. No, she would never allow that to happen to Samuel. She would do whatever she could to make sure it never happened to her darling Samuel.

She had met him tonight because she couldn't go much longer without seeing him. It was hurting her too much. She'd paid a boy a dollar to bring Samuel her note. Now she looked up into her lover's eyes as he asked once again to go away with him.

"I can't, Samuel, not now—I just can't, you have to understand. But sometime soon, sometime soon I'll be able to. Will you please wait a little while longer? Please, my darling, you have to know how much I love you. . . ."

He raised her reddened hand to his lips and kissed it. "I'll wait for all eternity for you, Lettie, you have to know that. I could never feel for another woman the way I feel for you."

She reached up and kissed him on the cheek. "I have to find out what Sarah Jane is planning, Samuel. We need to make sure my father won't be able to follow us. Once I know, then I will go away with you."

Once the words were out of her mouth, she knew

*they were true, and she felt as though a weight had been lifted from her shoulders, that she could now fly if only he asked her to, she could do anything.*

*He smiled down at her. "If I have to wait until the end of time, Lettie, I will wait for you."*

*Tears started to again roll down her cheeks, and impulsively she reached up and kissed him again, before turning and walking away, through the dunes, heading back to her home. She turned once and blew him a kiss. Samuel caught it with his hand and placed it on his lips. Oh, how she loved him!*

*The night was cold, and the hardened snow on the ground crunched under her feet. She stopped walking when she reached the road and looked up at the dark clouds in the night sky above her head. It would all work out, she realized as she stood there, looking back down the road and seeing Samuel's dark shape cross the road into the wooded area, on his way back to his rooming house. She stuck her hands into her pockets, and felt the ring she'd meant to give him. She cursed herself for forgetting. It wasn't much, a thin gold band with a small ruby set into it, something her mother had given her shortly before she died. Lettie had intended to give it to him as a token of her love. For just a moment, she debated whether to run after him or just wait until the next time. But when would the next time be?*

*"I want him to have it tonight," she whispered out loud.*

*She turned and headed back down the road to the place where Samuel had entered the wood. Snow was falling again, and the wind was rising, so she put her head down and walked faster. The woods were silent, no sound other than her shoes crunching though the layer of snow. An eerie silence chilled her blood. She wasn't superstitious, but she'd always thought the woods were haunted, that there was evil there, ghosts of the pirates and smugglers who had founded Provincetown. She told herself she was just being ridiculous, that there was no such thing as ghosts or spirits or anything of that nature. She thought about calling after Samuel, but the night was so still she was afraid her voice would carry. It wouldn't do to have anyone asking questions as to why the senator's daughter was wandering unchaperoned through the woods so late at night.*

*Lettie started walking faster, not paying attention to where she was placing her feet, so she never saw the tree root buried in the snow. She lost her balance and fell forward. The last thing she remembered before hitting the ground and losing consciousness was a sound just ahead of her she couldn't identify.*

*She opened her eyes and sat up with a groan. Her head ached, and when she reached a hand to her forehead, she felt the stickiness of blood. Pulling herself up by a tree trunk, she leaned against it as a wave of dizziness washed over her. She scooped a handful of snow and pressed it to her aching forehead. Taking a deep breath, she continued following the footsteps Samuel had left, illuminated by the moonlight. She reached the edge of the woods and stepped out into the road—*

*—and saw a body lying on the other side of it.*

*She stifled a scream and ran across the road, her heart in her throat. The body was that of a man, but when she drew nearer she could tell it wasn't Samuel— the coat he was wearing was different, and he wasn't nearly as tall as Samuel—and she sighed in relief, but for just a moment. The jacket was soaked with blood, shredded in places, and through the tears in the jacket and the shirt underneath she could see slashed, angry bloody wounds in the skin. Just then, a shaft of clear cold moonlight revealed his face.*

*It was Orville Axelrod.*

*The scream died in her throat.*

*Had Samuel done this?*

*She ran—ran hard until she collapsed, sobbing, in the snow once again.*

*"Please, God," she prayed as she staggered to her feet. "If you exist in the heavens and can hear my prayer, please, God, let it not have been Samuel who did this, I beg of you, dear God. . . ."*

The house was silent when Jessie got home, although the lights were on in the attic, and she could see Karen silhouetted in the eave window, her head bent down, obviously typing away at her laptop. She stood there at the gate, looking up at Karen for just a moment.

*Karen, what's going on in your head? We've been antagonists since you came to this house. But how much of that has not been us—but the echo of Lettie Hatch's own hatred of her stepmother? Is it too late now for you, Karen? If only I had reached out earlier—but I felt frozen. Frozen in hate. How much of it was my own?*

Jessie didn't want to think of an answer to that question. Now all she felt was sympathy for Karen, who came to this place hoping for a life of love—and instead found death. Was it even Karen who sat there at her computer? Or did Sarah Jane Hatch stare down in amazement at the wondrous technology at her fingertips?

Jessie sighed. She entered the house, pulling off her snowy boots and heading up to her room, where she switched on her own computer. She opened her mail program and started to type.

*Chris:*
*It was awesome to be with you again.*

*What happened between us that night—well, it's obviously hard for me to talk about, but please forgive me for writing it in an e-mail. It wasn't something I was ready for, and I don't know why it happened . . . I like you a lot, Chris, but I've never even had a boyfriend before—and we really don't know each other well enough to do what we did that night. I'm not saying that maybe it wouldn't have happened at some point, depending on how our feelings for each other continued to grow—but it was too soon, much too soon.*

*I don't want to hurt your feelings—please understand me, that is the last thing in the world I would want to do, I owe you so much! But I can't help but feel that somehow we became Lettie and Samuel that night. It was their feelings for each other that somehow came through us, and that somehow it was part of everything that is going on. It was just one more link in the chain that is tying us to the past, and we weren't ourselves. I don't think you would have wanted to do it any more than I would have if we were in control of ourselves. . . .*

*I'm sorry I've not answered your e-mails. I was afraid to—I was embarrassed by what happened, and I didn't want to hurt you, but by not answering you I hurt you anyway. Why does everything always have to be so complicated? I do want to keep seeing you, I hate being apart from you, and maybe we could, once this is all over—well, we'll have to see.*
*J*

*If we're still alive to see what happens,* she thought, clicking Send and then turning off her computer.

She stood up and walked to her door, slowly turning

the knob so the latch wouldn't click, and eased it open.
The entire house was silent and enveloped in darkness.
She crept down the hall to her father's room, feeling
her way through the darkened hall. She listened at her
father's door, which was ajar. Philip was lying on his
back snoring and Karen, finished with her work, now
lay beside him. From what Jessie could tell she was
asleep. The blanket over her rose soft and steady with
her breathing.

Jessie's heart leaped in her chest. The coast was clear.
She crept back down the hallway to the attic staircase.
Hesitating for just a moment, she took a deep breath
and started to climb the stairs, praying that none would
creak on her way up.

She hadn't set foot in the attic since the day she'd
found her mother.

Jessie opened the door at the top of the stairs and
reached in for the light switch. For just a brief moment
before she flicked it on—

*—her mother's face, blackening, her eyes bugged
out, the tongue protruding from her mouth, which was
open in what looked like a horrible scream, her body
turning slowly in the light from the windows, her hair
hanging down, the rope—*

*Stop it, Jessie, stop.*

She sighed with relief as light flooded the room.
Jessie stepped into the attic and pulled the door shut
behind her. Tiptoeing over to the desk, she looked down
at Karen's computer. The screen, darkened, seemed to
accuse her, so she closed the laptop. Then she pulled
out the wide center drawer and readied herself to see
the diary—

But all the drawer contained was pens, pencils, paper
clips. Jessie closed it quickly, then tried the top drawer
on the right, but found it locked.

*Bingo*, she thought, and opened the center drawer

again. There was a tiny gold key sitting on top of the
open box of paper clips, and she inserted it into the tiny
lock. It turned, and when she pulled on the drawer, it
opened.

The diary was the only thing in the drawer.

She reached in and pulled it out, and a burst of joy-
ous energy shot through her body, an exultant shout
rising within her she had to struggle to contain. Glancing
quickly over at the door, she opened the diary and started
to read.

*Breathing hard, Lettie shut the kitchen door behind
her, and stood there, gasping, her heart racing. She'd
run all the way back to the house. Could Samuel have
done it? Could he have killed Axelrod to protect her?*

*The room suddenly filled with light, and blinking,
she glanced up at Sarah Jane, standing in the doorway
to the kitchen. Her stepmother, in her robe, looked
down at the puddles of melted snow tracked across the
kitchen floor, Lettie's still wet boots sitting on a mat
next to the door.*

*"Where have you been?" Sarah Jane asked her.*

*"I took a walk."*

*"In this snow?"*

*"I like the snow."*

*"I was waiting for you," Sarah Jane told her.*

*Yes, Lettie thought, trying to catch her sneaking
back in? But she wasn't going to let this woman intim-
idate or scare her anymore.*

*That's when Lettie noticed another set of boots by
the door, snow still caked along the edges. They were
Sarah Jane's.*

*"You were out this evening, too, Sarah Jane?" An
idea came to her. Could it have been Sarah Jane who
killed Axelrod? Had he been blackmailing her in some*

way? But the body had been so mutilated. Was Sarah Jane strong enough to do such a thing?

"I went looking for you, Lettie." Her stepmother raised an eyebrow. "I heard you go out, so I dressed and went looking for you. I came back here when I couldn't find you."

"You don't need to play guardian with me."

"Why will you never let me be your friend, Lettie?"

"Because I don't trust you! Because I can see through your schemes!"

"You have barely spoken to me since I arrived! You have never given me a chance! I want to help you, Lettie! Help you go to college—"

Lettie laughed. "You have been spying on me. You want to bring trouble upon me with my father."

Sarah Jane folded her arms across her chest. "And what do you think your father would say if he knew you were sneaking out of the house at night, Lettie? To meet some fisherman out on the dunes? How do you think he'll take that, Lettie?"

Lettie raised her chin defiantly. "I don't know what you are talking about, Sarah Jane. I merely like to take walks in the evening, that's all. Your suspicions reveal more about how your mind works than perhaps you'd care for anyone to know." She narrowed her eyes. "And somehow I doubt that was your intent in going out this evening, Stepmother dear. Perhaps you were meeting your own 'friend'?"

For once Sarah Jane looked concerned, as if Lettie had touched a nerve. Was she really so foolish as to think no one knew about her and Axelrod?

"Don't take that tone with me, young lady." Sarah Jane came across the room so quickly that Lettie wasn't prepared for the hard slap that suddenly crossed her face.

"How dare you?" Lettie hissed, and slapped her stepmother back with all her might.

*Her hand to her cheek, Sarah Jane stepped back. "Oh, you'll be sorry for that. When your father finds out about your little trysts, it won't be college he sends you to. It'll be off to a convent school for you."*

*"And why would he believe anything you say?" Lettie stepped closer to her stepmother. "He already knows all about you, and what you are. Are you so confident, Sarah Jane, that he'll take your side? Do you think my father will be pleased to know you are off every night meeting a bootlegger? How will that look? I'm sure my little indiscretions of taking solitary walks will be considered nothing compared to yours."*

*Lettie saw the deep hatred that creased Sarah Jane's face.* This is a woman who is capable of murder, *she thought. In that instant, she was convinced that Sarah Jane had killed Axelrod, with an anger and a hatred so powerful that she had stabbed him over and over again.*

*Saying nothing more, Sarah Jane turned and swept out of the room.*

*Lettie sank down into a chair. Then the tears came, all the energy draining out of her. She turned her eyes toward the ceiling. "Please, Samuel, we need to go soon," she whispered. "We need to get away from here as quickly as we possibly can."*

The sun was coming up when Jessie slid the diary back into its drawer, locking it and putting the key back in place. She tiptoed back to the door, turning off the light. She crept back down the stairs. There was no sound coming from the master bedroom, so she headed across the hall as quickly as she dared. Her eyes ached from reading Lettie's cramped handwriting but, tired as she was, her mind was racing.

*She didn't do it.*

*Lettie Hatch didn't kill her father and stepmother!*

Jessie had read the end first. That idea of Karen's to read it only a page at a time was crazy. Jessie had to know what happened. But on the day of the murder, there was no confession—no description of the horrible deed. Lettie was as stunned as anyone—at least that's how she appeared, from the stark, one-line entry she wrote: *They're dead. Father and Sarah Jane. How— why ???*

And she'd filled the rest of the page with odd little flowers and smiling faces.

The rest of the diary had been just as surprising. *Karen lied to Bobbie,* Jessie thought. *Lettie wasn't a spoiled little brat who hated her stepmother for no reason, Sarah was cruel and mean to her, Lettie was just a misunderstood young girl whose mother died and was lonely, and she was in love. "S"—Samuel—was her whole life. She only wanted to be with him. She didn't know how to handle it, didn't know how to make something so impossible for her to work out. She wanted to get away from everything, run away with Samuel.*

*She was not a killer. She didn't kill them.*

Jessie shut the door to her room and collapsed onto the bed, staring at the ceiling. Her last thought, just before her exhausted mind went to sleep, was:

*If Lettie didn't kill them—who did?*

# Chapter 23

*"What a pleasant surprise, Mrs. Hatch."*

*Sarah Jane entered the little studio with a smile on her face. The sun was streaming through the windows.*

*"Well, Mr. Axelrod, I simply got tired of waiting for an invitation to see your studio." She walked over to a stack of canvases covered by a white sheet, which she tapped with her hand. "I understand you are quite a gifted painter, and I would love to see some of your canvases."*

*Axelrod smiled. "Just give me a moment to put a shirt on, and I'd be delighted to show you some of my work." He couldn't help but notice the way she was looking at him. It wasn't the first time a woman had looked at him in that way, and he was certain that it wouldn't be the last, either. She was a beautiful woman, with her long curling blond hair, her wide blue eyes, and porcelain-white skin. Of course, he'd noticed her before, on the times when he made deliveries to the senator, a man he detested. He'd noticed she always seemed to be around when he arrived with the senator's liquor, and he hadn't thought her interest was in the whiskey. It would, he thought, be quite a nice feat to seduce the senator's wife and, if he was not mistaken, not incredibly difficult.*

*She turned to look at him again, and a seductive smile played on her lips. She glanced at his bare chest. "No need to cover up on my account, Mr. Axelrod. I've seen more than my share of male torsos, and I have to say, yours is quite a good specimen." She stepped closer to him, until they were almost touching, and he could feel her breath on his skin. She tilted her head back, her lips pursed.*

*Easier than he ever imagined . . .*

*He put his arms around her, pressing his lips to hers. At first she struggled against his embrace, out of some stupid pretense at convention—but as the kiss deepened, her resistance lessened, and her arms came around his neck and pulled him deeper into her.*

*He ran his hands down the length of her body, unbuttoning the dress. She didn't resist him, as he knew she wouldn't. . . .*

Bobbie opened his eyes groggily.

*Okay, now that was the weirdest dream I've ever had . . .*

*Kissing a woman?*

He became vaguely aware of beeping sounds, that he wasn't at home. His mind was drifting, and he struggled to reel himself back in. As his eyes focused, he noted the needle in his arm, the long tube running up out of it into a bag filled with a reddish substance. His eyes moved from left to right and he recognized the smell of the place, and awareness began to pierce through the sleepiness.

*What the hell am I doing in the hospital?*

He tried to sit up farther, but when he moved, pain ripped through him so quickly and blindingly that he gasped, his eyes watering. He sat back, closing his eyes. *What the hell happened here?*

The last thing he remembered was going for a walk in the snow.

"Oh, good, you're awake." A female figure hovered above him, and he focused his eyes to see a smiling woman in her early forties. She was short and rather stocky, wearing a blue nurse's uniform. She was checking the IV and the monitors. Her facial expression was cheerful, if a little tired. "Are you comfortable, Mr. Noble?"

"What—happened?" The effort of talking exhausted him, and Bobbie closed his eyes again. He took a couple of deep breaths, trying to focus. *Snap out of it, Bobbie, you've got to get a hold of yourself.*

"You were wounded, I'm sorry to say." The nurse monitored his pulse, then placed his finger into an electronic thermometer. "Temperature's a little high, but that's normal." He heard a tearing sound, then felt the cold rubber circling his arm as she started taking his blood pressure.

"How was I wounded?" he managed to ask.

"You were stabbed. Fortunately, you were wearing a thick coat, so it took most of the force of the blow, but the wound was still pretty deep, and you lost a lot of blood. Can you move your right arm for me?"

Bobbie concentrated, lifting his arm, but the pain struck again, sharp and throbbing. With a gasp, he dropped his arm. He started taking deep breaths again, keeping his eyes closed.

*Someone stabbed me? Who? Why? In Provincetown? But this kind of thing never happens here . . . Was it an anti-gay attack?*

"Still in pain, I see," the nurse said.

Bobbie opened his eyes and blinked away tears. "Yeah, that's an understatement."

388 *Robert Ross*

"Here." She handed him a little paper cup with a pill in it, and he used his left hand to put it in his mouth. "This will help."

"Water?" he asked.

She shook her head, handing him a cup of ice chips and slipping one through his dry lips with her fingers. "Nothing fluid for a few more hours, I'm afraid, Mr. Noble. Now, try to move your arm again."

He lifted it until the pain started to throb once more.

"Excellent," the nurse declared. "We were worried about possible nerve or muscle damage, but you seem to be fine."

"Fine? I've been stabbed! Why? When can I get out of here?"

She sat down in the chair next to him. "We're still giving you some transfusions, Mr. Noble, but you were out there in the snow for a long time, and you've got frostbite in your toes. No, don't worry, we were able to save them, but you were very cold, and almost had hypothermia. You're going to be with us for a few days for observation, I'm afraid. Do you feel strong enough to talk to the police? They've been waiting to talk to you."

"The . . . police?"

"It won't take long, they promise."

"Yeah, I guess so. . . ." He felt horribly afraid all of a sudden.

Jessie. She had worried she might try to kill him. . . .

Was this . . . the start of what they were all fearing?

The nurse stood and headed toward the door. "I gave you a pain pill, so you're probably going to get drowsy again. Don't worry about it—you need to get a lot of sleep so your body can heal itself. I'll be back in to check on you later."

Bobbie nodded his head. The nurse gave him a reassuring smile before walking out of the room. A policeman walked in seconds later—young, maybe twenty-eight or twenty-nine, kind of attractive with reddish blond hair and pinkish red skin. *You've got to be okay, Bobbie*, he told himself, *if you can still check out whether a guy's attractive.* Bobbie managed to give the cop a weak smile as he started to ask questions.

Already Bobbie's mind was fading into a blur. The attractive policeman was asking if he knew of anyone who might want to hurt him . . .

*Jessie.*

*No, I can't say that. I can't tell him about Jessie. . . .*

No, I can't think of anyone who would want to hurt me. . . .

No, I generally don't go out for walks alone late at night, but I just really needed to get out of the house and think, so I went for a walk. . . .

No, I didn't see anyone . . . I heard something behind me, but I thought it was just an animal or something, or just the wind . . . it was snowing . . . blowing . . .

No, I don't remember anything else . . . no, no, nobody wants to hurt me. . . .

Yes, I had my wallet, yes, I think there was twenty dollars in it, my debit card, maybe a couple of credit cards—Visa, Discover, those are the only ones I had. . . .

They took my wallet? So it was just a robbery? Awesome, awesome . . .

I just mean I'm glad . . . glad that it wasn't . . .

Was it?

No tracks in the snow?

You have no suspects?

Good, good . . . I'm really tired, can we finish this later?

The door shut behind the cop, and as Bobbie drifted off into sleep again, his last thought was:

*No, Officer, it wasn't a robbery . . . it was something else, but I can't think of what it was right now.*

When the nurse came back in, Bobbie was sound asleep.

*He started meeting Sarah Jane every afternoon in his studio.*

*He wasn't in love with her—he wasn't really capable of loving anyone other than himself. But he loved being with her, of making her beautiful silky body tremble with his mouth and his hands. He found himself looking forward to the afternoons when she would appear. Her cover story was that she was sitting for him. In case anyone wondered what the senator's wife was doing in the artist's studio. It made all the sense in the world.*

*Except Orville didn't paint portraits.*

*Part of her appeal to him was definitely her beauty. Orville couldn't remember the last time he'd seen a woman as beautiful as Sarah Jane Hatch. But the fact that she was Horace Hatch's wife made it even more intense for him. He hated the senator with a blind rage. Every time he'd made a delivery to the Hatch house, and Hatch stood there counting out his money, Orville smiled obsequiously, while inside he burned with anger, with rage, wanting to wipe the condescending smirk off Hatch's face, to punch him and pound him until he was nothing more than a bloody pile of flesh on the ground.*

*So he'd paint a portrait of his wife for him, as Sarah Jane suggested, so she could give it to Horace as a Christmas present.*

*She, of course, had no idea he was painting her nude.*

*Horace Hatch was the reason Orville had come to Provincetown in the first place. His soul burned with a desire to destroy him and his entire family. Orville's father had been destroyed by Hatch in a business deal that ended with the family in bankruptcy, ruined. Their* name was Marren then, and Orville had watched his father—or what was left of him—decline until he finally died, a broken husk of the man he had once been. Orville Marren had vowed over his father's grave that if it took him the rest of his life, he would get even with Horace Hatch.

He'd changed his name to Axelrod, and one fine summer had come to Provincetown to paint. There wasn't any family money left—Horace Hatch had seen to that—so Orville became a whiskey runner, occasionally sailing out to the Canadian or British ships off the coast of the Cape and hauling in the cases of whiskey. How ironic that his biggest client was Horace Hatch!

Destroying Ellen Hatch had been easy . . . practically too easy. She'd been an incredibly stupid woman, one of the mighty Chamberlains of Beacon Hill, with her condescending airs and attitude of superiority. He'd followed her, just as he started again followed the second Mrs. Hatch. He'd meet her eyes whenever it was possible. Oh, how easy it had been to convince the first Mrs. Hatch that a portrait would be the perfect gift for her husband. Oh yes, Ellen Hatch had been remarkably easy.

Her unhappiness was plain on her face the first time Orville saw her, walking up Commercial Street with a basket over her arm. She looked like she was ready to cry at any cross word. Of course, he figured, being married to a world-class bastard like Horace Hatch would destroy any woman. Orville watched her for a few days before approaching her.

"You are quite beautiful, madame," he said, presenting her with a single yellow rose. "As an artist, I must pay tribute to beauty whenever I see it."

She looked at him, her face pinched into a frown. "Do I know you, sir?"

"My name is Orville Axelrod, and I am a painter."

*He took off his hat and bowed. "And your beauty is so exquisite, madame, I would like to capture it on canvas."*

*"I should think not, sir. Good day." She turned quickly and walked away.*

*Her rejection only spurred him to try harder. Each day, when she made her way down to the markets, he managed to stop and speak to her. At first, she ignored him, but after a few days his looks and charm began to have the desired effect on her. Ellen Hatch began to thaw, allowing him to walk with her in the beginning, talking to him about art and painting, and about her daughter, whom she loved very much. She never once mentioned her husband—local gossip held they were estranged, with the senator rarely returning to the Cape from Washington. Certainly Mrs. Hatch never ventured down there. It took a few weeks before Ellen finally agreed to sit for him, but it had to be a secret—she didn't want anyone to know. Which was more than fine with Orville.*

*He continued to charm and flatter her until he was certain she was attracted to him, and then he took her one day into his arms and gave her a kiss, a kiss he was certain was unlike any she'd ever received from her foul husband. In moments he was undressing her, and then they were on the floor.*

*Afterward, she'd wept with shame.*

*But she returned the next day.*

"Bobbie?"

He opened his eyes and gave Karen a weak smile. She sat down in the chair next to his bed, placing a box of candy on the little table next to a bouquet of red roses. Her eyes were watery and bloodshot. "Are you okay?" She touched his arm. "I was so worried when I heard about what happened!"

"Okay—I'm okay," he croaked out. "Some water . . ."

Karen grabbed a cup full of ice chips and slid one into his mouth. "The nurse said you should only have ice chips for now—maybe later on you can have some juice." Her eyes filled with tears again. "Oh, Bobbie, I was so worried—"

He tried to focus. Karen . . . It was Karen . . .

The old Karen. His friend.

He thought it was, anyway. . . .

His eyes closed automatically as she began to prattle. "When I heard . . ." Her voice trailed off. "Well, I was scared. But . . . now that I see you're okay, I'm less so. The nurse said you'll be fine. I'm glad, Bobbie. Very glad."

He forced his eyes open. If there had been a flash of the old Karen, it was gone again. Something about her lips, the way she smiled. The way she held her head.

"When you get out of here, Bobbie, I'm going to cook you a wonderful dinner. My cooking class has been going supremely. I made beef burgundy last night, it was so good, even Alice said so, and you know how cross she can be."

"No," Bobbie said. "I really don't . . ."

"Oh, but she can. She and Jessie. In cahoots together. But no mind. I've risen above it. Everything has been going so well."

He tried to focus on her. "Are you writing, Karen?"

"Oh yes. It's going wonderfully. It's good to have a hobby, you know."

"It's a hobby?"

"When you get out of here, I'll bring over a pot of the beef burgundy. You'll be better in no time!"

"Karen, we need to talk . . ."

"No, no, no. No talk, Bobbie. You just rest. Don't worry about anything. I'll pick up your mail, water your plants. Is there anything you want from the house? I'll get it, Bobbie, I'll take care of everything and anything you need—"

Her voice stopped suddenly and Bobbie managed to open his eyes and look at her. She had her hands balled into fists and she was pressing them into the sides of her forehead.

"Headache?" he croaked. "Still with the headaches?"

"No, no, no more headaches." But her face was still scrunched up and her fists pressed harder into her temples. "I'm fine, Bobbie. I'm fine."

"Karen, the diary . . ."

"Don't talk, Bobbie. Just get well."

"Karen . . ." But his eyes were closing again.

"I'm going to go now, Bobbie, but I'll be back, okay? You get some . . ." She paused again for a moment, and through his half-lidded eyes Bobbie saw her take a deep breath, then compose herself and smile down at him. "Everything's going to be okay, Bobbie. You'll see."

He closed his eyes.


*"I can't wait to see it."* Ellen's dark eyes danced with excitement.

Stupid, stupid woman, *Orville thought, and with a smile, he pulled the white sheet off the painting.*

*Her face went white. "Orville—what—what . . ." She sat down hard on the chair, her eyes wide in horror.*

*"Don't you like it, Ellen? It's one of the best nudes I've ever done. I'm going to exhibit it next month."*

*"You—can't," she whispered. "You can't do that."*

*"But why not, Ellen? Don't you like it?"*

*"I'll—I'll be ruined." She stood up. "What will Horace say?"*

He made a show of not understanding her distress. "I think he'll appreciate a piece of art when he sees it, especially when he sees how beautiful I've made his wife." He reached out and touched the mole on her bare shoulder, which was clearly represented on the canvas as well. "And how true to life, too."

Ellen started to sob, then suddenly flew into a rage, picking up a paint scraper from his table and lunging at him. He took the weapon away from her as easily as if she were a child. "I think you ought to go home, Ellen. You're not yourself."

She staggered out of the studio. He watched her weave up the sidewalk, walking into people as though she didn't see them, walking as if she were drunk.

He didn't expect her to hang herself. Pity, really. He read about it in the newspaper the next day. What an interesting turn of events. He thought he'd only get to shame Horace, maybe blackmail him . . . but this was even better. The town gossips blamed the good senator for neglecting his poor wife. Surely Horace heard the scuttlebutt.

Orville considered delivering the portrait to Horace anyway. Let him deal with his grief by knowing his wife was a common harlot, giving her favors away to any man. Or perhaps it should be sent to one of his political enemies.

But he finally destroyed it. It was no use to him now that she was dead. He'd just bide his time. Horace had a daughter, after all, who was getting older every day, and she was a pretty little thing. . . .

Bobbie opened his eyes. Weird dreams again, but he was feeling better. His head was still a little foggy. Instead of sitting up, he used the control panel to raise his bed into a sitting position. He turned on the television, flicking through the channels when his door opened. Jessie and Alice walked in. Jessie was carrying a bouquet of flowers, which she set down on the table next to the roses Karen had brought.

"Are you okay?" Alice asked, sitting down in the chair and staring at him.

"Better now." The cup of ice chips had melted. He picked it up and took a drink. "Thanks for coming." His eyes caught Jessie's but they didn't linger.

"Bobbie, I don't know what to think of this," Alice said.

"Neither do I," he said, and resisted looking at Jessie again.

"The police are saying it might have been a hate crime. You know, with how . . . public . . . you are about . . . well, you know, the act . . ."

"You mean Zsa Zsa? Who would want to stab Zsa Zsa?"

Alice looked as if she might cry. "Bobbie, I haven't always been very open-minded about your lifestyle. But I'll tell you. If you were harmed because someone hated you just for being who you are, well—I'd see them rot in jail!"

Bobbie managed a smile. "Thanks, Mrs. W—Alice." He sighed. "But I'll be honest. I wish I could say it was just a simple old thing like a hate crime. Never thought I'd say that, but . . ."

"You think it has to do with the circle of time. What happened to Axelrod . . . the echoes of the past tried to do to you."

Jessie had stepped forward and stood beside his bed. This time their eyes held.

"I didn't do it," she told him.

Bobbie smiled. "Sweetie, you might not have even known it if you did. . . ."

"I didn't do it, Bobbie."

"It wouldn't be you doing it, baby. It would be Lettie."

Jessie's face was stern. "Lettie didn't do it either."

Bobbie made a face in puzzlement.

"I read the diary, Bobbie." Jessie sat down on the side of his bed carefully, so as not to jounce him. "Karen lied."

"Lied? How?"

She shook her head. "Bobbie, she told you it sounded as if the diary gave evidence that Lettie was planning to kill Horace and Sarah Jane. It wasn't like that at all. I mean, it was pretty apparent Lettie didn't care for Sarah much, that she resented her and all, thought she was common, but that's just a small part of it. Lettie didn't care much about her father and his new wife at all. All she talked about was 'S'—Samuel."

Bobbie looked from her to Alice. "Karen had such a different read of it . . ."

"Lettie was in *love*, Bobbie, and I know . . ." She hesitated. "I know everyone thinks she killed them both, but after reading the diary, I can't believe it myself. There's just no way—I mean, it was—" She barked out a laugh. "It was just a teenaged girl's diary. All she really talked about was Samuel, and how it wasn't possible for them to be together, that her father would never allow it, but she loved him—she was even thinking about running away with him, to California. Does that sound like someone who a few weeks later was going to commit such brutal murders?"

"Maybe they found out," Bobbie offered, "and tried to stop her in some way. We don't know for sure—we may never be sure."

"I'm sure." Jessie got up and walked over to the window, looking out. "It's snowing again."

"Did you read the end? Karen never read all the way to the end. . . ."

"Yes," Jessie said, without looking around. "The diary ends just a few days afterward. Lettie was clueless about the murders. Why? she asked. How? There was nothing leading up to that day to indicate she was planning on killing anyone."

"Nothing?"

Jessie turned around. "She did start writing more and more in code. She was clearly frightened. Something happened. Something she just called 'what I found.' Even that she started abbreviated as WIF."

"What do you think she found?"

Jessie shrugged. "She was anxious because Sarah Jane was spying on her. She found out about Samuel. She and Lettie had a big argument one night. But I don't think Lettie was capable of murder."

Bobbie wasn't convinced. He just looked at her. "Where were you, sweetie, when I got stabbed? I'm not accusing you, doll. Just tell me where you were."

"I was walking home."

"With Alice?"

"No," Alice said uneasily. "I had gone on ahead. She stayed behind to talk with Chris."

"So you were with Chris?"

"Only for a few minutes; then his roommate picked him up to take him back to school." She sighed. "I have no alibi, Bobbie. No one was with me. But I have not felt shadowed in several days. My mind has been clear. I have not been Lettie. You're just going to have to trust me that I didn't try to harm you."

"So who did?"

She shook her head. "All I know is, that diary convinced me that I'm not the one my father and Karen have to fear. Someone other than Lettie killed Horace and Sarah Jane. So someone else in our little circle of time . . ."

"Oh dear," Alice Winn said.

"If everything is replaying again," Bobbie said, "then that leaves you, dear Alice, our good buddy Chris, and yours truly."

"But we—none of us—" Alice was blathering.

"Or maybe there's another piece we just can't see," Jessie said.

"I've been thinking," Alice said. "If Samuel loved Lettie, if he wanted to take her away, and the only obstacle to their being together was her father, then why didn't they marry each other after the trial?"

"Maybe he thought she was guilty," Bobbie offered. "No one's been able to find out anything about Samuel."

"Samuel would never think Lettie was guilty," Jessie said firmly. "I know that. No matter how bad it looked. They *loved* each other."

Bobbie was once again finding it hard to keep his eyes open.

"We'd better let him get some sleep." Alice stood up, and leaned down and kissed his cheek. "We'll be back, Bobbie."

"Yeah," he said. "Listen, Karen was here . . ."

They looked down at him, waiting for what he might say.

"She's fighting it. But she's having a hard time . . ." He fought to keep his eyes open a moment longer. "We're going to have to help her."

"If Sarah Jane is controlling her mind, she wants revenge," Jessie said. "On whoever killed her. I don't think we can trust Karen."

"But if we can reach her, I mean, the real Karen . . ."

"You need to rest, dear," Alice said.

"But why has she become so . . . so . . . domestic? Such a Stepford wife? Sarah Jane wasn't like that, was she?"

Jessie raised her eyebrows. "It's true. She's become almost ingratiating to my father. Cooking for him, giving him massages, flattering him like a stupid fan . . . It is weird. Sarah Jane was a crusader for women's rights."

Bobbie was nodding off. "It doesn't fit . . ."

"Just rest, Bobbie," Alice said again. "We'll be back."

And he was asleep before the door even shut behind them.


*So he waited.*

*He watched Lettie every chance he got. But then he caught a glimpse of the senator's beautiful second wife. And once he had her in his studio, well—three times a week she came to see him.*

*As the weather turned colder, he became aware of something in her that was cold and hard. Sometimes when he looked into Sarah Jane's eyes, it was as if they were dead. He saw the same look in his own eyes sometimes. This woman wouldn't be so easy as her predecessor. From what he knew of Sarah Jane Hatch, she had been one of those firebrand suffragettes—but here she was, being made to play provincial hostess, the little woman to a great man. No wonder she had hardened. Orville wondered why she had married him. Probably thought she could effect change through her husband, influence policy, gain access to power. Stupid woman. Doesn't she know that when a woman marries a man she becomes his chattel?*

*When he looked into her eyes, he almost felt afraid. Had she been a man, he would have been truly concerned, but there wasn't a woman alive he couldn't master.*

*He didn't tell Sarah Jane about her stepdaughter's little tryst in the dunes—although it did amuse him. He'd wait to see where that bit of information would best serve his ultimate plan.*

"I can't wait to see it," Sarah Jane said, her eyes

*dancing with excitement as Orville gestured toward the painting, covered on its easel by a sheet.*

*"Just a moment longer, my dear," he told her.*

*Outside, the snow continued to pile into huge drifts. It had been snowing for days; almost a foot of it lay on the ground. Yet still Sarah Jane had come running to his studio, tramping through the snow drifts, when he sent word that her painting was complete.*

*He flipped the sheet off. "I hope you think I've done you justice."*

*Her eyes narrowed appraisingly. She pursed her lips. Stepping closer to the canvas, she asked, "So, this is how you see me?"*

*He watched her in silence, fascinated.*

*She turned and gave him a dazzling smile. "My breasts are larger and better shaped than these."*

*He was thunderstruck. She didn't seem upset in the least.*

*"You—you don't think it a good likeness?"*

*She laughed. "I tease you, Orville. I think it's an excellent likeness." She looked back at the painting. "I think Horace will be quite pleased."*

*"You do?"*

*"Yes, of course." She glanced at the clock on the mantelpiece. "Oh dear, look at the time! I need to get back—the doctor's coming to have a look at Lettie. She's not been well lately, I fear."*

*He looked at her in wonder.*

*"I'll be back for the painting soon, dear. I wouldn't want it to get ruined by the snow. Ta-ta!" She gave him a quick kiss on the cheek and was out the door.*

*From the cupboard Orville grabbed a bottle of whiskey.*

*She's playing me somehow,* he thought. *She's going to run to Horace now and scream at what a horrible thing I've done! She's got a plan. A scheme.*

Schemers can always recognize each other.

*He took another swallow of the whiskey, then snatched a can of turpentine and splashed it onto the canvas until the colors began to run and bleed together. He kept on splashing until finally it was just a smear of colors, except for her smiling face, which seemed to be laughing at him. With his fist he punched through the canvas, then threw the whole thing into the fireplace.*

*Now he had a score to settle not only with Horace Hatch, but with his little bitch of a wife, too.*

*That night, whiskey bottle in hand, Orville went for his nightly walk through the woods out near the dunes. He was quite drunk. He couldn't figure what scheme Sarah Jane was up to. But there had to be something. To just shrug off the painting like that? She was using him somehow. Orville had thought she was just using him to escape the loneliness of a loveless marriage. But it was more than that. She was cunning. Clever. She wanted out of the marriage with Horace. She wanted her freedom back. And maybe a divorce wouldn't shame a woman like that. Maybe she'd welcome her freedom!*

*Orville Axelrod decided he'd better lie low for a while. Leave Provincetown, go to Boston, or New York—*

*The knife hit him so quickly that he almost didn't feel it.*

*"What?" He spun around, and there she was.*

*Sarah Jane Hatch, a long bloody butcher knife in her hand, that same smug smile on her face.*

*"You shouldn't have done that, Orville," she whispered. The knife blade glinted in the moonlight, and it came down, slicing into his chest. Orville staggered backward, landing on the ground with a thud that knocked what was left of his breath out of him. He was*

aware of the whiskey bottle breaking, and the knife was coming down again,

And again.

And again, until he lost consciousness, and the last thing he saw was her smile, that horrible, horrible smile.

# Chapter 24

*Dear Jessie:*

*Attached to this e-mail are various family trees—Sarah Jane McConnell's, as best we can figure out, the Hatches, Karen's, and finally yours. My mom showed me how to get lots of info off the Internet. She thinks I'm writing a paper on demographic changes in the family over the last century. She's so psyched. Poor clueless Lois.*

*Anyway, the most interesting thing is that according to an obituary, Karen's maternal grandmother was adopted. . . . Maybe that's where the link comes in. There's no other place it could be since there are no McConnells in Karen's family. What do you think? I looked up yours too—but everyone in your family is accounted for. No connections there. Maybe this idea that it's the bloodline—that somehow you or Karen are related to somebody from the past—is wrong.*

*How's Bobbie doing? I hope he's better. I called him at the hospital, but he doesn't answer his phone. Josh and I are going to try to get up there this weekend to see him—but I don't know. The anniversary of the Hatch murders is coming up, and we've got to be ready. What do you think?*

*Oh, and by the way, I still love you. Me, Chris. Not Samuel.*

*Talk soon,*
*Chris*

Jessie downloaded the attachment, then printed it out. She looked at the e-mail again and sighed. She clicked the icon to respond.

*Chris:*
*Thanks for sending the family trees. I'll print it out and take it over to Bobbie's tomorrow. He's coming home today, but Karen's picking him up, so I have to wait until the coast is clear. She's still acting sweet, but she just gives me the creeps. Even my dad seems mystified by her change in behavior. He looks at her funny a lot.*

*I managed to track down some McConnells in Cooper Road. I'm going to call them after I send this. Alice's daughter had a car accident—she's fine but broke her collarbone—so Alice is driving down to Hyannis to be with her and help with her kids for a bit. I'll talk to Bobbie about our plan for the anniversary. I'm not sure coming here for that day is a good idea. I think maybe the best thing would be for all of us to be out of town, don't you?*

*Thanks,*
*Jessie*

She backed over the *thanks* and quickly typed in *love*, and clicked Send before she could change her mind.

Taking a deep breath, she picked up the telephone and dialed. She'd gone to the Internet phone directory and looked up McConnells in Cooper Road, Louisiana; there were three. The first was MCCONNELL, GARY. Jessie braced herself before punching in the number, glancing at the clock. Louisiana time was an hour behind, so it was only two o'clock there. Carrying the cordless phone over to the window, she stared out over the bay, which was roiling with whitecaps. The sky was filled with fast-racing dark clouds. The wind was whipping around the house. *Looks like a bad storm coming.*

She had her cover story down. Alice had helped her come up with it, and she'd rehearsed it several times so she could say it without having to resort to her notes. The phone started ringing.

"Hello?"

"Yes, may I speak to Gary McConnell?" she asked politely.

"This is Gary."

"Mr. McConnell, my name is Jessie Kaye, and I'm doing a research paper for a class in women's studies at Boston University, and I'm trying to trace the family of a woman named Sarah Jane McConnell, who was born in Cooper Road in 1899. I was wondering if you could help me."

Gary McConnell laughed. "I dunno, ma'am. You oughta talk to my grandma if you're talking family history."

"Great. Is she available?"

He laughed again. "She done passed away five years ago."

"Oh, I see. I'm sorry."

"No apology needed. I'm only twenty-eight, so I don't know if I can help you, Miss Kaye. But I can tell you there's been McConnells in Caddo Parish since before the Civil War, so chances are, if she was born in

Cooper Road, she's a relative of mine. What was her name? Sarah Jane? Let me think for a minute—can you hold on?"

"Sure." Jessie could hear her heart pounding in her ears.

He was riffling through pages, maybe a phone book. "The person you need to call is probably my great-uncle Ira. He's pretty old, but sharp as a tack, so if this woman was a relative of ours, he might know. Would you like his number?"

Jessie looked down at her list. Ira McConnell was the next person she'd found. She asked Gary if the number she had was correct. It was.

She thanked him and hung up quickly, dialing the other number. It rang twice, and then a quavering, older male voice answered, "Yes?"

"Mr. McConnell?"

"Yes."

"Your nephew Gary suggested I call." She gave him her spiel, about doing a paper on Sarah Jane McConnell, and then the voice on the other end was silent.

"Mr. McConnell? Are you there?"

"Yes, I'm here." He paused. "It's just quite a shock, you know? I haven't heard that name in years."

"Then she was a member of your family?"

"Oh yeah, she was definitely one of us—she was my father's older sister. He was crazy about her. She went away before I was born, though. I never knew her." He sighed. "Daddy always thought she'd come back one day. But she never did. He always wondered what happened to her. How do you know about her?"

"She became a suffragette. A crusader for women's rights."

"Well, I'll be doggone. Good for her." He paused. "I guess there's no harm in telling you about her. It was a

long time ago—a very long time ago. Daddy said she
was the prettiest girl in the parish, and back in those
days, the McConnells weren't much, you know? My
grandma died young, and my grandpa was a hopeless
drunk. It was my daddy who made the farm finally pay,
turned us into a family of substance here in Caddo
Parish—but Sarah Jane was gone by then. She got herself mixed up with a rich boy, thought he was gonna
marry her, you know?"

"Rich boy . . . ?" It couldn't have been Horace
Hatch. That was later in Sarah Jane's life.

"Yep, a filthy rich land-grabbing son of— Well,
you're a lady, I won't use such language. But this boy
was only after one thing from poor Sarah Jane, and
once he got it, he was quit of her."

"That's terrible," Jessie said.

"Yuh-huh. What made it worse was he got her pregnant."

Jessie's jaw dropped. "Pregnant?"

"Yes. That's the saddest part. Grandpa liked to have
blown a head gasket—so he went to the local priest and
found a place where girls in her situation go to—run by
the nuns, you got to know. Here's what we always wondered, even more than about Sarah Jane. Whatever
happened to her baby?"

"Her . . . baby?"

"Yeah, a girl, we were told. Poor child was placed in
an orphanage. After Sarah Jane had the baby she was
supposed to come back home, but she never did. She
had that baby and walked out of that place, and we
never heard from her again. Daddy went down there,
you know, and was pretty heartbroken that she was
gone. He just adored his sister. He always swore she'd
come back one day, but she never did."

"What year was this, Mr. McConnell?"

"It was a couple of years before Daddy married Ma, so I guess it woulda been 1919, 1920? Sometime back around then. Sarah wasn't more than a girl herself."

"Thank you, Mr. McConnell." Jessie's mind was reeling with the information.

"So she went on to be a big women's libber, huh? Good for her. Maybe help some girls who had to go through what she did. Did she get married?"

"Um, yes. . . ."

"Any children? I mean, besides the one she had to give up?"

"No. . . ."

"And when did she die?"

Jessie took a deep breath. "In 1922."

"Not long after then. Poor girl. She went up North, did she?"

Jessie couldn't bear to tell him that she'd been one of the bloody corpses in the celebrated Hatch murders. So she just thanked him and hung up the phone. She reached for the printout of Karen's family tree. And there it was—Karen's maternal grandmother, Iris Villere Laborde, born 1920, parents unknown. Adopted.

*It has to be the connection.*

*The bloodline.*

*Sarah Jane's daughter. The bloodline. Karen is Sarah's great-granddaughter, returned to the house where Sarah Jane was murdered.*

A chill went down her spine.

She heard Sophie's message again in her head. *Bobbie, I was wrong, wrong about everything, tell them, the bloodline, it's the bloodline.*

Her head spinning, Jessie got up and walked over to the bed. Maybe, just maybe, if she concentrated hard enough—

*Lettie, are you there? Lettie, can you hear me?*

She sat down on the bed, leaning back against the headboard.

If the past was replaying, the person in the present who stabbed Bobbie was the person who murdered Orville Axelrod.

*Karen.*

*It had to be Karen.*

*And Karen was bringing Bobbie home from the hospital.*

She dialed the hospital, but Bobbie had already checked out.

*Will she try again to kill him? Maybe I should call the police. Yeah, right, and tell them what? My stepmother is channeling an evil spirit that's driving her to kill? And then when the guys in the white coats get here, maybe they'll believe me.*

The wind howled outside. Hard icy sleet started pelting her window. A flash of lightning lit up the room, and thunder rolled behind it.

*Lettie—are you there? Please, for the love of God, Lettie, talk to me! You've come inside my head before, why not now? Where are you? Why have you gone away? I know you didn't kill them! You have to help me! Please!*

She walked back over to the phone and punched in Bobbie's number. Nothing. It didn't even ring. She hung up, clicked it on again, but there was no dial tone. The phone was dead.

She walked over to the window just as another flash of lightning ripped through the sky. The lights in her bedroom flickered, and then went out.

*Lettie, are you there? Please, Lettie, I need to know, Lettie, please, talk to me.*

And out of the corner of her eye, she saw something in the darkened room, and the hair on the nape of her neck stood up. But when she turned her head, there was nothing there.

*Lettie, please, I know you didn't kill them, Lettie, please.*

Thunder shook the whole house, and the sleet came down harder.

*The storm raged outside.*

*Lettie kept pacing, every so often glancing out the window. Where was she? What could be keeping her?*

*Her father had arrived home last night, tired and grumpy as always. He'd greeted Lettie in his usual brusque manner, and given Sarah Jane a kiss on her lips. Lettie noticed how her stepmother stiffened in his arms, the look of distaste that crossed her face. But when she spoke, it was in a sweet, fawning tone that Lettie couldn't believe her father didn't see through. She'd changed in the last couple of weeks – she was so sweet, so gushing to him. Cooking for him, cleaning, massaging his big hairy shoulders—but it wasn't real. Lettie could see through it, why couldn't Horace Hatch? One would think with all of his experience in Washington dealing with fawning acolytes and people who wanted things from him, he'd have the brains and the experience to see through her—but no. He seemed to like this change in her. He kissed her hand. He called her "sweetheart." It made Lettie sick.*

*All through dinner, Sarah Jane kept feeding her husband questions about Washington and politics, asking for his opinion. Horace was more than happy to pontificate. The whole time, Lettie had wanted to scream. Would Sarah Jane tell about Samuel? What scheme was going on in her head?*

*Lightning flashed, and in the reflected glare she saw Mrs. Windham hurrying up the walk. The front door opened and a blast of wintry air and sleet pushed into the house. Lettie ran to meet her tutor. Mrs. Windham closed her umbrella, shoving it into a stand, then withdrew a thick envelope out from under her jacket.*

*"At last!" Lettie cried, grabbing it from her hands. She looked down at the return address: the Pinkerton Agency office in Boston.*

*"Isn't that your traveling dress?" Mrs. Windham's sharp eyes looked Lettie up and down. She missed nothing.*

*"Yes, it is." The grandfather clock in the hallway struck ten o'clock.*

*Mrs. Windham smiled. "So. Tonight's the night. He'll be by here to pick you up? You'll finally get away?"*

*She glared at Mrs. Windham.*

*"Oh, I've known about you and young Samuel from the very beginning." Mrs. Windham shrugged. "Nothing much gets past me, young lady. Don't worry, I haven't said anything to them. The sooner you get out from under her influence, the better." She looked up at the ceiling, making a tut-tutting noise in her throat. "Are they still abed? At this hour?"*

*Lettie nodded, walking back into the living room and tearing the envelope open. She sat down and started reading the report.*

*Dear Miss Hatch:*

*It wasn't an easy task, but we were able to find the information you were looking for. Sarah Jane McConnell was born to Abraham and Martha (nee Davis) McConnell on their farm just outside Cooper Road, Louisiana, in 1899. Mr. McConnell is held in some general contempt by his contemporaries. His farm does not sustain itself, partly because Mr. McConnell is the town drunk. His wife died several years after the birth of her young-*

*est child, probably around 1907. The people in
Cooper Road remember Sarah Jane McConnell
well. She was not particularly well liked. They remember her as being haughty and holding herself above everyone else in the town, despite the
fact, as one of them says, "the McConnells never
even had a pot to piss in."*

*Miss McConnell apparently set her cap for
Arthur Rutledge, the son of the wealthiest man in
town, and was seen frequently in his company.
Once his father caught wind of the relationship,
he put a stop to it, and shortly after that, Sarah
McConnell disappeared from Cooper Road. There
were many rumors about Sarah's fate, but by ply-
ing her father with whiskey, our operative from
New Orleans was able to discover that Miss
McConnell had been with child, and was sent to
the St. Terese Home for Girls in Chalmette, just
outside of New Orleans. Miss McConnell gave
birth there. The very next day she walked out of
the home and never returned. The child, a baby
girl, was put up for adoption and was taken by a
local family. (A copy of our operative's report is
included.)*

*Miss McConnell next appeared in Washington,
D.C., and became a member of the Ladies Suffrage
League there, making her home at a hotel for
women and working as a secretary for a congressman. There were rumors in Washington about an
illicit relationship between Miss McConnell and the
widowed congressman, but we have no proof of
such a relationship. (See the attached report.) After
being discharged from his employ, Miss McConnell
began to be seen around the city with your father,
Senator Horace Hatch, who after a year or so,
married her.*

*If we can be of any further service to you, Miss Hatch, please feel free to let us know.*
*Sincerely,*
*Victor Brownworth*
*Pinkerton Agency*

*Lettie stared at the letter, then paged through the reports. It was all there, more evidence than she ever could possibly have wanted. This was what she needed. This was the key to get her out of here once and for all.*

*"Mrs. Windham," she said slowly, "I need you to do me a favor. I need you to run down to Mrs. Straub's boardinghouse and get a message to Samuel. . . ."*

Jessie shook her head, her eyes swimming back into focus.

*Lettie . . . somehow I feel she found out the same thing I have. About Sarah Jane's baby . . . She found out . . .*

The storm hit the windowpanes, threatening to break the glass. A mix of sleet and snow. The day darkened. Without power, the room was falling into darkness, even though it was the middle of the day. Jessie walked over to her desk and retrieved some candles from one of the drawers. Placing them in holders, she lit them with a methodical deliberation, as if by her very calmness she could draw more truth from Lettie's shadow. The flickering light helped alleviate the gloom somewhat. Jessie stared into the flame.

*Come on, Lettie, tell me more.*

*She watched through the window as Mrs. Windham hurried down the sidewalk. Holding the papers in her hand, Lettie slowly climbed the stairs. The clock showed fifteen minutes past ten. Mrs. Windham was right—it was unusual for them to still be in bed this late. Sure, her father had been tired from his long trip, and he'd drunk more whiskey than he usually did, but why was Sarah Jane still in bed? They hadn't come down to breakfast, which at the time had seemed a godsend, but now it concerned her. It wasn't like her father to sleep so late—he never stayed in bed this late. Was everything all right? Lettie wondered, and finally steeled her nerve. She walked down the long hallway to their bedroom door. Hesitantly she raised her hand to knock, then changed her mind and turned the doorknob.*

*Her father lay sleeping soundly on the bed.*

*But there was no sign of Sarah Jane.*

*She closed the door and headed back down the stairs. Where was she? She hadn't seen her stepmother leave the house. Lettie had risen early, but had gone down to the market to buy butter before the storm hit. Had Sarah Jane slipped out of the house while she was gone? Mrs. Windham would have said something had she seen her. A thought struck Lettie. Had Sarah Jane left the house during the night?*

*Where could she be? Where could she have gone?*

*Lettie walked into the kitchen, puzzled. She'd packed her bag last night, prepared to take very little with her: a few changes of clothes, some photos of her mother, and some of her jewelry. Now it was just a matter of waiting for Samuel. With the storm, perhaps the roads would be difficult to pass, but Samuel had promised to get a good car. She wanted out of here—desperately.*

*Her father had always treated her so badly, his disappointment that she wasn't a boy always apparent, even when she'd been young and her mother still alive. She'd hired the Pinkertons to find out about Sarah Jane's past, and she'd use it as leverage against the both of them if they tried to stop her from leaving. All she could think about now was getting out of the house, getting off the Cape, getting as far away from Provincetown and her father as she possibly could. If they tried to stop her, she would release the information to the society columnists in Boston. That was her threat, her key to getting away once and for all.*

*But could she do it? Why had the Pinkerton report so disturbed her? She had to stop letting her emotions rule her. She needed to get out of this house. Today!*

*Oh, she wouldn't miss this house of horror, the house where her mother had died, where Lettie herself had been so miserable all of her life. No, she had to get away. California. Hollywood. Where dreams were made. Los Angeles, the City of the Angels, that was the place she and Samuel would go, where they would begin their life as husband and wife. The City of the Angels. It was almost too perfect to be believed.*

*She sat down at the table and poured herself a cup of coffee. She looked down at the report on Sarah Jane. Why did it bother her so much?*

*Despite herself, Lettie found herself feeling sorry for Sarah Jane. What must it have been like to grow up poor, on a farm with a drunkard for a father? There was no questioning that Sarah Jane was a smart and beautiful woman, and perhaps she'd thought the rich boy was her ticket out of poverty. Instead, he'd treated her like a whore and cast her aside—how hard must it have been for Sarah Jane to bear a child without marriage, to just walk away from the child? It couldn't have been easy—Lettie wasn't sure she would be able to do the same. No, for all her faults, Sarah Jane was more to be pitied than hated.*

*"I don't need it," Lettie whispered to herself. "I don't need to use it. I can get away on my own. Samuel*

*and I will go to Los Angeles and make our own dreams.
I don't need to have any final confrontation with my father. I'll just slip away."*

*She looked again at the report.* No, I can't do that to
you, Sarah Jane, as much as you might have done it to
me.

*She stood and walked over to the stove. Hesitating
only a moment, she opened the lid and dropped the
Pinkerton report inside.*

*Being married to Horace Hatch was enough punish-
ment for Sarah Jane.*

*That's when Lettie noticed that one of the big knives
was gone from their holder.*

Jessie shivered.

Lightning flashed again. She carried a candle with
her out into the hallway. Her father . . . where was he?
He had said nothing since the power went off.

She had little feeling for her father. Always so distant. Jessie thought he'd wanted a son instead of a
daughter. Her lack of interest in his writing had always
displeased him. Jessie thought she reminded him too
much of her mother for him to ever really be close to
her. Oh, sure, the world thought he doted on her. That's
the impression he gave in interviews, in talking about
Jessie on the road. "I can't wait to get home to my
daughter!" he'd say. But once here, he'd sequester himself in his room and barely speak to her. More than
once Jessie had longed to be free of this house of hor-
rors, where her mother had died.

How far her father had been corrupted by the echoes
of the past, she couldn't tell. Alice was urging her to
talk to him, to share with him what was happening. She
argued that Philip Kaye was a writer of the supernatural—he'd surely listen with an open mind. But Jessie

knew better. Her father might write about supernatural subjects, but he rejected out of hand the existence of any force beyond the physical one—he called it kookiness. "I make my millions off people who actually believe this crap," he'd said more than once.

Now, when he'd kiss Karen's hand after she made him a superb dinner, Jessie had to wonder: *is that kookiness, Father? Or should I call you Senator Hatch?*

She walked down the corridor to the bedroom her father shared with Karen. In the candlelight, she checked her watch. *Why hasn't he come out? He can't be working without any power. . . .*

She opened the door. Her father was lying, fully dressed, across the bed, breathing shallowly, apparently asleep.

*That's weird,* Jessie thought. *He never sleeps during the day . . . he always says that if he naps during the day he can't sleep at night.*

She shrugged and walked back downstairs. She wondered if Horace Hatch ever slept during the day. Something in her mind told her he did.

The house was so still and quiet. Jessie walked into the kitchen and lit some more candles. *I wish Alice were here.*

Jessie suddenly felt terrified.

*I wish Chris was here,* she thought.

She looked out into the blinding snowstorm and wondered where Karen and Bobbie were. The four-wheel-drive SUV should get through the storm okay.

But could Bobbie survive Karen?

She was the one. Jessie felt sure of it. Karen stabbed Bobbie.

Or rather, Sarah Jane stabbed Bobbie.

But that didn't make sense either. Maybe Sarah Jane killed Orville Axelrod, but then who killed Sarah Jane and Horace?

Was she really so sure Lettie was innocent?

The diary hadn't really exonerated her. She had written *How? Why?*

But maybe it was a message to her own confused mind. . . .

Jessie shivered again. She was scaring herself with these thoughts. The house was so spooky, with the flickering shadows thrown by the candles, the lightning, the sleet, the thunder. She walked over to the window and looked out into the gloom. Everything was covered with a thin layer of ice.

She sat down at the kitchen table and closed her eyes.

*Lettie, are you there? Talk to me, Lettie.*

This time, no images came, just feelings—sadness, loneliness, and an incredible yearning. *Come on, Lettie, you can do better than that. What else happened that day? Tell me.*

The sadness came over her like a wave, so strong Jessie almost cried out, and her own eyes filled with tears. It was so strong, she couldn't fight it off, no matter how hard she tried. And then—

—*the waves were coming in, whitecapped and angry, pounding away on the shore. She was stupid for coming, she knew, but every night she kept coming back, braving the wind, hoping that somehow it would be this night, that he would come and her suffering, her long unbearable suffering, would end.*

*"You swore you'd come for me," she whispered, the tears flowing freely down her face. They froze on her face. "You swore!"*

*He wasn't coming. All their plans—dashed. And now they'd never get away. That much was dawning on her. Could she blame him? Given what she had done?*

*Or rather, what Samuel had done? What he had done for her?*

*The look on his face that last time Lettie saw him. It wasn't love in his eyes, not anymore, but horror—horror for what he'd done, for what she'd asked him to do.*

*Wouldn't it be better to do what her mother had done? Take a rope and go up to the attic, loop it over one of the beams, then tie the other end around her neck? She'd climb up on a chair and kick it away, letting her neck snap. Her face would turn black and her eyes and her tongue would bulge out. Yes, that would be better than this.*

*All through the trial she'd said not a word in her defense, refusing to testify, refusing to answer their questions. She had just sat there like the sweet girl, the grieving daughter, glancing over at the jury behind her lace handkerchief. Her lawyer had always known she'd go free—but she wasn't free, she would never be truly free.*

*She knew everyone in town thought she'd killed the two of them, and that she'd gotten away with it. So she never left the house, that horrible house of unhappiness, which she hated, with all its reminders of how close she'd been, so close to truly being happy for the first time in her life. The only time she ever left the house now was at night, to come down here to the dunes and walk, and hope. But he wasn't coming, she knew now he never would. It was just a foolish schoolgirl's dream that love would finally win out, and her dreams would finally come true.*

*"Samuel, you promised!" she shrieked, finally collapsing to her knees in the sand, not caring if someone did come along. They all thought she was crazy anyway, so let them think what they wanted. Lettie didn't care about them anymore—the hateful villagers with their accusing eyes, the stupid song their children*

*shouted at her house on Halloween: "Lettie Hatchet took a butcher knife, and with it took her father's life. To put an end to all her strife, she used it then on her father's wife."*

*How they delighted in torturing her. Sometimes they threw rotting eggs at the house, sometimes broke windows, and when the police officers came, she could see the way they looked at her. As if she deserved everything that she got. They thought she was evil and crazy—a killer—and maybe she was. She had certainly killed Samuel's love for her. He'd gone away and never come back, and sometimes even Mrs. Windham would say to her, "I'm sorry, Lettie—I never expected it to turn out this way."*

*Mrs. Windham was the only person who knew the truth, knew about the hell Lettie's life had turned into. Her eyes were always sad, and sometimes Lettie wondered what she would do when Mrs. Windham died.*

*She thought she saw something out of the corner of her eye, and Lettie turned, looking hopefully down the beach. Hope does spring eternal, but it was just a man walking along, picking up pieces of driftwood. It was not Samuel. It never would be Samuel, ever again.*

*Wiping the tears from her face, Lettie started walking back to the house.*

Lightning flashed.

"What did you do, Lettie? What did you ask Samuel to do?" Jessie whispered in the silence.

She shivered. The sadness—she couldn't shake the sadness. No, Lettie didn't kill anyone. Jessie was almost certain of it. Yes, there was guilt Lettie was feeling, but not the guilt of a murderess.

"What was the guilt, Lettie? Why did Samuel never come back for you?"

Fingers of sleet scratched at the windows. She didn't like being alone in the house like this. Her father in that unnatural sleep—why did she sense Horace Hatch had slept like that, too, toward the end? And Karen out there in the storm with Bobbie. She debated for a minute about getting her coat and running over to Bobbie's house. Maybe they had gotten back by now.

*Close the circle, Jessie.*

Jessie looked up in a start. "Lettie?"

*The hatred . . . it lives, Jessie.*

The voice was stronger than ever before in her head, and for the first time, it addressed Jessie by name.

*The hate has trapped us in this house all these years, all of us . . .*

"Who's all of us? You, Lettie? And Sarah Jane?"

*All of us. All of us who hated, who found ourselves trapped. Like you, Jessie . . .*

"But what can I do?"

*Everything has come back into place . . . everything . . .*

"Lettie?"

*Close the circle, Jessie. . . .*

"How?"

The lights came back on. Startled, Jessie almost screamed; then they flickered and went back out again.

*The circle must be closed. . . .*

Out of the corner of her eye, Jessie saw something move. She turned quickly, holding up the candles. A flash of skirt, of a tall laced boot, moved into the shadows. Then it was gone.

*She's here. Lettie. And Sarah Jane . . . she's over there with Bobbie.*

Jessie closed her eyes tightly and concentrated.

*Chris, I need you, please, Chris, please hear me, I'm scared and I'm alone in the house, and I'm so scared. . . .*

But would he come? Samuel had never come back for Lettie. And now, the past was being replayed in the present.

"Why didn't Samuel come back, Lettie?" Jessie asked out loud. "Why won't you tell me that? What happened that night?"

But the only sound was the wind rattling against her windows.

# Chapter 25

"Power lines are down all over New England in what some meteorologists are calling the worst winter ice storm to hit the area in decades." The pretty blond weather forecaster was offering a very grim expression on her face. "In parts of Massachusetts, the rain has turned into ice and hail, breaking windows and bringing down power lines. Authorities are requesting that people stay indoors if at all possible, and to not get on the roads, which are covered with ice. Roads are being closed all throughout New England. These conditions will continue to worsen as the rain gets heavier and the temperature continues to drop. We here at Channel Three will keep our viewers posted throughout the night as this storm continues. And now back to our regular programming."

Josh clicked the television off and yawned. "Looks like we might be trapped here for a while."

Chris just grunted, not bothering to look up from his computer screen. He was trying to finish a paper for his history class, due in the morning, and he couldn't be bothered. *Just the conclusion and I'm done,* he reminded himself, *and this is what you get for waiting to the last minute again, asshole.*

Classes had been canceled because of the storm, which was lucky for him. He'd have been up all night otherwise finishing the damned thing. He focused on what he was doing, his fingers flying over the keyboard, and finally he sat back with a sigh of relief, clicked Save, and printed it out. "Finally."

He stood up. There was a knot of tension in the middle of his back between his shoulder blades from hunching over the computer, and his right forearm was aching. His lower back cracked, and he sighed again. He walked over and collapsed onto his bed. "I just hope the power doesn't go out before it finishes printing."

"Yeah, that would suck," Josh agreed. "But I don't think we're going to have class tomorrow anyway." He gestured to the window. "Look at that shit coming down. TV said roads were closing because of the ice— which won't be gone by tomorrow."

Only two weeks of school were left before the Christmas break, and Chris would be glad when finals were over. He was pretty well prepared for them—he'd stayed caught up on his reading and studying all semester, and with the history paper done, all he'd really have to do was review his notes to prepare. And then he'd be heading up to Boston for the three-week break. And he hoped to be able to get down to Provincetown to see Jessie.

Her last e-mail, which he'd gotten that morning, had been signed *love*, which made him smile, in spite of himself. He wished he could be with her, but maybe she was right. Maybe they all ought to be as far apart from each other on the day of the anniversary of the Hatch murders.

If anyone had told him six months ago he'd be believing all this supernatural stuff, he'd have told them they were crazy. But the attack on Bobbie had cinched it for him. He couldn't doubt it now.

And he was part of it. He was Samuel. Whatever role Samuel had played in the past, Chris would play now. It's what that role was that worried him.

Josh thought he was crazy. "Dude, you're way in over your head. You sure this chick isn't just loose in the brain?"

"Jessie's not crazy," he told his roommate. "If she is, then all of us are."

"Well, she is pretty," Josh said, taking the joint out of his mouth, pinching it out, and tossing it into the ashtray. "I'll give you that." He shook his head. "See, this is why I don't get mixed up with girls seriously. They fuck with your head too much. A couple of dates, that's all, and if they put out sooner than that, you don't even have to ask her out again."

Chris smiled. "Just not my style, man."

Josh shook his head. "You've got it bad, man."

*I do have it bad*, Chris thought as Josh clicked the television back on and started flipping through the channels. *But I know it's me, not Samuel, who has these feelings, and it's Jessie, not Lettie, who I care about.*

He tried not to think about how it was all going to end. The family tree search he'd done on Karen seemed to bear out what Madame Nadja's last message had been about—*Karen* was the bloodline. When he'd finally gotten Bobbie on the phone and told him about all of it, Bobbie had seemed really pensive. Karen was coming to pick him up from the hospital. But he'd insisted to Chris there was nothing to worry about over it. Karen was his friend, Bobbie said. He'd reach her. She was fighting whatever it was that might be inside her head. Bobbie insisted he had nothing to fear from Karen Kaye.

*But what about Sarah Jane Hatch?* Chris thought.

He'd been trying to figure out what happened. Okay, so maybe Sarah Jane had killed Orville Axelrod. That left two unexplained deaths. Horace and Sarah Jane herself. If Jessie was right and Lettie didn't do the dirty deed, who did? Chris could buy the idea that if Sarah Jane killed once, she could do it again, and certainly she had the motivation to kill her husband. But all the evidence was that one person killed both Sarah Jane and Horace. Who?

"It was Lettie who done it, everybody knows that," Josh had said to him. "Don't you remember that TV movie a few years ago? Wasn't it Valerie Bertinelli who played Lettie Hatch? Of course she did it. She was the only one with the means and the motive. My dad has made enough whodunit flicks that I know what to look for."

"Jessie said it wasn't Lettie," Chris had argued. "She knows. She's clued in to her."

"Even if I buy your whacked-out theories, Muir, which I don't, I would think that if the ghost of Lettie Hatch was talking to your girlfriend, she's gonna do a good job of convincing her she's innocent. She's not going to admit to offing her parents."

Chris shuddered. He didn't like to think that way. But it was true. If Lettie's shadow was on Jessie, if Jessie was really under the influence of Lettie's echoes from the past, she wouldn't blame Lettie. She'd want to cast suspicion on someone else. . . .

His head hurt. "I think I'm gonna try to take a nap. Wake me up for dinner, okay?"

"Sure," Josh said. He was watching a rerun of *Everybody Loves Raymond*, the audience laughing uproariously at something Doris Roberts had just said.

Chris closed his eyes and rolled over onto his side.

* * *

"You really mean it?"

Samuel knew he was grinning like an idiot. He'd waited so long to hear her say it.

"I mean it." Lettie gave him a brilliant smile. "I have to get out of that house. I can't stand not being with you anymore, Samuel. I love you so much! Tonight, I am going to pack some things, and then tomorrow afternoon, when you get in from the boat, I want you to come by the house. And I am going to tell them that we are leaving together."

"I'll borrow a car from a friend," Samuel promised. "A good car that will take us through the snow far away from here."

"Yes! To Los Angeles!" Her eyes swam with happy tears. "The City of Angels! Oh, Samuel, for the first time in my life I'm going to stand up to him. Really stand up to my father!" She gave him a quick kiss on the cheek. "I have to get back, but at this time tomorrow we'll be together and on our way."

He hurried back to the rooming house and started packing all of his belongings into a big duffel bag, his heart singing. His landlady commented on his mood, and the other boarders couldn't help but notice. Even Pedro saw how happy he was, when they sailed out on the boat the next morning.

"What'a has happened to you, Sam? You're practically dancing as you tie the nets. A woman, no?"

Samuel smiled. "A woman, yes."

A storm was blowing up, so they called it an early day and headed back into port. After unloading the fish, Samuel rushed back to his boardinghouse and cleaned up. Leaving cash on the dresser of his room to pay the rest of the month in full, he swung his duffel bag over his shoulder. He pulled on his jacket and cap,

*hurrying out the back door into the cold rain. He prac-
tically ran down toward the east end of Commercial
Street. He glanced at his watch. It was only two; he
was a little early, but that would give them a head
start—a head start to freedom.*

*Lights shone through the gray, sleety afternoon from
the windows of the Hatch house. He rapped on the
door. Would she be ready? Had the confrontation taken
place? He was nervous, his palms sweaty inside his
gloves. Senator Hatch was a formidable man, but surely
Senator Hatch wasn't going to stand in the way of his
only daughter's happiness? Surely no father could be
that cruel.*

*He adjusted the hat on his head. When no one an-
swered the door, he knocked again.*

*All that came in response was the howling wind
around his ears.*

*Samuel moved over to a window and pressed his
face up against the glass, trying to see inside. The front
entryway wasn't lit, so all he could see were dark
shapes and reflected light coming from other parts of
the house. He stepped back, uncertain what to do. He
was early—maybe Lettie wasn't even home yet from
whatever errands she'd needed to run before leaving.
That must be it. He looked at his watch again. She had
told him to come by at four; it was only two-thirty.*

*"Great," he muttered to himself. "Samuel, you oaf.
In your eagerness you may have spoiled her plan. Come
back when she told you. Lettie said to come by at—"*

*Suddenly he heard a cry from inside the house, fol-
lowing by thumping, like a heavy weight falling down
the front staircase.*

*Concerned, Samuel turned the doorknob and pushed
the door open. He gasped. At the foot of the stairs lay
the body of Sarah Jane Hatch, her clothes spattered*

*with blood. In her right hand was a huge butcher knife, drenched in blood that was pooling underneath it.*

*"Samuel."*

*He looked to the top of the stairs. There he saw Lettie, her face white.*

*"Lettie?" He couldn't speak beyond that. His eyes moved back and forth between Lettie at the top of the stairs and the bloody form at the bottom of them.*

*"Close the door, Samuel," Lettie told him.*

*He did as she commanded. He stood there facing the nightmare before him.*

*Holding the handrail for support, Lettie came down the steps. Twice she staggered, and if not for her grip on the railing, she would certainly have tumbled down the rest of the way to fall on top of the dead body of her stepmother.*

*"Samuel," she said numbly. "It was terrible. What I heard in there . . ." She winced, pressing her hands over her ears. "I can still hear it!"*

*He grabbed her hands, which were ice cold. "Lettie, what happened?"*

*Lettie stared down at Sarah Jane. "Is—is she dead?"*

*Not taking his eyes off Lettie, Samuel knelt down and reached for Sarah's throat. It was sticky with blood. He felt for a pulse; there was nothing. Sarah Jane's head lolled to one side; her eyes were open and staring. He turned his head, unable to look at her any longer.*

*"Is she dead?" Lettie asked again.*

*"Yes." Samuel stood up and backed away from her.*

*"Don't look at me like that! I can't stand it!" Lettie started to tremble.*

*He grabbed her and pulled her into the living room, pushing her down on the couch. "Lettie, where's Mrs. Windham?"*

*Lettie turned her eyes back to him. "I—I sent her to bring you a message. Didn't you get it?"*

*Samuel shook his head. "No."*

*Lettie started to cry.*

*"Where's your father?"*

*"Upstairs."*

*"Stay here." Samuel carefully stepped over Sarah's body, and took the steps two at a time. There were pools of blood all along the hallway, but that still didn't prepare him for the charnel house that was the master bedroom. Horace Hatch lay across the bed, still in his nightgown, and the blood was everywhere. Splattered on the furniture, on the walls. The bedsheets were soaked in it. Horace's eyes were open, and the wounds—there were so many, it looked as if a rabid animal had been at him. Samuel felt the gorge rising in his throat, and he gagged.*

*He was halfway down the steps when the front door opened and Mrs. Windham walked in, closing her umbrella. She let out a half scream when she saw Sarah, and then she noticed Samuel on the steps. She gave him a strange look, then knelt down beside Sarah's body. She felt for the pulse, then looked up at Samuel. She slowly rose. "I'm going for the police."*

*"No, Mrs. Windham, no!" Lettie had come to the living room door. "It wasn't Samuel . . . no, never Samuel . . ."*

*Mrs. Windham lifted her chin and looked down at Lettie. "Where's your father?"*

*"He's dead." Samuel continued down the steps. "You don't want to go in there, Mrs. Windham. No one should ever have to look upon that."*

*"I'll tell you what happened," Mrs. Windham said. "This whore here on the floor . . . this trash . . . she killed her husband, then took her own life."*

*"No," Lettie mumbled. "No, that's not it. . . ."*

*"Of course it is!"* The stern old woman was shrill. *"It can't be any other way!"*

Lettie was staring down at the dead body of Sarah Jane. *"I tried to feel sorry for her ... it wasn't her fault ... not really ..."*

*"It's all her fault!"* Mrs. Windham was looking back at Samuel. *"Were you here when she killed Senator Hatch?"*

Samuel looked sharply at her. *"When who killed Senator Hatch?"*

*"His wife! Sarah Jane!"* Mrs. Windham was insistent. *"Who do you think I mean?"*

*"No,"* he said. *"I wasn't here."*

Mrs. Windham reached down and picked up the butcher knife. She didn't seem to mind the blood and gore. *"She killed him because he'd found out about her past. You still have the report, don't you, Lettie?"*

*"No,"* the girl said. *"I burned it."*

Mrs. Windham glared at her. *"Why would you ever do such a thing? Foolish girl, it was your protection."* She sniffed. *"No matter. The Pinkerton people will still have a copy in their files."*

Samuel had crossed over to stand beside Lettie. He looked down at the blood on her dress and her hands.

*"Tell me the truth, Lettie. Is how she describes it the way it happened?"*

Her eyes held Samuel's. *"I don't know ... I heard them fighting ... It wasn't Sarah Jane's fault. She was as trapped as I am."*

Samuel struggled. He looked at her. *"Damn it, Lettie. Just get your things and come with me. The car is waiting."*

*"Think, you fool!"* Mrs. Windham hissed. *"Who do you think the police are going to look for? You can't run away. You've got to stay here and show Lettie's innocence."*

*Samuel looked from her back to Lettie, then across the floor at the dead body of Sarah Jane.*

*"Come into the living room and listen to me," Mrs. Windham said. Samuel put his arms around Lettie, who was cold and trembling. "I have been praying for deliverance of this house. Ever since your poor sainted mother took her life, in defiance of all that is holy, the devil's mark has been on this house. This blood is not a stain, children. It is a purifying water! It cleanses us of our sin! That woman was Satan in disguise, tempting your father—you—all of us!"*

*Samuel looked over at the dead woman and started to weep softly.*

*Mrs. Windham seemed almost in rapture. "Today we have been delivered from sin! Satan struck out and took poor Senator Hatch, but you, Lettie, you have been saved!"*

*She stood, walking back over to the dead woman's body. "Let us rejoice in our salvation!" Mrs. Windham lifted her umbrella from the floor and stuck the point at the top into Sarah Jane's blood. She began drawing flowers and smiling faces upon the wall.*

*"She's insane," Samuel uttered. "Lettie, we've got to get out of here."*

*"I can't," Lettie said weakly. "I can't go."*

*He looked at her. "It didn't happen the way she said it did, did it?"*

*Mrs. Windham threw the umbrella into the fire and returned to them. "Lettie," she said. "Where is the dress you were wearing this morning?"*

*"In the other room. I hung it there to be sent out for cleaning. . . ."*

*"It has not been touched by any of this blood, has it?"*

*"No, it's just a bit soiled. . . ."*

*"Good. Because you need to get out of that blood-*

stained dress you're wearing and back into that other one. The milkman saw you wearing it this morning, remember? You took the delivery at the back door. You must be seen in the same clothes you were wearing this morning."

Lettie nodded weakly.

"Samuel," Mrs. Windham said, "does anyone know you were coming here?"

"No. I left a note for my landlady, but she shouldn't find it until tomorrow morning."

"Good." Mrs. Windham sat down, exhausted, in a chair. "The Lord has given us a gift in this horrible weather! Everyone has stayed inside! Lettie, you and I have been at my cottage all day, working on some sewing, do you understand? We left the house this morning after breakfast and the senator and that woman were fine when we walked out of the house. We've been together all day, never out of each other's sight, do you understand that?"

"But—"

"It's the only way!" Mrs. Windham shouted. "You two foolish children! You'll both be hanged if you don't listen to me!"

"But Samuel wasn't here!"

"He was when I came through that door." Her cold eyes fixed on them. "But we must make sure no one ever questions anything. They must believe this was a crime of revenge—perhaps by one of the senator's political enemies. Otherwise they'll say poor Lettie did it, and then Satan will really have won."

"I'll do anything to protect Lettie," Samuel said.

"Fine," the old woman said, leveling her eyes at him. "Then take the knife and stab Sarah's body as many times as you can stomach."

"What?" Samuel's stomach lurched. "I—I can't do that."

"You have to." Her face was grim. "You must make it look as though the crimes were committed by the same person, with the same motivation. Remove all of your clothes before doing so, however. Not a drop of blood must touch them. Then get dressed again and hurry out the back way to your boardinghouse. Lettie and I will go out the same way, down to my cottage, and then come back up here and find the bodies." She sighed. "Lettie and I will alibi each other. And if you get back to your rooming house and remove that note, no one will ever connect you with this either."

"No," Lettie said, her voice breaking.

"What choice do we have?" Mrs. Windham looked back out into the hallway. "I curse the day that woman came into our lives! Lettie, don't you understand? This is our only hope! The only way you and I can go on living! We can go back to our lives, so saintly, so peaceful, so quiet—the way they were before that woman arrived and changed everything."

"Do what she says, Lettie," Samuel said, but his voice sounded different to him. "I won't see you hanged."

Mrs. Windham beamed. "Now you're listening to reason!"

Samuel stood, taking off his coat. "You ladies ought to go now."

"We'll go into the other room so that Lettie can change. We'll take her bloody dress and burn it in my cottage. Then we'll slip out the back way."

"Samuel," Lettie said, her voice breaking.

"Go on, Lettie," he said. "Get out of this place."

After they were gone, Samuel slowly undressed. His stomach was lurching and his heart was pounding so hard he could hear it. He swallowed his fears. Wearing only a leather glove, he picked up the knife from the floor. He brought it up into the air.

"Dear God," he prayed out loud. "Forgive me."

*He swung the knife down through the air and began stabbing the dead flesh.*

Chris sat up in bed, wide awake. His heart was thumping. "Christ!"

"You okay, bro?" Josh asked from in front of the television set.

Chris reached for the phone and dialed Jessie's phone number. "We're sorry, that line is temporarily out of service." He slammed the phone back down, then dialed Bobbie's number, only to get the same electronic message.

"Fuck!" He threw the phone across the room. "Their phones are out."

"Phones are out all over, dude. That's what they just broke in to say. From Rhode Island straight across Cape Cod. They're really getting hit hard over that way." Josh clicked off the television. "What's up?"

"We've got to get up there." He grabbed his coat. "You've got to drive me up to Provincetown."

"Whoa, man. In this storm? We'd never get permission—"

"Josh, they're all so worried about the damned storm no one's going to even think about trying to stop us." He crossed the room and grabbed Josh by the shoulders. "Jessie's in danger, man. It's going to be tonight— it's going to be tonight."

"What's going to be tonight?"

"The murders! It's happening again!"

"Oh, right. Your whacked theories. But I thought you said the anniversary of the Hatch murders wasn't for another week."

"It's the storm." Chris let go of him and began pacing around. "The circle—it doesn't care about exact dates and things. If it did, Bobbie wouldn't be gay."

"Huh?" Josh asked.

"Never mind. But there are lots of things that are slightly off. What matters is the context. I get that now. And today—this storm! The Hatches were murdered during a storm like this. And I know who killed them."

"How do you know?"

"I just do."

"Then who?"

Chris lunged at him, grabbing him by the sweater. "Please, Josh! Take me to Provincetown!"

"Okay, man, I'm in," Josh said. "Explain in the car."

The boys ran down the hallway and down the back steps. The sleet was hammering hard, the parking lot slick with ice. Josh unlocked the doors, and they climbed in. The car started immediately, and the windows immediately fogged up. Josh turned the defroster on.

"Are you sure you want to do this, man?" Josh asked.

"Are you scared to drive in this?"

Josh bristled. "No way, man. This is not a problem. It's just that if we get caught, we get expelled. Now, my folks won't care one way or the other. But your mom would freak."

"I can't worry about Lois. For once in my life I'm not going to worry about Lois." Chris looked straight ahead. "We've got to get up there."

"You're the boss, man."

Chris closed his eyes.

*Talk to me Samuel, tell me something, anything, tell me that Jessie's going to be all right, damn it, talk to me!*

But the only sound was the car's engine as Josh revved it and slammed it into gear and they were on their way.

*That's why no one was ever able to figure it out, why no one could solve the murders. Sarah Jane must have killed Horace—that's what Lettie heard. Maybe he had hit her again, and she freaked out. Then, when Lettie found them, Sarah Jane had tried to attack Lettie. Lettie had grabbed the knife, slashed her across the throat, killing her in self-defense. That's why Samuel had to stab her dead body again. So that the murders would look the same. Back then they didn't have the technology to realize that Sarah Jane was already dead when she was stabbed repeatedly in the stomach.*

Chris felt nauseated, and not from the way the car was swerving on the icy surface of the parking lot.

*Jessie, please be okay. I'm on my way, I'm on my way.*

They approached the school gate, which was just a wooden bar. The gatehouse was deserted. Josh pulled up and stopped. "Chris, get out and lift the gate."

Chris opened his car door, the wind knifing through him, but he managed to force the gate up high enough for Josh to drive the car underneath it. He jumped back into the car. "It's fucking freezing out there," he chattered.

"Yeah." Josh shifted the car into gear and they flew out onto the county road. "So, bro, tell me—who killed the Hatches?"

Chris closed his eyes and started talking.

# Chapter 26

*Bobbie's my friend,* Karen thought as she steered the car along the icy stretch of Route 6 between Truro and Provincetown. *Bobbie was the first friend I made here. Bobbie's my friend.*

Why did she have to keep saying that to herself? Of course Bobbie was her friend. Why did the thought keep coming to her mind?

She looked over at him in the passenger seat. Poor wounded bird. She'd take good care of him once they were home.

Oh yes, she'd take care of him.

What did that mean? She hated these moments. She'd been having them frequently the last few weeks. Moments of strange doubts, confusing fears. They'd intrude into her good mood—the good mood that she'd finally embraced. It was so much better than the anxiety and insecurity she'd first felt, when Horace first brought her here to this godforsaken place.

She smiled over at Bobbie. "You know," she said, "I was thinking you ought to try painting for a hobby. I'd be glad to pose for you."

Bobbie looked uncomfortably over at her. Orville Axelrod—Jessie had told him that Axelrod had been a painter.

Maybe he shouldn't have agreed to let Karen drive him. He still didn't believe that she was the one who stabbed him—he refused to believe it, even though he knew it was the only explanation that made sense—but Karen was his friend. He could reach her. He knew he could.

"Sweetie," he said, "I appreciate your concern, but I have to tell you, darlin', I'm concerned about you, too."

"Me?"

"Yeah. You. You're not yourself."

She flashed him a grin. "Whatever do you mean?"

"Like that." He looked at her sternly. "Karen, you're speaking in a southern accent."

She laughed. "I'm jes toyin' with y'all."

"Well, it freaks me out. You have to know what it makes me think."

"No, what?"

He sighed. "Karen, you haven't talked about Lettie Hatch's diary for weeks. About all that crazy stuff . . . about how you felt somehow some connection to Sarah Jane."

"Poor Sarah Jane," Karen said dreamily. "Poor Sarah Jane."

*How horrible Horace had been. Horrible Horace. That's what she called him to herself. To think she had brought herself to be so sweet to him. He had bought her phony happy housewife persona. How she had loathed touching his hairy shoulders, massaging his fleshy body. After what he had done to her—he had raped her! Her own husband had raped her!*

*But she had found a way out. She would win him over the only way that would work. He was such a sap for a pretty woman. Always was. She'd make him forget that mistress down in Washington by whimpering sweet around him, playing the little lady. She'd cooked for him. She'd fluttered her eyelashes at him. She'd let him have his fumbling, disgusting way with her in bed. And it had worked. He was beginning to trust her again. Trust her enough to let her fix him a drink when he got back home, tired and exhausted, from Washington. A special drink that made him relax . . . and sleep . . . oh, how Horace slept. Long and deep enough for Sarah Jane to go through his briefcase and read all of his private papers, learn all his political secrets. She saw what bills he was working on. She saw what was coming up, the strategies he planned to use to get policies passed. She learned enough to know who were his friends on Capitol Hill, and who were his enemies. . . .*

*He'd even promised her one night, after she'd cooked him a dinner of beef burgundy and given him a foot massage, that she could come back with him to Washington next time. She had kissed him like a good wife and thanked him for being such a good husband.*

*At last! She'd go to Washington with him. And that's when she'd spring it on him. She'd go to his enemies, give them information on his political plans. They would ruin him. There was so much that could bring him down—the kickbacks he was getting from lobbyists, the brokering for votes in the smoky back rooms of the Senate, his extramarital affair with a Washington widow . . . The powerful Senator Hatch would be brought down, and Sarah Jane would be free!*

*How she longed to be back in the corridors of power, away from this backwater of a town. But then it all had changed. She had come upon Horace as he read a report from Pinkerton's Detective Agency—a copy of*

*what that damned spying little bitch daughter of his
had paid for. Even now Sarah Jane had to laugh at the
girl's naïveté. Did Lettie really think the Pinkerton
people would investigate her stepmother without in-
forming the mighty Senator Hatch?*

*Not that Horace hadn't known most of what the re-
port revealed—his own spies had done their job well
enough—but the bit about the baby surprised him. No—
it had infuriated him. "You never told me there was a
child from your whoring!" he bellowed, and she knew
in that moment all her weeks of kissing his big fat hairy
behind would do her no good.*

*He had staggered toward her in blind fury, as if he
suddenly suspected her nature these past few weeks
had been all a ruse. "It's one thing to take a wife back
to Washington with a sordid past—but that she has also
borne a child out of wedlock? It would destroy me!"*

*His eyes had bulged from his red face. "And when
this child grows up and makes a claim for my estate?
Then what?" He bore down on her hideously, his stinking breath in her face.*

*Sarah Jane panicked. In that moment, her whole life
had flashed before her.*

He's going to find her. My daughter. And what
would he do to her?

To my baby?

No, not my baby . . .

I'm Karen Donovan.

Karen Donovan Kaye.

She turned onto Shank Painter Road in Provincetown.

"Bobbie," she said weakly.

"What is it, babe?"

"Sometimes . . ."

The headache again, overpowering her.

"Sometimes what, Karen?"

The pain . . . She tried to steady her thoughts as she gripped the wheel. She had to focus; otherwise they'd run off the road in this ice and snow.

Such a godforsaken town here at the end of the world. In storms like this, the end of the Cape was cut off from the rest of the world. Karen struggled to concentrate, but the headache was too strong.

Sarah Jane had had such plans, such dreams—and now here she was, trapped in this place—

"Sometimes what, Karen?" Bobbie asked again.

"Sometimes I think you're jes the cutest ol' thang," she sang out, still in that ridiculous accent.

Bobbie shuddered. He wasn't reaching her. Maybe he was too tired. Maybe he just need to rest before trying again.

And maybe, he feared, she was unreachable.

They pulled up in front of his house. Bobbie gave her a faint grin and opened his car door. "Well, thanks, Karen. I really appreciate the ride. Give me a call later, okay?"

She gave him a strange look as she turned off the ignition. "Bobbie, don't be crazy. With this storm coming on so strong, I'm not leaving until I have you all settled in—and I'll make you a nice sandwich and maybe some soup. Wouldn't you like that?"

"I'd kind of like to be alone." He bit his lip. *What I mean is, I don't want to be alone with you.*

"Don't be silly," she said, opening her door and taking off her seat belt. "It's the least I can do."

Sharp sleet stung their faces as they hurried to the door. Karen followed in behind him, feeling for the light switch. Bobbie prayed the power wouldn't be out here in the west end. It had looked suspiciously dark as they'd come through the center of town. Thankfully the room filled up with light as Karen hit the switch. "Now, you just make yourself comfy on the couch," she said, "and I'll see what's in the kitchen."

"I'm not hungry, Karen." Lightning flashed, followed by a roll of thunder that rattled the entire house. Bobbie sat down on the couch, stretching his legs out and pulling a comforter over him. He turned the television on, to see a grim-faced news anchor, with SPECIAL WEATHER BULLETIN scrolling across the bottom of the screen.

"This is a highly dangerous storm. According to the National Weather Service, already power and telephone lines are down throughout the northeastern United States. Reports of hail, sleet, and ice are coming in from all sections of Connecticut, Rhode Island, Massachusetts, New Hampshire, Vermont, and Maine. Roads are being closed throughout the region. The coast guard is urging any small craft out on the water to make for a safe port until this storm passes. State officials are urging residents to stay off the roads, and to stay indoors if at all possible. The temperature is continuing to drop, which will freeze the water on the ground. We will keep you updated as often as possible on this dangerous storm— the worst according to meteorologists that the area has seen in more than ten years."

Bobbie switched off the television and got to his feet. He was still a little wobbly, but his back didn't hurt anymore; he could move his right arm without too much stiffness, but only so far. He stood in the doorway watching Karen. Her back was to him as she stirred something in a pan on the stove. The empty red and white can sitting on the counter read CHICKEN NOODLE.

"Karen, really, I'm fine. You should probably get home. This storm is getting worse." He shivered. "You might wind up being stranded here."

"Oh, pish." She didn't turn around. "I'm from Louisiana, remember? I've been through hurricanes and tropical storms. This is nothing." She snapped her fingers. "Besides, I only have to drive a few blocks."

"I'd feel better if I knew you were safe at home."

She walked over and pinched his cheek. "You're so sweet to be so worried about me, but it's fine, Bobbie." She laughed. "If I didn't know better, I'd think you were trying to get rid of me."

*If you only knew how much it scares me to be alone in the house with you.* He shook his head. *No, it couldn't be. Karen couldn't have been the one to stab me, look at her, cooking me soup and trying to take care of me, it's stupid to even think that, maybe we're all just kind of losing our minds here—*

Lightning flashed, and the lights flickered, dimmed, and went out.

"Well, shit," Karen said just before the thunder drowned her out. "So much for the soup. Sorry, Bobbie."

He decided to level with her. "Karen, listen. Stuff is happening. You have to feel it. You're not yourself."

"Stop saying that," she said, sounding genuinely annoyed.

"But it's true, sweetie. I'll admit to you I'm scared."

"Of what, Bobbie?"

He fumbled for words. "Are you still reading Lettie's diary?"

Her face looked pained. "Why are you asking about that?"

"She didn't kill the Hatches, did she?"

Thunder crashed over the house.


Karen looked down at the man standing in the doorway to the kitchen. Who was this man? Why was she here? What was this place?

"Of course Lettie killed the Hatches," she heard herself saying. "Who else could it have been?"

"Is that what it says in the diary? You've never told me. Did you ever reach the end? What did you find out, Karen?"

She eyed him. He looked familiar. Yes, she knew him. That painter . . .

"What did you mean," she asked this man, "when you said that stuff is happening?"

He gave her a frightened expression. "It's almost the anniversary of the Hatches' deaths," he said.

She felt the headache behind her eyes again. "The anniversary . . ."

*Lettie didn't kill the Hatches, did she?*

What *had* the diary said? Karen couldn't remember. Had she ever gotten that far?

No, no . . . she had stopped reading it. Stopped reading because she already knew the outcome. . . .

She knew who killed Horace and Sarah Jane Hatch.

*He was going to find my baby.*

*He was going to find the little girl I had given up to a new world, sent far away from the misery I had known, a little girl who would grow up loved and happy . . .*

*He would find her. Horace would find her. . . .*

"Really, Karen, why don't you just go on home?" the man in the doorway was pleading.

*Karen? Why does he call me Karen?*

*Oh yes, Karen Donovan.*

*Darling, sweet Karen Donovan.*

*My own blood. Part of my bloodline.*

And Philip had treated Karen very badly. Lying to her, humoring her, belittling her work. *Just as Horace had done to me.*

*He'll pay. They'll all pay.*

\* \* \*

*There it is again*, Bobbie thought. *That look in her eyes*.

"Look, Karen," he said. "I just want to go to sleep. Forget about all of this, all of this mystery of the past. Go home and we'll talk about it later. I'll be fine here. . . ."

She was smiling again. "And leave you alone in the dark, with the power out? What a lousy friend you must think I am! I was raised better than that, Bobs. Do you have candles?"

He nodded. "Top drawer, next to the stove." He could barely make out her form moving through the darkness, but he heard her rattling around in the drawer. His stove was gas, so the lit eye glowed eerily orange and blue in the darkness. He saw her place the end of a candle into the flame until it sparked and caught. She handed it to him, then repeated the process, as Bobbie placed the candles into holders. The room flickered with a soft golden light.

"Bobbie," Karen said.

"Yeah?"

"What you said about the anniversary of the Hatches' deaths."

He eyed her. "Yeah, what about it?"

She shivered. "I'm frightened too. I don't know why."

*That's her. That's Karen.* "Oh, sweetie." He took her into his arms.

"Maybe I *will* go home," she said. "I'm sorry about lunch. I'm not that great a cook anyway."

"It's going to be okay," Bobbie said, placing his hands on the sides of her face and looking into her eyes. "We have a week. I'm going to call a friend of Sophie's who came to her funeral. He's a parapsychologist."

She looked confused.

"It means he deals with the supernatural. Sweetie, I know it all must seem weird to you, but I've been talking with—with people." He figured he wouldn't bring Jessie into it. Just to be safe. "Stuff really is happening, babe. I believe it now. Anyway, this Dr. Hobart has a place here on the Cape. Down in Fall's Church. He seemed like a nice guy. Maybe he'll know what to do, have something to suggest . . ."

"You think . . . something is going to happen on the date of the Hatches' anniversary?" she asked slowly.

"I don't know. It's crazy."

"You think . . . Philip and I . . ."

"No, baby, I don't think anything. I shouldn't have said anything. . . ."

"The anniversary, Bobbie," she said, and for a moment her deep brown eyes seemed to hold the answer. "I don't think it matters."

"What do you mean?"

"The anniversary itself . . . it doesn't matter."

"I'm not following, honey."

But she fell silent. She slowly moved out of his arms.

"Karen, are you okay?"

She looked at him. *Bobbie is my friend.*
*Bobbie is my friend!*

Her eyes moved across the kitchen to where he kept his knives in a basket beside the microwave oven. Long, sharp blades that reflected the candlelight . . .

"I think I *will* go home now, Bobbie," she said, a wave of unexplained fear passing through her.

"We'll talk more tomorrow," he promised.

She looked at him.

Orville Axelrod.

How innocent he tried to come across standing there, looking at her that way. But she knew he'd been double-crossing her. She had learned how to sniff out underhandedness, and the man across from her was stewing in it. She could feel the waves of guilt emanating off of him. Foolish man, to think he could pretend with her . . .

There was another flash of lightning, this time so close that the thunder roared almost immediately after the light died.

"All right," she said, in a voice she didn't recognize. "Will you at least get back on the couch before I go?"

Bobbie sighed, picking up a candle and walking back into the living room, but she noticed how he never fully turned his back to her.

*Smart move, sir*, she thought, a smile creeping across her face.

Bobbie set the candleholder down on the coffee table and stretched out onto the couch, pulling the comforter over him once more. He smiled up at her. "Happy now?"

*I could kill him right here. He's too weak to fight me off. I could take one of those knives from the kitchen and plunge it through his scheming heart. To think I believed he had cared about me. I thought someone here in this land at the end of time actually cared about me. But I was wrong. He was going to try to fool me the way I had been fooled by Arthur . . . but I'll never be fooled again.*

The headache once more screamed behind her eyes.

"Karen," Bobbie said. "I'm fine now. You can go."

She looked down at him with strange eyes. Her own? Or Sarah Jane's? Bobbie couldn't tell.

"What's going on, Bobbie?" She set her candle down next to his and sat down in the recliner opposite him. "What is it that you're so frightened about?" She stared at him through the darkness, her eyes glittering in the candlelight. "I mean, if you're mad at me about something, you'd tell me, wouldn't you?"

"Karen, let's talk later," he said.

"But now you've gotten *me* frightened."

Had he been wrong to bring it up with her? She seemed herself one minute, then possessed by Sarah Jane the next. He couldn't do this alone. He needed help. Maybe Dr. Hobart—somebody—anybody. He just knew he didn't want to be alone with her.

"I'm sorry," Bobbie said. "But the pain medication is really kicking in. I'm just really tired. Don't be frightened about anything, Karen. We'll talk later."

"Fine." She stood, annoyed. "You've made it clear I'm not wanted." She pulled her coat back on and headed toward the door.

"Karen—wait." *Let her go, let her go*, his mind screamed, but he couldn't let her leave like that. She was his friend. *Karen is my friend!*

She sat back down in the chair again. He could see her eyes, and his heart leaped into his throat and his blood froze in his veins.

Her eyes were blue!

*Karen—my brown-eyed girl—has blue eyes!*

Bobbie swallowed, opened his mouth, but nothing came out.

One of Karen's eyebrows went up and she was smiling. "You wanted to say something?"

*Her voice is different, colder—that isn't Karen! If Karen had been struggling to come through, she's not there now.*

"Something more you were going to say?"

*She's Sarah Jane Hatch—and I'm alone in the house with her!*

And then another thought came to him.

*The anniversary doesn't matter. That's what she said. The anniversary itself didn't matter!*

They were wrong to think they still had time. It wasn't the date—it was the storm! It was during a storm like this that the Hatches were killed.

It was happening now!

"Bobbie," she said, unnaturally calm, "I'm waiting."

*I can't let her go*, Bobbie thought. *I have to keep her here. I can't let her go back home without warning Jessie—*

Lightning lit up the room.

"Well?" Karen smiled. "What did you want to tell me, Bobbie?"

He looked at her. Her blues eyes blazed in the candlelight.

"Nothing," he muttered.

"Oh, come now, Bobbie. I'm sure you were going to say something. Words never fail you, and they never have. Always so quick with the comeback. A charmer. That's what you are."

He just stared at her.

"Maybe what you're going to say was that the circle of time had finally come around, that the echoes were set to become so loud that they would drown out everything else? Is that it, Bobbie? Is that what you were going to say?"

He stared at her. Karen laughed, a hideous sound.

"Oh, Bobbie. Finally everything is going to be as it should be. The way it was meant to be."

"You're not Karen," he managed to say.

"We are all many people, Bobbie. We have all led many lives."

He stood warily. She watched him with a smile on her face.

"I told you I wanted you to rest, Bobbie," she said. "You mustn't strain yourself."

"I'm going to stop you, Sarah Jane." His heart was pounding as she stood to face him. "There will be no more death as there was in the past."

She gave him a sympathetic face. "There wasn't supposed to be death then either. But we had our own echoes to confront. All of us live with the echoes of the past. There's no changing that. And I'm afraid no—what did you call him?—parapsychologist can change that fact."

Lightning flashed again, and for that instant Bobbie saw her standing there as she really was, in a long blue silk dress, her curling blond hair cascading past her shoulders, and those oh-so-cold blue eyes. . . .

"Lettie?" Jessie called softly. "Are you there?"
Nothing.
*Something's happening. I can feel it.*
A loud bang suddenly sounded from the master bedroom.

Jessie tensed in terror. Every instinct in her body told her not to look. Her mind screamed to shut her bedroom door and lock it, shove a chair under the doorknob, climb out the window, anything—just get the hell out of the house. Instead, she took a deep breath and picked up the candelabra and walked out into the hall. The candles flickered as she squared her chin and proceeded toward her father's room.

Her father was lying on the floor, next to the bed.
"Dad?"

She hurried to his side, kneeling down and setting the candelabra on the floor. "Dad? Can you hear me,

Dad?" She felt for his pulse. It was there, faint—but there.

His eyelids fluttered and he made a sound in his throat.

"Dad? What's happened with you?"

He opened his eyes and looked at her. "Lettie . . ."

"No, I'm Jessie, Dad, I'm Jessie. . . ."

"Lettie," he rasped. "She gave me something to drink and then I slept . . ."

His voice was different. Deeper, thicker, older. He was fighting to stay awake. Jessie was held by his eyes. They were different, too—black eyes.

"Father," she said.

"I never told you I loved you, Lettie, and for that I am sorry."

She laughed. "You never loved me, Father. There is no use in pretending now."

"I did love you, Lettie." He struggled to stay awake despite the drug. "And your mother, too. But it got swallowed up by the hate. Don't you see? It's the hate that has lived on, the hate that is echoing still . . . hate that lives in this house."

For a moment Jessie and Lettie existed together, in the same place. Jessie fell quiet, letting Lettie speak. She knew it was a moment that Lettie had waited for.

"I did hate her," Lettie said, and Jessie felt her hot tears run down her cheeks. "And I allowed my hatred to consume me, as it consumed her. But I never meant it to go so far. . . ."

Her father grabbed her hand. Their eyes locked.

"Forgive me, Lettie."

She stared at him. She had spent most of her life despising this man, but once, when she was a very little girl, he had seemed a beneficent giant, picking her up in his arms, his great smile filling her vision.

"I forgive you, Father."

A terrible crash of thunder startled them both.

"Jessie," rasped Philip Kaye.

"Dad . . ."

He managed to lift an arm and place it around her shoulder. "Jessie," he gasped. "I won't let her hurt you. . . ."

He felt back into his drugged sleep. Jessie grasped his arm, tugged him to his feet, managing to get him back up onto the bed.

*I've got to get help. It's starting. It's going to be tonight. It's the storm, just like the day the Hatches were killed.*

She looked down at her father. Was he dying?

"I forgive you, too, Dad," she said softly. "No more hate."

"Can't we go any faster?" Chris demanded, slamming his fists down on the dashboard.

"Chill, bud, chill. I'm going seventy now—and that's probably not smart with the roads this slushy." Josh gripped the wheel tightly. "Let's hope that German engineering was tested on icy Alpine roads, shall we?"

Chris closed his eyes and tried to remain calm. *She's going to be all right, everything is going to be just fine. I'm just freaking because I had a dream. It's more likely I'm going to be killed in a car than by some shadow of the past. . . .*

He opened his eyes again. The sleet had turned to mostly rain. Every once in a while the ubiquitous lightning would fork across the sky as the car hurtled through the night. He looked over at Josh, whose face was frowning with concentration.

He closed his eyes again.

*Samuel? Are you there?*

\* \* \*

*He'd had to throw up when he was finished, but the job was done. Sarah Jane Hatch lay stretched out on the floor, her body mutilated with stab wounds. Samuel washed himself thoroughly of the blood, then dressed again and hurried out of that house of nightmares. He found Lettie at Mrs. Windham's cottage, wearing her old dress and huddling by the fire. She wouldn't look at him—and he found he couldn't look at her either.*

*"Throw the knife off the pier on your way back to the boardinghouse," Mrs. Windham instructed in that cold voice of hers. "And you two are going to have to stay away from each other for a while."*

*"I'm not going to ask how it really happened." His voice sounded a million miles away, hollow and empty. "I did what I did to protect Lettie."*

*"You know how it happened," Mrs. Windham insisted. "Sarah Jane killed the senator, then came at Lettie. Lettie managed to take the knife from her and killed her in self-defense." She smiled. "But because of your bravery, Samuel, now even that much will never fall upon sweet Lettie's frail shoulders. For an investigation will conclude that a girl as delicate as Lettie would never have the strength to stab and slash so many times, and with such force."*

*Lettie started to cry.*

*"They'll blame it on an intruder, an enemy of the senator's." Mrs. Windham looked very pleased with herself. "We are delivered from that whore's evil! Praise God!"*

*Samuel looked down at Lettie crying on the couch. He wanted to take her back into his arms, cover her face with kisses, but somehow he couldn't make himself go do it. His arms, his hands, his feet all felt numb—as if the life were fading out of his body. Every time he closed his eyes, he could hear the sound of the knife crunching into Sarah's body, and he'd wept the whole time as he desecrated her body. And in that horrible instant he knew his dreams of escaping to California with Lettie were never going to come true.*

*She was sitting there looking up at him with her tear-filled eyes.*

*"You'll—you'll come back for me, won't you, Samuel?"*

*"I'll come for you."*

*He turned and left the house, trudging through the snow out into the dunes, where he and Lettie had met so many times in secret, where they'd known so much pleasure, so much joy. He headed back out to the harbor, walking along the windswept pier and dropping the knife off the end into the churning waters of the bay. The freezing rain soaked his clothes, dripped down his back, but still he walked, until he was finally tired of walking. He staggered back to Mrs. Oliver's rooming house, walking in through the front door only to collapse at the foot of the stairs.*

*Mrs. Oliver found him there, burning with a fever and muttering deliriously. Another roomer carried him up the stairs and put him into bed. The fever developed into pneumonia . . . and as Samuel ached and burned and suffered, sometimes he hallucinated that Lettie was there with him. He tried calling to her, but nothing ever seemed to come from his throat except bile and phlegm. Then everything started fading away, and all Samuel could see was a blazing white light, warm and loving and gentle, and a sweet voice saying gently in his ear, "Lay your burden down, Samuel, let it down, and rest."*

*And as he let go, he thought of Lettie and his promise. Lettie, I will come for you . . . and then there was nothing but that pure, beautiful light.*

\* \* \*

Bobbie slipped out the back door, locking the dead bolt behind him. Immediately, the icy rain soaked him, and he wished he'd gotten a coat before he slipped out. He could hear Karen—Sarah Jane—calling for him inside the house. Through the windows he could see the flickering of the candles and the form of a woman with a butcher knife in her hand.

"Jesus," he muttered. "She wants to kill me."

Shivering, he turned and started to run down to Commercial Street, slipping every few steps, struggling to maintain his balance. *I've got to get to Jessie, I've got to warn her. . . .*

When he reached the corner at Commercial, he looked back over his shoulder and saw the lights of Karen's SUV come on. *She's in the car. She's coming looking for me!*

He vaulted the short fence of the corner house, feeling the pain from the stitches in his back, and ran behind the house, huddling down, hiding behind a snow-covered thicket of holly bushes. The SUV moved slowly down the street, and Bobbie scrunched down farther, whispering a prayer as he did. She was looking out the window, her eyes scanning the street. She stopped at the corner. Bobbie could see her through a break in the bushes, and her eyes were level with his. He prayed that she couldn't see him. Then she made a face in frustration and turned right and headed slowly up toward Bradford Street.

Bobbie let out a long sigh.

*I've got to warn Jessie.*

He began to run down Commercial Street through the snow and rain.


With a shudder and a screech, the power came back on.

Jessie almost screamed with relief, and grabbed for the phone on the nightstand, but there was still no dial tone. "Dad," she said, slapping him softly on the face. "Come on, Dad, wake up, I've got to get you out of here."

He moaned, opened his eyes briefly, and then closed them again.

*The hate lives. She won't let it go.*

Jessie spun around. There, in the far corner of the room, stood Lettie Hatch, in black dress and high-buttoned shoes. Her mouth was opening and closing as if she were speaking, but there was no sound coming from her lips. Only in Jessie's head could she hear her.

*She's coming. She's on her way back. You've got to get out of here, save yourself, you can't save him. . . .*

"I will save him!" Jessie shouted. "He's my father! I lost my mother! I won't lose my father too!"

The power flickered and went off again.

Headlights flashed through the windows.

*She's back!*

"Chris!" she screamed. "Help me!"


*Chris, Chris, help me, oh God, Chris, please help me!*

"Fuck!" Josh screamed.

Chris opened his eyes just as the car shot past the WELCOME TO PROVINCETOWN sign, and it began to slide. Josh fought the wheel, but the car was spinning around and around and then it was off the road, still spinning. Chris could see they were heading for a telephone pole. There was a loud crash and the car slammed to a stop. Chris was thrown forward, his head coming close to the dashboard, but his seat belt stopped him just short. It catapulted him back into his seat, slicing into his chest. Stars flashed in front of his eyes and everything went dark.

*Chris! Chris, help me!*

He opened his eyes. His entire body was screaming with pain. He was getting wet, so he turned his head to his right and saw that his car door was open and Josh was shaking him. "Dude, are you okay?"

"I—I think so." The whole front end of the car was crumpled, and the telephone pole was leaning dangerously.

Josh popped Chris's seat belt off. "You've got to get out of there, man, that pole could go at any minute."

Chris climbed out of the car. His neck hurt, and the pain across his chest from the seat belt burned like hell, but he stood up, shivering in the wind. They backed away from the smoking car, the icy rain pelting down on them. "Josh, your car . . ."

"It's insured." His friend shrugged. "I'll go see if I can get some help. You wait here—"

"No—I've got to get to Jessie." He closed his eyes and he heard her calling his name again, and a chill went through him.

"Chris—"

*"I always said I would come for her,"* he heard himself saying, but the voice didn't sound like his own. *"I failed her and I will not allow that to happen again!"*

Josh, his eyes wide and his face white, backed away from him, holding up his hands. "Okay, man, whatever."

Chris turned and started running.

Jessie shut the bedroom door and pushed the lock closed. It wouldn't hold anyone—it could be popped with a credit card or a pin—but it might slow Karen

462          *Robert Ross*

down. She ran over to the window and saw Karen climbing out of the SUV. Lightning flashed.

She was carrying a butcher knife.

Jessie whimpered in fear. She started looking around the room. There was nowhere to hide, nowhere to run.

There, still standing in the shadows of the corner, was Lettie.

*Find a weapon. Find anything to defend yourself with. Fight back. She wants to kill you. All of her plans went wrong eighty years ago and now she's consumed with hate. The hate still lives. It's what has lived on in this house . . . the hatred that consumed all of us. Now you've got to stop her. You've got to close the circle. That's what the psychic meant. You've got to put an end to echoes of hate.*

Jessie heard the front door slam shut, then footsteps on the stairs. "Jessie?" Karen called softly. Her voice seemed normal. "Where are you? Is your father awake?"

Jessie stood facing the door, her entire body starting to shake.

*Chris, please, oh God, Chris, please hurry, she's coming for me.*


Shivering and soaked, Bobbie let himself through the back gate of the Kaye house and ran up to the back door, praying it wasn't locked.

*Thank you, Jesus*, he thought as the knob turned in his hand. He pushed it open slowly and stepped into the darkened kitchen.

"Jessie, where are you?"

It was Karen's voice from upstairs—but no, it was Sarah Jane's voice. Bobbie glanced around in the darkness, spying the pot rack hanging from the ceiling on the far wall. He crept over to it, carefully freed a <u>frying pan</u>, feeling a little stupid.

*A weapon is a weapon*, he rationalized as he walked into the hallway.

He could hear soft footsteps upstairs. He slipped his shoes off, clenching his jaw to keep his teeth from chattering, then slowly started to climb the stairs.

*Chris, please, she's coming for me, please hurry, oh, dear God, hurry!*

Chris's lungs were screaming for air, but still he ran. He slipped and fell more than once, hitting the pavement with a thud but bouncing back up and starting to run again. As he ran, his mind kept flashing with images that made no sense to him as he focused on running, on getting to Jessie.

*I don't care if she killed them. It doesn't matter. I love her.*

"And I love Jessie, Samuel," Chris shouted into the wind. "I'm doing this as much for me as I'm doing it for you!"

Ahead of him sat the big white house on the bay. The SUV was parked in the driveway. The entire house was dark, except for the flickering of a candle in what he knew was the master bedroom—

He jumped over the fence and threw open the front door.

The knob on the door shook.

"Philip?" came Karen's voice. "Jessie?"

Jessie watched in horror as her father staggered to his feet.

"Dad, don't! Don't open the door!"

"Sarah Jane," he murmured, and he unlocked the door.

He moved aside. Karen came into view just as the power flickered back on. Jessie caught a look at her stepmother's eyes. They were blue.

She screamed.

Philip slunk down onto the bed as Karen stepped forward into the room.

"Lettie Hatch." Karen's face twisted with hate. "You made my life miserable, when all I wanted to do was help you. I should have killed you then. Maybe then I could have been free."

Jessie stepped toward her, her fear evaporating. She allowed Lettie to speak.

"But you didn't kill me, Sarah Jane. In that moment, in that final moment, you stepped back from your hatred and your fear."

Sarah Jane's eyes blazed at her. "I had such plans . . . I had gotten away from so much . . . only to find all my dreams destroyed by this house." She grimaced. "This room . . ."

Lettie shuddered. The sounds she had heard in this room. What she had seen when she opened the door . . .

Her father, his eyes swollen and bleary.

His papers were all over the floor. Sarah Jane still held some of them in her hand.

Her father was moving at her, ripping at her blouse. Sarah Jane screamed.

"I won't let you!" she shouted at him. "Not again!"

From her deep pocket she produced a knife.

"I vowed never to let you touch me again!" she screamed, and brought the knife up into the air. Horace Hatch, drugged and slow, couldn't move out of the way in time. Lettie watched in horror as the knife came down through the air and pierced his chest. He rasped out in pain as blood spurted over his papers on the floor.

She was a madwoman, Sarah Jane. How she had stabbed him, over and over, his blood spraying everywhere, onto her clothes, onto the bed, onto the floor. She seemed oblivious of Lettie's presence as she knelt there, raising the knife again and again, plunging it deep into Horace's body. Lettie couldn't move. She couldn't scream. She could only watch in horror.

"You!" Sarah Jane shouted when she realized she had a witness. She stood menacingly. Lettie backed out of the doorway into the hall.

"You bitch! You scheming little witch!"

Sarah Jane advanced at her, the knife held aloft. Lettie backed up toward the stairs.

"You'll tell the whole world now, won't you?" Sarah Jane shrieked. "You'll tell what you saw and I will hang!"

"No, please, Sarah Jane, put down the knife, I won't tell. . . ."

"I didn't leave the hell of Cooper Road to hang!" She made a move to stab Lettie, but the girl caught her arm, pushing her away.

The two women held eyes, the way they would hold them again more than eighty years later in the same room.

*In that moment, in that final moment, you stepped back from your hatred and your fear.*

"No more," Sarah Jane cried. "No more."

And she lifted the knife to her own throat, and sliced her jugular vein.

Lettie screamed.

Sarah Jane's body shook for a moment, then tumbled down the stairs.

"You stepped back from your hatred," Jessie managed to say.

Fire burned in Sarah Jane's blue eyes. "Now my hatred is all I am," she seethed.

Jessie cowered back into the corner as the knife came toward her.

"No," Philip rasped, taking hold of Karen's arm, turning her around.

"You!" She spun on him. "I heard you! I heard what you said to that man! Belittling Karen's work! You truly are Horace Hatch!"

"No," Philip mumbled. "I never said . . . never . . . belittled . . . I am . . . not Horace . . . I am . . . Philip Kaye."

Karen had turned to face Philip, her back to the doorway. Jessie saw Bobbie there suddenly, his eyes wild.

"Now you will die like Horace Hatch!" Karen screamed, raising the knife over her husband.

"No!" Bobbie lunged into the room, grabbing Karen's arm. But he was too weak, still too wounded, to knock her over. She fought back, elbowing him in his stitches. Karen saw fresh blood from Bobbie's wound seep through his shirt. He screamed, crumpling, the pain overwhelming him.

But his quick action gave Jessie enough time to run to her father, who was fading back into a drugged faint. Philip collapsed on the bed. Jessie tried to pull him to safety, but everything was happening so fast. Karen was approaching them again with the knife.

"They were all so cruel to you, weren't they, Sarah Jane?" Jessie suddenly cried out. "All of them. Starting with Arthur. He got you pregnant but didn't care. How you suffered. Your father. The people of Cooper Road. And Horace Hatch, too. You killed him because you had to. Because he would have raped you again."

Karen stood still, the knife held over her head.

"He would have found my baby," she said in a terrible, raspy voice.

"But he didn't. She lived. She had a good life. A good life because you made sure she could grow up away from the pain you had known. She lived, Sarah Jane! She lived a life of freedom, a woman free to make her own choices—she lived the life you fought so hard to make possible!".

Karen's grip on the knife was faltering.

"She lives on," Jessie said, "in Karen."

"Karen . . ." Sarah Jane's voice was weak.

"You stepped back once before from the hatred, Sarah Jane. Do so again. Your life was taken from you, but the life you brought into this world—it lives, it flourishes."

Jessie wasn't sure if it was her voice speaking, or Lettie's.

Or, more likely, a combination of them both.

"The way it ended before," Sarah Jane said dreamily. "The way it must end now. The only way . . ."

She turned the knife away from Philip and Jessie and brought it to her own throat.

"No!"

It was Chris!

Jessie watched in amazement as Chris lunged through the door and grabbed Karen's arm. He twisted her wrist, and the knife fell on the floor. Bobbie, still clutching his side, managed to grab it and hold it.

Karen staggered. She closed her eyes and put her hands up to her head. "It hurts, oh, it hurts so bad."

Bobbie had managed to stand. "Let go, Sarah Jane, let the suffering stop," he said softly. "Give us Karen back."

Karen opened her eyes, and Jessie stared at her. Her eyes were brown again!

"Bobbie?" Karen was shaking all over. "Is that you?"

"Yeah, doll face. It's me." He took her into his arms. Jessie saw him wince from the pain, but he held her tight.

"Jessie?"

Chris was standing over her. She looked up at him and started to cry. Chris put his arms around her, and it felt so right. . . .

It felt so right.

"Are you okay?" he asked.

"You came." She buried her face in his chest. He was cold and wet, but she didn't care. "I called for you, and you came."

"Of course I came." He looked into her eyes.

She just cried harder, clinging to him.

# Epilogue

The storm had lessened in its fury. There hadn't been any thunder or lightning in almost an hour, and the rain had let up. The wind was still howling around the house, rattling windows and shaking the outside doors, but it didn't seem an enemy anymore.

*It's almost as if Sarah Jane conjured the storm with her hate*, Jessie thought, taking a sip of her coffee, which was strong and black. *Now that it's all over, the storm is fading away too.*

She had dug through her father's closet to find sweats for Chris and Bobbie to wear while she threw their soaked and frozen clothes into the dryer. Chris was a good seven inches taller than her father, so the sweatpants reached just as far as his knees, and the sleeves of the Harvard sweatshirt stopped just short of his elbows. She couldn't help but smile.

In the living room, Karen was sleeping on the couch under a pile of blankets. Chris had carried her down here; she had been too weak to make the stairs herself. She had fallen into a deep sleep. Bobbie was sitting beside her. He was still in pain, but Alice had shown up moments after it was all over—just as Mrs. Windham had all those years ago—and thankfully she had some gauze and bandages in her car. She'd wrapped up Bobbie's wound again. Once the storm subsided a bit more they'd take Bobbie back to the hospital for more stitches.

"It's over," Chris said, taking Jessie's hand. "Can't you feel it?"

Jessie nodded. The shadowing was gone. The echoes in her mind were silent. Lettie was gone. All of them were gone. And so was the hate.

She stood, walking over to the couch and kneeling beside Karen.

"She's okay?" she asked Bobbie.

"I think so," he said. "She just needs to sleep. Her mind is exhausted."

"And Dad?" Jessie asked, looking toward the stairs.

"I just checked on him," Alice said. "He's coming out of it. He seems fine. His pulse is strong and he's breathing all right."

Across from them sitting in front of the fireplace was Chris's roommate, Josh. "I don't know what went down here today," he said. "But I do know Chris and I aren't getting back to school tonight. Or maybe not even tomorrow. My car is totally wrecked, people."

"I'll drive you back," Bobbie offered.

"No, no, no," Alice said. "You're going to bed, young man, and I'm going to take care of you. I'll take the boys back to school when the roads are better."

Bobbie smiled. "Yes, Mrs.—Alice."

Chris was suddenly behind Jessie, snaking his arms around her waist. "I just want some extra time with you," he purred in her ear.

She smiled. "Not at the risk of getting expelled, mister. What would Lois have to say about that?"

"We won't get expelled," Josh said. "I've already

called my dad. He's putting in a story that he came and got us and in the storm couldn't find anybody in authority to let them know. They'll believe him. He's giving a big chunk of cash to the school this year. They'll believe whatever he says."

"Look," Bobbie said. "We need to talk about Karen." He shivered. "I still can't believe she stabbed me, and tried to kill me again tonight—tried to kill all of us."

"It wasn't Karen," Chris pointed out. "It was *Sarah Jane*."

"You're right, but if Karen wakes up with memories of all she did . . ." Bobbie sighed. "We've got to be there for her. We've got to support her. All of us." He looked over at Jessie.

"All of us," she agreed.

"That's right," came a voice.

It was Philip, coming down the stairs. They all looked over at him.

"I never believed in all this," he said, walking slowly toward them. "But now . . ."

He sat down on the couch beside his wife, looking down at her face.

"For the past few weeks I've had Horace Hatch in my mind. I spoke like him, thought like him. I even treated my wife the way he treated his."

He cupped Karen's sleeping face in his hand.

"Or maybe, I was never all that different from Horace Hatch."

He looked around the room.

"I don't even know most of you people, but I am indebted to you. To all of you." He looked over at his daughter and offered his hand. She took it. "And most of all to you, Jessie."

She felt her eyes sting with tears.

Philip looked back at Karen. They all backed away to give him time alone with her.

In the kitchen Chris refilled his coffee mug.

"Poor Lettie," he said. "All those years people believing she killed them. . . ."

"And trapped with that crazy Mrs. Windham," Jessie said, shuddering. "What was even more sad is that Jessie felt responsible, even though she hadn't been the one to wield the actual knife. She felt she had played her own part in the hatred of this house, so she shared in the blame."

"And Samuel never came for her . . ." Chris said.

Jessie held his eyes. "You know, I think if I hadn't been so scared of what was happening when all this started, maybe I would have realized the only emotion Lettie communicated to me was sadness. Sadness and loneliness over Samuel's rejection of her. He must've always doubted whether she was truly the killer, and couldn't bear to see her again. Poor Lettie—it breaks my heart to think about it."

"Well, you're wrong about Samuel." Chris pulled her down onto his lap. "Samuel didn't just run off and forget about her. He loved Lettie—she was his whole reason for living, all he ever thought about. Until the day he died." He sighed. "I have a feeling if we went down to Provincetown Town Hall and checked the death records for a few days after the murders, we'd find that Samuel died of pneumonia."

"But he did finally come back for her," Jessie said, looking into Chris's eyes.

"It wasn't just Samuel who came back, Jessie," he told her. "I want you to know that."

She smiled, circling his arms around her neck. "I know that, Chris," she said, and they kissed.


Karen opened her eyes to see Philip looking down at her.

"Philip?"

"Are you all right, darling?"

She tried to move. She felt stiff, and her muscles ached. But the headache was gone.

"I think so," she managed to say.

She looked into his eyes. How long had it been?

"Darling," he said. "I never meant to . . . I mean, I . . . I love you, Karen."

"I love you, Philip."

He bent down and took her into his arms. "Whatever I may have said, however I may have acted, can you forgive me?"

"Forgive *you*?" She placed her hands on his cheeks. "Can you forgive me?"

"We're going to change the energy of this house, darling. We're going to change the legacy that has lived here too long."

They kissed.

For the first time in weeks, Karen felt herself in control of her own mind. She could remember the horrible events she'd been through only in patches . . . but she knew Sarah Jane was gone now. Her power over her mind and thoughts was ended.

Bobbie was standing over them with a cup of coffee. "Is that my honey pie speaking?" Philip moved aside so that Bobbie could join them on the couch. He handed Karen the coffee, and she took it gratefully. "That will revive you, baby doll."

She took a sip, then looked at him in his eyes. "Bobbie, I'm so sorry. . . ."

"It's all gone, Karen. It's in the past, and we're leaving it there."

She looked from him to Philip, then back again. "I have to pay for what I did," Karen insisted as terrible memories flooded her mind. "I could have killed both of you." A shudder ran through her body. "I don't know how I'm going to live with that on my conscience for the rest of my life."

"Sweetie, it wasn't you. We've all been living with these echoes in our heads. Every one of us here. We know the full story now. We know it wasn't you."

She felt a twinge of fear as she remembered how it began . . . the thoughts in her head, the raging emotions over which she had no control. The hate. The blinding hate—toward Philip, Jessie, Mrs. Winn, even Bobbie . . .

And the diary. How it had possessed her. Her dreams of glory, of fame and fortune. She would have been profiting off the hatred and misery of others. She would give the diary to some historical society, get it out of the house as fast as she could. She trembled when she thought of it in her desk upstairs. . . .

"Are we sure it's over?" she asked, holding the hot mug in her hands, clinging to its warmth. "Are we sure that tomorrow night, or next week, it won't start all over again?"

"We're sure." It was Jessie now standing over her. "The shadowing is gone. For the first time in months, I feel completely like myself again. Don't you feel the same way, Karen?"

Karen nodded. "Yes. I feel . . . myself."

Philip squeezed her hand.

Yes, she felt herself again. Finally. The girl from New Orleans who had fallen in love with her literary hero only to find him a man like any other. Who was promising now to love her, like a man. Like a new man. Yes, she would get rid of the diary and all that it represented. Karen thought she could bring a whole new set of insights to Vicky now—she'd write a great novel on her own, without any help from the Hatches.

She felt Jessie's eyes on her. Karen looked up at her stepdaughter.

"Karen," the girl said. "I'm sorry."

"What on earth for? Jessie, I'm the one—"

Jessie took a deep breath. "No, we're all the ones. I let my own resentments and frustrations dictate how I acted when you first came here. You tried to be my friend, and I cut you off. I want to change that. I'd—I'd like for us to be friends."

Karen smiled at her. "I'd like that too, Jessie."

Setting the coffee mug down on the floor, Karen reached out and took Jessie's hand into her own. With her other hand, she clasped Philip's. Jessie looked at Chris standing beside her and with her free hand gripped his tightly. For his part Chris placed his other hand on Bobbie's shoulder just as the older man knelt beside the couch. Alice Winn moved in to stand next to Bobbie, who rested his head upon her thigh.

With that, the circle of time was finally closed.

# More Books From Your Favorite Thriller Authors

# More Thrilling Suspense From Your Favorite Thriller Authors

# BOOK YOUR PLACE ON OUR WEBSITE AND MAKE THE READING CONNECTION!

We've created a customized website just for our very special readers, where you can get the inside scoop on everything that's going on with Zebra, Pinnacle and Kensington books.

When you come online, you'll have the exciting opportunity to:

- View covers of upcoming books
- Read sample chapters
- Learn about our future publishing schedule (listed by publication month *and author*)
- Find out when your favorite authors will be visiting a city near you
- Search for and order backlist books from our online catalog
- Check out author bios and background information
- Send e-mail to your favorite authors
- Meet the Kensington staff online
- Join us in weekly chats with authors, readers and other guests
- Get writing guidelines
- AND MUCH MORE!

**Visit our website at
http://www.kensingtonbooks.com**